SHELTERED BY HER TOP-NOTCH BOSS

BY
JOANNA NEIL

RE-AWAKENING HIS SHY NURSE

BY
ANNIE CLAYDON

MILLS & BOON

When **Joanna Neil** discovered Mills & Boon®, her lifelong addiction to reading crystallised into an exciting new career writing Mills & Boon® Medical Romance™. Her characters are probably the outcome of her varied lifestyle, which includes working as a clerk, typist, nurse and infant teacher. She enjoys dressmaking and cooking at her Leicestershire home. Her family includes a husband, son and daughter, an exuberant yellow Labrador and two slightly crazed cockatiels. She currently works with a team of tutors at her local education centre, to provide creative writing workshops for people interested in exploring their own writing ambitions.

Cursed from an early age with a poor sense of direction and a propensity to read, **Annie Claydon** spent much of her childhood lost in books. After completing her degree in English Literature, she indulged her love of romantic fiction and spent a long, hot summer writing a book of her own. It was duly rejected and life took over. A series of U-turns led in the unlikely direction of a career in computing and information technology, but the lure of the printed page proved too much to bear, and she now has the perfect outlet for the stories which have always run through her head, writing Medical Romance™ for Mills & Boon®. Living in London, a city where getting lost can be a joy, she has no regrets for having taken her time in working her way back to the place that she started from.

SHELTERED BY HER TOP-NOTCH BOSS

BY

JOANNA NEIL

MILLS & BOON

First published in Great Britain 2013
by Mills & Boon, an imprint of Harlequin (UK) Limited.
Harlequin (UK) Limited, Eton House, 18-24 Paradise Road,
Richmond, Surrey TW9 1SR

ISBN: 978 0 263 89912 2

Harlequin (UK) policy is to use papers that are natural, renewable and recyclable products and made from wood grown in sustainable forests. The logging and manufacturing process conform to the legal environmental regulations of the country of origin.

Printed and bound in Spain
by Blackprint CPI, Barcelona

Dear Reader

I'm sure a lot of people have skeletons in their cupboards, scandals that affect their families, or things they might have done long ago that they regret when they're a bit older and wiser.

And that set me to wondering… What would happen if my heroine's former indiscretions came back to haunt her? And how would she cope if those transgressions promised to ruin her career and maybe destroy her chance of happiness with the man she loves?

Well, to find out what happens you'll need to read all about Ellie and James and their troubled path to true love.

Happy reading!

Joanna

Recent titles by Joanna Neil:

RETURN OF THE REBEL DOCTOR
HIS BRIDE IN PARADISE
TAMED BY HER BROODING BOSS
DR RIGHT ALL ALONG
DR LANGLEY: PROTECTOR OR PLAYBOY?
A COTSWOLD CHRISTMAS BRIDE
THE TAMING OF DR ALEX DRAYCOTT
BECOMING DR BELLINI'S BRIDE

CHAPTER ONE

ELLIE SHIFTED RESTLESSLY on the barstool, crossing one long, elegant leg over the other. How much longer would it be before she could decently slip away from here? She cradled a cocktail glass between her fingers and watched her friends enjoying themselves. She was the only one out of kilter here.

The party was in full swing, the heavy beat of music drowning out the buzz of conversation, though every now and again a burst of laughter broke through the din. Some people were on the dance floor, and everyone seemed contented, eager to let their hair down.

If only she could feel the same way. She'd had an awful day, though, and she desperately wanted it to end. This was the last place she needed to be.

'I'm glad you managed to get here tonight after all,' Lewis said, moving closer. 'I know you had to work late today.' His hazel eyes were warm as he gazed at her. An errant lock of brown, wavy hair fell across his forehead.

She nodded and made an effort to put on a cheerful expression. But how much more small talk could she make? She'd spent the last hour doing that, and all the while she'd been hoping for the chance to say goodbye and leave the party relatively unnoticed, some time soon.

'I had to try,' she said. 'I know how keen Zoe was to have us all come to her celebration.' She smiled, seeing her friend circle the room, chatting to people who'd been her colleagues for the last few years. 'I'll miss her, but I'm glad she managed to get the promotion she wanted. It's just sad that she'll be moving away from here.'

'Well, she's only going as far as the next county—I dare say she'll be coming back to Cheshire to visit us every now and again.'

'Yes, I suppose you're right.' She drained the last of her drink and then said, 'I haven't seen your wife here tonight. Couldn't she make it?'

Lewis shook his head and looked uncomfortable. 'She…uh…had to go to another do. A family thing.' His voice trailed off, and just as Ellie was absorbing that, Zoe came over to them.

Ellie's eyes widened a fraction as she glanced at the man who accompanied her. His brooding gaze wandered over her in turn, and there was something about him that caused a frisson of awareness to shiver down her spine. Did she know him from somewhere? Snatches of memory flickered through her mind and dissolved as fast as they had come into being.

But how could she have forgotten him? He was tall, and exceptionally good-looking, wearing an immaculate dark suit. Peeping out from beneath his jacket sleeves, the cuffs of his shirt were pristine, fastened with stylish gold cuff links. But the feeling remained, niggling at the outer edges of her consciousness. She felt strangely uneasy.

'Ellie, I must introduce you to James,' Zoe said, bubbling with enthusiasm, her blonde hair quivering with every small movement she made. 'He's taking over from me at the hospital—honestly, I'm already regretting taking the new job. Would you credit it? Just as I'm leaving, *he* turns up?' She rolled her eyes in an *'Isn't he to die for?'* kind of way, and James laughed, a soft, rumbling sound coming from the back of his throat.

He looked at Ellie, appreciation sparking in his smoke-grey eyes before he tilted his head in acknowledgement to Lewis.

'It's good to meet you, Ellie,' James said, his voice a deep, satisfying murmur that whispered along her nerve endings and turned her insides to jelly.

'Likewise.'

'I understand you work with Lewis?'

She nodded. 'We're in different departments, but we're both at the hospital. I'm a registrar in A and E.'

Ellie studied him from under her lashes. She could see what Zoe meant. He had the kind of looks that had her stomach doing peculiar flips, despite her initial misgivings about him, while her senses were falling over each other as they clamoured for attention.

He *was* gorgeous, there was no doubt about it. He had black hair, beautiful grey eyes and perfectly proportioned, angular features, along with a body that was lithe and muscular, radiating energy. Even in her present unhappy state of mind she managed to register all those things.

James turned to Lewis. 'Hi,' he said. 'Are you and Jessica still coming over to the house this weekend?'

'Yes, we are.'

'Good. We'll look forward to seeing you there.'

Lewis nodded. 'James is my cousin,' he explained

to Ellie. 'He's always taken it on himself to watch out for me. I lost my parents when I was in my teens, you see, and his father took me in.'

'Ah, I see.' She hesitated. 'I'm sorry to hear about your parents, I never knew that. I guess there must be a strong bond between you and your cousin because of that—you're a bit like brothers, I suppose?'

'That's right.'

'I make sure he stays on the straight and narrow,' James said with a smile. 'Though I've been away for a while and perhaps I need to catch up with the latest news. I'd no idea he was working with such a beautiful woman.'

Seeing their absorption with one another, Zoe gave a satisfied smile and walked away from them, taking a reluctant Lewis along with her. 'I want you to meet a friend of mine,' she told him.

Ellie set her empty glass down on the bar and glanced at James. 'I thought I caught a glimpse of you earlier,' she murmured. Even then, she'd been on edge without knowing why. Perhaps it was all down to the horrible day she'd had.

He smiled. 'Same here. I saw you come over to the bar a few minutes ago. The truth is,' he confided, 'I've been badgering Zoe to introduce us ever since.' His glance wandered over her, drifting down over the dress that clung where it touched, over her long, silk-clad legs, still crossed at the knee, and came back up to linger on the mass of burnished chestnut curls that lightly brushed her shoulders.

Her skin heated as though it had been licked by flame. No man had ever had this effect on her, turning her body to fire with a single glance.

She struggled to get control of herself, and then looked at him once more. Perhaps she knew him from seeing him around the hospital?

'I heard you've already started working in A and E,' she said, 'but I don't think we've actually met before this, have we? Somehow, I had the feeling...' She added quickly, 'It gets so busy in the emergency unit, I don't always have the opportunity to meet up with new people straight away.'

'I've been working the night shift,' he answered, 'getting to know the lie of the land. Officially, my job as consultant doesn't start for a couple of days.' He studied her once more. 'I feel I do know you already, though. I often watch your TV programme—*Your Good Health*.' He gave her a crooked smile, and there was a mischievous glint in his eye.

'I have to tell you, you're my very favourite TV presenter—you look terrific both on and off camera, and you make medicine seem like child's play. I imagine every red-blooded male who watches the programme secretly yearns for you to be there to mop his brow.'

She laughed. 'I very much doubt that, but thank you anyway. I enjoy doing the show. It makes a change from A and E and I hope I might be doing some good, maybe helping people to look after themselves.'

'I'm sure what you do is extremely useful.' He looked at her empty glass. 'Can I get you a refill?

She shook her head. 'Actually, I was just about to leave. It's been a long day, one way and another. I think I'll ring for a taxi.'

'You're not enjoying the party?' He frowned. 'I wondered if there was something amiss when I saw you earlier. You seemed preoccupied, a little despondent maybe? Is it something you want to talk about?'

'Not really.' She eased herself off the barstool, pulling down the hem of her dress and smoothing the material over her hips. His gaze followed the movement of her hands and she said huskily, 'There's no reason for me to spoil your evening by involving you in my problems. I've had a difficult day and I should never have come here, but I didn't want to let Zoe down.'

'I understand.' He frowned. 'I'm sorry you're feeling that way. Maybe I could see you home? I have my car outside. Whereabouts do you live?'

'Ashleigh Meadows, but I don't want to put you out. I'll be fine, really. You should stay and enjoy the party.'

'That's okay. It's no trouble. I didn't intend to stay long anyway.' He glanced at the gold watch on his wrist. 'I have to be on duty at the hospital in just over an hour, and Ashleigh Meadows is on my way.'

'Oh, I see.' She hesitated. It wouldn't hurt to accept his offer, would it? 'Well, in that case, okay. Thanks.' She glanced quickly around the room. 'I'd better take a minute to go and say goodbye to Zoe.'

He nodded and went with her, and a few minutes later they were both sitting in his luxuriously upholstered car, with the air-conditioning switched on and soft music coming from the CD player. She gave him directions to her house, and after driving for a few minutes James turned the car onto the Ashleigh Road. Ellie sat back, lulled by the soft purr of the engine, trying to relax and let the music soothe her battered soul.

James slanted her an oblique look. 'Are you sure you don't want to tell me about it? Whatever it was, it seems to have made a powerful impact on you. Was it personal or something that happened in A and E?'

Her first instinct was to stay closed up and keep things to herself. She certainly wasn't going to tell him her worries about her brother and his constant battle with debt. Noah had phoned her first thing that morning, worried about the way things were going with his finances. She loved her younger brother and would do anything she could to help him out, but his situation troubled her.

But as to the other problem—what was the point in keeping it to herself after all? No one could make it better, but perhaps talking it over with a colleague might help her to come to terms with what happened.

She gave a shuddery sigh. 'A patient died,' she told him. 'I know it happens from time to time, and as doctors we should be able to deal with it, but this was someone I knew—the aunt of an old schoolfriend of mine. I knew her quite well and it was such a terrible shock when she died. It was upsetting that I couldn't save her. I kept asking myself if I did everything possible.'

His brow creased in sympathy. 'I'm sorry. It must have been terrible for you to go through that, especially with someone you knew.' He turned off the main road and the car's headlights picked out the country lane, stretched out like a ribbon before them, throwing the overgrown hedgerows on either side into deep shadow.

She nodded. 'But it was worse for Amelia. Her aunt virtually brought her up, and she was devastated when she died.' She hesitated, her voice dropping to a hoarse whisper. 'She blames me for letting it happen.'

He exhaled sharply. 'You mustn't take it to heart. It's the shock—sometimes people just can't accept it when a loved one dies. They say and do things while they're emotionally upset and often come to regret it afterwards. I'm sure you did everything you could for your friend's aunt.'

Ellie winced. 'I'm afraid Mel doesn't see it that way. Perhaps if she knew me better she might have more confidence in me, but we lost touch after we left school and moved in different circles.' She frowned, thinking back over what had happened. 'She thinks I should have changed her aunt's medication and sent her for surgery, but I'm not sure if there was anything I could have done to change the outcome.'

'What was wrong with her aunt?' He slowed the car as a cluster of houses came into view, yellow points of light illuminating the village in the darkness.

'There was an inflammation around her heart. She was brought to A and E in a state of collapse, with severe chest pain and breathlessness. I put her on oxygen and monitored her vital signs, did blood tests and sent her for a CT scan, as well as echocardiography.' She sucked in a breath.

'The tests showed that she had an acute bacterial infection that had caused the pericardium to become congested with purulent matter. I put her on strong antibiotics and started to drain the pericardial fluid, but in the end her heart simply stopped.' Her voice choked. 'I think her age and general frailty worked against her. Her heart couldn't take the strain.'

'And you explained all that to your friend?'

She nodded. 'Yes, but I don't know whether she took it all in. I fetched her a cup of tea and sat with her for a while, and tried to explain, but it was as though she was frozen. She seemed not to hear what I said. She was upset and angry at the same time.'

He pressed his lips together in a grim line. 'It happens that way sometimes.'

'I suppose so.' She looked out of the window as the cottages drew near. 'Mine's the old farmhouse,' she told him. 'Turn next left, and it's at the end of the track.'

A short time later he pulled the car up on the gravelled drive outside the brick-built house. A lantern in the wide, slate-roofed porch gave off a welcoming glow, highlighting the ivy-covered walls and the tidy front garden.

'Judging from what I can see by the light of the moon, you have a very attractive place here,' James commented.

Ellie nodded. 'I'm glad you like it. I'd had my eye on it for a while, and when it came on the market I jumped at the chance to buy.' She gave a wry smile. 'It needed a lot of renovation, so at least it was within my budget. I like it because it's not crowded out by other properties—there's just the converted barn across the courtyard at the back of the house.'

She paused then asked hesitantly, 'Do you have time to come in for a coffee before your shift starts? I could give you a quick look inside, if you like.' She'd only just met him, but he had a warm and sympathetic manner, and she wanted to be with him just a little bit longer.

'That would be great, thanks. I like these old farmhouse cottages—they have a lot of character.'

'That's how I feel, too.' She slid out of the car, leaving its comforting warmth for the coolness of the summer evening, and together they walked to the front door.

'Though cottage is perhaps a bit of a misnomer—it's quite cosy inside, but there are two storeys.'

The door opened into a large entrance hall, and she led the way from there to the kitchen, where James admired the golden oak beams and matching oak units.

'This was the first room I renovated,' she said, spooning freshly ground coffee into the percolator. 'The beams were dark with age, so I had them cleaned up and then picked out cupboards to go with the new, lighter colour.'

James nodded. 'They make the room look warm and homely.' His gaze went to the gleaming range cooker that she'd lovingly restored and which had pride of place in her kitchen. 'That must help heat up the kitchen.'

She nodded. 'It does. I love it—I spend lots of time experimenting with new recipes—it's kind of a hobby. Cooking helps me to unwind.' She smiled. 'Though I live here on my own, so I often have to share what I've made with the family across the way…the people who live in the converted barn.'

He looked her over, amusement sparking in his eyes, and once again she experienced that odd feeling of familiarity, as though she knew him from somewhere in the past, but once again the circumstances eluded her.

'You cook as well?' he said. 'Wow. Fortune's following me around today—I must have stumbled on my dream woman!'

She chuckled. 'I wouldn't get too carried away, if I were you—I didn't say I was any good at it.'

He laughed, and while the percolator simmered, she showed him the living/dining room that was tacked on to one end of the open plan kitchen. 'I had the wall taken down,' she said, 'to make the place seem bigger. I was a bit worried it might not work out too well.'

'I don't think that's a problem at all.' He stood close to her as they surveyed the room, and all she could think about was his nearness, the long line of his strong and lean body, the way his arm inadvertently brushed hers and sent a ripple of heat surging inside her.

He glanced at her, and there was a stillness about him that made her wonder if he'd experienced that same feeling. He seemed distracted for a moment or two and then appeared to force his attention back to the subject in hand.

'It all seems to work pretty well. The dining area goes on from the kitchen, and the living room is part of the L-shape, which makes it kind of separate. All the rooms benefit from the extra space.'

She nodded, struggling to regain control of herself. 'That's what I was hoping for. There's a small utility room as well, so I have just about everything I need here. I'm really fortunate to have this place, but it's the extra money from the TV show that funded all the renovations.'

'I can imagine.' His mouth made a crooked line. 'But as an avid fan, I'm convinced you're worth every penny they pay you. You explain things in a way people can understand, and make the programme lively and interesting at the same time.'

'I'm glad you think so, but it's all down to teamwork really. It doesn't take too long to make the programmes, so it's worked out pretty well for me, all in all.' She sent him a quizzical glance. 'Perhaps it's something you'd like to try? The producers are always looking for new presenters.'

He shook his head. 'I don't think so. I'm busy enough as it is. I've enough going on outside medicine to keep me occupied. So time out for a spot of rest and relaxation would be first on my agenda, and I like to spend it on my boat, where I can get away from everything and everyone.' He sent her an oblique glance, his mouth making a teasing curve. 'Is there any chance you might want to join me? I could set aside a few days especially for you and we could maybe spend a long, lazy weekend together.'

She gave him an answering smile. 'That's a tempting proposition, James, but I'd really have to give it some thought.' It had definite appeal, but some innate sense made her hold back.

She'd been in relationships before, which had promised so much and then proved to be a huge letdown. Perhaps her background, the disintegration of her family life had made her cautious about expecting too much. 'We barely know each other, after all.'

'That could soon be remedied.'

They walked back to the kitchen, and Ellie poured coffee, smiling faintly as the tempting aroma teased her nostrils. Despite her reservations, she liked being with James. She'd been feeling thoroughly down in the dumps and somehow he'd managed to pull her out of the swamp of depression.

She handed him a cup and he added cream and sugar, stirring thoughtfully. 'So how did you get into the TV business?' he asked, as they sipped the hot liquid. 'Were you spotted by a talent scout prowling the emergency unit?'

She laughed. 'No such luck. I know someone who works at the studios, and she suggested I might like to try it. I'd written a few articles for magazines and made a couple of videos for students that turned out all right, so she thought I might take to it.'

'And I guess she was right.'

'Mmm, it seems so.' She rummaged in the fridge and the cupboard, looking for something to nibble on. 'Would you like something to eat? Biscuits and cheese, or a slice of quiche maybe?'

He shook his head and took a quick sip of coffee. 'Not for me, thanks,' he said, and there was a hint of resignation in his tone. 'I'm afraid I must be going very soon.'

'Oh, of course. Okay.' She felt a pang of disappointment because he was about to leave. They drank their coffees and talked about her TV work for a while longer. Then he put down his cup and started to head towards the door.

'You said you lead a busy life,' she murmured as she walked with him. 'What is it that takes up most of your time outside work?'

'I help to manage my father's estate. The manager has taken extended leave to deal with a family crisis in Ireland, so I've had to step into the breach in the meantime.'

His father's estate. She frowned, and all at once alarm bells started to ring faintly inside her head. Memories of her past came flooding back to haunt her, causing a feeling of nausea to start up in her stomach, and she tried to quash the thoughts that were crowding her mind. There wasn't necessarily anything untoward in what he was saying.

'His estate?' she said in a guarded voice. 'That

sounds like something quite involved. What kind of estate is it?'

'Farming, mostly, with a dairy and creamery on site. There are other things going on there as well—there's an orchard, and a lake where people can go to fish.' He glanced at her, as though gauging her reaction. 'My father isn't too well at the moment, so he's finding it difficult to oversee things. He tried to get someone to take over the management on a temporary basis, but that hasn't worked out so I've had to get involved.'

'You're talking about Lord Birchenall's estate, aren't you?' She said it in a hoarse whisper, while the blood drained from her face. 'You're his son?'

'That's right.' He studied her, his expression solemn. 'Does it matter?'

'I thought there was something about you—that I knew you from somewhere. I just never dreamt…' She pulled in a shaky breath and then looked up, her gaze meeting his. 'You've changed. You're so much more…' She broke off. The gangly youth she remembered was gone.

This man was muscled, toned, his features etched by the trials and tribulations of the years that had passed. 'I don't suppose you remember me?' He'd headed off to medical school when she had been around thirteen or fourteen years old. Why would he have given her a second thought?

'Of course I do. It was a long while ago, and you've filled out in all the right places, but how could I forget you, Ellie? You were always up to something, climbing trees, camping out in the woods. I watched out for you, in case you landed yourself in a scrape.'

He'd watched out for her? She cast that thought to

one side. 'Why didn't you tell me you knew who I was all along?' A flash of bitter defiance shot through her, making her green eyes spark with anger. 'You should have said something right at the start, when Zoe introduced us.'

'And lose the chance of talking to you?' His dark brows lifted. 'I may be many things, Ellie, but I'm not a fool.'

'No, you're Lord Birchenall's son—and you've been brought up to believe in his values and everything he stands for.'

'And what would those be, Ellie?'

'That all that matters is his own comfort, his own perfectly organised way of life.' She bit out the words through clenched teeth as she gave vent to her feelings of resentment and betrayal. 'Nothing must get in the way of his wellbeing, must it? Woe betide any hapless worker who falls foul of Lord Birchenall.'

'Aren't you being a little melodramatic?'

She gasped. 'How can you say that to me? My father was Lord Birchenall's estate manager for a dozen or more years until your father sacked him and threw him off his land. We lost everything…the house that went with the job, our livelihood, our unity as a family.'

'I know that must have been a tremendous blow to you, but are you so sure your father didn't bring it on himself? I remember my father being angry, at the end of his tether. Things had not been running smoothly, there were glitches, problems. I don't know all the reasons why it happened, Ellie, but I'm sure my father wouldn't have acted without due cause.'

'And you didn't care what became of his family afterwards?'

'That's not true. I did care. But I went away to medical school around about that time, and I didn't know what went on after I left. I asked my father what happened to you and he said you'd moved to a house in the village.'

She opened the front door and stood to one side to let him pass.

'What else could we do? We had to move in with friends for the first few months. He ruined our lives, that's what happened.' She pressed her lips together to hold back the anger that was taking hold of her. 'I'd hoped I could put it behind me after all these years, but now it's come flooding back with a vengeance.'

She stiffened, bracing her shoulders, and her gaze locked with his. 'You should go,' she said.

He stepped outside into the porch, and then turned to face her once more. 'I'm sorry you feel this way. It was all a long time ago. Maybe it's time for you to let it go.'

'I don't think that's possible.'

'That's unfortunate.' He frowned, studying her face in the moonlight. 'Goodnight, Ellie.' He nodded briefly and then strode across the gravelled drive to his car.

She watched him go. She'd thought the day couldn't get any worse…

CHAPTER TWO

'THANKS FOR THIS, Ellie.' Noah folded the cheque Ellie had given him and slid it into his wallet. 'I'll pay you back as soon as I can, I promise.'

Her brother looked earnest, his youthful features lit with relief. 'It's just that things are difficult for me right now, with the magazine closing down—it was my best source of income. But I'll make a go of this freelance work, I know I will.'

'I'm sure you will, eventually.' Ellie finished off the last slice of toast and brushed the crumbs from her fingers. It was worrying, the way things had been going for him lately. They'd been through a lot together, and she'd always looked out for him. If only there was some way she could help him get out of this mess.

'Perhaps you could look for something a bit more secure in the meantime? There must be some regular jobs in photography—in advertising, maybe, or even something like illustrating medical books. I know it's not what you're used to.'

He pulled a face, his hazel eyes troubled. 'I'll try, honestly I will—I know I need to sort something out. I've spent the whole weekend looking for alternatives. But photojournalism's what I'm really interested in.'

She nodded, and began to clear away the breakfast dishes. 'Did you want any more tea, or shall I empty the pot?'

'I'm fine, thanks. I should go and try to appease the landlord.' He patted the wallet in his pocket. 'This will keep him off my back for a while at least.'

'And I must get ready for work.' Her green eyes clouded momentarily and Noah gave her a thoughtful look. 'Is something wrong? You don't look too happy about that. I thought you loved your work?'

'I do…mostly.' Her patient's death still haunted her, and the whole episode with Mel's unsettling reaction had thrown her off balance somehow. It would take her some time to get back into her stride.

But that wasn't it.

'The new consultant's starting work today.' She winced. 'I met him at Zoe's party—turns out he's Lord Birchenall's son.'

'Birchenall?' Noah bit out the word with distaste. 'No wonder you're out of sorts. I thought we'd seen the last of that family.' He frowned. 'Perhaps I should have guessed. I read in the paper that he was back home to take care of his father—the old man is suffering from some kind of heart condition, apparently.'

'Is he? James said he was unwell, but he didn't go into detail.'

'James? You're on first-name terms with him?' Noah's lips tightened. 'I wish you didn't have to deal with him at all. How do we know it won't turn out to be like father, like son? You could go along with him thinking everything's fine, and then when something goes wrong you find he's turned against you. It's all in the genes.'

'You could be right,' she acknowledged thoughtfully. 'We'll see. I suppose I'll just have to be cautious around him until I get to know him better.'

'Yeah, well, it's a pity you have to know him at all. I'm sorry you've ended up having to work with him.' He frowned. 'I'd better go. Thanks for breakfast, and good luck.'

'You, too.'

After he'd gone, Ellie finished tidying the kitchen and glanced at the clock on the wall. It was about time for her to set off for work, but just as she reached for her jacket, the doorbell rang.

'Lily.' Ellie was startled to see her neighbour standing there. Lily was heavily pregnant, and right now she looked flushed and her breathing was fast, making her struggle to drag air into her lungs. Her face appeared a little puffy, and when Ellie glanced down at her hands, she saw that there was some swelling there, too. Her brown curls were faintly damp around her face, and Ellie became increasingly concerned. 'Are you all right? Is it the baby? Are you having contractions?'

Lily shook her head. 'No, but I have to go to hospital—the ambulance will be here any minute. The midwife sent for it. I have a terrible headache, and my ankles are swollen. She said something about hypertension and pre-eclampsia—she thinks they'll keep me in for a few days.'

'I'm so sorry, Lily.' Ellie put a comforting arm around her. 'Do you want to sit down? Shall I get you a chair?'

Lily shook her head. 'No, thanks. But I do need to ask a big favour.' She gave her a worried look.

'It's okay. Anything. What is it? What can I do for you?'

'It's Jayden—he's at nursery school right now, and my friend will pick him up and look after him after school, but I wondered, just in case they do keep me in, if you would have him stay with you for the next few nights? I know it's an awful lot to ask, but Harry's away in Switzerland, trying to sort out some problems with the company, and my parents are on holiday abroad. I don't know what else to do.'

Ellie thought about the small guest bedroom upstairs. She'd have to bump up the heating in there and get in a few provisions to satisfy a four-year-old's diet, but otherwise there shouldn't be a problem. 'That's okay. I can do that for you. I'll be glad to help. And Jayden often comes here to see me, so he's used to being around the place. Don't worry about it. Just concentrate on getting yourself well again.'

'Oh, thanks, Ellie,' Lily said in a relieved tone. 'I don't know what I'd have done without you. Here, have my key—you'll need to pick up some clothes for Jayden and some of his toys.' An anxious look crossed her face. 'He always takes his teddy to bed with him. He won't sleep without it.'

'I'll make sure he has it. Rest easy, and take care of yourself.'

The midwife came to help Lily back to her house across the courtyard as the ambulance arrived, and Ellie went with them, waving her neighbour goodbye before setting off for the hospital. It was worrying, seeing her in that situation, but at least the paramedics were with her and would take care of her.

The A and E department was busy as usual when she

arrived there a short time later. She'd had a weekend away from work and she found she was apprehensive coming back to it, a little bit uneasy about dealing with patients who were very ill, after her experience with her friend's aunt. Although she felt she'd followed the correct procedures, her confidence had been badly shaken by Mel's outburst. It was difficult getting back into the fray, but after an hour or so she had more or less settled into the routine and her anxiety eased a little.

From time to time she caught sight of James, working with the most seriously ill patients, and she did her very best to steer clear of him. In a way she was regretting her outburst the other night, because he hadn't done anything to deserve her wrath. It was just his family connection that had thrown her into a state of shock.

But she had to put all that aside if she was to do her job properly. Just now she was tending a young woman who'd fallen from a horse. Until the accident the girl had been enjoying a holiday at a pretty lakeside resort nearby, but her fall meant she'd ended up in the emergency unit, being treated for a broken arm.

'That was unfortunate, wasn't it, Natalie?' Ellie murmured. 'But the good news is that the X-ray shows a straightforward break. We'll re-align the bones for you under anaesthetic and then immobilise them with a cast. We should soon have you feeling more comfortable.'

'Thanks.' Natalie pulled a face. 'I guess that's put an end to my horse riding for a while.'

'I'm afraid so. It'll probably take six or eight weeks to heal, and you should be careful with it in the meantime. So…' she smiled '…I'd avoid abseiling or water-skiing for the time being.'

The girl laughed. 'I'll bear that in mind.'

Ellie left her with a nurse while she went to type up her notes on the computer. After a moment or two as she sat at the desk, she became aware of someone approaching, and looked up to see James coming to stand beside her. Her whole body tensed.

He was immaculately turned out, having discarded the scrubs he'd been wearing earlier and replaced them with a dark, expertly tailored suit and a crisp linen shirt that gave him an aura of authority. He wore a subtly patterned tie that picked out the colour of his smoke-grey eyes.

Maybe he was dressed this way because he had a meeting to attend. Either way, Ellie found his nearness extremely distracting. It unsettled her. She didn't want to be aware of him, especially not as a virile, energetic and powerful man.

'How are things going?' he asked. His expression was serious, his eyes cool and watchful. 'Are you getting back into the swing of things? I know it must have been difficult for you. I noticed you were a little hesitant at first when you were dealing with patients.'

Her eyes widened. Had he feared she wouldn't be able to cope? She stiffened.

'I'm fine,' she answered. 'There's no problem, none at all.'

'Hmm. You must tell me if things change.' He looked doubtful, and she guessed he thought she was covering up. 'After all, it's my job to see to the welfare of the staff, as well as the patients. I don't want you to feel that you must struggle on your own.'

'As I said, I don't foresee any difficulties.' If she'd known who he was the other night, she would never have admitted her worries to him. It had been a bad mistake. No doubt from now on he'd be watching her like a hawk.

She turned her attention back to the screen in front of her. With any luck, he might take the hint and leave her to get on with her work.

But things definitely weren't going her way. Instead, he sat down on the edge of the table and out of the corner of her eye she caught a glimpse of his long legs, the material of his trousers stretched tautly over his strong thighs. Disconcerted, she quickly averted her gaze.

Her fingers tapped jerkily at the keypad, and she realised straight away she'd made mistakes so that she had to delete what she'd just typed.

'Um, was there something else?' she queried. Having him so close jangled her nerves.

He inclined his head. 'I think you and I have some unfinished business,' he said quietly. 'I know you feel a lot of resentment towards me and my family, and I'm concerned that might be a problem for us at work.'

'I…I'm sure we can both act in a professional manner towards one another,' she said. 'Perhaps I was wrong in extending your father's actions to you, but I can't simply forget what happened, as you suggested. My parents' marriage fell apart because of it. My mother blamed my father for losing his job and making us all homeless.'

'Your mother felt that way, and yet you still put the blame on my father for letting him go?' His gaze was quizzical, those dark eyes studying her and taking in the slightest hint of vulnerability.

Her chin lifted in defiance. 'I think there were reasons why my father acted the way he did. He's a good man, and he always took a lot of pride in doing his job well. When things started to go wrong, your father should have talked to him a bit more and tried to get to the bottom of what was going on with him.'

James was sceptical. 'It doesn't seem as if your mother had much faith in her husband, so why should my father have been any different?'

Her eyes narrowed. 'My mother suffered from depression. She was always a difficult person to live with. She was so wrapped up in her woes that she left me and my brother to fend for ourselves. We took care of one another, and did pretty much as we pleased, but through all that my father was the cement that kept us all together. That is, until he…'

'Until he lost the plot.' He stood up. 'I'm sorry, Ellie. I know how much you must love him, but you're making excuses for his behaviour and taking your resentment out on my family. You need to get things straightened out in your head.'

'Do I?' Her gaze was frosty. 'I believe my father was ill. That's why he appeared to change and became lax in his work where before he had been a perfectionist. But nobody seemed to care enough about him to find out what was going on.'

She stood up as her pager bleeped. 'I'm afraid you'll have to excuse me. I have a patient coming in.'

She was annoyed with herself as she walked away. How could she have lost her temper that way? Surely she could have handled things better? And now, instead of smoothing the way towards a better working relationship, she'd probably set them off on a course of downright antagonism.

She had to force that to the back of her mind, though, and concentrate on answering her pager. She couldn't let her personal life interfere with her work.

Her patient was a pregnant woman who was bleeding heavily. 'She was out shopping when she collapsed,' the nurse told her. 'She's very shaken up. She's thirty-three weeks. Her heart rate is very fast and her blood pressure's dropping way too low.'

'Thanks, Olivia. Let's get a couple of intravenous lines in before she goes into shock—and we need to set up foetal monitoring.'

'I'll do that right away.' The nurse hurried to fetch the equipment while Ellie did an ultrasound scan to find out what was causing the problem. 'I know this is upsetting for you, Phoebe,' she said gently, 'but try not to worry.'

Phoebe nodded faintly. Small pearls of perspiration had broken out on her brow, dampening her dark hair, and Ellie gave her a reassuring smile. 'We'll take good care of you and your baby.'

A short time later, she turned to the nurse once more. 'I'm going to call Dr Reynolds for a consultation,' she said in a low voice. 'The placenta's covering the birth canal. It's come away slightly, and that's what's causing the bleeding. We need to admit her and make sure that she rests—that way the bleeding might stop on its own.'

She began to take blood for testing and quickly labelled up the samples for the lab. She was handing them to a porter a few minutes later when Lewis came to join her.

He smiled. 'Hi, Ellie. It's good to see you. You have a patient for me?'

'Yes.' She returned his smile. 'I'm glad you're here, Lewis. It's reassuring to know you're around to look after our pregnant ladies.' She handed him the patient's file. 'Phoebe has placenta praevia. I've arranged for her to be admitted.'

He glanced at the woman's notes. 'Okay, I'll go and have a look at her.'

He came back to Ellie a few minutes later as she stood by the central desk glancing through reports.

'We might have to do a Caesarean,' he said, 'but I'd prefer to leave it until it's absolutely necessary to give the baby the very best chance. In the meantime, we'll put her on steroids to help the foetus's lungs to mature.'

'I'll organise it,' she said. Remembering her neighbour, she said quietly, 'Have you admitted a new patient this morning—Lily Harcourt? She's my neighbour. She would have come in by ambulance, suffering from pre-eclampsia? I wondered how she was doing. With any luck I'll be able to look in on her some time today, but I'm a bit concerned about her. She didn't look too good this morning.'

'She's your friend?' Lewis's dark eyes clouded. 'I'm sorry, I didn't know. Yes, she came to my ward. We have her on oxygen, and we're monitoring her heart and blood pressure. Unfortunately, she had a seizure when she first arrived, but we're giving her medication to control her blood pressure and also to try to prevent any more convulsions. It's too early for her to deliver this baby at the moment, so we need to get her condition stabilised.'

Ellie frowned, disturbed by his account. 'It doesn't sound good, does it?'

He laid an arm lightly about her shoulders. 'You shouldn't worry, Ellie. We're doing everything we can for her.'

'I know, I'm sure you are. Thanks, Lewis. Will you keep me updated?'

'Of course.' He gave her a quick hug and then headed back to the maternity ward. Ellie watched him go and then glanced across the room and saw James standing by the doorway, his eyes narrowed as he watched her.

How long had he been standing there? He must have seen Lewis put his arm around her, and for some reason he didn't look at all pleased. Was he bothered in some way about her friendship with his cousin?

She turned away. Why should she be concerned about what he was thinking? He may not have the same temperament as his father, but he obviously had the Birchenalls' way of taking control and keeping a check on everyone. He'd only been in the job five minutes and he was making sure he knew everything there was to know about the staff. She'd seen him looking at others in that calm, assessing way that seemed natural to him.

She looked in on Lily before she finished her shift, and reassured her that she would take care of her little boy. Her friend still looked slightly flushed and seemed a bit restless, but that was probably because she was worried about her son.

'We'll come and see you as soon as the doctor says it's okay,' Ellie promised. 'In fact, I could get him to talk to you on the phone if that will make you feel better?'

'Oh, it would. Thanks, Ellie.'

'You're welcome.'

Ellie drove home, soothed by the beautiful Cheshire countryside, with its wooded hillsides and rolling plains. It helped put her in a relaxed frame of mind, so that for a little while she could forget that James Birchenall was a thorn in her side.

She stopped to pick up Jayden from his friend's house, and from then on any illusion of peace was shattered.

'Can we make play dough?' the four-year-old asked. 'I liked it when we did that before when I comed to your house.' He looked at her with shining grey eyes, full of eagerness and expectation.

'Okay. That sounds like a good idea.' Ellie remembered the last time, when loose bits of brightly coloured dough had escaped and gone off in all directions. She'd kept on finding bits of it all over the place for a couple of hours afterwards, mainly thanks to it being trampled underfoot by eager young feet. He'd even managed to get it tangled up among the curls in his dark hair.

'I thought we'd have spaghetti for tea. That's your favourite, isn't it?'

'Mmm. Yes. I always have s'ghetti. Every day.' He gave her a big-eyed look and she hid a smile.

'Do you? Really?'

'Yes.' He looked away uncertainly, as though he thought she might stop believing him if he held her gaze for too long.

'Well, we'll see what we can do. Let's go and collect your things from your house first and get you settled in.'

'All right.'

Some time later Ellie helped him to get ready for bed. They'd had a busy time, having fun with play dough, followed by a baking session, and by now she was worn out even if he wasn't.

'Mummy always tucks me in,' he said with a quiver in his voice, as he climbed into bed and looked around the strange room.

'I know, sweetheart, and I know she wishes she could

be here with you now, but you talked to her on the phone, didn't you? Remember, she said she'll see you when we go to the hospital?'

He nodded solemnly, his eyes overbright.

'How about I read you a bedtime story?' Ellie said. 'Give teddy a cuddle and slide down under the duvet, and we'll see what Noddy's getting up to in his little red car.'

'Yeah.'

He'd fallen asleep before she finished the story, and Ellie switched off the bedside lamp and crept out of the room.

Downstairs, she cleared away Jayden's toys and tidied the kitchen, and just as she was thinking about making herself a well-earned cup of coffee, the doorbell rang. She frowned. She wasn't expecting anyone. Could it be Noah, in more trouble? Feeling apprehensive, she went to the door and found James standing there.

'Oh…I…um…'

He'd changed out of his suit, into casual, stylish clothes, stone-coloured chinos and a navy long-sleeved shirt, but there was still that air of authority about him. Somehow she sensed he wasn't there for a social visit. 'Is something wrong?'

'In a manner of speaking. Would it be all right if I come in? I don't mean to disturb you, but I need to talk to you about something and I'd prefer not to do it at the hospital.'

'Yes, of course.' He seemed serious, and she was troubled now, wondering what was so important that he'd come to see her at home. 'We'll go through to the kitchen and I'll put the coffee on.'

She led the way and waved him to a chair by the oak

and granite topped table. 'It sounds as though I should be worried,' she said as she prepared the coffee. 'What's happened?' She put some freshly made fruit scones on a plate and passed it to him. 'Help yourself. There's butter and some strawberry jam.'

He looked at the golden-topped scones and smiled. 'A sample of your home baking? I thought there was a wonderful smell in the kitchen.' He sent her a quick, appreciative glance. 'How could I resist? Thanks. I haven't eaten yet this evening, so these will fill a hole.'

She raised her brows. 'You've not eaten? How did that come about?'

He shrugged. 'I was busy. I had a difficult case to deal with—a perforated appendix—and there were a couple of meetings I had to attend—one of them straight after my shift finished. It happens like that sometimes.' He cut a scone in half, spreading butter on each portion, and then added a spoonful of jam.

'Hmm. Perhaps you could introduce a snacks trolley so staff can grab a bite to eat if they can't make time to go to the restaurant. It shouldn't cost much and we could all chip in to fund it.' She poured coffee and slid a cup towards him. She wasn't going to sit down. That would be too much like supping with the enemy.

'That's a good idea…a very good idea.' He bit into the scone and for a moment, as he chewed, a look of absorbed bliss came over his face. Ellie's breath caught in her throat. There was a boyish look about him that tugged at her heart and for a moment or two she floundered. 'These are delicious,' he said, smiling his satisfaction.

'Hmm.' She pulled herself together and studied him. 'Does that mean I get to keep my job?'

His brows met in puzzlement and she added, 'There was something you needed to tell me?'

'Ah.' He finished off the scone and swallowed some of the coffee. 'I wish I didn't have to tell you this, but…' He paused. 'Amelia Holt came into the hospital today and made a formal complaint. She believes her aunt didn't receive the proper care and attention she needed, resulting in her death.'

'Oh, no.' Ellie went pale, and felt for a seat opposite him, sitting down as her legs seemed to give way. 'I know she was upset, but what does she think I should have done?'

'She says you should have done a pericardiectomy. She's obviously been looking things up or talking to someone who knows a bit about medicine.'

'But that kind of surgery is usually a last resort.' Her mouth was dry and her heart had suddenly begun to thump heavily against her rib cage. She swallowed hard. 'Removing the pericardium is a risky procedure, and her aunt's heart was already weak.'

'I agree. It wouldn't have been the first course of action I'd have taken, but we have to acknowledge the complaint, I'm afraid.'

'So what happens now?' Ellie's palms were clammy, and she rubbed them against her jeans. Inside she was shaking.

'We have to set up a meeting with her to discuss the issue. If she accepts your viewpoint, there won't be anything more to be said, but if not, we have to take it through an independent review procedure.'

'All right. I understand. I…I just have to wait and see how…how things…'

He reached for her hand and captured it between

his. 'Ellie, it's going to be all right. You've done nothing wrong.'

'I know, but…' The warmth of his caress comforted her, and for a while she lost herself in that gentle, yet firm, grasp. 'I still…'

'I'll go with you to the meeting, if that will help. You don't need to worry about this. I'm on your side.'

She nodded. 'Yes. I'd appreciate that. Thank you.'

He held her hand for a while longer, until she seemed to have calmed down. She let out a soft, shuddery sigh.

'Okay, then,' he said, gently releasing her. 'I'll arrange everything. Don't think about it again until the meeting.' His gaze meshed with hers. 'Promise me you'll cast it from your mind?'

'I'll try.' In spite of herself, she was already missing that warm embrace. Of course, she should never have let him comfort her—she didn't want to get close to the man whose father had destroyed her family. And yet…

'Good. I'm sorry I had to bring bad news.'

She nodded. 'I suppose we all have troubles to bear.' She glanced at him. 'I hear that things aren't so good for you back home. I know you said your father was unwell, but it's quite serious, isn't it?'

'His heart is failing, so life is difficult for him.' He braced his shoulders. 'It's not as bad as it sounds—as you know, people can live for years with heart failure. It's more a matter of quality of life that needs to be addressed.'

'Yes.' When someone's heart began to fail, it meant that the heart couldn't cope with pumping blood around the body, resulting in breathlessness, discomfort and fatigue.

'Still,' she said, 'he must be glad to have you back home. Are you living at the manor house?'

'I am.'

'And is that working out all right? You get on well with him, don't you?'

'Yes, I do.' He gave a wry smile. 'I'm his only son and he's relying on me to take care of things and secure the family's heritage.'

She thought about that. 'I suppose you've had your career to keep you busy up till now. Becoming a consultant is a huge step.'

'It is.' He might have said something more, except that a small sound alerted them to the fact that they were no longer alone in the kitchen. They turned round.

Jayden stood in the doorway, clutching his teddy bear in the crook of his arm and rubbing his eye sleepily with his free hand. 'You putted the light out,' he said accusingly, looking at Ellie. 'I has to have the light on.'

Ellie hurried over to him and crouched down, bringing herself to his level. 'Oh, Jayden, sweetheart, I'm sorry.'

She'd turned the lamp out in case the light disturbed him. 'Let me take you back to bed. I'll leave your bedroom door open a little and put the hall light on. Will that be all right?'

The little boy nodded, and Ellie took hold of his hand to gently lead him back upstairs. She glanced back at James. 'I won't be long.'

'That's okay.' He said it slowly and she saw that he was staring at Jayden in some kind of shock, his eyes wide, and a small frown creased his brow. Then he seemed to get himself together. 'Actually, uh…no need to rush. I should go. I have to go on to a dinner party.'

'Oh, I see. Of course…if you must.'

Jayden looked up at him. 'Who that?' he asked, holding onto Ellie's leg for protection as she stood up.

'I work with him at the hospital,' she told him quietly.

James made an effort to relax and said with a smile, 'Hello, Jayden.'

Jayden didn't answer, but gave him a cautious look from under his lashes.

'Come on,' Ellie murmured. 'Let's take you back to bed. You have to get up for school in the morning.' She glanced at James once more. 'Give me a minute and I'll see you out.'

'That's all right. I can see myself out. You go ahead.' He walked towards the door. 'I'll see you tomorrow.'

'All right, then. Bye.' She couldn't quite understand the expression on his face, a mixture of disbelief and conjecture, and it was only after James had gone that it finally dawned on her…he thought Jayden was her child. But he'd gone, without giving her a chance to explain.

CHAPTER THREE

'IS THERE SOMETHING on your mind?' Lewis studied Ellie thoughtfully as they walked together towards A and E. 'What's wrong? Is it something to do with your TV programme? You look worried.'

'Do I?' Ellie covered her feelings with an attempt at a smile. 'No, I'm not worried. Everything's fine.' And that was true, at least as far as her TV career was concerned. She was to record the next programme in the series in a few days' time.

As to the rest, things were unravelling fast, and she couldn't begin to tell him about that—where would she start? With the fact that in the last few days she'd discovered that her hospital career was under a cloud, or that her boss was the very last person she'd want to work with? Or maybe she could blame her troubles on the cryptic text message she'd received from Noah that morning—one that had left her wondering what on earth was about to explode in her face and cause all manner of fallout. He must have sent it yesterday, but she'd been busy looking after Jayden and hadn't checked her messages.

Things are on the up and up. Just had a huge scoop—the Sunday Supplement printed my article and photo exposé about the Birchenalls. Will get a copy to you.

Despite her bad feelings towards Lord Birchenall, she would never have condoned putting forward any piece of writing that drew a negative picture of his family. It wasn't in her to take that kind of revenge.

Unfortunately, though, it looked as though she was too late to put the brakes on Noah. Today was Monday, which meant the paper had already gone out. Whatever the article contained, it didn't sound good, and she could only hope James hadn't seen it.

'Is it to do with your meeting with Amelia Holt tomorrow?' Lewis persisted. 'It must be on your mind.'

'I suppose it is, but I'm trying not to think about it.'

'I can understand that.' He glanced at her. 'Perhaps we could have lunch together tomorrow, and you can tell me all about it?

She nodded. She certainly didn't want to talk about any of her problems to Lewis, though, so she did her best to change the subject as they walked into the emergency unit.

'How is Lily getting on?' she asked. 'I went to see her over the weekend, and although she hid it from Jayden, it seemed to me she was a bit down.'

Jayden had been overjoyed to see his mother. He'd given her a picture he'd made, showing her sitting up in bed, with a teddy bear of her own to cheer her up. He'd beamed brightly when she'd given him a hug and a kiss in exchange.

Lewis pulled a face. 'It's only to be expected, I suppose. She has an intravenous drip to contend with, she's not enjoying the enforced rest, and she wants to be with her child. And, of course, her husband's still away. That can't be good for her peace of mind, and it has a bad effect on her blood pressure.'

Ellie frowned. 'He offered to come straight home from Switzerland to be with her, but she was worried about the effect on the business. He owns the company, so it's their livelihood. Unfortunately he's had to deal with a lot of difficult situations in the Swiss branch lately.'

'That's bound to cause a conflict of loyalties, I suppose.'

She nodded. 'I told her I'm okay looking after Jayden, and she hasn't gone into labour, so she told him to finish what he went there for. He says he's going to come over here to be with her and then go back to work next day. Of course, they talk all the time on the phone, so that helps.'

'Well, we seem to have stabilised her condition for now, but I'm keeping her on bed rest—her blood pressure does vary and we need to keep it down. As soon as I feel the time is right, we'll deliver her baby by Caesarean section.'

'At least I know she's in safe hands.'

He smiled and said teasingly, 'You know I'm taking extra-special care of her just because she's your friend.'

Ellie laughed and they parted company as she set out to work her way down her list of patients and Lewis went off to answer his pager call.

James watched her approach the desk. He was there looking through a sheaf of papers, and as she came closer she saw they were lab reports.

'Hi, there,' she greeted him, but he only nodded in return, his eyes half-closed as he watched Lewis head towards one of the treatment bays. She looked at him in confusion. That wasn't the reaction she'd expected. Again she had the feeling that there was some reason he didn't want her being friendly with Lewis. Or was there something more to it?

'I have to go out,' he said, 'so perhaps you could deal with the angina patient in room three?' His tone was curt and she sent him a quick glance. His whole body was taut, she noticed, and a muscle was flexing in his jaw.

'Okay.' She frowned. 'Will you be coming back at all today?'

'I don't know. My father was taken ill yesterday, and just now I had a call to say he's taken a turn for the worse. I have to go and be with him.'

'Oh, I'm so sorry,' she said, a flood of sympathy washing over her. 'That must be worrying for you.' A horrible thought struck her. Had he seen the Sunday papers?

He didn't answer her, but his smoke-dark gaze met hers like the lash of a whip, and she felt her throat go dry.

'James…'

'I've examined the patient briefly and he has unstable angina. He'll probably need to be scheduled for cardiac catheterisation as soon as possible. I've given him blood-thinning medication, but he'll need a beta-blocker and—'

'I'll see to it,' she cut in. 'Really, you don't need to be concerned. I'll do everything necessary.' Didn't he trust her? Was he having second thoughts about her competency now that Mel had made an official complaint?

'I'm not concerned. Not about that, at any rate.'

'Then what is it that's troubling you?'

'Perhaps you should talk to your brother about that. His article in the Sunday paper wasn't even based on truth—my father's business dealings are all above board. He would never harass anyone. And as for myself, what gives him the right to lay out my private life in the tabloids for all to see? What he did was irresponsible—unforgivable—especially given my father's precarious state of health.'

He dropped the papers back in the tray and strode away before she could answer him. All at once her stomach felt like lead. So he *had* seen the newspaper. Now, more than ever, she wanted to know what Noah had written.

'He's well and truly put out, isn't he?' Olivia said, frowning, as she came to look at a patient's file. She pushed a stray lock of fair hair behind her ear. 'I've not seen him like that before—mind you, if you've seen the paper… I guess you must have—there's a copy in the staff lounge.'

'I haven't seen it,' Ellie answered quietly. 'What's it all about?'

'Well, it's to do with both him and his father. James has this upper-crust girlfriend, Sophie Granger—'

'He does?' Unexpectedly, Ellie's heart plummeted. It hadn't occurred to her that James was spoken for. But why would he not be involved? After all, he was an extremely eligible man.

Olivia nodded. 'She's from a well-to-do family—you know the sort of thing, born to money. They're close friends of the Birchenalls, apparently. Anyway, there were several photos of him with her, but then there are also pictures of him leaving a private dinner party with another beautiful young woman. The article sort of makes him sound like a philanderer.'

Ellie absorbed all that. Perhaps there was no truth in any of it. Her brother might have seen James with these women and made up his own mind about what was going on. On the other hand, she'd already had one bad experience with her ex. Shouldn't she have learned a lesson from that? How was James any different from him?

'And his father? What does the article say about him?'

Olivia winced. 'It makes him out to be a ruthless businessman. Apparently he's been trying to obtain some land from his neighbour so that he can expand the dairy farm and add more trees to the orchard. The only problem is, the owner of the land doesn't want to part with it, and complains he's being harassed.'

'Oh, dear.' Ellie groaned inwardly. What had Noah been thinking? He must have followed James over the last few days in order to get this scoop, and had somehow managed to delve into his father's business dealings.

'I feel sorry for James,' Olivia said. 'He's not been here long, but he's been fair to everyone and treated us well. He's always there to listen if you need to talk.' She smiled. 'He's even started to bring in cakes and pasties for when we need to grab a quick bite to eat. I asked him who's paying for it, and he said he was.'

Ellie closed her eyes briefly. Was she wrong to see James as the enemy? His father had hurt her family badly, but was that anything to do with James? She would have to try to do something to put this right. Maybe if her neighbour could keep Jayden for a little longer this evening, she should pay James a visit. She would give her a call and find out.

She'd no idea what she would say to James, but surely she had no choice but to try to make amends? She had to work with him, after all.

And as to Noah... He'd never behaved this way before. Did his dislike of the Birchenalls go so deep that he would go against his principles? Maybe in the cool light of day he would come to regret what he had done.

As soon as she found time to take a break, she called him. 'What were you thinking, Noah, going ahead with a piece like that? Don't you realise how much trouble you've caused?'

'I just took advantage of circumstances,' Noah protested. 'I was in the area and I saw Birchenall standing there with his arm around this pretty young woman. It's exactly the sort of thing that sells.' She could feel the frown in his voice. 'I thought you'd be pleased. It means I can pay you back the money you loaned me.'

'How could I be pleased? You said yourself Lord Birchenall has a bad heart. How did you think he would be affected by what you wrote? And as for myself—James is my boss! I have to work with him. Heaven knows how far this has set us back.'

'He'll come round.' Noah shrugged it off. 'His kind of people are used to this sort of thing. They're in the public eye all the time.'

It was clear he didn't understand her point of view, and eventually Ellie cut the call, feeling more disturbed than ever. She would have to do something to try and smooth things over.

When her shift finished at the end of the afternoon, she checked on Jayden at her friend's house, and then hurried home to change into something presentable. It was important that she look her best, because she had to muster all the confidence she possessed if she was to face up to both James and his father.

In the end, she chose a midnight-blue dress that swathed her figure in gentle folds, and added a light touch of make-up to lend a soft flush of colour to her cheeks. Her hair fell loosely about her shoulders, the silky, chestnut curls gleaming with health.

It was several years since she'd been anywhere near her former home, and as she drove along the Birchenalls' sweeping drive in the early evening, memories of her childhood came flooding back.

Her family had lived in the lodge, a neat cottage situated in the grounds, and she'd spent the summers exploring the surrounding woods with her friends. They'd fished for tiddlers in the brook that ran through the estate, and picked wild flowers in the meadows. They had been blissful times, until her father had lost his way and their world had fallen apart.

The manor house came into view and she gazed at it with a mixture of awe and apprehension. How would James and her father respond to her turning up here? She would be their least favourite person at the moment.

She drew the car to a halt on the cobbled drive and stepped out to look around. She'd always loved this beautiful old house, with its white-painted walls and pretty leaded windows. The building was wide and symmetrical, with an extended middle portion whose tiled roof met at right angles with the main roof structure. In front of that was a large covered porch, again with its own roof canopy.

Steeling herself, she approached the front door and

rang the bell. Then she waited, her heart beginning to pound. Why on earth was she feeling so nervous? There was no explanation, except that perhaps this place—and its owner—had been at the root of all her family's troubles.

'Ellie?' James frowned when he opened the door then pulled it wider. He was wearing dark chinos and a shirt that was open at the neck to reveal his lightly bronzed throat.

Ellie swallowed and tried to work out what she was going to say.

His gaze ran over her briefly as he tried to read her expression. 'Has something happened at the hospital—something I need to know about?'

'No, not at all,' she said quickly. 'It's nothing like that.' She hesitated. 'I just wanted to know if your father had recovered at all? I felt I had to come here and say how sorry I am that my brother caused you and your father any distress. I don't think—'

'Come in,' he said. He ushered her into a large hallway and then led the way to a sitting room. In here, the evening sunlight filtered through diamond panes of glass, glinting on crystal vases and fluted goblets set out in a display cabinet. Table lamps shed small pools of golden light over mahogany occasional tables, and lit up the open fireplace where an original oak beam formed the main feature. Overhead there were more beams, lending an old-world look to the room.

'How is your father?' she asked.

'He had a nasty setback, but thankfully he's feeling much better now.'

'Can I ask what happened?'

He nodded. 'I think the stress of reading the article

overloaded his heart, so that he had trouble getting his breath. I gave him oxygen and medication to relieve the symptoms. It took a while, but eventually he began to pull round. Then today he was bombarded with calls from the press. They even camped out on the driveway.'

She frowned. 'I didn't see anyone out there.'

'No. I called the police and had them moved on.' His expression was bleak. 'My father can't take the strain these days.'

'No. I realise that. I feel bad about all this. I don't think Noah really understood the implications of what he was doing.'

'Hmm.' His glance shimmered over her, taking in her worried look and the silent plea in her green eyes. He laid a finger gently under her chin. 'It's actually Noah who should be here apologising. You didn't need to take it on yourself to come here in his place.'

'N-no…' She stumbled over her words, distracted by the soothing touch of his hand. It was almost like a caress. 'But I felt it was necessary. I would never have wanted this to happen.'

He released her and went over to a cabinet at the side of the room. 'Can I get you a drink?'

She shook her head. 'I'm driving but thanks. Maybe a juice of some sort if you have it.' Her mouth was dry and she needed some kind of pick-me-up.

'Okay.' He took out a tall glass and added a generous portion of ice, topping it up with fruit juice. He handed it to her with a paper coaster and poured himself a small measure of whisky.

She looked around the room. 'This is a lovely room. It seems strange, but I don't think I've ever been in this house more than a few times over the years,' she murmured. 'I would go to the back entrance when I had messages to pass on from my father, and your housekeeper would slip me a cookie or a fruit tart if she'd been baking. I think it's down to her that I developed the urge to learn to cook.'

He smiled. 'Harriet's still with us, though she works fewer hours now. I'm very fond of her. She took me under her wing and helped me a lot after my mother died. She became like a second mother to me.'

Ellie nodded. 'I remember how kind she was.' She hesitated. 'I noticed there are some pictures of your mother around the room. You couldn't have been very old when she died.'

'No. I was ten or eleven.'

Ellie's heart went out to that young boy who must have been through so much anguish. 'That must have come as a real shock to you.'

'Yes, it did, though she'd been ill for some time, and I remember wishing that I knew more about medicine so that I could make her better.'

Ellie laid her hand gently on his arm. 'I can't imagine how awful that must have been for you.'

His expression was wistful, acknowledging her compassion. 'Perhaps there was a silver lining, after all. I guess that's what made me decide to become a doctor.'

She nodded and let her hand slide away from him. 'How did your father react to that decision? I imagine he would have preferred you to stay here and run the estate when you were of age.'

'That's right, he did. It caused a few problems to begin with. But, going back, I think my mother's passing had a huge effect on my father. He became bitter and more intolerant of other people.'

'I think I can see how that would happen.' So perhaps that was why he'd let her father go without a second thought?

The door opened then and to her dismay Lord Birchenall came into the room. He had steel-grey hair and regular features, and Ellie noticed that he walked with a slight stoop.

'James,' he said, then stopped suddenly as he saw Ellie standing there. 'Ah, I thought I heard voices.' He looked her over, his dark eyes assessing, missing nothing. 'I don't think I have had the pleasure,' he said with a smile. He glanced towards his son, clearly expecting an introduction.

James inclined his head a fraction. 'This is Ellie,' he responded. 'She's changed quite a lot over the years, so you perhaps won't remember her but she's John Saunders's daughter.'

Lord Birchenall stiffened. His jaw clenched and he turned his attention back to Ellie, saying tersely, 'I can't imagine why you would show your face here after the piece your brother wrote about us.' His breath rasped in his lungs, and the colour rose alarmingly in his cheeks.

She was taken aback by the vehemence of his words but she tried to ignore his obvious hostility. 'I haven't read the article,' she said, 'but I do understand that it must have been upsetting for you.'

He gave a snort of derision.

Ellie pulled in a deep breath and started again. 'I came here to apologise for my brother's actions. I don't think he thought things through. You must understand that he feels a lot of resentment towards you after what happened to our father. I think he seized an opportunity to tip the scales, as it were.'

Lord Birchenall's brows rose sharply in angry disbelief and she hurried to add, 'I'm not condoning what he did in any way, but I'm just trying to explain what might lie behind it.'

'Why would he choose to do this now, after all this time?'

Ellie moved restlessly, suddenly uncomfortable. 'I think it was because James…because your son started to work at the hospital with me. It has thrown us into close contact after all this time, and it seems to have stirred everything up again.'

She hesitated then went on. 'Noah was quite young when my father lost his job and it had a huge effect on him. Perhaps now, as an adult, he felt the need to express his feelings. But I realise that you've been ill and I'm sorry that he hurt you.'

'Hmmph.' Clearly Lord Birchenall wasn't appeased. His eyes narrowed on her. 'I remember you now. You're that wayward little madam who ran amok through the village, getting into all sorts of trouble after you left here. I suppose you'll say that was my fault, too?'

Ellie's face paled. It was true her behaviour had deteriorated badly when their family life had fallen apart. But she hadn't been expecting that full-on assault and she didn't know how to answer him.

James stepped forward. 'Ellie came here to apologise,' he said in a quiet reprimand. 'I don't see that there's any need to add more fuel to the fire.'

Lord Birchenall ignored him and pressed on. 'Your father simply didn't do his job properly,' he told her. 'He was warned what would happen if his work didn't improve, but he chose to ignore those warnings.' He struggled to get his breath. 'Whatever happened is on his head.'

Ellie braced her shoulders. She was very conscious that this man was unwell, and she didn't want to exacerbate that situation in any way, but she was goaded into defending her father.

'He worked for you for many years without a problem. If his behaviour became erratic after that, there had to be a reason and the truth is he was ill. That's what caused things to go wrong, and being dismissed and thrown out of his house with no means of fending for his family led him on a downward spiral.'

His mouth flattened. 'I'd have expected you to make excuses for him.'

He turned away from her, glancing at his son. 'I came in here to tell you that Sophie phoned earlier when you were out.' Becoming unsteady on his feet, he began to reach behind him for a chair, and James came forward to lend him a supporting arm.

He sat down, taking a moment to pull air into his lungs. 'She's upset about the article, too, so I persuaded her to come along and have dinner with us. We'll have to do our best to sort things out.'

James frowned. 'I'm sure Sophie won't be upset for long.'

Ellie's stomach clenched involuntarily. He didn't seem too concerned. Maybe he was confident enough in his relationship with his girlfriend to be certain he could smooth things over with her. That thought made her feel strangely out of sorts.

'I think I'd better go,' she said, putting down her empty glass. 'I have to pick up Jayden from a friend's house.'

'Of course.' He glanced at her left hand and must have seen that it was bare of rings. He seemed puzzled, but she was in no mood to explain things, especially with his father looking on.

She wasn't sure quite what she'd achieved by coming here. Lord Birchenall was still aggrieved, and it looked as though she was in the way because James was about to get ready to greet his girlfriend.

'Goodbye, Lord Birchenall.'

He nodded. 'Goodbye, Miss Saunders.'

'It's actually Dr Saunders,' James murmured, but his father didn't bother to acknowledge that comment.

James took Ellie lightly by the elbow and led her to the hallway. 'I'm sorry about the way my father spoke to you,' he said as they walked to the door.

'It's all right.' His hand on her arm was comforting, and for one wild moment she wished she could turn to him and let him soothe away all her problems. Of course, it would never happen.

James gazed down at her. 'He's always been very forthright—I'm afraid it's a quality that can be both a blessing and a curse.'

'Yes, I imagine it is.' She half turned towards the door. 'Goodbye, James.'

'Goodbye.' He held open the door for her and she stepped out onto the porch. She was desperate to leave.

More and more she was seeing that it had been a mistake to come here. Perhaps in a naive way she had been hoping for some kind of redemption, but instead she felt more dejected than ever.

It was odd, because she had no idea why she was feeling that way.

CHAPTER FOUR

'WHEN'S MY MUMMY coming home?' Jayden spooned breakfast cereal into his mouth and looked at Ellie with wide grey eyes.

Ellie made a small start. Her thoughts had been far away, with James and the way her body responded to his slightest touch. It was disturbing to have so little control over her emotions and she would have to guard against that. After all, he had a girlfriend. It ought not to have bothered her to discover that, but it had.

She met Jayden's innocent gaze and decided it was best to be truthful. 'I'm not sure,' she told him. 'But she's feeling a lot better now, and once the new baby is born it won't be long before they'll both be able to come home.'

He pulled a face. 'Why can't she leave it at the hospital?'

Ellie's brows shot up. 'Do you want her to do that?'

He nodded.

'But why?'

'I don't want Mummy to have a baby,' he said, wriggling his shoulders. 'Why can't she just give it to a nurse?'

'Um, I really don't think she would want to do that.'

She looked at him in consternation. 'Are you sure you don't want a little brother or a sister? After all, it might be quite nice for you when it's a bit older. You'll have someone special to play with.'

He wrinkled his nose. 'I don't want anyone else to play with. I like playing with Josh.'

'Well, I'm glad you get on well with him,' she said. Jayden went to school with Josh, her neighbour's child, every day, so it was good that they'd forged such a strong friendship.

She stood up and affectionately stroked his hair. This was a difficult one, and maybe it was something she had better not share with his mother just yet. The way things were going, she might have a few days yet to bring him round to accepting the status quo.

A short time later she dropped him off at her neighbour's house and kissed him goodbye. Molly was good with children and she knew she could relax, leaving her to take him and Josh to nursery school.

Jayden's reluctance to accept the new baby was on her mind, though, as she drove to work, and when she arrived at A and E she told Olivia what he'd said.

'At least he's come out into the open with it,' Olivia commented. 'It could be worse, I suppose, if he were to bottle it all up. You hear such stories about children being jealous of their siblings.'

Ellie nodded in agreement. 'I wish I could find some way to help him get over it.'

At least her discussion with Jayden had helped take her mind off the meeting she had to attend later that morning. Amelia Holt was coming to the hospital so that they could discuss her complaint, and every time she thought about it, her insides lurched. No matter how convinced she was that she'd done everything possible to save Mel's aunt, if this complaint was taken further to a second hearing there was always the chance that her career could be badly damaged.

Through the course of the morning she became more and more apprehensive. James had said he would be with her when the time came, and that helped, but it also added to her confusion. Her emotions were all over the place where he was concerned.

She forced herself to concentrate on her work and later, as she was passing by one of the treatment rooms, she saw that James was working on his own in there.

He was talking to his patient, a man who had been vomiting and was now struggling to breathe. It was clear that James was doing his best to make him feel better. Beads of sweat had broken out on the man's brow. He looked very ill and as though he was in great pain, and Ellie could see from the monitors that his heartbeat was very fast and his blood pressure was dropping.

All the time James was gentle and supportive and Ellie stood still for a moment, struck by his caring manner.

Then, all at once, things started to change. The man appeared to collapse suddenly and monitors all around him started to make shrill bleeping sounds. Ellie hurried into the room.

'Would you like some help?' she asked.

'Thanks.' James was reaching for the intubation equipment.

'What are we dealing with here?'

'I suspect from his history that it's acute pancreatitis—he was complaining of abdominal pain and continual vomiting.' He frowned. 'He looks anorexic.'

'Yes, he does, except for the swelling of his abdomen.'

'Will you put in a nasogastric tube?' James asked as soon as the patient was intubated. 'He's been vomiting so much I need to be sure he's not going to choke.'

She nodded. 'I will.'

She set to work, and as soon as he was sure that the man was receiving adequate oxygen and was connected to the ventilator, James prepared his patient and began to insert two central lines so that he could be given medication and other essential substances.

'He's dehydrated,' he said. 'At this rate, his kidneys will start to fail—we need to get him on normal saline right away.'

She nodded. 'I'll set up a drip. Has he had a painkiller?' She checked the man's notes. His name was David Langley and within the last month he'd been to his GP complaining of abdominal pain.

'I'm doing that now. I'm going with meperidine.'

Watching him at work, Ellie could see why he'd reached the level of consultant. He was exceptionally skilful and thorough in everything he did. She sighed inwardly. If only she could share some of his calm expertise. Ever since Grace Holt had died, she had begun to question everything she did. Even something like placing a catheter could be hazardous if the correct sterile techniques weren't followed.

'Are you okay with helping me?' James was watching her, and she guessed he was wondering about her hesitation.

'Yes. I'm all right.'

She dragged her thoughts back to the task in hand and started to insert a catheter into the man's arm. As soon as that was done, she set up the saline bag, hooking it up to a metal stand. Then she connected the IV tubing to the catheter and checked that the infusion was working correctly.

Once they had seen to their patient's immediate needs, James said, 'I'll get a CT scan done. It's possible that gallstones have passed into the bile duct and caused the inflammation, but from his condition I suspect there's a lot more going on here.'

'Like what?'

'Maybe an abscess and certainly general inflammation. If that turns out to be the case, we'll have to drain it, but I'm going to give him a strong antibiotic as a precaution. I'm pretty sure there's an infection of some sort. Anyway, I'll take him along to Radiology.'

He glanced at her. 'You're very quiet. Are you sure you're all right?'

'I'm fine.'

'Good.' He scanned her features a moment longer as though he still had some doubts. 'As soon as I've finished here, I'll help you prepare for the meeting with Miss Holt. Whatever happens, remember that you did the right thing. It's not your fault that her aunt died.'

She nodded. For a few minutes as they'd worked she'd been able to forget about it, but now her anxiety had come back with full force.

He glanced at his watch. 'It's not for another hour yet. We should have plenty of time.'

He went off to Radiology with Mr Langley, while Ellie returned to her own patients.

When it was almost time for the meeting, she handed over to another registrar and went to seek out James once more. She was feeling jittery and wishing their appointment was over and done with.

'Do you have Mr Langley's results?' she asked.

James nodded. 'Yes, I have the radiology report and some of the lab tests are back. Alongside the bile duct obstruction there's a large abscess resulting from infection of fluid that has collected in the abdomen.'

He glanced at the patient's chart. 'I've put in a drain tube to draw off the infected matter and called for a surgical consultation. A renal specialist is going to come down and look at him, too.'

She frowned. 'He's not doing very well, is he?'

'No.' He shook his head. 'I've arranged for him to be transferred to Intensive Care as soon as we can manage it.' He glanced at her. 'You're very pale. Are you worried about seeing your schoolfriend?'

'I don't think she thinks of herself as a friend any longer.' She guessed he could read her body language and she made an effort to calm herself. 'I'm a bit apprehensive,' she admitted. 'I've been trying not to think about it all morning.'

He lightly squeezed her hand. 'I'll be there with you,' he said. 'Between us, we should be able to persuade the woman that there's no case to pursue.'

'I hope so.' She appreciated him trying to cheer her up. It made her feel a lot better, but she wasn't as confident as he was that Amelia would be easily appeased. She'd always been a volatile, over-emotional person and her love for her aunt had made her fiercely defensive.

'Try not to worry.'

'I'll try.' She glanced at him. His smile was encouraging, coaxing her to have faith, and it warmed her inside to know that he was such a caring, thoughtful man. How was it that he could be so different from his father?

She hesitated as he glanced through the radiology

report. 'How is your father?' she asked after a while. 'I hope he hasn't had any more setbacks. I was a bit worried I might have done more harm than good when I went to the manor house yesterday.'

'Is that what's been bothering you?' He made a wry face. 'None of it was your fault, and I'm sorry he spoke to you the way he did. He's been more tetchy of late and I think that's down to his illness. His heart has been failing for some time, and he isn't used to being so restricted and helpless. I've come to realise that all I can do is try to make his life more tolerable. It grieves me that it's come to this, but in the end we just have to make the best of things.'

'I realise it must be difficult for him. I have to remind myself that he's ill and I need to make allowances.'

He laid the report down in the wire basket. 'Let's go to my office,' he suggested.

She went with him along the corridor to a room that looked out over a large quadrangle, decorated with tubs of colourful flowers, pretty fuchsias and scarlet geraniums.

His office was furnished with a large, polished mahogany table and three comfortable leather-backed chairs, and on the walls were a couple of watercolour paintings showing peaceful country landscapes. It was a restful room, and Ellie imagined that patients and their relatives would soon begin to feel at their ease in here.

James poured coffee from a machine at the side of the room and handed her a cup. 'Help yourself to cream and sugar,' he said. 'It might be a good idea to eat something, too.' He took a packet of biscuits down from a wall cupboard and tipped some of them out onto a plate. 'Food might calm your nerves.'

'Thank you.' She didn't feel like eating, but it was thoughtful of him to offer.

'How are your parents these days?' he asked, coming to sit down opposite her, and she had the feeling he was trying to divert her thoughts from the meeting ahead.

'My father is working as an estate manager again,' she told him. 'It's nowhere near as large as the Birchenall estate, but he seems happy there.' She paused, swallowing her coffee. 'I see him often—he comes over to the house for dinner with me and Noah and vice versa.'

'And your mother?' he prompted.

'I haven't seen her for some time,' she murmured. 'She went into a deep depression when we had to leave the lodge, but after a while she was admitted to hospital and had some treatment that seemed to help. Then, when she was back on her feet, she moved away from Cheshire to a small village in Wales. We didn't have much contact with her after that. I don't think she could handle the responsibility of a family.'

'I'm sorry.' He was quiet for a moment, deep in thought. 'Perhaps that's why you went off the rails for a while? It must have been really hard to bear when your mother left.'

Her cheeks flushed with heat. 'It was, though she gave Noah and me a choice. We could have gone with her, but she had never seemed to have our interests at heart. Whereas my father has always been a loving man, despite his problems, so we both decided to stay with him. It's something I don't like to think about too much. And I did behave badly afterwards, I admit. I rebelled against everything. Your father was quite right when he pointed it out.'

Perhaps the biggest legacy of that time was her feeling that no one was to be trusted with her heart. It had been shattered by her mother, the one person who should have cared most of all, so how could she rely on anyone else to cherish her?

And back then, filled with feelings of rejection and despair, she'd responded by running amok and getting into as much trouble as she possibly could.

James gave a faint shrug. 'My father didn't look for reasons back then, and I don't recall too many of the details. Like I said, I went away round about that time. Wasn't it something to do with drink and wild stunts? Late-night partying and that sort of thing?'

'Something like that,' she murmured. She shuddered, thinking of a couple of times when her exploits had been featured in the local paper.

He frowned. 'It must have been difficult for you. I know something of what it's like to lose a mother, but I had my father and Harriet to help me through the bad times. Does your mother still not keep in touch?'

'No, not really. An occasional note and maybe a card at Christmas.'

Just then there was a knock at the door and a nurse showed Amelia Holt into the room.

She seemed tense, obviously uptight, and though Ellie stood up and went to greet her, Amelia didn't make eye contact. Her black hair was cut in a tidy, layered bob, and she wore a dark blue suit with a jacket nipped in at the waist. She looked neat and businesslike.

James did his best to put her at ease. 'We're here to try to understand the nature of your complaint and see what we can do to sort things out,' he said, after inviting her to sit down and offering her a cup of coffee. 'I'm hoping that we might be able to resolve the situation to everyone's satisfaction.'

They talked at length, but it soon became clear that Amelia was adamant in going ahead with her complaint. 'I know that if more had been done for my aunt, she would be alive now. I accept that she was very ill but if Dr Saunders had acted sooner, things would have turned out very differently.'

James frowned. 'I've read through the medical notes that were made that day,' he said, taking out Grace Holt's file and skimming through its contents, 'and I have to say I feel that Dr Saunders acted in the best interests of your aunt. She worked very quickly to diagnose the nature of the problem and then followed all the treatment protocols. I'm very sorry—we're both sorry—that your aunt is no longer with us, but I don't believe Dr Saunders could have done anything more to save her.'

'I'm not satisfied,' Amelia said, pressing her lips together. 'I want to take this further. I want the matter to be dealt with by somebody who is completely independent.'

'That is your prerogative, of course.'

Ellie felt a wave of nausea rise in her stomach. This business could go on for months, and all that time she would be under a cloud. Would her colleagues begin to talk among themselves and start to ask what it was that she'd done wrong?

'It's what I want,' Amelia insisted. She stood up, preparing to leave. 'You'll let me know when the next hearing is to take place?'

James and Ellie stood up. 'I will,' James said. He showed Amelia to the door and she left without looking back.

Ellie curled her fingers into a tight ball in her lap. Her one-time friend hadn't once looked at her.

James shut the door and came back to her. 'Well, that could have gone better,' he said in a rueful voice.

Ellie nodded, but couldn't bring herself to say anything just then. She bent her head as though that would shut out all that had just happened, and her chestnut curls momentarily fell across her cheeks and hid her face. She was glad James could not see her desperation. In the back of her mind she'd hoped that by talking things through with them Mel would come to see sense, but without a doubt that wasn't going to happen, now or in the future.

'I can see you're upset,' James said. He laid an arm around her shoulders, and she lifted her head, raising a shaky hand to brush the hair back from her cheeks. 'I'm sure it's not nearly as bad as it seems,' he went on. 'No one in the medical profession is going to decide in her favour. You did everything you could to save Mrs Holt.' He gave her an encouraging smile. 'Why don't we go and have lunch and see if we can't talk this through?'

'Mel seemed so determined,' she said quietly. 'It seems hard to believe that we were once friends, that we went to school together. We used to confide in one another and she'd comfort me whenever I was in trouble.'

'It's the shock of losing a loved one.' He reached for her hand. 'Lunch?' he said again.

'I'd like that but I can't,' she said, suddenly remembering that she'd arranged to meet Lewis. She was disappointed. She wanted to go with James, so that they could spend some more time together. He seemed to understand her and was there for her, and that made her feel good inside.

'I'm supposed to be meeting Lewis,' she said, conscious of his hand engulfing hers. 'He said he wants to hear how the meeting went, and I'm hoping he'll be able to give me news about one of his patients...my neighbour. I've been really worried about her. She was admitted with pre-eclampsia and I think he might be doing a Caesarean soon.'

James frowned. 'Are you sure it's wise for him to do that?'

'A Caesarean?'

'To discuss a patient's details.'

'Oh, I see.' She shook her head. 'It'll be all right. He won't tell me any confidential details.'

He studied her, his expression brooding. 'You see a lot of Lewis, don't you? He seems to be a good friend.'

She nodded. 'He is. We've known each other for a long time.' She studied him closely. 'Is that a problem for you?'

'I'm not sure. Do you think he might be getting a little too fond of you?'

She stared at him. 'What do you mean?'

'Well, he seems to be very familiar with you.' His gaze meshed with hers. 'Perhaps you don't notice it.'

'No, I don't. I haven't.' Her brows met in a worried line.

'Hmm.' He sounded as though he didn't believe her. 'You know his marriage is in trouble, don't you?'

Her mouth dropped open a little. There had been rumours, but she'd taken no notice of them. If Lewis had any problems, she was sure he would manage to sort them out somehow. 'I imagine all couples have their ups and downs. You're adding two and two together and making five.'

'I don't think so. I'm simply telling you what I see, and I'm asking you to steer clear of getting too deeply involved with him. He's my cousin, and I care for him like a brother—I don't want to see him get hurt. He's vulnerable right now, and if you give him half a chance, he might do something he'll come to regret.'

She gave a small gasp, pulling her hand away from his as though she'd been scalded. 'You're warning me off? How can you say such things to me? Do you really think I would get involved with a married man?'

'I was just offering some friendly advice,' he said quietly. His eyes scanned her face. 'I'm concerned about him. The grapevine is already buzzing with rumours about you and him being together—I wouldn't want either of you to be hurt, that's all.'

There were rumours going around? She stiffened. 'Thank you for your concern, but I'm quite capable of conducting my own relationships without any help from you—and so is Lewis. Whatever we do, it's certainly no business of yours—cousin or no cousin.'

She wrenched open the door and went out into the corridor. How could he even suggest that she was involved with Lewis in that way?

She was still angry when she walked into the cafeteria a few minutes later, but she made a supreme effort to calm down as she picked up a tray and loaded it with various items of food. She'd been a fool to allow herself to be pulled into James's web of charm. She might have known it would come back to hit her in the face.

'Hi, Ellie.' Lewis put his tray down on the table and came to sit opposite her. 'I've had a really difficult morning. My placenta praevia patient had another bleed and I had to take her to Theatre straight away. It was either that or risk losing the baby.'

'Phoebe? What happened?' She was shocked. 'Are they both all right?'

He nodded. 'Thankfully, yes. Phoebe needed a transfusion, but she seems to be rallying now. The baby's fine. A bit of a concern to us at first, but he's okay now.'

She smiled. 'That's good to hear.' She dipped a fork into her lasagne. 'Is there any news on Lily? I don't like to ask her too much when I visit, especially with Jayden listening in.'

He grimaced. 'I'd prefer it if I could say she was completely free of symptoms, but she still needs to be closely monitored for the usual things: blood pressure and protein in the urine. It's still a tad too early for us to elect to deliver the baby, so we're being very careful with her.'

'She hasn't had any more seizures, though?'

'No. We have her on medication to try and prevent those.'

She talked to Lewis for a while longer, and all the time she was asking herself if what James had said could possibly be true. Was Lewis being over-familiar with her? She couldn't see any evidence of it, though, and made up her mind to dismiss it from her thoughts.

'I should go,' she said, glancing at her watch. 'I'm due back in A and E.'

Lewis smiled. 'It wouldn't do for you to be tardy and have your new boss put a black mark against your name, would it?'

She gave a wry smile. It was a bit too late for her to worry about that, wasn't it? James must have tacked her outburst onto the list of reasons why she was a difficult person to have on his team. He already had a number of items on that list! In the short time he'd been here he'd learned that a complaint had been made against her, she'd upset his father, and he'd discovered she was subject to quick bursts of temper.

She didn't see James for the rest of the afternoon. He and the senior house officer were dealing with a crush injury, leaving her to tend to a girl who had broken her ankle.

She left for home at the end of her shift feeling weary and out of sorts, and when Noah rang just as she arrived home he picked up on her mood. 'Are things not going well?' he asked.

'You could say that.' She told him what had happened.

'Do you think you might be reading too much into what he says? After all, you've a lot on your plate just now, what with looking after Jayden and the TV work, and so on—maybe you're a bit stressed?'

'Maybe.'

They talked for a while longer, and when she finally cut the call she was at least reassured that his career was on the up and up. 'I'm getting lots of commissions now,' he'd told her. 'The tide seems to have turned in my favour.'

She set about her chores in the kitchen while Jayden sat at the table, happily sticking tissue and coloured paper shapes to small pieces of card.

'Look what I did,' he said, after a while. 'It's a card for Mummy.'

'Let me see.' She looked at the collection of white tissue-paper flowers he'd carefully stuck down onto a folded piece of blue card. 'Well, that's just lovely,' she told him. 'Shall we put a yellow middle on the flower?'

He nodded eagerly. 'She likes daisies,' he said.

'Good. I'm sure she'll love it. You can give it to her when we go to the hospital next time.'

'Yeah. I've putted lots of kisses, see?'

'Oh, yes.' She smiled. Half the page was filled with pencilled crosses.

He finished off the card and a little while later she sent him to the bathroom to get ready for bed while she made him a drink of hot chocolate.

'I'm not tired,' he complained, as she tucked the bed-covers around him a few minutes later. 'I don't go to bed this early…ever.' Again, there was that wide-eyed look of innocence that she was coming to recognise.

'Well, you don't have to go to sleep. We'll just look at the storybook together for a while, shall we?' And as usual he fell asleep within minutes.

Leaving his door slightly ajar, she went quietly downstairs and started to tidy up.

The doorbell sounded as she finished washing dishes and she went to answer it, wondering who would be calling on her at this time of the evening.

'I hope you don't mind?' James said, giving her a quizzical look. 'I've just finished work at the hospital and was passing by on my way home. I thought it might be good if we could talk.'

She opened the door for him to enter. 'You'd better come in.'

She showed him into the sitting room. 'Have a seat,' she said, whisking a couple of toy cars from the settee and waving him to the space she'd cleared.

James glanced around the homely room and then sat down. 'I suppose Jayden must be in bed by now?'

She nodded. 'He always complains that he has to go to bed too early, and yet he's asleep within minutes every time.' All the time she was talking she was busy scooping up magazines and a newspaper, which she dropped carefully into a wooden rack.

'I guess you have your hands full, with work at the hospital, your TV programmes and looking after a child, as well.' James watched her as she moved around the room. 'You do all this on your own?'

'I'm sure lots of women do it all the time.' She picked up a cushion and plumped it up just so that she could keep busy…anything rather than sit down and talk to him face to face.

'I expect so.' He hesitated, and then asked, 'Might I ask—is his father around?'

'He's in Switzerland, sorting out some major problems with his business—financial troubles and difficulties with the workforce, that sort of thing. He's managed to get back a few times over the last couple of weeks.'

'Oh, I see.'

'I don't think you do.' She stopped tidying up and came to sit opposite him, in one of the armchairs. 'Jayden is my neighbour's little boy. She's in hospital, suffering from pre-eclampsia.'

'Ah.' He gave a rueful smile. 'I had it all wrong. That will teach me not to jump to conclusions.'

'Maybe.'

'How's it going with the boy? Are you coping all right?'

'I'm not sure. I think so—he seems happy enough,

though he's upset about his mother having a baby. He thinks she should give it away.'

He laughed. 'Well, that's not good.'

'No.' She was silent for a moment then said, 'Actually, I've been racking my brains for a way around the problem. I don't like to see him upset, and his mother has enough to contend with right now.'

'Hmm.' He thought for a while. 'I suppose there must be storybooks about children having to face up to a new child in the family. There must be one out there that will help him see the situation in a new light.'

She exhaled as though a small weight had been lifted from her. 'You're right. Why didn't I think of that? I'll go along to the bookshop and see if I can find one or two.' She sent him a quick glance, beginning to feel a little better about having him there.

'Was there a reason you came to see me?' she asked.

He nodded. 'I realise I upset you earlier today, and I wanted to apologise for that. You were quite right. I was out of order. How you and Lewis relate to one another is none of my business.'

She thought about it. 'Perhaps I was a bit touchy,' she conceded. 'With one thing and another—Mel taking the complaint further, and work, and the stress of working on a TV series—it's possible I could have overreacted.' Now that she'd had time to get a grip on herself she was beginning to regret her quick flare of annoyance. Perhaps she'd taken on too much and it was showing in the way she reacted to situations.

'We're okay, then?' He stood up and went over to her. 'I wouldn't like to think that things are strained between us.'

She nodded, getting to her feet. 'That would be awkward, seeing that we have to work together, wouldn't it?'

'It would.' He laid his hands gently around her arms, his long fingers making bands of heat on her bare skin. 'I'd much rather we had a good working relationship.' He smiled. 'In fact, we'll probably be working together more than you think.'

'Oh? How is that?' His touch was doing strange things to her nervous system. She was finding it more and more difficult to concentrate.

'I have to go to the TV studios on Saturday,' he answered. 'I'm going to record a programme about the Birchenall history—didn't you mention that you were going to the studios that day, too?'

'That's right.' She looked at him curiously, and as she moved slightly, he drew her into the circle of his arms. 'How did it come about that you're doing a show—didn't you say you hadn't time to do that sort of thing?' His nearness was disconcerting. At the same time he was so near, it seemed, and yet so far away. She was beginning to yearn for something much more intimate.

'I did say that.' He half smiled. 'Obviously I spoke too soon, but my father's keen for me to do it. He's very proud of his heritage—though he doesn't often allow the cameras into his home.' His grey gaze moved over her, warming her with its shimmering heat.

Perhaps he, too, was finding their closeness distracting, because all of a sudden he appeared to have trouble thinking straight. 'I think the skirmish with the press made him realise he has to work on his image, so when this opportunity came up, he asked me to stand in for him.' His hand wandered along the length of her spine, coming to rest in the small of her back. 'I want to put his mind at ease, so I agreed.' He drew her closer and the breath caught in her throat as the softness of her curves collided with his toned masculine frame.

'I get the feeling the weight of the Birchenall dynasty lies squarely on your shoulders.'

'Oh, yes.' Again, there was that rueful quirk to his mouth. 'My father is determined that we live up to our heritage.'

'I guess it means everything to him,' she murmured.

'Yes, it does.' He looked down at her, his glance sliding over her flushed face and coming to dwell on the ripe fullness of her lips. All the time his hands gently stroked her, smoothing over the rounded swell of her hips, and her heart began to thump heavily in her chest so that she could feel it banging against her rib cage.

This was much more than a friendly, soothing touch. It was a caress, gossamer-light and incredibly compelling, enticing her to move into the shelter of his strong, male body.

He bent his head towards her, and she realised what was about to happen. It was as though everything was in slow motion.

'Ellie?'

She didn't know if it was a sigh or a question, the way he said her name. Either way, there was plenty of time for her to make a move, to stop him there and then, but recklessly she did nothing.

'I can't think straight,' he said huskily. 'You've bewitched me.'

She was mesmerised by his warm, comforting presence, and more than anything right now she wanted him to sweep her into his arms and make her troubles fade away.

He didn't let her down. His lips softly claimed her mouth, brushing over it with tender expertise and tantalising her with his coaxing, possessive kiss. Her hands slid upwards, over the flat plane of his stomach and onto his hard rib cage.

He groaned softly and crushed her to him as he deepened the kiss, and she clung to him, her fingertips tracing the line of his powerful biceps. There was strength and control there, arms that could hold a woman fast and promise her heaven on earth.

'You taste so good.' He murmured the words against her lips, and a quick, unexpected ripple of desire flowed through her, shocking her to the core. She'd never felt this way before, never had such a deep-seated longing overwhelm her and cast her inhibitions to the wind.

'Ellie, I want you. I could make life so sweet for you. Give you so much.'

'You don't have to give me anything,' she murmured. She revelled in the way his hands moved over her, shaping her, enticing her to lean into him, to feel her soft body melding with his hard frame.

He kissed her again, a fervent, passionate kiss that stirred her senses and had her almost begging him for more, much more.

'You don't need to be with my cousin,' he said raggedly. 'He's not right for you—let me be the one to make you happy.'

Ellie froze in shock. What was he saying? How could he say those things to her? Did he truly believe she was making a play for Lewis? Was that why he was holding her, kissing her? Just so that he might divert her away from him? Was that what he planned all along?

She stared at him, scarcely able to believe what was happening.

He frowned, conscious of her sudden withdrawal, but when he might have coaxed and cajoled her once more, his phone began to ring. He stood very still for a few seconds while the ringtone burbled. Then, as if he had been woken from a trance, he said quietly, 'I'm sorry about this. I have to answer it. It might be… Excuse me.'

He answered the call. He listened for a moment and then said, 'Sophie, what's wrong? No, I'm at Ellie's house. Yes, I told you about her. We work together.'

He broke off again as Sophie began to speak. Then, 'It's just a few minutes away. Why?'

Sophie answered him and after a short time he interrupted her quickly to say, 'It's all right, I'll come home. Loosen any clothing around his neck and prop him up with pillows. Has he had his glyceryl trinitrate spray?'

He shut off the phone a second or two later and Ellie looked at him worriedly. 'Your father? Do you need an ambulance?' Her mind was a whirl of confusion.

James frowned. 'I'm hoping we can get through this without sending him to hospital—he hates being there. But he went out to visit friends today and now he's having a bad episode. Can't get his breath. It's lucky that Sophie was with him—she has a key to the house so that she can come and go and keep an eye on him for me.' He sucked in a quick breath. 'I'll try him with a stronger diuretic to see if that will help reduce the load on his lungs.'

She went with him to the door. 'Is there anything I can do to help?'

He shook his head. 'I have everything I need.

Thanks.' He glanced at her briefly. 'Ellie, about you and I. You need to know—'

'Go to your father, James,' she cut in. 'He needs you.'

He drove away and she went back inside the house. She couldn't get her head around what had just happened between them. What had she been thinking of, falling for him that way, when all the time he had been leading her down a false trail?

CHAPTER FIVE

'I WANTED TO wish you good luck, Ellie. I hope the filming goes well for you today.' Lewis was cheerful on the phone, and Ellie smiled.

'Thanks. I've looked through my notes and checked with the studio that all the props are in place, so hopefully it will all go smoothly.'

'It'll be great. I always enjoy watching your shows.'

'I'm glad—though I think you're a teeny bit biased, Lewis!'

'Yeah, maybe.' He chuckled. 'Anyway, I'll let you get off. I know you have to be there a couple of hours beforehand to get your make-up done and so on. I suspect that's why you took the job, so that you could be cosseted every now and again.'

She laughed. 'And why not?'

She finished the call a short time later and went out to the courtyard to say goodbye to Jayden. He was with his grandmother, getting ready to go to his grandparents' house, and she wanted to give back a couple of toys that he had left behind.

'I think you forgot your jigsaw puzzles and the new storybooks,' she said, handing them over.

'Thanks.' He looked in the bag and passed it to his

grandmother. 'We're going to see Mummy at the hospital this afternoon,' he said. He frowned. 'I think the baby's coming today.'

'Really? You'll be a big brother—imagine that! It's very important, being a big brother, you know.' Ellie smiled at him and he nodded cautiously.

'Yeah. Mummy said that.'

Ellie looked at his grandmother. She was in her early fifties, a slender woman with neat brown hair feathered around her face. 'He's been a joy to have around,' Ellie told her. 'I shall miss him.'

'We're really grateful to you for looking after him. Thank you so much.'

'You're welcome. If you have any problems and need to have him sleep over any time, just let me know.'

She watched them get into their car and waved as they drove away. Then she slid into her own vehicle and set off for the studios.

The road passed through wooded hills and vales, by gentle waterways, and in the distance she could just about make out the misty peaks of the Pennines. The countryside was beautiful, serene, and incredibly peaceful.

The only blot on her landscape was that James was going to be at the television studios and she hadn't worked out quite how she was going to avoid him. It could be managed, though, because they would be using different studios for their recordings.

Whatever happened, she'd made up her mind that she wasn't going to let him get to her. How could she have been such a fool as to let him work his way into her heart like that, only to have him turn the knife when she least expected it? And why had she even thought about getting together with him when it was clear he wasn't averse to playing around? Wasn't he just like her ex?

Well, it was enough. She'd learned a lesson. He wouldn't get the chance to hurt her again.

Soon the scenery changed from rural to urban, and a few minutes later she slowed the car as she approached the impressive building where the show was to be filmed.

Everything looked spacious, with architect-designed buildings made up of brick and marble and a huge expanse of plate glass, all surrounded by landscaped terraces.

'It's good to see you again, Ellie,' the receptionist said as she walked into the grand foyer. 'They're ready for you in Make-up—you can go straight through.'

'Thanks.'

She drank coffee and chatted while the hairdresser styled her hair, teasing her silky curls into a loose topknot, and then she relaxed while the make-up girl, Alice, set to work, giving her a light touch of foundation and adding a gentle sweep of blusher to her cheeks. At least, she tried to relax.

'I was watching James Birchenall in the garden studio a little earlier,' Alice confided. 'I couldn't resist listening in on his interview. They're going to do some more filming at the house and then piece everything together, but today he was talking about how the land passed to his family in the sixteenth century, and telling us about the gentry who have lived there over the years. Of course the house has been altered in that time, with bits added on here and there.' She sighed. 'How the other half live! I certainly wouldn't mind being *his* other half.'

Ellie chuckled. 'I expect a lot of women feel that way.' Excluding herself, of course. She was immune to him now, wasn't she? But from the sound of things she could rest easy because his programme was over and done with and he was most likely on the road home by now.

After Alice finished working on her make-up the hairdresser came along to add a few finishing touches to her style, and then Ellie went off to record the programme.

She talked about cardiovascular health and how people could look after themselves by eating the right kind of food and getting enough exercise. Then she talked to a nutritionist about fruit and vegetables and cereals, and measured people's blood pressure after cycling and various kinds of exercise.

The programme finally came to an end, and Ellie collected her bag and jacket, ready for the journey home.

'Oh, you mustn't go just yet!' the producer exclaimed. 'I'd like to talk to you about doing another series. I was thinking maybe something on pregnancy and women's health—what do you think?'

She nodded. 'Sounds good. I'd need to expand my list of experts who could take part—but I could ask my friend and colleague Lewis about that.'

'That's great,' he said. 'Look, why don't I join you in the Green Room in half an hour or so and we can talk about it some more? We've laid on quite a spread in there, so you must sample it while you're waiting. There are some prime cuts of meat and great desserts.' He lowered his voice, speaking in a confidential tone. 'You'll have to forget about all the stuff you were saying in your programme just now and live a little, but with your figure it won't hurt, will it?'

She laughed. 'I suppose, if you're going to twist my arm…'

'That's my girl.' He waved her towards the door. 'You won't regret it.'

She went to the Green Room and took advantage of the free time to make a quick call to Lewis.

She told him what the producer had suggested, and asked him about people who might agree to appear on the show.

'That's great news, Ellie,' he said. 'I can think of a few people offhand, who might like to take part. I'll drop by your house one evening—maybe Friday, because Jessica will be out then. We can talk about it and I'll let you have a list of names.'

'Thanks, Lewis.'

When the call ended, she went to help herself to the buffet, filling her plate with thin slices of roast beef and a generous helping of rice and salad.

'Ellie—I hoped I would see you here today.' James's deep voice smoothed over her, and she looked around to see that he was right by her side.

Hot colour swept along her cheekbones. She'd been congratulating herself on managing to steer clear of him so far, and now he'd turned up when she was trapped with absolutely no excuse to rush away.

'I was rather hoping the opposite,' she murmured.

'You're angry with me?'

'How did you guess?'

His plate was filled with a selection of meats and savoury pastries, she noticed. He had a healthy appetite and never seemed to put on an ounce of fat, and she guessed he burned it up by being constantly on the go.

A waiter offered a selection of wines and fruit juices and she chose a small glass of Bordeaux, as she would be driving later.

She went to sit at a table by the window, overlooking one of the terraces. There were ornamental cherry trees out there, graceful weeping willows and banks of flowers, and every now and again benches were placed where people could sit for a while and relax. She studied the view for a while, trying unsuccessfully to ignore the fact that James had come to sit opposite her. She was way too conscious of him.

'I don't want to see Lewis getting into something he can't handle,' James said, offering her a bread roll from a wicker basket. 'But that doesn't mean I blame you for anything. I meant what I said to you. You're a beautiful, caring, thoughtful woman. What man wouldn't want to be with you? What would be the harm in you and I getting together?'

She could have mentioned his girlfriend—the woman who spent so much time at the manor house and who, according to Noah, had been singled out for him, coming from a well-to-do family that had been linked to his in friendship for many years. But James was clearly pushing any such thoughts to one side for the time being. Wasn't that what she might have expected, given the way men went from one woman to another, at least in her experience?

Instead, she murmured, 'I can think of a few things offhand.' She speared a cucumber slice and then recounted the list of reasons. 'Let's see; you're devious, conniving, an opportunist—and as you pointed out, should I be foolish enough to be caught out a second time, the rumour mill will start to work overtime at the hospital.'

'We can overcome all those things,' he said. 'They're nothing.'

'Hmm. You would say that, wouldn't you?' She savoured her wine, letting it rest on her tongue for a second or two. 'Of course, there's always the fact that your father hates me.'

'He doesn't. Anyway, my father isn't the one who wants to date you,' he said, his mouth making an amused quirk.

'That's definitely true.'

She glanced across the room and James must have caught her look of surprise because he turned to follow her gaze and said in a low voice, 'Well, there's a turn-up for the book. What's my father doing here with Sophie?' He frowned. 'I warned him there's no way he should be here.'

'That's what I was thinking,' she said in a puzzled tone. 'I wouldn't have thought he was well enough to be out and about—it was only the other night you had to rush off to help him.'

James nodded. 'I don't know what he can be thinking.'

He stood up. 'Excuse me. I'd better go and invite them over, if that's all right with you?'

'Be my guest,' she said.

It was probably a good thing that she was no longer going to be alone with him. She wouldn't put it past him to wheedle her into believing that she was mistaken in everything she knew about him and that he was actually a saint. Of course he hadn't wanted to prise her away from Lewis. That would have been the furthest thing from his mind. Yeah, right. She had deluded herself into thinking he really wanted her and instead it had simply been a ruse.

Lord Birchenall walked slowly towards her. 'May we sit here?' he asked, and she nodded.

'Please, do.'

'Are you sure we won't be intruding?'

'Not at all. I'll have to leave soon anyway, to go and talk to one of the producers.'

'Thank you.' It was clear that walking had taken the stuffing out of him. She heard the breath wheeze in his lungs, and he paused for a moment to gather strength before saying, 'This is Sophie. She's the daughter of a family friend. She was kind enough to bring me here today.'

'Hello, Sophie.' Ellie tried a smile. Okay, so she might be James's girlfriend, but that didn't matter to her any more, did it? Her stomach churned at the lie, but she had to accept that James was no longer on her radar and, besides, wouldn't Sophie be upset to know that he had been kissing another woman? Another reason why Ellie had to steer clear of him. What kind of man was he who could do that?

Sophie nodded acknowledgement, her gaze moving over Ellie from head to toe. Ellie had the feeling she was being thoroughly assessed. Thank heaven she'd dressed carefully that morning, in a cream-coloured skirt with a matching jacket that nipped in at the waist to flatter her figure. Beneath the jacket she wore a pretty, lace-trimmed top.

Sophie was truly beautiful, a slender girl with honey-gold hair held loosely with a clip at the back. She had deep blue eyes, a perfect, oval face and a full, rose-pink mouth. No wonder James had chosen her.

Sophie sat down, and once she was settled, Lord Birchenall took his seat next to her.

'Would you like something to eat?' Ellie enquired, turning her attention to James's father. 'I could get something for you.'

He shook his head. 'Not for me, thank you. I'll just have a drink. A coffee, perhaps.'

'I'll get it for you,' James said. He stood for a moment by his father's chair. 'It's good to see you, but I can't think what possessed you to come here today. You know I warned you that it might be too much for you.'

'Yes, but…' Lord Birchenall paused, his breath coming in short gasps. 'I wanted to watch the recording. After all, it was our heritage that you were talking about.'

James patted his shoulder. 'I know how much it means to you, but I don't want to see you struggling. I could have shown you the recording later.'

His father smiled. 'Ah, yes, but it wouldn't have been quite the same. And Sophie offered to bring me, so I jumped at the chance.'

'And was it worth it?'

'Oh, yes. It will be a good programme.'

'I'm glad you think so.' James smiled and went to fetch food and drink for Sophie and his father, leaving Ellie to chat with them for a while.

'Did you enjoy the show, Sophie?' she asked.

'I did. I thought James was wonderful and he chose the best video footage that shows the manor in all its glory.' Her gaze drifted over Ellie once more. 'I take it James invited you to come and watch the show?'

Ellie shook her head. 'Actually, no. I came here to make a recording of my own. I do a medical programme that's airing once a week at the moment. Perhaps you've heard of it—it's called *Your Good Health*?'

'No, I'm afraid not.'

Lord Birchenall was intrigued, his face lighting up with recognition. 'So that's it. I thought I knew you from somewhere, other than when you lived at the lodge. I watch that series. You should be pleased with yourself. It's very well done.'

'Thank you.' She was surprised he was being so generous, given the way he'd reacted to her when she'd visited the house, but perhaps James was right when he'd said the shock of the newspaper article had made his father more tetchy than usual. 'I can't take the credit, though—there's a whole team who helps put it together.'

She sipped her wine and glanced at him once more. He seemed to be breathing a bit better now that he was sitting down. 'Have you fully recovered from your upset the other day? It sounded as though you were very ill.'

'I'm much better, thank you. It's a sad fact that my health is not good these days, but I'm fortunate in having James to watch over me.'

James came back just then with a plate of food for Sophie and two coffees.

Sophie was deep in thought. 'Is it right, that you lived at the lodge?' she asked, turning to Ellie.

Ellie nodded, and Sophie reclined back in her seat. 'Of course,' she said. 'I remember hearing something about that. Your father worked for Lord Birchenall, but he left, didn't he?'

Lord Birchenall gave her a sharp look and shifted

uneasily in his seat. 'Ahem,' he said, but Sophie ploughed on.

'Wasn't there some sort of problem?'

Once again, Lord Birchenall tried to intervene. 'I don't think we need to go into that,' he said. 'It was all a long time ago.'

'Oh, but—' Sophie continued, and this time James interrupted.

'As my father said, Sophie, I don't think we want to delve into the past. Ellie's worked hard to make a career for herself. She works in A and E, as well as doing a TV series.'

'Really. How interesting.' She frowned and looked at Ellie once more. 'You've done well for yourself, haven't you, considering your troubles over the years? I heard a little about the family who lived in the lodge.'

'As James said, I've worked hard to overcome all that,' Ellie responded. 'As to my father, we didn't know it at the time, but he was actually quite ill. Later on he had to go into hospital for a few weeks.'

Sophie delicately sliced the meat on her plate. 'I'm sorry to hear that. What was wrong with him?'

'He had Addison's disease. It's an endocrine disorder that makes the patient very ill.'

Lord Birchenall looked shocked. 'I'm so sorry, my dear. I didn't know that.'

She nodded briefly. 'None of us did at first.' Even now it haunted her that she hadn't seen what had been happening to her father, that she hadn't realised he was ill. She'd been angry with Lord Birchenall for the way he'd treated him, but wasn't she just as guilty for not recognising that something was wrong?

She said carefully, 'It's quite rare, and it was some time before his condition was properly diagnosed.'

'I recall you told me something of this last time we met, when you came to the house.' He frowned. 'I'm afraid I wasn't myself that day, what with all that business of our family splashed over the Sunday papers.'

Sophie laid down her fork. 'It was very distressing that you had to go through all that,' she said. 'It's no wonder you weren't yourself.'

Ellie pushed her chair back carefully and stood up. 'If you'll excuse me,' she said, 'I can see my producer's just arrived. I'd better go and join him.'

James stood up with her. 'I'm glad we met up today,' he said, moving with her away from the table. He laid his arm lightly beneath her elbow. 'You mustn't take any notice of Sophie. She doesn't always think before she speaks. She's one of these people who say what's on their minds without considering the effect on other people.'

'Like your father said, it was all a long time ago.'

'How is your father these days? Is the disease under control?'

'I believe so. Of course, if he gets an infection or if he's stressed, his symptoms flare up and he becomes very tired and doesn't cope so well. When I spoke to him last week, he was feeling fine.'

They'd almost reached the bar, where her producer was ordering a drink, and Ellie stood still, ready to part company with James.

'Do you ever think about making a new start with your mother?' he asked. 'After all, you said she was in hospital for a time. Perhaps her illness affected her and made her distant and unable to cope.'

'It's possible, I suppose, though I think you're being ultra-kind about her. She chose to leave us, after all. I'm afraid I'm not like you. I find it hard to be generous in those circumstances.'

He lightly ran his hand over her arm. 'It's understandable. I don't know how I would have reacted in that situation.' He smiled. 'The same way you did, probably.'

She thought about the way she had responded when her mother had gone away. Over the next few years she'd turned to drink and wild parties in town that had sometimes spilled out onto the street. Her picture had ended up in the local paper when the rowdiness had annoyed the nearby residents. She gave him a wry smile. 'And risk bringing your family into disrepute?' She shook her head. 'I don't think so somehow.'

'Oh, I don't know. I think I'd quite like the opportunity to be disreputable with you,' he said, amusement glimmering in the depths of his eyes.

'Chance would be a fine thing,' she murmured. 'Anyway, I think you have other obligations right now.' She glanced at the table by the window where Sophie and his father were chatting.

Every now and again Sophie would shoot a look in their direction, and Ellie began to feel uncomfortable. Whatever James's feelings might be, Sophie was definitely interested in him.

He followed her gaze. 'You're right,' he agreed, bracing his shoulders. 'I just felt that I needed to put your mind at rest over Sophie. She's very forthright, but she's not bad at heart. She genuinely doesn't realise she might be upsetting people.'

'No, but she might be quite upset if you don't go and join her at the table very soon,' she said.

He nodded. 'Maybe I'll see you later?' he suggested.

'Possibly.' But she knew she wouldn't. As soon as she'd finished talking to her producer, she would slip away and drive home. She needed to put some space between herself and the Birchenalls…and Sophie.

CHAPTER SIX

ELLIE DROPPED THE letter into the wire tray. So the second meeting with Amelia Holt was to take place in another six weeks' time. Six more weeks of waiting to find out if her career was going to be safe.

She hadn't voiced her thoughts out loud, but James must have guessed what she was thinking.

'Don't let it get to you,' he said. 'No sensible person could see her getting anywhere with such a complaint. She's just not thinking straight. Losing her aunt must have shaken her really badly and turned her mind.'

'Perhaps you're right.' She gave a rueful smile. 'Maybe she'll come to her senses before too long.'

'I'm sure she will.'

But that wouldn't happen any time soon, Ellie reflected, if the email she'd received from Mel that morning was anything to go by. She wasn't going to tell James about it. *'Why don't you face up to things and accept you were in the wrong? Why prolong the inevitable for another six weeks?'* Mel must have been informed of the date of the next meeting at the same time she had been.

The phone rang in A and E and Olivia went to answer it. 'There's an emergency coming in,' she said.

'It's a woman complaining of chest pains and difficulty breathing.'

'Okay. Room Two is free, so I'll see her in there as soon as she comes in.' Ellie left James to go and look after his own patients and went to make preparations. Then she hurried down to the ambulance bay to receive her patient.

The woman was very distressed and fearful, and Ellie hurried to reassure her. 'We'll take good care of you, Angela,' she said, checking her name from the notes. 'I'll take you in to the examination room and then we'll do what we can to make you feel more comfortable.'

'Thank you.' Angela struggled to say the words, exhausted by her struggle to get air into her lungs, and Ellie could see that she was gravely ill.

When they were in the treatment room, she gave her oxygen through a mask to help her breathing and gently questioned her about the events leading to her illness.

'I had a…chest infection,' Angela said in a halting voice, moving the oxygen mask briefly away from her face. 'Everything feels…so tight in my chest. It's such a…sharp, stabbing pain. It feels really…bad.'

'Perhaps you'll feel a bit better if we sit you up,' Ellie said, noticing how the woman tried to lean forward to relieve the pain. She raised the bed head while Olivia brought more pillows to prop her up, and Angela gave a small sigh of relief as she sank back against them.

Ellie examined her, and became increasingly worried. 'You're feverish,' she said. 'I'm going to order some blood tests and a CT scan so that we can find out what's going on in your chest. In the meantime, I'll give you a painkiller and start you on antibiotics, because I suspect you have a nasty infection.'

Angela nodded, restless with pain and discomfort, too ill to say much more, and Ellie set about preparing the injection.

She was writing out the lab forms when James came into the room a little later. 'Is everything all right in here?'

He introduced himself to the patient, putting her at ease, and then moved away from the bedside so that he could talk to Ellie.

'How's it going?' he asked, and she turned away so that the woman wouldn't see or hear what she said.

'I've examined her, and the heart sounds are very faint. There's a rubbing sound, too, and I think there's fluid in the pericardium and around her lungs.'

'So you're thinking…?'

'Pericarditis.' Her heart began to thump heavily as she said it. 'The same as Grace Holt,' she added, 'though maybe with a different cause.' Memories rushed to fill her mind, and all at once she was starting to feel shaky inside and chills were shooting up and down her spine.

She knew the colour had drained from her face. Was she up to dealing with this? Had she gone wrong before somehow when she'd treated Mel's aunt? Was she to go through it all again and finish with the same outcome?

James studied her pale features, his dark eyes giving nothing away, but she knew he must be weighing up her response to the situation. 'You're doing tests?'

She nodded. 'It'll be a while before we get the results from the lab, but I'll do a scan and go from there. I have her on anti-inflammatory medication and diuretics to reduce the fluid volume.'

'Okay. Let me know as soon as you hear.'

'I will.'

He touched her arm briefly as he left the room, and that small act of encouragement helped her to feel a tiny bit better. She wasn't alone, he was silently telling her, and she was grateful for his support. Even so, she was worried sick.

The CT films made her even more anxious when she brought them up on screen some time later. She'd been right about the fluid around the heart and lungs. This was beginning to look exactly like Grace Holt's illness.

'I've looked at your scan,' she told Angela, 'but we're going to do another test, an echocardiogram, so that we can see how your heart is working. It's nothing to worry about and it's a painless procedure—the technician will glide a device over your chest and a picture will come up on the monitor.'

James came to look at the films with her later on when some of the lab reports had also come through.

'You were right,' he said. 'It is an inflammation around the heart. The infection is stopping the heart from pumping properly. We need to prep her for a pericardiocentesis.' He sent her a quick glance. 'Are you okay with that?'

'Yes.' She wasn't, but she had to prove to herself that she could do it, and for Angela's sake they had to drain the fluid from around her heart as quickly as possible. It would have been more usual for James to take over at this point, being the senior doctor, but she guessed he saw this as a way of getting her to face her demons. 'I'll get the equipment ready.'

He helped her to prepare the patient for the procedure, and when they were finally ready, and Angela had been given a local anaesthetic, Ellie ran the ultrasound probe over her chest, glancing at the computer screen to make sure she had the right location.

'I'm going in through the fifth intercostal space,' she said, checking the point of entry between the ribs. Then she inserted a long spinal needle into Angela's chest, checking to see that the woman was coping with the procedure.

Ellie had to take the utmost care to avoid puncturing vital organs and arteries, and she positioned the needle carefully so that it entered the pericardial space around the heart. She could see it all on the screen. 'Are you all right, Angela?' she asked again.

The woman nodded and slowly Ellie began to draw off fluid into the syringe.

'Her vital signs are improving a little,' James said. To Angela, he commented, 'You should start to feel more comfortable as the pressure eases off your heart.'

Ellie handed him the filled syringe and exchanged it for a new one.

'We'll send that for analysis,' James said, and added in a low voice, 'You're doing great. Keep going.'

She nodded, glad of his encouragement. A faint film of perspiration dampened her brow and James said quietly, 'I'll wipe that for you.' He gently dabbed her forehead with a cloth.

'Thanks.' When she had drained as much fluid as possible, she put a catheter in place and connected a drainage tube and bag.

'How does that feel?' she asked her patient.

'It's so much better,' Angela said, sounding exhausted. 'It's such a relief not to feel that pressure and that awful pain.'

'I'm glad.' Ellie was thankful that everything had gone without complication. Angela wasn't out of the woods yet, though. The infection that had caused the build-up of fluid was still active, and the antibiotics needed time to work. In Grace Holt's case, the infection had proved overwhelming, and she had died of a sudden heart attack.

Ellie left the woman in the care of a nurse and walked back to the main desk to check her list of patients.

'I think you deserve a break,' James said, getting into step alongside her. 'You haven't stopped since first thing this morning. Let's go and get some lunch.'

'Okay. That sounds like a good idea.' Perhaps she ought not to spend time with him, but it was hard for her to put up any resistance. Whenever she was near him she found herself wanting to prolong that contact.

They went to the restaurant, where they filled their trays with a selection of food from the chilled cabinets.

'It's warm today,' James said. 'Shall we go and sit outside?'

'Perfect.' She chose a bench table close by a spreading old beech tree. Its trunk was wide and its branches were thick and long, and sunlight filtered through the leaves. There were tables dotted around at intervals on the grass, but they were all deserted, and she guessed this was because it was well past the usual time for lunch.

James smiled at her as he started on his chicken salad. 'You did well back there. How do you feel?'

'I'm not sure.' She'd been holding her breath for so long, it seemed, and now that she could breathe freely again she was still cautious, anxious in case anything went wrong.

'You did everything right,' he said. 'Just as you did last time. Relax.'

'Yes, I'll try.' She tasted the grated cheese on her plate and washed it down with a chilled fruit juice.

The sun was warm on her bare arms, and gradually, as they talked, her spirits began to lift.

'What's happening with your neighbour?' James asked. 'Didn't you tell me she's had her baby?'

'That's right. Lewis did a Caesarean a couple of days ago. She had a little girl.' She smiled. 'She's a beautiful little thing, all soft, downy skin and curly brown hair. They'll be discharging Lily from hospital later today, provided her blood pressure is stable. I think Lewis plans to keep her there most of the day, just to be certain she's all right. Anyway, I said I would look after Jayden while her husband goes to fetch them from the hospital. I think they're planning on stopping by her sister's house to show her the baby.'

'Aren't the grandparents around to look after Jayden?'

'Not today, unfortunately. His grandfather has gone down with some kind of stomach bug and they're steering clear so as not to infect anybody.'

'That's bad luck.' He looked at her curiously. 'You don't seem to mind looking after him.'

'No, I don't, although it can be a bit tiring, because four-year-olds don't have an off button and they just never seem to stop.' She chuckled. 'He's very easy to entertain, though.' She mused on that for a while. 'I think we might do some baking this evening. He likes doing that, and I expect Lily and her husband will enjoy eating the cakes afterwards.'

'I'm sure they will.' His dark gaze wandered over

her. 'Have you ever thought about having a family of your own?'

She pondered on that for a while. 'Yes, I have.' She returned his glance fleetingly. Until now, she'd never met a man she would want as the father of her children, but James was different from anyone she'd ever met. He was extra-special, and she could definitely see him in that role. A small ripple of awareness ran through her, and she had to pull herself together and answer his question properly as he was looking at her expectantly.

'As far as my mother is concerned, I don't have a great example of parenting to work from but that just makes me want to make up for it with my own family. I definitely want to have children at some point.'

Her gaze met his once more. 'What about you? I expect your father hopes you'll have a son one day to continue the line.' Her mouth curved. 'How do you feel about that?'

He gave a soft laugh. 'Oh, yes, there is that. But putting my father's wishes to one side, I'd like a family of my own one day.'

He pushed his plate away and started on his dessert, a cream-topped strawberry trifle. His expression became serious. 'Have you thought any more about visiting your mother? From the way you reacted to my father in the beginning, I sense there's a lot of pent-up emotion stemming from your teenage years. Perhaps it would do you both the world of good to talk things through.'

She shook her head. 'Perhaps, some time in the future, I might seek her out. The way I feel at the moment, though, is that she chose to leave and for any reconciliation to be meaningful she should be the one to make the first move.' A small tremor of unease ran through her. Was she being fair to her mother in thinking this way? Hadn't her mother had problems to overcome, too?

He nodded. 'I suppose I can see the logic behind that.'

They talked for a while longer but then their pagers began to bleep simultaneously, a warning of another emergency patient coming in.

'Hey-ho,' James said. 'Off we go again.'

Ellie looked after her patients through the course of the day, and just before her shift was due to end she went to check on Angela. The drainage tube and bag were filling up, showing signs that the infection was still raging, but she wasn't as breathless as she had been earlier, and though her heart rate and blood pressure were still giving cause for concern, her condition was relatively stable for now.

Ellie went home and picked up Jayden from her neighbour's house, but she didn't stop to chat for long because Lewis had said he was going to drop by later on and she needed to get organised. She wasn't expecting Lily to be home for a few hours yet.

'So what do you think of your new sister?' she asked Jayden when they were home.

He wriggled his shoulders. 'She's all right, I suppose. She doesn't do anything, though, except sleep and yawn, and sometimes she cries.'

Ellie nodded. 'Babies do quite a lot of that,' she said. 'It's their way of letting us know they need something.'

She changed out of her work clothes into jeans and a top, and after they had eaten she showed him the cookery book and let him choose what they were going to make.

'Cupcakes,' he said, his eyes growing round as he looked at the pictures. 'Those with the pink stuff on top.'

'Hmm. Pink for a girl. That seems about right.'

Just over an hour later she set the cakes out on a tiered cake stand and they inspected the finished results. 'They look pretty good, don't they?'

Jayden nodded. 'Can I have one now?'

'Of course you can. I think you've earned it after all that work.'

The doorbell rang and she went to greet Lewis. Jayden came with her to see who was there, and looked disappointed for a second or two when he realised it wasn't his mother. He held onto Ellie's jeans and she put an arm around his shoulders, recognising that he was shy of strangers.

'Lewis,' she said, 'I wasn't sure if you would remember. It's good to see you.'

'And you.' He gently touched her arm and while she appreciated the tender gesture of affection she felt a momentary quiver of unease. Could James have been right when he'd said Lewis wanted more than friendship from her? Surely not?

'I wouldn't forget,' he said. 'Sophie invited my wife to some sort of women's fashion evening, so I told her I'd come to see you and drop off that list of names you wanted for the TV series.'

'Oh, you have it with you? That's great,' she said. 'Thanks.' She shook off her worries about him. Lewis had never given her any reason for concern.

He smiled at Jayden. 'Hello, young man. I don't think we've met before, have we?'

Jayden shook his head. 'I'm Jayden,' he said. 'Who are you?'

Lewis chuckled. 'I'm a friend of Ellie's,' he said. 'I've come to talk over a few things with her.'

'Okay.'

They went into the living room, and Ellie settled Jayden down with some paper and crayons. Once he was busy drawing, Lewis suggested that they sit down and talk about the experts on his list.

'I've made a few notes about each one and where they might fit in with your kind of programme,' he said. 'For instance, there's a doctor who knows all about scans and how to interpret the images, and another who could talk about gestational diabetes.'

'That sounds good.' They went through the list and talked about how the programmes might take form.

'Thanks for this, Lewis,' she said after a while. 'It'll be a great help when we come to set up the series.'

'You're welcome. I'll do whatever I can to help out.' He glanced at his watch. 'I should go. Jessica will be home soon from her fashion thing—'

'All right.' They stood up and Jayden came over to them, thrusting a piece of paper into Ellie's hand.

'It's a car,' he said. 'My car—for when I'm big. It goes really fast.'

She looked down at the drawing. It was a blue streak of a car with a rainbow trail of fumes coming from twin exhaust pipes at the back. She smiled at him. 'It's beautiful, Jayden. Is that you in the driver's seat?'

He nodded, beaming with satisfaction as he walked with Ellie and Lewis to the front door. Ellie glanced at Lewis. 'Between us we've managed to come up with some great ideas for programmes. I can't wait to tell my producer about them.'

'He'll love what you have planned.'

She opened the door, and as they were saying goodbye they were both distracted by the sound of a car door slamming at the end of the drive.

Someone shouted, 'Ellie Saunders? This way, Ellie. Look over here.'

Startled, Ellie looked to where the sound was coming from and saw a man pointing a camera in her direction. All three of them were caught in the flash that followed. The camera whirred a couple more times before she realised what was happening and she quickly ushered Jayden back inside the house. She was completely taken aback by what had just gone on.

'Who is he? What's going on?'

Lewis shook his head. 'I don't know, Ellie, but he looks to me as though he might be someone from the press. Perhaps it's something to do with the TV programme. You're getting to be quite famous after all, a household name.'

'Oh, heavens. What am I to do?'

'Leave it to me. I'll see to it that he goes away,' Lewis told her, his mouth making a grim line. 'You go back inside the house.'

'Are you sure?'

'It'll be fine. Goodbye, Ellie.' He strode down the path and the man must have read the dark intent in his features because he dived into his car and revved the engine before screeching away down the road.

Ellie watched Lewis drive away and then shut the door, leading Jayden back to the kitchen.

He said happily, 'That man took a picture of me.'

'He did, sweetheart. He took a picture of all of us.' She settled him down at the kitchen table and he started eagerly on another picture.

She was jittery, completely unsettled by the intrusion, and for a while she paced the floor. Would he come back? He had what he wanted, after all.

She felt dreadful. The episode had upset her, and she couldn't quite fathom the reason. Perhaps it was fear of the unknown. What was the man intending to do with the photos? What did he want with her?

The doorbell rang for the second time that evening and she jumped nervously. Had he decided to return after all to cause more trouble?

Jayden looked at her. 'Is it the man?'

'I don't know.' She stood up and made an effort to stay calm for Jayden's sake. 'How's your colouring coming along?'

He lifted his book to show her. 'It's a boat on the water, see? And there's a frog sitting on a leaf.'

She nodded and said absently, 'It's called a lily pad. And you've coloured the picture really well.'

The doorbell rang again, sending a small shudder through her. She had to face up to it and go to see who was there. There was more than one kind of demon to be faced, she was discovering.

She was ultra-cautious when she opened the door, and felt a surge of relief when she saw it was James standing there.

He gave her a searching look. 'You're white as a sheet,' he said. 'What's happened? Are you ill?'

'I'm fi—' she began, and he cut in sharply.

'And don't tell me you're fine because I can see quite plainly that you're not.'

'I've had a strange visitor,' she said, opening the door wider and waving James inside. Seeing him standing there had been like the sun breaking through clouds on a dull day. Somehow, with James around, she immediately felt safe, as though nothing else mattered.

'It was just a photographer,' she explained. 'He called my name and started clicking away with his camera. I've no idea what he was doing here, but he took several photos of us.'

'Us?' James echoed.

'Lewis was here.' She led the way to the kitchen and went to the sink to fill the kettle. It gave her something to do and the mundane task was comforting somehow.

James frowned. 'Perhaps it was a good thing he was here with you. It looks as though you've had a bit of a shock.'

She nodded. 'I can't think of any reason for him to turn up here. Lewis thinks it could be something to do with the TV series. He says I'm newsworthy now that I'm getting to be a household name.'

'Could be, I suppose.'

James glanced at Ellie as she busied herself making tea, and she sensed he knew she was staying on the move so as not to give way to her anxieties.

'I came to see if you needed some help with the young lad,' he said, 'but it looks as though you have everything under control.'

She nodded. 'We've had a busy time, haven't we, Jayden? I can't remember how many cakes we made.'

'Lots,' he said, then crinkled his brow. 'This many.' He held up his hands, his fingers spread wide. 'But I had two of them.' He bent two fingers downwards.

'I think we should offer some to James, don't you?'

Jayden frowned, looking first at the cake stand and then at James. 'Yeah, okay,' he said after a while. He watched anxiously as James picked out a pink-topped cupcake covered in edible silver balls, but looked relieved when he seemed satisfied with just one.

Ellie set about making a pot of tea, and when she turned round she saw that James and Jayden were busy picking out the cakes that had the best decoration.

'That can't be one of yours,' James said, shaking his head. 'It's way too special. You're only…what is it, four years old? You couldn't have done that. Could you?'

'I did! I did it!'

'What, all by yourself?' James put on an incredulous face and Jayden jumped up and down in his seat with delight.

'Yeah, all by myself.'

'Wow!' James laughed and turned to Ellie. 'It sounds as though he's had a great time.'

'I guess he did.' It was heart-warming to see the way James and the little boy interacted. James clearly had a knack for dealing with young children.

She picked up Jayden's discarded colouring book and pencils and dropped them into his schoolbag. 'There are some toys in the box in the sitting room,' she told the boy. 'Why don't you go and choose something to play with?'

Jayden slid down from his seat at the table and went off to find the box, and Ellie watched as he settled down in a far corner with some construction blocks. Because of the L-shaped design of the house she could still keep an eye on him from the kitchen if she walked over to the worktop.

She poured tea from the pot into two ceramic mugs and passed one to James. 'It was thoughtful of you to come and see me,' she said.

He swallowed some of the hot liquid. 'Well, I know

you've had a difficult day, in more ways than one, so I wondered if you might be glad of a helping hand. Like you said, four-year-olds can be wonderful, but exhausting sometimes.'

He placed the mug down on the table and moved towards her. 'You've a bit more colour in your cheeks now, at any rate.' He slid his arms around her waist. 'I hope that's down to me and not Lewis.'

Much as she liked having his arms around her, her brows drew together in a frown at his comment. 'I thought we'd discussed all that.'

'Did we? I'm not so sure we're both singing from the same song sheet somehow. Lewis is a married man, but he was here, after all. It seems he can't keep away.'

'He was here because he brought me some information for my TV series.' She felt exasperated. 'I don't know why I'm bothering to explain things to you.'

'Maybe it's because you and I both know he could have given you any information you needed at work.'

'But there's absolutely no reason why he shouldn't bring it here.'

'No—except he seems to find it hard to keep away. He needs to be protected from himself.'

She scowled at him. 'I give up. You're impossible. I'm pretty sure Lewis can sort out his own marital problems without any help from you.' She tried to wriggle out of his grasp but he only wound his arms more closely about her.

'But, like I said before, you don't need Lewis hanging around—you and I could be wonderful together if you would give us half a chance.' His hands made gentle forays along the length of her spine. 'You're like one of those gorgeous cupcakes—perfect in every way, deliciously tempting, and definitely more than I can resist.'

She gave a soft laugh. 'You make them sound positively sinful.'

'Mmm…that, too,' he murmured, nuzzling the sensitive flesh behind her ear. 'I could lose myself in you, Ellie.' His lips drifted sensually over the column of her throat, and as she turned her head a fraction he swooped to claim her mouth. Her body tingled as his lips pressured hers, and his kiss made her blood sizzle, sending ripples of pleasure surging through her from head to toe. She was lost in that kiss, swirling in a mist of heady delight.

'I ache for you, Ellie,' he said, his voice roughened with desire. His hands shaped her, exploring the rounded contours of her body and bringing her up closer to him so that her soft curves meshed with his powerful frame. 'You make me feel so good.'

It was sheer bliss to have him hold her this way, and for a while she felt exhilarated in the delicious sensations that quivered along her nerve endings, yearning for this moment to go on and on.

But with a four-year-old just a short distance away and liable to come into the kitchen at any moment, it would have been madness to go on.

'James, we can't do this,' she said in a low voice. 'Jayden is…'

'I know.' He sighed raggedly. He held her for a few seconds longer before reluctantly easing back. 'I want you all to myself.'

She looked up at him, a bemused expression on her face. She was besieged by a whole array of conflicting emotions, not least of which was where Sophie fitted into any of this.

'What is it?' he asked, giving her a quizzical look.

'You said you want me all to yourself, but aren't you dating Sophie? That's what Noah's article said and Sophie seems to be at the manor house quite often.'

Her question must have caught him unawares because he was serious all at once, and he appeared to be deep in thought. 'Sophie's family has been linked to ours socially for many years,' he said at last. 'Her parents are on very friendly terms with my father.'

'But you've taken her out? That's true, isn't it? You've been out with her recently?'

'Yes, I have.' He frowned. 'The situation with Sophie is complicated. She helps out a lot with my father so I see her quite regularly, and there are social occasions when we meet because of my father's friendship with her parents. But none of that has to affect you and me.'

'Doesn't it? I think you might be wrong there.'

She moved away from him. She wasn't sure he'd given her a straight answer, and as far as she was concerned, that meant he was out of bounds from now on.

'Why, Ellie? You were with me all the way just now. You wanted me every bit as much as I want you. I felt it. So what went wrong?'

'Nothing. You're right, I did want to be in your arms but I came to my senses. I can't get involved with any man who casts his net wide. I've been caught that way before, and I vowed I would never let it happen to me again. I went out with a man for quite a while, and I really liked him, but then I went out with some girl friends and saw him wining and dining another woman. They were holding hands and whispering to one another, and they walked out of that place with their arms around one another.'

He sucked in his breath. 'I'm sorry that happened to you, Ellie. But this isn't the same. It isn't what you think. It's all to do with heritage and family links—all the sort of things my father holds dear. I don't want to cause him any upset while his health is in such a precarious state. But my seeing Sophie doesn't mean anything, believe me. She's just the daughter of a family friend.'

'I wonder if Sophie understands that?'

He frowned. 'She doesn't have anything to do with what's between you and me.'

'No? It doesn't sit well with me, James.'

'Ellie—the truth is, I'm not ready for any sort of commitment yet. I have a lot of responsibility as well as having to look out for my father and overseeing the management of the estate. But I don't see any reason why we can't have fun and enjoy things the way they are.'

'I understand that but I'm not sure I can go along with it.' She frowned. 'I need time to think, so perhaps you should go. I think we've said all we need to say. I was carried away for a moment, but it won't happen again. I wasn't thinking straight.'

'You know I like being with you.'

'And I like being with you, but I'm pretty sure this is not going to work out the way you were perhaps expecting.'

She'd made up her mind, and he must have seen that because he went to say goodbye to Jayden and left the house soon afterwards.

Ellie shut the door behind him and felt a bleak wave of emptiness wash over her. She missed him already.

CHAPTER SEVEN

'ELLIE, WHAT'S GOING on?' Noah sounded really concerned. 'I saw the papers this morning and wanted to talk to you about what I read in there. I've been ringing you for ages but I couldn't get through.'

'It's the press, Noah. They won't leave me alone.' There was a note of desperation in Ellie's voice. 'They've been calling all morning and I stopped answering the phone, until I saw your name on the caller display. I switched off my mobile phone because they even managed to find that number. It's driving me crazy. And it's not just that. They're camped out at the front of the house, too.'

'Have you tried calling the police?'

'Yes, they've moved them on once, but they keep coming back. It's been going on since six o'clock this morning.' She gave a heavy sigh. 'At least they've stopped knocking on the door. I've locked myself in. I don't know what else to do.'

'I suppose you could try speaking to them.'

'And have more rubbish printed about me? I can't do that. It's bad enough that they dragged up all the stuff from my past—they even found pictures from the local newspaper back then. They made me look like the all-time drunken party girl. That headline: *"TV's Ellie Saunders as you have never seen her before."* It made me feel sick.'

'I guessed you must be feeling pretty bad. It must have been a tremendous shock.'

'Yes, it was. But it's Lewis's wife I feel sorry for. They've tried to make out that Lewis and I are having an affair—they even linked Jayden with both of us. Can you believe it? How could they do this?' She frowned. 'It just makes me realise how Lord Birchenall must have felt when the press bombarded him after your story was printed. Until now, I hadn't imagined just how bad it could be.'

'I know. Me, too.' He was contrite. 'I feel terrible about what I did. But I was just so full of anger at the time. I kept thinking how he threw us out and the family broke up. All I could think about was that here was a way of getting back at him at last, but I'm really sorry for it now.' He pulled in a quick breath as a thought struck him. 'Do you think he could be behind all this stuff in the papers?'

'Surely not? I don't think he would stoop to something like that. Lewis is his nephew. Whatever he is, he's not vindictive, and even if he was, I can't see James letting him do something like this.'

'I guess you're right. So, do you have any idea who might have gone to the papers?'

'No. I can't think straight. It's been such a shock.'

'Is there anything I can do to help, Ellie? Shall I come to the house?'

'No, there's no need for you to do that, Noah. I expect they'll get tired of waiting and go home before too long. And I think I'll switch off the landline phone.'

They spoke for a little while longer, and then Noah rang off. Ellie pulled the plug on the phone connection and began to pace the room. She'd tried to sound confident that they would go away, but she wasn't.

She'd had to draw the curtains to stop journalists peering in at her and taking photos through the windows, and she'd had to switch on the lights even though there was daylight outside. She was a prisoner in her own home.

Occasionally, she peeped out through the curtains in the hope that the crowd of photographers and journalists might have gone away but, no, they were still there. She clenched her fists in frustration. What was she going to do?

Then there was a loud rapping at the front door and she froze. She wasn't going to answer it but the knocking went on and a man called out, 'Miss Saunders? I have a letter for you. It's important. Will you please read it now?'

She walked across the hallway and stared at the white envelope lying on the mat. What now? Was this some new ploy they'd dreamed up? Almost in anger, she snatched up the envelope and ripped it open.

Ellie, I guess things are pretty bad for you right now, so I've asked Charles to come and fetch you. Go with him and he'll bring you to the manor house. You might want to bring an overnight bag with clothes for a couple of days. James.

Relief surged through her. James was there for her, he was thinking about her and offering to help free her from the mob outside. She felt an overwhelming rush of gratitude, and joy, too, that he would come to her rescue, despite what had gone on between them the last time they'd been together. She'd believed she was alone in this, but he'd been thinking of her all the time.

She opened the door a crack. 'Are you Charles?' she asked the young man who was standing there, and when he nodded she beckoned him inside, shutting and locking the door again quickly as the men and women from the tabloids rushed forward in a frenzy of excitement.

'I'm a friend of James,' he explained as they went to the kitchen. He was tall, with a strong physique, and looked capable of handling himself in a difficult situation. Was that why James had chosen him? 'He didn't come himself in case they recognised him. He thought they might follow you to the manor house.'

'That makes sense.' She waved a hand towards the coffee percolator. 'Help yourself to a drink while I go and pack a few things. It's all set up and should be hot.'

'Thank you.'

She was shaking as she bundled a change of clothes into a holdall. How were they going to get through the baying pack outside? After all, Charles was only one man against the crowd.

She pushed her cosmetic case into a corner of the bag and zipped it closed. Then she hurried downstairs and went to find Charles once more.

'I can't think how we're going to get away from here,' she said. 'Even if we're quick, they'll surround us.'

He nodded. 'We thought of that. I parked round the

back and walked to the front of the house so they didn't see me drive up. They'll probably assume my car is one of those parked on the road out front. If we go out of here the back way we might be able to fool them. Your car's out front, so they won't be expecting you to leave any other way.'

'Okay. That seems like a good plan.'

A few minutes later they slipped out through the kitchen door and hurried to Charles's car, a long, black saloon with tinted windows.

'So far, so good,' Charles said, as he started up the engine. Then he smoothly drove across the courtyard and out through the stone archway onto the road, where he picked up speed.

'They must have heard us,' Ellie said, looking through the rear-view mirror. 'They're running towards the road.'

Charles smiled. 'Don't worry. They'll never catch up with us now.'

About twenty minutes later they arrived at the manor house and as James came out to greet her, Charles said goodbye. 'You take care.'

'Thank you—thanks for everything,' she called after him, and he acknowledged her with a wave and a smile.

'Hi.' James took hold of her bag and she noticed he, too, was carrying a holdall, the long strap slung over his shoulder. He reached for her, taking her hand in his firm grasp as he led her towards his streamlined silver coupé.

'Hi.' She'd never been so glad to see him. He was long and lean and tautly muscled, every bit her saviour, and she felt safe for the first time in hours. 'Thank you for this,' she said, looking at him with heartfelt gratitude. 'I felt so trapped and frightened, and then all of a sudden you were there for me, giving me a way out.' She would be forever in debt to him for this.

'I knew you must be worried sick. I'm sorry you had to go through all that.' He unlocked the boot of his car and began to stow their bags inside.

She frowned. 'Where are we going?'

'Where no one will find us,' he said. 'Relax. We're going on a boat trip.'

He held open the passenger-side door, and she slid into the seat. 'A boat trip?' she echoed. 'But what about work in the morning? We have to be at the hospital.'

'Not any more,' he said, starting up the car. 'I've arranged for us to take a couple of days off and brought in locums to take our places.'

Her mouth dropped open. 'Why would you do that?'

He gave her a sideways glance. 'I figured the press will lose interest after a couple of days if they can't find you, and then they'll move on to some other news story.'

She stared at him, wide-eyed. 'This is all so hard to take in. How did you know I was in trouble?'

'I saw the papers this morning. I tried ringing you, but you had your phone switched off and the landline was constantly engaged, so I guessed you were having problems. Then I rang Noah and he told me what was going on, so I thought the best thing would be to come and get you, except I didn't want the press to recognise me and put two and two together, so that's where Charles came in.'

'I really appreciate you doing this for me.' She looked at him earnestly and he gave her a brief smile as he turned the car onto the main road. 'I felt so alone and then you sent me that note and it was as if a great weight had been lifted from me.'

'I guessed you needed some help.'

'Thanks again, anyway.' She looked out of the window at the passing landscape, seeing the rolling hills gradually give way to lowland meadows and serene countryside where a river meandered lazily through a gentle valley.

'Where are we headed? What kind of boat trip did you have in mind? I remember you saying once that you have a boat. What kind is it? Is it a yacht?' She looked at him doubtfully. She wasn't sure she wanted to go sailing on a wide, choppy sea.

'Nothing as grand as that. Ever since I was a child I've enjoyed cruising the inland waterways, so a couple of years ago I decided to buy a canal boat. Now, whenever I get the chance, I like to spend leisurely weekends on the water. That's where we're going.'

'It sounds great.' She smiled. 'It'll be a new experience for me.'

'Then I hope you like it. The boat's fitted out with most things we might need for a comfortable journey.'

Ellie thought about his leisurely weekends. Had Sophie spent time with him on the boat? Her stomach lurched and she quickly pushed the unwanted image from her mind. James was doing this for her and she should be grateful for that. It wouldn't help to dwell on the woman who was unwittingly driving a wedge between them.

They finally arrived at their destination and James parked the car at the marina, where a dozen or so colourful boats were moored.

'Here we are. This one's mine, the *Louise Jane*.'

Ellie made a quick guess. 'Is she named after your mother?'

He nodded. 'That's right. I wanted something special to keep her memory alive.'

Unexpectedly, Ellie's eyes dampened. It was a wonderful gesture, a loving tribute from a son who had lost his mother at a young age. It was something his mother would have truly appreciated.

The boat was long, and a pleasing dark green, with distinctive artwork painted across its length. There were pictures of flowers in bright reds and yellows, and other canal art showing watering cans and colourful tubs.

'Let's go on board,' James said, 'and I'll show you around.'

He held her hand, supporting her as she stepped onto the deck, and then he closed the rail and led the way down wooden steps into the galley. Immediately, she missed his warm hand clasping hers. 'I had her fitted out with a top-of-the-range cooker and fridge and as many cupboards as possible.'

'This is really impressive, James.' All the equipment was modern, and the stainless-steel surfaces gleamed softly. The floor was covered in warm-looking, solid oak timbers.

He acknowledged her praise with a faint inclination of his head. 'I stocked the fridge and the cupboards recently and I've brought a few essentials with me, so we should manage well enough.'

She pulled in a deep breath. It was only just beginning to dawn on her that she and James would be alone on this boat for the next couple of days. It wasn't something she might ever have imagined, especially since they had left each other in strained circumstances just a short time ago. Now, though, her treacherous body responded by being both excited and unnerved at the same time.

'Come through to the main cabin,' he said, ushering her into what looked like a cosy sitting room.

There were plush, upholstered bench seats on opposite sides, decorated with bright cushions, and in one corner there was an oak table large enough to accommodate four people.

'The seats lift up, so there's more storage space underneath,' he explained, and she looked around admiringly.

'Do you sleep in here?' she asked, imagining sleeping bags laid out along the length of the seats. And that gave rise to a worrying question in her mind. Where would they both sleep tonight? How would she cope, being so near to him?

'No. There are separate sleeping berths—partitioned off to allow some privacy. I'll show you, and you can choose which one you want.' He glanced at her, his mouth making a devilish twist. 'Unless, of course, you'd like to share with me? It can get chilly out on the water at night, and I'd be more than happy to keep you warm.'

Heat washed through her from head to toe at his suggestion. 'I'm sure you would,' she murmured, 'but somehow I don't think that would be a good idea.'

'A pity, that,' he said, giving her a rueful glance. 'I thought it was an excellent one. But if you should change your mind…'

'I'm sorry, but I won't.' It grieved her to say it, but

she'd made up her mind not to get involved with him. Her reputation was in tatters, and getting close to him would only lead to heartache in the end because they were worlds apart. He came from a family of meticulously respectable ancestors, and she simply wouldn't fit in. Especially now, since her face had been splashed over all the papers.

And yet he'd taken her rejection of him with good humour, as always. It was so heart-warming to have him look after her this way. He'd asked nothing of her. He was a truly wonderful man, like none she'd ever known. Who else would have taken care of her like this, without expecting something in return?

He took her through to the sleeping quarters, each room furnished with a double bed and overhead cupboard space, and lastly he showed her what he called 'the head', which was where the bathroom facilities were housed. Again, these were the best quality with pearl-white porcelain fittings.

'I'll start up the motor and get us under way,' he said, as they walked back towards the galley. 'Then when we're away further along the canal we'll stop for a bite to eat. I'd suggest we stop at a pub, but with your picture being splashed over the papers, people who've seen you on TV might be tempted to hassle you. What do you think?'

'I think you're probably right,' she said in a dejected tone. 'I feel as though my life's been turned upside down. I just don't know why any of this is happening or who could have done it. Who would want to ruin my life, and my TV career?'

He put his arms around her and gave her a quick hug.

'I can't imagine anyone who would want to do something like this. Everyone I know likes you. You're sweet, kind and thoughtful, and you certainly don't deserve to be pilloried this way. Neither does Lewis. It's abominable how they've pointed the finger at him.'

He released her all too soon, and Ellie struggled to bring her chaotic senses under control. She followed him up on deck.

James untied the mooring rope and started up the motor, steering them slowly along the watercourse. He looked perfectly at ease at the wheel, completely in command. He was wearing khaki chinos and a dark T-shirt that emphasised his powerful biceps, and Ellie had a strange compulsion to run her hands over his strong arms and feel his body tauten next to hers.

With a supreme effort of will she resisted the urge. Instead, she said quietly, 'I rang Lewis's wife and told her there's no truth in the stories. She seemed thoroughly shocked by what's happening and Lewis is doing his utmost to put her mind at rest.'

'They've been struggling lately,' James remarked. 'I don't know exactly what the problem is, but Lewis admits they've been arguing far more than usual. They've been married for about five years, and up till now things have gone well for them, or so it seemed.'

'And you blame me for getting in the way?'

He gave her a sideways look. 'He may not have said anything, but Lewis is very susceptible to your charms. I think he's flattered because you're a good listener, you have a sympathetic ear, and it's easy to see how his head might have been turned.'

'But that's all in your imagination. Surely you know

that? There has never been anything going on between Lewis and me. Why would you think otherwise?'

'Because Lewis is vulnerable, and it would be very easy for him to be open to temptation. It would ruin him if he succumbed, because he really does love his wife. Far better, then, for you to try to steer clear of him.'

'Don't you think Lewis and I can sort things out between us?'

'Unfortunately, no. But I certainly feel more at ease knowing you're on this boat with me, rather than getting together with Lewis to offer each other sympathy and understanding. Lewis is already in a fragile state emotionally. Having you close at hand could make any man go weak at the knees.'

She frowned, uneasy at what he was saying. 'Is that why you brought me here?'

'I brought you here to make sure you were safe and out of reach of the press. Keeping you out of reach of Lewis is an added bonus.'

She bit back a sharp comment. After all, she could hardly take him to task for that when he had saved her from being trapped in her own home. She didn't want to be at odds with him, but inside she fretted at his lack of faith in her. What made him doubt her? Was it some subconscious conviction that women weren't to be relied on? That they would somehow manage to cause hurt? A sad relic of his mother leaving him, perhaps, albeit that she'd done it unwillingly?

Surely she was the one who was most likely to be feeling insecure in that way? Her mother had deserted her—hadn't that led to the wild teenage years that were her undoing now?

She sighed. 'Shall I go below and put the kettle on? I could prepare some food if you like. I don't know about you, but I haven't eaten today. I lost my appetite when I saw the papers, and the rest is history.'

'That's a good idea, if you don't mind doing that. There are cooked meats in the fridge and some bread. Help yourself to whatever you want. I expect sandwiches will be the easiest. I'll come and give you a hand as soon as I find a place to moor the boat.'

'Okay.'

She went to the galley and looked inside the fridge and the cupboards. As he'd said, they were well stocked. There was rice, a variety of meats, peppers and vegetables, some mushrooms and onions. Pushing back the sleeves of her blouse, she washed her hands and set about making a meal. She could do better than sandwiches.

'Hey, something smells good,' James said, coming down the steps to the galley some time later. 'What's cooking?'

'Chicken risotto. It seemed like the easiest thing to do. And I've made a fruit salad for dessert. All of a sudden I'm starving.'

He grinned. 'Me, too. I can't wait to try it. Shall we eat up on deck? We may as well make the most of this lovely weather while it lasts. Before we know it, we'll be into October and it'll be coats and scarves at the ready, unless we're lucky.'

'Yes, okay. Shall I make us a drink to take up there?'

'I'll open a bottle of wine. You serve up and I'll see to the drinks and carry everything up top.'

'All right.'

They sat on bench seats by the boat rail and tucked into the meal while watching ducks dip in and out of the reeds at the water's edge. The canal had opened out here and wildlife flourished. Birds flew down to catch insects that hovered over the thistles and sedge on the banks, and a somnolent, leisurely atmosphere pervaded overall. Ellie leaned back and relaxed, watching nature at its best.

'This is delicious,' James said, savouring the different flavours of the risotto. 'When you said you liked cooking, I didn't know you could throw a few ingredients together and make something like this. It's mouth-watering.'

'I'm glad you think so.'

He poured wine, chilled from the fridge, and they clinked glasses together in a toast. 'Good health and good times,' James said.

Ellie echoed the toast. 'Yes, let's hope for those,' she said, sipping the wine and feeling its soothing coolness slide down her throat. 'I wonder what sort of times lie ahead. You have your future mapped out for you, I expect, as it has been through the generations. And at least I have my hospital career to rely on.'

He was preoccupied for a moment, thinking about that, and then he said quietly, 'Have you heard anything from your TV producer?'

She shook her head. 'No. But all this is bound to affect my future there. He was planning to go ahead with a new series, but I dare say this will have put a spoke in that idea. He won't want a disreputable doctor presenting the programmes.'

'Surely most people will realise that you were still

a teenager back then? If they knew something of your background they would understand why you behaved as you did.' He watched the variety of expressions flit across her face. 'Perhaps it's time to bring all of that out into the open—talk about how you felt lost and alone, and this was your way of expressing all your teenage angst. You rebelled against the system and against the adults who had let you down. Why would people hold that against you?'

'I don't know. But someone obviously wanted it shouted to all and sundry. They must have known it would ruin my career in television.' She frowned and sipped more wine, then looked at him pensively. 'You're being very understanding about all this. I would have thought that with your background and everything, with your father being a stickler for the right way of going about things, you might disapprove of me.'

'I'm not my father.'

'No.' But she knew there would never be any place for her in his life. Throughout their long history, his family had been proud, deeply traditional, and conservative in outlook. They would never countenance accepting a notorious individual into their midst.

That thought had dropped into her mind without any warning. When had it happened that she'd started to yearn for more than a casual relationship, for something meaningful and secure?

James topped up her wineglass and ate the last of his risotto. 'Anyway, I feel that we're partly to blame for what happened to you and your family and I can understand why Noah felt so strongly.'

'He said he regrets what he did. I don't think he

realised until now how devastating it can be to come across things that have been written about you and spread out in the papers for all to see.'

'I know. He apologised to me this morning, and asked me to pass on his regrets to my father. He said he's going to write to him.'

'Will it make a difference to your father?'

'Possibly. He certainly feels some responsibility for your father's troubles since he discovered that he had been ill.'

They started on their desserts and waved to a passing canal-boat crew, though Ellie turned her head a little and let her hair draw a curtain over her features to stop her from being recognised.

'Why am I doing this?' she said in exasperation when the boat had travelled into the distance. 'I can't hide for ever, can I? Sooner or later I'm going to have to face up to things, and the public.'

'There's time enough to work out how to do that,' James said. 'Just take it easy for now. You've been through a traumatic time today, and you need to come to terms with it in your own mind before you take on the world again. I'm sure we'll think of something.'

She smiled, letting her gaze wander over his face and explore his perfect features. She wasn't alone. He was by her side, and he would help her to get through this. It made her stronger, simply knowing that.

The following day they travelled further along the canal, negotiating a series of locks along the way. Each time James jumped onto the towpath and turned the key to open the sluice, while Ellie helped pull the lock gates into position to allow them through to continue their journey.

'I can see why people take to this way of life,' she said that evening as they ate supper on the deck in the moonlight. 'There's no hurrying, no rush to do anything. You have to take your time, and after a while, without realising it's happened, you find the tranquillity has seeped into your bones.'

'It's certainly a good antidote to working in A and E,' James said with a smile. 'I'm glad you've taken to it. You definitely seem more relaxed now, more at ease with everything.'

'It's been perfect. I hadn't realised how much I needed to get away—to get right away—from everything and everyone. I feel so much better now, ready to face up to things.'

'That's what I was hoping for.' James took a long swallow of his chilled lager and offered to top up her wineglass with what was left in the bottle cooling on ice.

'Thanks.' She was in a dreamy, hazy state of bliss, at peace with herself for the first time in ages. 'And thank you for all this, James. It's been a great experience.' It had been wonderful just to be with him and she wanted this time to go on and on and never end.

She drained her glass and reluctantly got to her feet. 'It's late,' she said. 'I should go to bed. I'm wiped out—in a good way.' She didn't want to leave him but she was afraid to start something that might get out of hand. She cared deeply for him, was falling in love with him, but she was desperately afraid of being hurt.

'Goodnight, Ellie.'

She couldn't be sure, in the shadows cast by the silver light of the moon, but it seemed there was a yearning, regretful glimmer in the depths of his smoke-dark eyes.

She felt the same aching need for him as she lay restlessly on her bed, all too conscious of him in the next berth. The air was warm, and heavy with an electric tension, a vibrant, throbbing sense of unfulfilled, heady desire.

In the morning she woke up after hearing a knock on the door and some words that she couldn't make out through the drowsy mist of sleep. She stretched lazily, feeling slightly disorientated and with her head filled with remnants of dreams. They had been good dreams that in her semi-conscious state made her feel upbeat, as though the world was her oyster.

Some time later she became aware of the appetising smell of frying bacon, and James was knocking on the partition door once again, saying, 'Wake up, sleepy-head. Your breakfast is ready. You need to get yourself in here now.'

She scrambled out of bed and hurried to splash water on her face and wake herself up. Then she threw on a short silk robe that she'd had the presence of mind to bundle into her holdall, and went in search of that wonderful smell.

'Ah, there you are.' James must have caught sight of her out of the corner of his eye as he lifted a frying pan from the hob. 'I was thinking I'd have to come and haul you out of bed.'

Then he looked at her properly and suddenly became still, an arrested expression in his eyes and in the silent whistle that hovered on his lips. He put down the pan he was holding. 'On second thoughts, it's just as well I didn't come to get you.' His gaze shimmered over her, lingering on the silk that clung to her curves, before drifting down along her bare legs to her carefully painted toenails. 'That way, we'd never have got around to breakfast.'

She laughed, and looked at the preparations he'd made. The table was set with cutlery, a rack of toast and a covered teapot alongside two cups. 'Is there anything I can do to help?'

'Uh, yeah, maybe you could cover yourself with a sack and then I might be able to concentrate better.'

She chuckled, leaning negligently against the doorjamb. He looked pretty good himself, tall and flat stomached, strong and capable, a feast for her senses first thing in the morning. 'Is something disturbing you?' she enquired teasingly.

'Oh, yes, I'd say so. A slinky, sensual, gorgeous creature with curves in all the right places and a mane of hair that is sinfully sexy.' He shook his head as though freeing himself of a troublesome image and began to absently dish out golden-centred fried eggs, sliding them onto plates that had been warmed in the oven.

Then he gave up the fight with his willpower and left everything where it was, and came over to her. 'What the heck. I'm just a man and you're a temptress beyond imagining. What am I to do, Ellie?'

'Hmm…let's see. You could kiss me,' she said huskily. 'Do you think that would solve your problem?'

'I think it might go a long way.' He didn't need a second bidding. He took her into his arms and his whole body seemed to quiver with pent-up need, so much so that for a fleeting second or two she wondered if she should have thought this through. She could be taking on a whole lot more than she could handle.

Then his mouth crushed hers in a kiss that heated her blood and turned her whole body to flame, while his hands drew her up against his firm body and pressured her soft curves until it felt as though they had meshed together as one.

'I need you, Ellie,' he said raggedly. 'I want you so much.'

His hands sought out the smooth arc of her hips and swept upwards, seeking out the soft swell of her breasts. He cupped her gently, caressing her with exquisite expertise, bringing a low moan of contentment to her lips. His thumbs made a light, circling motion, tantalising her with sweet forays into the pleasure zone,and rousing her until she trembled with desire.

She ran her hands over him, memorising every flat plane and velvet-covered muscle, wanting to lay her cheek against him and feel the thunderous beat of his heart.

He kissed her again, a glorious, passionate, seeking kiss, and she responded wholeheartedly, her lips parting beneath his so that she could savour his sweet, warm possession.

Then, like the dash of a sudden, cold shower, a hooter sounded, long and loud, and they broke apart, looking about them in time to see another canal boat gliding past.

Ellie was breathing deeply, trying to get over the shock of the sudden separation, and James simply stared into space for a moment, caught in a strange kind of limbo.

He braced himself and exhaled slowly. 'Ellie…'

'Perhaps it's just as well we were disturbed,' she said. The dreamy haze was rapidly clearing from her mind and she was coming to see that getting close to him had been a big mistake. 'I should never have started that. It was wrong of me. Can we put it down to some sort of temporary lack of judgement?'

'Was it?'

'I think it must have been.'

Imagining that she could be with him was just a dream, beautiful while it had lasted, but now she had to try and get back to reality. She didn't want a brief fling with him. She wanted the one thing he couldn't give her. Commitment.

CHAPTER EIGHT

'HAVE YOU THOUGHT any more about talking to the press and giving your side of the story?' James asked as they drove home late that afternoon. 'You could point out where they had their facts wrong, and explain about the things that happened in your childhood to make you get into trouble.'

'I can't do that,' she said. 'It means I'd have to talk about my parents—about my mother leaving us. I won't do it. I won't say bad things about my family to the world at large. They'll either have to take me as I am and trust in me to be the kind of person they want to believe in, or follow what the papers say about me. There will always be people who think the worst.'

Wasn't that what happened whenever James saw her with Lewis? His problem was that he had to learn to trust, and until that happened, their relationship was doomed.

'Anyway, I'd far sooner find out who started these tales and ask why they did it.' Her brows drew together. 'Do you think Mel could have been behind them? I can't think of anyone else who might bear a grudge against me.'

He gave it some thought. 'It's possible, I suppose.

She was certainly angry and upset, and she wasn't satisfied with the result of our initial meeting. But she'd most likely deny it if you asked her and the papers won't reveal their sources.'

'That's true.' She sighed, frustrated by the lack of any possible action. It was upsetting to think that a woman she had known so well throughout her teenage years could have done something so vindictive.

In a while they pulled up outside the manor house and James parked the car on the drive.

'I'll take you home in a while,' he said, 'but I'm anxious to see if my father's all right. That last phone call from him earlier this afternoon made me suspect something was wrong. He didn't sound like his usual self.'

'You're bound to be worried about him.' Ellie went with him into the house, marvelling once more at its understated grandeur. Solid oak beams pointed to its historic origins and the spaciousness of the layout added to the feeling of stateliness and old money.

Lord Birchenall was in the drawing room, talking on the phone, and it was fairly clear that he was annoyed about something.

'There's no question about me harassing you over the land,' he said sharply. 'It was clearly written into the agreement I made with your stepfather a long time ago. The land was to revert to me after a period of ten years. All I'm doing is asking you to honour that agreement.'

He cut the call a few minutes later, breathing heavily. Ellie could hear the wheezing in his chest, and noticed that his cheeks were drained of colour.

'You promised you would leave me to deal with that,' James gently admonished his father. 'There's no need for you to be getting yourself in a state about it. We'll let the lawyers deal with the matter.'

'You have enough to do, running the estate,' Lord Birchenall protested.

'That doesn't matter. You shouldn't be getting hot and bothered about these things when I can take the worry from you.'

Ellie could see that it was all too much for James's father. He looked feverish and his breathing was getting faster and more laboured. He put a hand to his chest and began to cough, all signs that his lungs were drowning in fluid as a result of his heart problems.

She caught James's glance. 'I'll go and get my medical bag,' he said, suddenly on alert. 'His GTN spray is in the bureau drawer.'

She went to get the spray and gave it to his father, who had sunk down into a chair. He used the medication, which was supposed to help relieve the pain, and then she took his pulse. It was erratic, and that was worrying.

'James won't be able to run this place as well as do his job at the hospital,' Lord Birchenall said, his voice rasping. 'We need to sort things out…get some system in place…'

Ellie loosened his collar and said softly, 'I'm sure James will manage very well. Try to stay calm. We're here to look after you. You should rest.'

'He needs to marry and settle down. Sophie's ideal for him, they're well suited, and she'll make him a good wife. He needs to ensure his future here.'

Ellie's heart contracted at his words. All this talk of James and Sophie played on her worst fears. Was his future all mapped out? Had the time he'd spent with her this weekend been a simple dalliance? But she didn't have time to dwell on any of that because James's father was gasping now, and she was desperate to calm him down.

Lord Birchenall leaned forward, clutching his chest. The spray obviously hadn't helped him.

'You don't need to worry about any of that right now,' she said. 'Just try to take things easy.' They needed to get him on oxygen and give him some medication to reduce the amount of fluid on his lungs. 'We'll give you something for the pain. It won't be long now.'

But before they could do any of that, before James had returned with his medical kit, Lord Birchenall suddenly slumped and slid down in his chair, gradually losing consciousness.

Ellie couldn't find a pulse this time, and urgently called out to James for help. Then, after using her mobile to call for an ambulance, she used all her strength to carefully tug his father down on to the floor so that she could give him CPR.

When James hurried into the room, she was on her knees by his father's side, doing chest compressions to try to force the blood around his body. 'His heart stopped,' she said. 'Do you have a defibrillator?'

'Yes, right here.' His voice was taut with concern because he knew as well as she did that once the heart had stopped pumping, blood couldn't get around the body, and if that happened, the patient would die within a very short time.

James hurriedly set up the defibrillator, attaching the pads to his father's chest. All the time Ellie went on with the compressions.

'It's charged. Stay clear.'

She stopped the CPR and moved back a little while the machine delivered a shock to the heart. To their dismay, nothing changed, and as the unit detected that it had been unsuccessful it began to charge again. A second shock, more powerful than the first, followed.

This time a cardiac rhythm showed up on the monitor and James breathed a sigh of relief. He gave his father oxygen through a mask, while Ellie injected their patient with a painkiller and a diuretic that would help to reduce the fluid in his lungs.

'The ambulance should be here any minute now,' she told Lord Birchenall, and he nodded, dazed and uncertain about what had happened to him but beginning to recover a little.

The ambulance arrived and the paramedics came to tend to him. 'Are you coming with your father to the hospital?' one of them asked James.

'Yes. I'll throw a few things into a bag for him. They'll want to keep him in.'

'Okay. You might want to go and do that while we get him on a stretcher and transfer him to the vehicle.'

'I will.' James turned to Ellie and lightly squeezed her arm. 'Thank you for what you did. You saved his life.'

'We did it together,' she said, going with him to the stairs.

'I'm sorry you walked into all this,' he murmured, 'and I wish I didn't have to leave you this way. It wasn't the way I wanted our two days together to end.'

'It's okay.' Her mind was filled with doubts now about that time. She wanted him more than ever, but she couldn't see any way that would happen. He wasn't ready for any lasting relationship, unless he was planning to be with Sophie, as his father had suggested. 'I just hope your father's going to be all right.'

He sighed. 'So do I. Look, I hate to let you down—I'll call for a taxi to take you home.'

'No, I'll see to that. You need to concentrate on your father,' she told him. 'Go and pack some essentials. The paramedics will be ready to go any minute.'

He went upstairs and Ellie dialled the number for a taxi. She was sad for James that this had happened. He loved his father and his mind must be in turmoil.

When he came back downstairs she quickly searched his face. Her heart went out to him and she laid a comforting hand on his arm, knowing how anxious he was. He reacted warmly, giving her a quick a hug.

'Thanks again for all your help, Ellie,' he said as they walked back to the drawing room. 'It's a worry. These episodes are becoming more and more frequent.'

'I know, but let's be thankful we were both here with him.'

His hands lightly circled her arms. 'You're a treasure…in lots of ways.' He gave a half-smile. 'These last couple of days have been extra-special.'

'Yes, they were.' Her expression sobered as she saw the taxi draw up outside and the driver hooted his horn. 'I had a lovely time. Thank you for helping me to get away from everything.'

'Any time you need me, I'll be there.' He walked with her to the door and hesitated, obviously reluctant to see her go, but he said quietly, 'I'll come and see you tomorrow after work, just to make sure everything's all right.'

'Okay.'

She climbed into the taxi and waved goodbye as the vehicle moved away swiftly. She tried not to think about what Lord Birchenall had said, but his words echoed inside her head. He wanted his son to marry the daughter of one of his dearest friends. Was that what James wanted, too?

Her house was mercifully free of journalists lying in wait for her when she arrived home, and she went inside feeling relieved about that and prepared to get back into her normal routine.

She sat down at the kitchen table. When she'd switched on her mobile phone for the first time in two days, a number of text messages had started to come in. One was from her father, offering support, and she answered that, pleased that he had contacted her. Another was from her TV producer, asking her to get in touch.

I can drop by your place on Thursday evening, he wrote. *I'll be in the area then. Will you let me know if that's okay?*

Her stomach knotted briefly, but she knew this was something she would have to face up to eventually. Bracing herself, she answered him, setting up the meeting for Thursday.

Still worried by what had happened with the press, Ellie double-checked that she had locked all her doors and windows before she went to bed. If someone disliked her enough to set the newshounds on her, what else might they do?

But nothing happened during the night, and she woke up and got ready for work as usual in the morning. She was on edge the whole time. What kind of reception would she get at the hospital?

'Ellie, I feel really bad about what happened,' Lewis said later that morning when he came and found her in Accident and Emergency. 'How have you been?'

'I've been all right.' She studied his worried expression. 'What about you and Jessica? It must have been very distressing for you.'

He nodded, taking her to one side where they could talk more privately. Even so, she was aware of James watching them from a distance as he came out of the resuscitation room. His gaze was dark and contemplative, and she wished she knew what he was thinking. He'd been tied up with an emergency all morning and she hadn't had a chance to speak to him yet.

'I suppose the only good thing is that it made Jessica and I talk about things more than we have been doing of late,' Lewis said. 'We've not been getting on all that well these last few months, and I suppose this brought things to a head. We haven't resolved our problems yet, but at least we're going some way towards it.'

'I hope you manage to work things out.'

'So do I. Thanks.'

He went back to his own unit after a few minutes, and Ellie started to read through the notes on her next patient, frowning a little as she saw the test results.

James came over to her. 'Are you getting on all right?' he asked. 'Are people treating you well?'

She nodded and gave him a quick smile. 'They've been marvellous, really. Those who saw the papers are angry that they printed the stories. They say it was all sensationalism. But, of course, that's what seems to sell papers these days.'

'I'm glad you're all right. If you do have any problems, let me know.'

'I will, but I think I can handle things now. I feel much stronger mentally.' She had to be strong to face up to losing her TV career. It was something she'd built up over the years and she felt she was reaching out to a lot of people through the medium of television. It would be a wrench to have to let it go.

She sent him a pensive glance, conscious that he had worries of his own. 'How is your father? Is he holding up?'

He hesitated. 'He seems to be making a recovery of sorts. It's difficult to predict exactly how he'll do because, as you know, his heart was already failing, and this latest attack has only made things worse. They'll be keeping him in the cardiac wing for a few days at least.'

'I suppose that was to be expected. Does he need anything? Can I help in any way, with books or magazines, or anything? Noah has a collection of audio tapes about stately homes that might interest him.'

'I'm sure he'd welcome those, if Noah doesn't mind him borrowing them.'

'It would be Noah's way of trying to put things right, perhaps. At some point we have to let go of the past and move on.'

'Thanks. It's a great idea and it will help to take his mind off things. Sophie's getting together some books for him, but I'm not sure he's up to concentrating on the printed word just yet.'

He glanced at her. 'You know, he's really grateful to you for stepping in and keeping his heart going for those vital minutes. He's been asking about you, and he asked me to thank you for what you did.'

'I appreciate that.' She was trying not to read anything into his casual mention of Sophie, but an image of the two of them getting together persisted. 'It's good that he came through it all right. It was a nasty experience for him.'

James smiled at her, and then straightened his shoulders, as though trying to shrug off a heavy burden. He glanced down at the file in her hands. 'Do you have any worries with any of your patients? You looked as though you were troubled when you were looking through those notes.'

She shook her head. 'Not really, except it looks as though this lady's symptoms are similar to my father's. To be honest, it brought back memories I'd rather forget.'

He frowned and she explained, 'It was a bad time for us as a family when he started to become ill, and I didn't really understand what was happening. We thought he had lost interest in his work. Now, though, when I see these symptoms in other people, I realise what my father was going through.'

She turned the pages of the patient's file. 'This lady, for instance. She often feels faint and can't summon up any energy. She's confused sometimes, and any slight infection or viral illness makes her feel much worse. She came here today by ambulance in a state of collapse, so obviously things are pretty bad for her. Her heart rate is very high, she's breathing rapidly, and she has a fever and joint pain.'

'You think she has Addison's disease?'

'I do. I've run some tests, and I'm going to give her an intravenous injection of hydrocortisone. She'll need an infusion of saline with dextrose, too. That should help to calm things down for the moment.'

He went with her towards the treatment room. 'Do you know why your father carried on without telling anyone he was ill?'

She shook her head. 'I think he believed he was just a bit under the weather and tried to muddle through.

He didn't want to admit to any kind of weakness. It was only after he lost his job and the marriage broke down that the stress became too much for him. He went to the doctor and was treated for various complaints over time—none of them the correct diagnosis. Then, finally, his body couldn't cope with the demand on his adrenal cortex any longer. That's when he ended up in hospital and they found the real cause of his illness.'

'He must have been in a bad way…mentally and physically.'

'Yes, he was. But thankfully things are under control now, and he seems to be keeping fairly healthy. He just has to be careful if he gets an infection—then he has to take corticosteroids and perhaps antibiotics.'

He draped an arm around her shoulders. 'All I can say is that I'm sorry you had to go through that. If we'd known, we could have done something to help.'

'Do you think your father would have kept him on? I have the feeling he wants things to run smoothly, and he'll see it happen at any cost.'

'That might have been true at one time, but I think he might have mellowed a bit since then.'

'Perhaps.'

She went into the treatment room to see her patient, and James said softly, 'I'll come and see you this evening after work, as I promised. Just in case the press decide to come back. I may be a little late because I'll look in on my father first.'

'Um, you might want to change your mind about that—my producer is coming to see me. I think I'm about to get the sack.' She would have liked him to be with her this evening—just having him there would give her the confidence to face anything, but he would most likely stay away if he knew she wasn't going to be alone.

He pulled a face. 'The tide will turn,' he said. 'Things can only get better.'

She thought about that when she was at home, getting ready for Ben's visit. She dressed in a pretty pintucked shirt and a pencil-line skirt, on the premise that if she started out looking her best, she would feel brighter about the way things might turn out.

'I guessed you must be feeling low after what's been going on,' Ben said when she showed him into the sitting room a bit later on. 'We've had a lot of emails and calls at the studio.'

'You have? I'm sorry about that.'

He smiled. 'Don't be. You have a lot of really steadfast fans out there—a lot of them are male, it has to be said, but there were a good many letters from female viewers, too. They think it was wrong for them to have printed articles about events that happened when you were still in your teens.'

'That's good to know.' She brightened a little and then said, 'But how do we go on from here? Does it mean an end to the next series you were planning?'

'I'm not sure,' he said. 'We'd need to find a way of ensuring that the viewers are all on your side, one hundred per cent. It means they'd need to know what went on back then to cause you to go off the rails. Perhaps if you start by telling me what happened?'

She told him and gave him a few minutes to let him absorb what she'd said. She made coffee and brought it into the sitting room on a tray.

'How are we going to let people know?' he mused.

'Do we put out a statement to the press, or maybe deal with it in a separate programme?'

'I can't tell them about my past and what happened to my family. It would be too much like a betrayal.'

'Even though, in a way, *you* were betrayed? After all, you lost your home and your mother left you and your brother. That must have been a terrible blow when you were so young, and it had to have played a big part in sending you off track.'

'Maybe.' She thought about it, trying to make sense of her chaotic emotions. 'It was really hard for us to come to terms with what was happening at the time, but when I look back on it now I realise that both of my parents were suffering, too. After all, my mother was ill with depression and simply couldn't cope with the situation and the responsibilities of a family. Everything must have overwhelmed her and my father. But, of course, I didn't see that then.

'I was bitter and resentful and reacted by doing exactly as I pleased, regardless of the consequences. No matter what's happened now, I can't dismiss my own failings by putting the blame on my parents and throwing it all back in their faces.'

She tried to think of some way she could put things right. 'I suppose I could apologise for my behaviour and explain that it all happened when I was young and immature. Perhaps say that I've managed to turn my life around.'

'Unfortunately, I don't think that will be enough,' he said with a shake of his head. 'It seems we have a problem.'

They talked for a while longer, trying to think of ways around the situation, and eventually he stood up to go, saying, 'I'll give it some more thought and see if I can come up with something. Maybe we could do a series of programmes about children's problems, psychological worries, teenage angst and so on.'

That sounded encouraging, unless, of course, he decided to choose another presenter to do these programmes. That would be a bitter blow after she'd worked so hard to establish a career for herself.

She'd had to drag herself out of that downward spiral of recklessness that had threatened to destroy her, and instead put her energy into doing something worthwhile.

When she had been at her lowest ebb she had realised she was throwing her life away. After yet another all-night party her friend had fallen and injured herself and Ellie had been horrified to see blood pouring from a head wound.

She had hardly been in a fit state to help her. She'd managed to call for an ambulance and had held a towel to her friend's head to try to stem the bleeding, but the whole incident had been a wake-up call.

After her friend had recovered, Ellie had decided she would sort herself out once and for all. That's when she'd made up her mind that she would study medicine.

Now, though, her TV career was in jeopardy, and all she could do was wait and see whether it would fail completely.

It would have cheered her to see James this evening, but there had been no sign of him. Even though she'd suggested he might want to stay away, she was saddened and disappointed by his absence. A part of her had hoped he would want to be with her.

But perhaps he had chosen to be with Sophie instead.

After all, Sophie was a regular visitor to the manor house, and she would want to sympathise with him over his father's heart attack. It was only natural that they would be together.

CHAPTER NINE

'WE'RE GOING TO need ice packs and cooling blankets, Olivia. Her temperature's way too high. She'll need paracetamol every four hours to keep it down.'

'I'll see to it.'

'Thanks.' Ellie frowned as she wrote out the prescription form. Her patient, a woman in her late thirties, was very ill. The ECG showed an abnormal cardiac rhythm and she was feverish and sweating profusely. She could scarcely get her breath and was being given oxygen through a mask.

'I'm going to put her on a dextrose drip. Her body's gone into overdrive and is making way too many demands on her system. Her heart's racing, her blood pressure's off the scale—if we don't act quickly, she's heading towards seizures and heart failure.'

Olivia pulled a face. 'Perhaps it's no wonder she's irritable. She told me to stop fussing around her and to leave her alone. She must be feeling awful.'

Ellie nodded. 'I think the irritability is part of the illness. I won't know for sure until the test results come back, but I think we're dealing with a thyroid storm here. Too much thyroid hormone in the bloodstream.'

Ellie set up the drip while Olivia went to fetch the ice packs.

'Jenny,' she said gently, trying to reassure the woman, 'I'm going to give you some medication to calm your heart's activity down a bit and we'll do what we can to make you feel more comfortable while we're waiting for the lab results to come back. In the meantime, I'll make arrangements for you to be admitted to one of the wards.'

'Okay. Whatever.' Jenny was too exhausted to say anything more.

Ellie recognised that her agitation was simply a part of her condition, and she went on trying to explain things. 'When you're more settled, I'll ask a nurse to take you along to Radiology for a chest X-ray so that we can see what's going on.' If the heart had been overworking for any length of time, there was a possibility of heart failure, leading to a build-up of fluid on the lungs.

Ellie made sure that everything possible was being done for the woman, and then she went to check up on her other patients. She glanced around to see if James was working in one of the treatment rooms, but there was no sign of him. In fact, she hadn't seen him all morning and that was puzzling—but perhaps it wasn't altogether unusual if he had a meeting to attend.

Even so, she missed him. She'd looked for him first thing, and when she'd discovered he wasn't here, she'd half expected him to ring her and say something about last night. Instead, there had been silence, and that was odd, especially when he knew she'd been concerned about the meeting with Ben.

There must be a reason why he hadn't come to see her or tried to get in touch.

Those two days she'd spent with him on the boat had been wonderful. They'd made her realise that she wanted to be with him all the time—that he was the only man who could make her truly happy. It had been just a couple of days, but it had been long enough for her to know that she'd fallen in love with him.

And that was a foolhardy thing to have done, wasn't it, because she had no way of knowing if he would eventually lose interest in her. She would be devastated if that happened…and yet he had warned her. He'd said all he wanted was a casual relationship, but the tragedy was she'd discovered that she wanted much more than that.

'I rang up and enquired about the two patients you were asking about,' Olivia said, breaking into her thoughts as she came over to the desk where Ellie was checking the computer for test results.

'You did?' She pulled herself together. 'Thanks, Olivia. I haven't found a minute to do it myself. What's happening with them?'

'The lady with the heart inflammation is beginning to respond to the antibiotics, and is generally much better. The consultant has removed the drain and is positive about her recovery.'

Ellie smiled, relieved by the news. 'That's brilliant. I was so worried when she came in.' Then she frowned. 'What about Mr Langley, our patient with pancreatitis? Did you manage to get an update on him?'

Olivia nodded. 'He's had surgery to remove the obstruction, and he's being resuscitated with fluids. He's on antibiotic therapy, too, and seems to be doing well.'

'I'm glad about that. Thanks for chasing it up for me.'

'You're welcome.'

Ellie glanced at her watch. 'Time's gone a lot faster than I realised. I'd better go and take my lunch break.'

'You're a bit late with that, aren't you?' Olivia raised a brow. 'I went for mine ages ago.'

'It happens that way sometimes when we're busy. Anyway, I'm going to have a quick bite to eat, and then I'll go over to the cardiac unit.'

'Is that where James's father's being treated?'

'That's right. I have some audio tapes for him.'

She went off and helped herself to a quick snack in the cafeteria and then headed over to the cardiac unit. With any luck, Lord Birchenall would be feeling much brighter by now and would enjoy listening to the tapes.

He was receiving treatment in the private wing of the hospital, and Ellie needed directions to his room, but the nurse on Reception seemed cautious about letting her see him.

'I don't think…uh…I mean…uh…his son is in there. I don't think he should be disturbed.'

Ellie frowned. 'Has he taken a turn for the worse?'

'Um…yes, I'm afraid so. In fact…he died just over an hour ago.' She frowned. 'I'm very sorry.'

Ellie put down the bag of tapes she'd been holding. She stood for a moment, taking it in, and then she said quietly, 'Is his son alone in there?'

The nurse nodded. 'He said he wanted to be on his own for a while.'

'I understand that but I wonder if he might want to see me? I'd like to let him know I'm here.'

If he still wanted to be alone, she would leave, but she couldn't bear to think of him grieving and without comfort of any kind.

The nurse was doubtful, but after a bit more persuasion she reluctantly agreed, and Ellie went along the corridor to find the room. She knocked lightly on the door and waited.

'Ellie?' James pulled open the door. His face was ashen, his whole manner distracted, as if he was having trouble gathering his thoughts, and for a moment or two she wondered if she'd done the wrong thing in coming here. His gaze was blank. Perhaps he really did want to be alone.

Then he reached for her and she wrapped her arms around him, holding him tight as he told her what had happened. 'He had another heart attack yesterday evening,' he said in a taut voice. 'And after that he never recovered. He just…faded away…'

'I'm so sorry, James. I really thought he had a chance.'

He shook his head. 'I just never thought… I mean, I've been half expecting it for months, but now it's happened it feels all wrong. He should have been at home where I could care for him.'

'You did everything you could for him. No one could have done any more.' She gently stroked his back, soothing him as best she could. 'Anyway, he was frustrated by his illness. He was a strong man and even I guessed he hated being held back by his frailty. Perhaps he's at peace now.'

'Maybe. I hope so.'

He straightened up, and stepped out into the corridor, shutting the door behind him. 'I need to make some arrangements,' he said, but she shook her head.

'Not now, James. It will all wait. Let me take you home.'

He sighed. 'Okay. You're right, of course.' He gave a shuddery sigh. 'But I can drive myself home, and anyway you'll be needed in A and E.' He paused, trying to bring his chaotic thoughts under control. 'Why don't you come over to the house straight after work? I'd really appreciate it if you would do that.'

'All right. I'll be there.'

'Thanks, Ellie.'

She went out with him to the car park and watched him drive away. His expression was bleak, his eyes dark and empty, as though his emotions were all wrung out.

Somehow Ellie managed to get through the rest of her shift, though she had to force herself to concentrate.

'A few of the thyroid test results are back,' she told Olivia. 'I think we need to arrange for an endocrinologist to take a look at Jenny Soames.'

'I'll give Dr Mason a call,' Olivia suggested. 'Have you any idea what the treatment will be?'

'I imagine he'll put her on anti-thyroid medication, along with glucocorticoids. And of course he'll try to find out what caused the problem in the first place.'

'She's looking a bit better than she did earlier, anyway. She's cooler now and not quite so agitated.'

'That's good.'

Ellie handed over to the other registrar on duty a short time later and set off for the manor house. It had been heartbreaking to see James in such a sorry state that afternoon, and she could only hope that he might be feeling less battered by now.

'Hi,' he said, coming out to greet her when she parked her car on his drive some half an hour later. 'Come into the house.'

'Are you all right?' she asked him. 'How are you holding up?'

'I'm okay.' He led the way to the kitchen, where he pulled out a chair for her at the table before filling the kettle with water and switching it on. 'I'd rather not talk about what happened. I'd sooner keep busy, occupy my mind with something else. Does that sound bad?'

'No, not at all. It's probably understandable. It's hard for the mind to take in something like this.'

'You want tea or coffee, or maybe something stronger?'

'Tea will be fine, thanks.'

'Okay.' He put tea bags into the teapot and added boiling water. 'So, how did things go with your producer last night?'

'It wasn't too bad,' she answered. 'It was better than I expected, but I'm still not sure what's going to happen. It all depends on whether we can restore my image in the eyes of the public. After all, who wants to take advice from someone with a dubious background?'

'I think a lot of people will be able to identify with teenage rebellion,' he said quietly. 'I wanted to be there with you but…' His voice trailed away. 'I had a call from the hospital…and you know the rest.'

'Yes. I'm sorry.'

'I'd not long left there. He seemed to be recovering. He was cheerful and making plans for when he was to come home.' He shook himself, as though trying to clear his head. 'Have you had any more trouble with the press?'

'It's not been too bad. A couple of men were waiting outside for me this morning, but I told them I didn't have anything much to say. Except that I would always try to make good programmes and I wanted to help viewers understand more about their health and enable them to make wise decisions about their lifestyles.

'I said I would be sorry if all that came to an end because of some stories about my youthful indiscretions. And I told them there came a point when I'd realised I had to pull myself up from the downward spiral and stop seeing myself as a victim. I had to take responsibility for myself and make something of my life.'

'Good for you.'

She gave a rueful smile. 'Well, I decided I wasn't going to hide away any longer. I'm going to face up to whatever's out there.' She shrugged lightly, sloughing off the burden that had been weighing her down. 'Apparently I've had quite a lot of fan mail supporting me. That makes me feel a lot better.'

He poured tea and slid a cup towards her. 'Help yourself to milk and sugar.' He frowned. 'I ought to offer you something to eat. Come to think of it, I haven't had anything today.'

'You haven't eaten all day?'

He shook his head. 'I haven't felt like it. But I suppose...'

'What do you have?'

'I'm not sure. Harriet does most of the cooking. She's away at the moment, though, and won't be back for a few days. She's taking a holiday and she's gone to be with her daughter and her family in Wales.'

Ellie stood up. 'Do you mind if I have a look at what's in the cupboards?' She'd have to take over. It struck her that he wasn't in any state to make the simplest of decisions right now.

'No, go ahead.'

She had a look around and after a minute or two she said, 'I can make spaghetti Bolognese. How does that sound?'

'Fine. What can I do to help?'

They worked together, chopping onions, carrots and celery and then tossing these into a pan. Ellie added minced beef to the mix, cooking it for a while, and then added a broth along with a dash of red and white wine. She showed James how to make a sauce with tomatoes and herbs, and they left all of that to simmer for a while. Finally, James placed spaghetti in a pan of hot water, and within a few minutes the meal was ready to serve.

'I think I'd like to have you around all the time,' James murmured as they sat down to eat, and he wound spaghetti around his fork. 'This is the best spaghetti Bolognese I've ever tasted.'

'Oh, really! You just want me for my cooking abilities?'

James smiled. 'I can think of a few other reasons,' he said.

Ellie would have answered but her phone's ring tone sounded, and she gave him an apologetic look. 'Sorry, I should have turned it off.'

'No, don't do that. You should answer it. It might be important.'

She glanced at the caller display, and pulled a face. 'It's Ben, my producer.'

She answered the call, and discovered that Ben was in an upbeat mood. 'Something's happened that you'll never believe,' he said. 'I've had a call from your mother.'

'My *mother*?' Ellie echoed. 'Why would my mother be getting in touch with you?'

'Well, she read all the stuff about you in the papers, and she was worried about the effect it was having on the programme. Some of the articles were hinting that the series would be stopped and she was worried about that. It seems she follows your programme religiously.'

Ellie was surprised. 'I didn't know that.'

'Anyway, it seems she wants to put the record straight. I think she wanted me to know that none of this was your fault—actually, I knew that already—but she was calling to let me know she's going to the newspapers. She says she wants to tell her story—that it was because she left that you went off the rails.'

'But why didn't she tell me what she was planning?'

'She thought you might try to stop her. I think she's overwhelmed with guilt about the past and she wants to make it right. She's planning on giving you and Noah any proceeds from the articles, so she's certainly not doing it for the money.'

Ellie frowned. 'But she'll ruin her own life doing that. She mustn't. What will people think of her?'

'It's too late to do anything about it now. She'd already contacted the papers before she rang me. The article will be in the weekend issues. All of which makes me positive that we'll go ahead with the programmes we've planned and make a new series based on teenage problems. This is good news for you, Ellie.'

Ellie wasn't at all sure about that. Ben cut the call a short time later, and she stared into space for a minute or two.

'I put your plate in the oven to keep warm while you were talking on the phone,' James said. 'I'll get it for you.'

'That was thoughtful of you.' She gave him a quick smile. 'Thanks.'

He lifted her plate from the oven and slid it onto the table, looking at her in concern. 'Is everything all right?'

'It depends how you look at it.' She told him what Ben had said, breaking off to eat her spaghetti now and again. 'It's strange, but I feel as though I want to protect her. That's odd, isn't it?'

'Not really. She's your mother, after all. Whatever happens, whatever they do, our parents are a deep part of our psyche.'

She reached out and covered his hand with hers. 'Yes.'

He responded by gripping her hand warmly, and it was as though they had formed a bond, something that brought them together in their time of need.

They were still holding hands when there was a brief rapping sound and then the kitchen door opened. Ellie gazed in surprise as Sophie stepped into the room. She hadn't expected her to appear out of the blue like that, but then she remembered that James had told her she had a key so that she could come and go as she pleased.

Sophie glanced at them and said, 'I didn't realise that you had company. I came to see how you are, James. This must have been a terrible day for you.'

James nodded, and slowly released Ellie's hand. 'Yes.'

'Well, I'm here for you now. You don't have to worry about anything. I'll help you with all the arrangements. There will be a lot to do, I expect.'

He nodded, standing up to greet her. 'Would you like some wine?' he asked, waving a hand towards the opened bottle at the side of the table. 'I'll get another glass.'

'Thank you.'

Sophie sat down at the table. 'I see you've already eaten,' she said. 'I was going to suggest that we get in a takeaway, but obviously that's redundant now.' She smiled as James handed her a glass. 'You must let me organise things for you. I'll go with you to make the arrangements—you won't be in any shape to take it all in. I think we should go first thing tomorrow. And then I'll organise the flowers and so on.'

Ellie shifted uncomfortably. James couldn't handle any of this right now. He wanted some time to grieve, to get himself together, before he launched into all the preparations that were such an unhappy necessity. Ought she to say something to Sophie?

She tried to catch her eye to give her a warning look, but Sophie wasn't making any eye contact with her.

'White lilies would be best, don't you think? With perhaps some white carnations slipped in among them.'

James went over to the window and closed his eyes briefly, as though trying to shut himself off from what lay ahead. He opened his mouth to answer but no sound came out, and Ellie decided it was time to intervene.

'I don't think James is ready to make arrangements yet, Sophie. He's still in shock. Maybe it would be best if he had a bit more time to take in what's happened.'

'Oh, of course. You're right. I should have thought of that.' Sophie stood up and went to stand beside James, laying a hand affectionately on his arm. 'Like I said, I'm here for you. We'll just take it easy for a while. Do whatever you want to do.'

'I know you mean well, Sophie. Thanks for trying

to help.' James smiled at her, and as they talked quietly Ellie began to feel like an intruder.

To cover her confusion, she set about clearing the table, stacking crockery in the dishwasher and wiping down work surfaces.

'I need to go and check on something,' James said after a while. 'Sophie's reminded me that there's a problem with the stove in the drawing room. I should sort it out if we want to go and sit in there.'

He and Sophie left the room, presumably to go to the drawing room, but Ellie went on with tidying up. She threw out some fading flowers and emptied the waste bin, putting in a fresh liner. Then she prepared the coffee machine to make a fresh brew.

Sophie came in as she was setting out a tray with cups and saucers. 'James is not saying much at all,' she said softly. 'He seems totally preoccupied. I think it's probably best if we leave him alone for a while. I don't think he's in the mood for company.'

Ellie frowned. 'I suppose that's understandable.'

'Anyway, I'll see to the coffee,' Sophie murmured, filling a jug with cream from the fridge and adding a bowl of brown sugar to the tray. 'I expect you'll want to get off home now. James will be fine with me. I'll take care of him.' She smiled. 'It is my role, after all.'

'Is it?'

'Of course.' Sophie seemed surprised by Ellie's lack of knowledge. 'James has been too busy for any kind of commitment up to now, but it's always been taken for granted that I'll be his wife one day. Now that his father's sadly no longer with us, he'll need me by his side so that he can take his place as the next Lord Birchenall.

It's not really a situation for a single man. I expect we'll make it a spring wedding.'

Ellie swallowed carefully, trying to take it all in. If any of this was the truth, why had James been so attentive towards her?

'You must be wondering why James has been so involved with you lately,' Sophie said, guessing Ellie's thoughts with pinpoint accuracy. 'It doesn't mean anything. He's a kind and thoughtful man, and he wanted to look after you when you were in trouble. But being with you would never have led to anything, you know. He might have had his head turned for a while, but that would never last.'

She looked in the wall cupboard and drew out a packet of mint chocolate biscuits and shook some out onto a plate. 'You should know, it's ingrained in his very being that he must marry someone with an impeccable background, someone who can carry off the role of being his wife with perfect ease. He needs a woman who can organise his dinner parties, entertain guests from the highest levels of society. That's why he's always kept me by his side. He needs me…'

Ellie tried to breathe slowly and evenly, to keep herself as calm as possible. If Sophie was making this up, she was doing it with an unsurpassed expertise.

She said slowly, 'Doesn't it bother you that he might have been seeing another woman?'

'It's a flirtation, nothing more. It doesn't mean anything. Once we're married, all that will come to an end. James has far too much integrity to jeopardise his future standing. Perhaps he's been testing the water elsewhere, but I'm not worried about it. I know that it was just a fleeting thing while he struggled to come to terms with settling down.'

Sophie poured coffee into two cups. 'Anyway, I won't delay you any longer,' she said. 'I'm sure you have things to do. I'll take good care of James from now on. You don't need to worry about that—I had his father's blessing, after all.'

That, at least, was true. Ellie frowned, not wanting to leave but conscious that James wasn't here, in the kitchen, asking her to stay. Perhaps Sophie was right in what she was saying.

'Goodbye, Ellie.' Sophie picked up the tray and started towards the door. 'Don't forget your jacket. It's turning chilly outside.'

Deeply troubled, Ellie stared at the door for a while after she'd gone. Sophie was so sure of herself, so accustomed to having the run of this place, that she made her feel like an outsider.

Slowly, she retrieved her jacket from the back of a chair. Maybe Sophie expected her to simply disappear from James's life, but she wasn't going to do that. And for the time being she would at least go and find James and say goodbye.

'It seems to be working well enough now,' he said, looking up from his inspection of the cast-iron stove as Ellie followed Sophie into the room.

He glanced at the tray Sophie was carrying and frowned. 'Only two cups?'

'I've just remembered there's something I must go and do,' Ellie said. 'So I'll say goodbye. If you need me at all, if you want any help with anything, just give me a call. Maybe I'll see you back at work when you've had some time to get yourself together. Don't rush things. You should take as long as you need.'

He went with her to the front door. 'I'd hoped you might stay,' he said, and she wanted to put her arms around him and hold him close.

Instead, she said quietly, 'I think Sophie's planning on staying with you.'

'Yes.'

She walked to her car, and then with one last look around she slid into the driver's seat and started the engine.

What Sophie had said made perfect sense. James had seen *her* as a pleasant diversion, but ultimately he would marry Sophie, just as his father had wished. Why would he risk tainting his family's aristocratic lineage by associating with a woman whose life story was being splashed all over the pages of a Sunday newspaper?

CHAPTER TEN

'IT'S REALLY GOOD to see you again.' Ellie drank in James's features as she walked with him towards the ambulance bay. She'd heard he was back at work, but she had been busy with patients and hadn't seen him all morning. Now, though, she was overwhelmed by her feelings for him.

He didn't respond as she'd hoped, though. She longed to see the warm, easygoing man she'd come to love, but it looked as though it wasn't to be.

Instead, he was tense, his dark eyes shuttered, and she wasn't sure if that was because he was still in mourning or… She hardly dared think about it. Could it be that he was putting up a barrier between them now that he had made up his mind to be with Sophie?

Then again, perhaps he was simply on edge because he was preparing to deal with an emergency patient. There had been a road traffic accident, and a young man was being brought into A and E.

She pulled in a deep breath. 'I missed you,' she said.

'Did you?'

She nodded. She'd missed him more than he could ever know. It had been heartbreaking to walk away from him that night, and over and over she'd kept asking herself if Sophie had been telling the truth. But wouldn't he have contacted her if he had wanted to see her again?

She said slowly, 'I thought the funeral went very well…if these things can ever be thought of that way. The service was lovely, and the flower arrangements were beautiful, especially those inside the church.' Her brows drew together. 'I suppose Sophie was responsible for that.'

'No. I wanted to deal with everything myself. I felt it was important that I should do that.'

Ellie sent him a quick, sharp glance. That revelation surprised her, given that Sophie had been so keen to have a hand in everything. But perhaps it was all deeply personal to him and he hadn't wanted anyone else making those decisions.

'I was hoping to see you afterwards,' she said, 'but you must have gone away straight after the funeral. Harriet told me you went to stay with relatives.'

'You came to the house?'

'Yes.' She lifted her shoulders. 'I realise now that I should have rung first. I expect Harriet forgot to mention it to you. She was a bit harassed at the time.' Her mouth made a rueful line. 'Sophie was there and I think she was trying to suggest a few changes to the menus Harriet was planning.'

He gave a wry smile, the first chink to show in his armour. 'That was probably a bad move. Once she's organised herself, Harriet hates any interference in the kitchen.'

'Yes, I guessed as much, though I've always got on well with her. She was good to me when we lived at the lodge.'

They reached the ambulance bay and waited. A siren sounded in the distance and Ellie knew it would only be a minute or two before it arrived.

'I went away to spend some time with the family,' James said. 'Aunts and uncles…cousins. I needed to take some time out to clear my head and the hospital authorities granted me some compassionate leave. I'll make it up to them with overtime over the next few weeks.'

'I'm sure they won't expect you to do that,' she said with a frown. 'Everyone understands that you've just lost your father.'

'Maybe.'

The ambulance stopped in front of the doors to the emergency unit, and as soon as the paramedics had wheeled the injured man from the back of the vehicle, James hurried forward to meet him.

'His name's Sam Donnelly,' the paramedic said. 'He came off his motorbike. When we first found him he was trying to talk but we couldn't make out what he was saying. He's become much less responsive now, though, and his heart rate is very low.'

'Thanks.'

They left the paramedic to go back to his vehicle and hurried to the resuscitation room, where James immediately began his examination of the patient. 'Let's get him on a cardiac monitor.'

'I'll sort it.' Olivia went to set up the machine.

'His blood pressure's dropping,' Ellie warned him urgently. 'I'll put in an IV line and take some blood for cross-matching.' Sam looked to be about eighteen years old, and she couldn't help wondering how his parents must be feeling, left behind in the relatives' waiting room, knowing that their son was unconscious and that he might be dreadfully injured.

'Okay.' He started to insert an endotracheal tube into the young man's windpipe and then connected the oxygen supply.

He frowned as he went on with his examination. 'His condition's deteriorating by the minute,' he said. 'He's very pale, breathing rapidly, and his pulse is weak and thready.'

'His body temperature is low, too,' Ellie remarked. Sam's skin was moist and clammy and she was beginning to be very concerned about him. He must have been hurt badly in the accident for this to be happening, but apart from some gashes on his face, arms and legs there were no visible signs of any major injury that would have caused his collapse.

'Clearly, he's going into hypovolaemic shock but there's no obvious reason for the instability. We'd better put in a couple of wide-bore cannulas and give him fluids to compensate.' James was thoughtful as he continued to check over the young man. 'He must be bleeding internally, but we need to find out where it's coming from. And we need to find out quickly.'

'Do you want to do an ultrasound scan?'

He nodded. 'Hopefully, that will tell us what we want to know.' He glanced at Olivia, who was monitoring the patient's vital signs. 'Would you give Theatre a ring and tell them we might have a patient for them? They need to be prepared.'

'Okay.'

He set up the equipment and said cautiously, 'He

probably has lower rib fractures so I think we should be looking for blunt abdominal trauma.'

'That sounds logical.'

The scan, though, wasn't particularly helpful, and James asked the nurse to get the equipment ready so that he could do a diagnostic peritoneal lavage.

Ellie helped him to prepare the patient, and James used a local anaesthetic as he made a small incision in Sam's abdomen, before carefully introducing a dialysis catheter into the peritoneal cavity. Then he flushed warm saline into the opening, before slowly aspirating it back into the transparent bag.

'There's a lot of blood in there,' Ellie observed with a frown, watching the saline slowly turn red. 'It could be that his liver was damaged by the broken ribs.'

'It looks that way. We'll send him up to Theatre right away for a laparotomy.' He turned to Olivia. 'Will you give them another call and make sure they're ready for him up there?'

'I will.'

Ellie prepped the young man for surgery. The sooner he was operated on, the better his chances of survival would be.

They watched as he was wheeled away to Theatre, and James took off his protective gloves and tossed them into the bin. 'You did well back there,' he said, glancing at Ellie. 'It's good to see that you have your confidence back.'

'I suppose that's true,' she said with a small frown. 'I didn't even think about what I was doing. It was instinctive. And yet…'

'And yet?'

She pulled a face. 'Earlier today I had some news that knocked me back a bit. Olivia told me she'd had a call from Mel this morning. She wants to come in and see me.' Normally, that would have been enough to put her off her stroke, but perhaps with James returning to work she'd had other things to think about.

'Did she say why?'

'No. But I agreed to the meeting.' She looked at her watch. 'She'll be here soon, in about fifteen minutes.'

'Do you want me to be there with you?'

She smiled with relief. 'Would you? I'm really not looking forward to seeing her. What if she was the one who went to the tabloids with the stories about me? She knew me well enough back then after all, and she does have a grudge against me.'

'We'll try to find out.' He looked at her, taking in the green scrubs and soft plastic overshoes she was wearing. 'Maybe we should get ready to meet her?'

She nodded. She wasn't exactly sure of the reason, but her spirits had lifted as soon as he'd offered to stay with her. He'd seemed like a stranger to her at first today but now he was back, the man she loved more than any other, and no matter how much her head warned her to be cautious, it was being firmly overruled by her heart.

'We'll see her in my office,' James said, when they met up again, dressed in normal, everyday clothes.

She nodded and went with him, and almost as soon as they had entered the room, Mel knocked on the door.

'Won't you take a seat?' James invited her with a reassuring smile. 'I've just made coffee, so perhaps we should get comfortable and then you can tell us what the problem is?'

'It's not a problem,' Mel said. 'It's more about a decision I've made.' She was dressed in a businesslike fashion, as before, but her hair was styled more freely this time, with a slight wave to soften her appearance. She wore a dress with a matching three-quarter-length jacket.

She sipped the coffee James gave her and seemed to be taking a moment to gather her thoughts.

'A decision?' Ellie prompted her.

Mel took a deep breath. 'I was very upset when my aunt died. I was angry and frustrated, because everything happened so quickly. One day she was talking to me, making plans to come with me on a weekend trip to the seaside, and within a few more days she had died. I couldn't take it in. She was like a mother to me, and I loved her.'

She reached for her coffee with a trembling hand and hesitated, as though she couldn't go on.

'Take your time,' James said. 'We know this is difficult for you.'

She nodded. 'I've been to see a lawyer,' she said at last.

Ellie's heart lurched, and a wave of nausea rose in her as her stomach clenched involuntarily. She could see her career, everything she'd worked for, beginning to dissolve. Sitting across the table from her, James's gaze caught hers. He knew exactly what she was going through.

'He looked into the hospital records,' Mel went on. 'He talked to an expert about my aunt's illness, and found out that there was an operation that could have been done, where a kind of window is made in the tissue around the heart to remove the infected matter.'

'That's true,' Ellie told her. 'It's usually done if the illness is chronic and drainage hasn't been successful. In your aunt's case, the infection was overwhelming and didn't respond to the antibiotics, but it was the fact that her heart was weak that was the biggest problem. Her heart stopped. She went into cardiac arrest, and I did everything I could for her, but unfortunately she wasn't able to respond to the treatment. I'm sorry.'

'I know.' Mel grimaced. 'I understand now. I think perhaps I didn't want to see it before. I was devastated when my aunt passed away and I wanted someone to blame.' She looked at Ellie. 'I'm sorry I put you through all that. I know it wasn't your fault.'

Ellie exhaled slowly. 'Thank you for coming to tell me.'

'I saw the stories that were published about you,' Mel said. She shook her head. 'I thought it was really unfair. I remembered some of those times, the parties, the rowdiness. We were together a lot of the time, and you were never bad. You always wanted to help people, even though you were upset about what was going on at home. I hope your mother's account has helped to put things right.'

'You saw the article?'

Mel nodded. 'At least she realised that she was partly to blame. Perhaps, at the time, she didn't understand what pain she was causing, but the truth seems to have come home to her now.'

'I think we've both gone some way to freeing ourselves from the past. She helped a lot by explaining what had gone on, and it must have taken a lot of courage for her to do that. It made me feel better about her.'

She smiled. 'We met up and talked and brought things out into the open, so at least we have some sort of understanding of one another now.'

They talked for a while longer, and then Ellie went with her to the door. 'Goodbye, Mel,' she said. 'Thanks again for coming to see me.'

She went back into the office and closed the door, resting her spine against it for a moment as she absorbed everything that had happened. She hadn't expected Mel to look at things from another angle, and it was a huge relief to know that she had withdrawn the complaint.

As to her mother, it had been good to see her again and have the chance to talk things through.

'I've wanted to do this for a long time,' her mother had said. 'I wanted to see you and try to put things right, but I wasn't sure how you would feel about seeing me.'

'I'm glad we've found each other again,' Ellie had told her. 'I feel as though a huge burden has been lifted from me. I know it took a lot for you to open up to the press like that, and I realise, now, that you had been ill for a long time. We were wrong to blame you.'

'Thank you for that.' Her mother had smiled. 'I didn't want to let you go. You and Noah were so young, but I didn't have the strength to go on. I'm better now, though, and I hope we can make up for everything that's happened.'

'We can. We will. We'll start afresh from here, Mum.'

She came out of her reverie and became aware that James was watching her.

'Are you okay?' he asked, and she nodded.

'I'm fine. Everything's good.'

'I'm glad.' His gaze was thoughtful. 'But we are left

with a small puzzle to solve. If Mel didn't go to the press and start all the hoo-hah,' he said quietly, 'who did?'

'I don't know.' She frowned. She was beginning to have a shrewd idea who might have been behind it, but she was going to keep that to herself for now. There was only one person who might have reason to sully her reputation after all, but James was close to Sophie and she wasn't going to accuse anyone without proof.

He came over to her. 'Anyway, I'm glad all that business is over. You can get on with your life now without any worries.'

'Yes. It's a huge relief. Thanks for standing by me.'

'I told you once before, I'll always be there for you, Ellie.' He looked at her steadily. 'You can rely on me.'

If only she could believe that. But he was going to be with Sophie, wasn't he?

'That's a comforting thought,' she said, moving away from the door, 'but you didn't seem too thrilled to be with me earlier. You were very tense, but perhaps there were things on your mind?'

His dark brows drew together. 'Maybe I *was* a bit preoccupied. The last time I saw you, you walked out on me. I'd been hoping you might stay over at the house. I wanted to be with you. But you left, and you didn't call the next day. I couldn't think why you would suddenly pull back from me, except you might have decided it was a bad idea to be involved with me.'

'No.' She sent him a quick, insistent glance. 'It was nothing like that. Sophie told me that you and she were getting together, that you were going to be married.'

'What?' It was an explosive sound. 'Good grief, how did she manage to come up with that idea?'

Ellie was confused. 'But you've been together for a long time—your father told me she was right for you, and he gave me the impression you would be marrying her.'

'My father had lots of ideas about how things should go, but we didn't always agree. And I certainly wouldn't do something simply because it was what he wanted. I loved him and respected him, but we're different people and I have my own way of going about things.' He frowned as someone knocked on the door. 'Not now,' he muttered under his breath.

Olivia came into the room. 'Sam Donnelly's back from Theatre,' she said. 'His liver and spleen were ruptured, but the surgeon was able to repair the damage. I thought you might want to come and check on him.'

'Thanks, Olivia.'

She left the room and he turned back to face Ellie. 'I need to go and see him. Look, Ellie, I'm going to talk to Sophie and get this sorted out. I'll come and see you this evening, as soon as I'm done.'

'All right.' What was she to make of all this? From the sound of things, Sophie had been making it up as she'd gone along...because she wanted Ellie out of the way? Well, she'd succeeded in that, hadn't she?

But James had been disappointed that she hadn't stayed with him. That was what had her heart singing. That was what sent her hopes soaring skywards. Was there a chance for them after all?

She went with him to see how Sam was doing, and felt reassured that his blood pressure and heart rate were improving. It would take him some time to heal and recover, but thankfully his life was no longer in danger.

She went home at the end of her shift, and stopped to say hello to her neighbour, Lily, who was just coming back from the shops with the baby and Jayden.

'Hi, there. How are things going?' Ellie chatted to Lily and admired Jayden's toy car, and peeped into the buggy to coo over the gorgeous new addition to the family. 'Hello, Amy. Aren't you a tiny little thing?' The only answer she received was a sleepy yawn and a delicate sucking sound as the baby pursed her pink rosebud mouth and went back to dreaming of creamy milk.

Both women chuckled, and after a while Ellie left to go and make herself look presentable for when James arrived. She wasn't sure what to expect. Would Sophie persuade him that she was only going on what he'd led her to believe over the last few years?

She made herself a snack and then went upstairs to shower and change into jeans and a pretty camisole top. She put on a light smattering of make-up, adding a pale bronze blusher to lend colour to her cheeks, and left her hair loose. Then, feeling a bit more sure of herself, she went downstairs to wait for James.

He turned up soon after, and she opened the door to him cautiously, not knowing what to expect.

'I wasn't sure whether you would already have eaten,' he said in a quizzical tone.

'Just a snack,' she told him. 'A couple of crackers and cheese. Why?'

He produced a white plastic carrier bag that he'd been hiding behind his back. 'I brought Chinese food. I'm starving, so I'm hoping you're ready for this, too.'

'I love Chinese food,' she said, sliding plates into the oven to warm and breathing in the wonderful aroma.

He slid the packages onto the kitchen table and she drooled over the contents. 'Beef with green peppers in black bean sauce, special fried rice, sweet and sour chicken… Oh, I'm in heaven…'

He laughed. 'I'll put the kettle on. Unless you want wine? I can go and get a bottle.'

'That's all right, I have wine in the fridge.' She went to get it, while James took cutlery from a drawer and set the table.

They sat down to eat and she tasted the sweetly battered chicken, following it up with a forkful of rice. 'This is delicious. Yum.'

He smiled as he speared a prawn with his fork. 'Yes, it is.'

They chatted about this and that, and finally she finished her meal and put down her fork. 'I wish I had more room in my stomach,' she said woefully. 'It's my favourite, and I can't do it justice.'

He laughed. 'I'll bring you some more, whenever you want.'

'So you'll be coming back?'

'Do you think you could keep me away?'

'I wouldn't want to.'

'That's good. That's what I really want to hear.'

She absorbed that with a smile of contentment, leaning back in her seat. 'Shall we take the wine and finish it off in the living room?'

'That sounds like a good idea.'

He went with her and poured more wine before coming to sit beside her on the sofa. Watching him, long and lithe and gorgeous, she was wistful and her expression became serious.

'Did you go and see Sophie?'

'I did.' He frowned.

'So, what happened?'

'She confessed that she'd lied to you. She also admitted to leaking the stories about you to the tabloids.'

'I thought she might have been behind it.' She was puzzled, though. 'But how did she know about me when I was a teenager?'

'She quizzed my father about your family being at the lodge and what happened after you left. He told her about the newspaper articles, so she passed that information on to the papers.'

She was still for a moment, taking it in, and then pulled herself together. 'She must have been very insecure,' she said.

He nodded. 'I'm sure she was.'

'So you never intended to marry her?'

'I didn't ever have a relationship with her, apart from a couple of dinner invitations with friends, never mind want to marry her. She just let it be known to anyone who would listen that she and I were together. I think that's where your brother came by the idea that we were a couple.

'I warned her that I didn't share her feelings,' he went on, 'but she didn't listen. Perhaps she thought I would change my mind. Either way, she must have been living in a fantasy world and it didn't help that she managed to work her way into my father's affections. She was always there for him.'

He thought about that for a moment. 'To be fair, she looked after him really well, making sure he had his medication, driving him around when he couldn't manage it himself and I wasn't available. But I think, all the time, she was working on the idea that we would be an item.'

'I almost feel sorry for her.'

He nodded. 'Of course, when you came along, she must have seen you as a threat. Anyone with half an eye could see that I'd fallen for you.'

'Had you?' She sent him a quick glance, her heart beginning to thump heavily. 'I don't know about that. I wasn't sure what you really felt for me. I mean, I know you wanted me, but you said you weren't ready for commitment and I started to realise that I didn't want to settle for anything less.'

His grey eyes homed in on her face. 'Are you saying you wanted to be with me?'

'Yes, I did. I do. But your father had such expectations for you. I felt as though my name had been tarnished, and he would never accept someone like me being involved with you.'

He gave her a rueful smile. 'It wasn't his decision to make. Anyway, after he got to know you better, and especially after you saved his life, he thought of you with affection. He told me he wished he could make it up to you and your family for the way he'd treated your father.'

'I'm pleased about that.'

He wrapped his arms around her, making her feel cosseted and cherished. 'I should never have doubted you,' he said. 'But I was afraid Lewis might persuade you he needed you, and somehow turn your head, and even though I knew you weren't the kind of person who would break up a marriage, I was consumed by this insane jealousy every time I saw you with him. It was total madness. I know Lewis would never do anything to hurt Jessica.' He frowned. 'Perhaps it was because I wasn't sure of your feelings.'

'I was just as guilty,' she said softly. 'I kept thinking you were dating Sophie at the same time that you were seeing me. I should have had more faith in you.'

'I don't want any other woman, Ellie. Only you.' He kissed her tenderly, his hands stroking her and bringing her closer to him.

'Is it really true?' She was desperate to believe him. 'You said you didn't want commitment and I was so afraid I was falling for you. I knew I would be devastated if you didn't feel the same way I did.'

'It's true, believe me. I never thought it would happen to me, but when we spent that time together on the boat I realised that I wanted to be with you all the time. It hit me hard, like a thunderbolt. I'm only really happy when I'm with you. I feel as though I'm at peace with the world and myself.' He kissed her again. 'It's as though I've found my soul mate. I love you.'

'Oh, James, I love you so much. I didn't know it could be like this.' She lifted her arms and let her fingers trail through the silky hair at the back of his head. 'I've been longing to hear you say you feel the same way, too.'

She kissed him lovingly, thrilled by the way his body meshed with hers, as though he couldn't get enough of her. With every part of her being, she yearned for him.

'Ellie, will you marry me?' he said huskily. 'I need to know that you'll be with me through everything, for all time.'

'Oh, yes, James.' She smiled up at him, her lips parting for his kiss. 'Yes, please. It's what I want, more than anything.' She sighed happily, losing herself in his arms, clinging to him as they kissed fiercely, passionately, with all the love and longing that spilled over into that wonderful, satisfying embrace. Like he'd said, they would be together for all time, she knew it.

* * * * *

RE-AWAKENING HIS SHY NURSE

BY

ANNIE CLAYDON

MILLS & BOON

All the characters in this book have no existence outside the imagination of the author, and have no relation whatsoever to anyone bearing the same name or names. They are not even distantly inspired by any individual known or unknown to the author, and all the incidents are pure invention.

First published in Great Britain 2013
by Mills & Boon, an imprint of Harlequin (UK) Limited.
Harlequin (UK) Limited, Eton House, 18-24 Paradise Road,
Richmond, Surrey TW9 1SR

ISBN: 978 0 263 89912 2

Harlequin (UK) policy is to use papers that are natural, renewable and recyclable products and made from wood grown in sustainable forests. The logging and manufacturing process conform to the legal environmental regulations of the country of origin.

Printed and bound in Spain
by Blackprint CPI, Barcelona

Dear Reader

It doesn't seem ten minutes since I first sat down to write one of these letters for my first book, and now I'm on number five it's becoming a regular pleasure.

It's often said that true courage is doing something despite your fear. If that's so then we are all heroes and heroines, because everyone's done something which has frightened them. And sometimes fear can be a good thing. It warns us of danger, helps to keep us safe. But when fear ceases to be a reaction to present danger and becomes a way of living it's exhausting and overwhelming.

Katya has lived through a terrible experience, and although her physical wounds have healed she has every reason to feel fearful still. Meeting gentle, handsome Luke might be one of the best things she's ever done, but it turns out to be one of the most difficult as well, when she is forced to confront her fears head-on.

Some of my own fears are in this book—both rational and irrational—and if writing about them was at times demanding, it was also a voyage of discovery for me.

I hope you enjoy Luke and Katya's story. I'm always delighted to hear from readers and you can e-mail me via my website at: www.annieclaydon.com

Annie

Recent titles by Annie Claydon:

THE REBEL AND MISS JONES
THE DOCTOR MEETS HER MATCH
DOCTOR ON HER DOORSTEP
ALL SHE WANTS FOR CHRISTMAS

These books are also available in eBook format from www.millsandboon.co.uk

DEDICATION

To all the staff and carers at the Sir Thomas Lipton Memorial Home, who prove daily that no kindness is too great to attempt or too small to bother with.

CHAPTER ONE

SOMETIMES IT WAS the little things that mattered. A decent cup of coffee to start the day. A woman's smile.

The days when Luke Kennedy opened his eyes to coffee and a smile were long gone and he'd got to the point where he hardly missed them. As he swung the door to the coffee shop open, he revised that sentiment slightly. He didn't miss his ex-wife any more. But there was something about the smile of the latest recruit to the ranks of early-morning coffee-makers that made him regret his resolve to do without those moments of simple pleasure until he was up and dressed and had driven to the high street.

'Hey, there.' Her head popped up from beneath the counter. 'Usual?'

'Thanks. Two shots.'

'I know.' She gave him a lopsided grin that told him he would be mistaken if he chose to underestimate her. 'You're early this morning, I've only just opened up.'

Luke shrugged. It would be way too much information to tell her that it was the thought of her iridescent green eyes that had jolted him into wakefulness this morning. 'Yeah.'

'Right.' The little quirk of her lips was far too knowing. As if she somehow understood that he'd made a decision not to get too close, and she didn't blame him. Or maybe he was just looking for meanings where there were none.

She set the coffee to brew and poured the milk, twisting the controller for the steam nozzle. The significance of the slight popping sound that came from the coffee machine registered too late, and by the time it did, her startled yelp had already jolted Luke out of his reverie and into action.

'Hey.' He rounded the end of the counter and she stumbled another couple of steps backwards, obviously panicking. 'Are you hurt?'

She was nursing one hand against her chest, still backing away from the steam that was issuing from the coffee machine. Luke turned, twisting the knob and shutting it off. 'Did you burn yourself?'

She jumped as her back hit the far end of the counter, but it seemed to bring her to her senses. 'I'm okay. I'm fine. Thanks.'

'No, you're not. Let me see.' He took a step forward, holding out his hand, and she seemed to flinch even further back, like a frightened animal caught in a trap.

The look in her eyes wasn't shock or pain. It was him that she was backing away from. Luke froze, instinctively spreading his hands, palms forward, in a sign that he would do her no harm. 'Why don't you put your hand into some cold water?' He reached slowly for the small sink behind the counter and turned the tap on.

She hesitated. 'Yes. Yes, I will. Thanks.' It was obvious that she wasn't going to come out of her corner yet and he had two choices. March over there, take hold of her and pull her over to the sink, if necessary, was the quickest, but something told him that if he tried that she'd only start to panic even more. Luke went for the second option and gave her some space.

By the time he'd made it back to the other side of the counter, she had her hand in the sink. And she was blushing. 'I'm sorry. I overreacted.'

Luke could let that go. Right now, with the flush spreading from her cheeks to the nape of her neck, he could let just about anything go. 'Are you all right? I didn't mean to scare you.'

'You didn't.' The answer was too defensive to be anything other than an excuse. 'I…I just got a bit of a shock. Someone must have forgotten to clean the steam nozzle properly last night and when I switched it on…' She tailed off. The tips of her ears were bright pink now and she was clutching at straws, trying to pretend that she hadn't panicked and tried to run when he'd only tried to help her.

'Made me jump, too.' Not entirely true, but he got a nervous smile in return. 'How's your hand now?'

He expected her to evade the enquiry, but instead she withdrew her hand from the water, squinted at it and then plunged it back into the sink. 'It looks fine. A little red, but it doesn't feel too bad.'

She couldn't have piqued his curiosity more if she'd tried. That sudden, perplexing reaction, followed by what seemed like a decision of sorts to trust him. 'Best to keep it in the water a little while longer.' She seemed far more comfortable now that the counter was separating them, and Luke planted his hands down on it, in a sign that he didn't intend to again invade what she so obviously considered was her territory.

She nodded, abstractedly. She clearly had something

on her mind, but it was impossible to tell what. Perhaps doing something practical would reassure her. 'Have you got a first-aid kit behind there?'

'Yes. It's here.' She reached under the sink with her free hand and pulled out a large plastic box, stretching across to slide it onto the counter.

Luke reached for the box and snapped it open. 'I may not be qualified to treat humans, but I can do some basic first aid.'

'Who are you qualified to treat?' She was looking at him gravely.

'Animals. I'm a vet.'

She nodded. 'Well, I've seen enough burns to know that this one's superficial. It'll be sore for twenty-four hours and then it'll be fine.'

'Good. Now we've got that out of the way, perhaps you'll let me dress it for you. It won't take a moment to put a bandage on it.' Luke couldn't usually reason with his patients and it was refreshing to do so now. More complicated as well. Animals didn't smell so good.

There was a moment of awkward silence and then the tension between them snapped. The quiet sound of her laugh was like fresh water poured over his burnt-out nerve-endings and sparking them back into life. 'I suppose I'd be better off if I had four legs and not two.'

'Much better. Or no legs. I'm good with snakes as well.' He gave her what he hoped was a reassuring smile.

'So how do you bandage a snake, then?' She lifted her hand out of the water, dabbing it dry with a napkin as she walked slowly over to the counter.

'Carefully. But that's a very old joke.'

She laughed again, her eyes dancing, and then held

her hand out towards him. Gently he touched the tips of her fingers and felt them tremble. Turning her hand to ascertain the extent of the damage, he applied his knowledge of first aid for humans and decided that he concurred with her assessment. It was a very minor burn.

Luke withdrew a small bandage from the first-aid kit. 'You'll not be wanting an Elizabethan collar?'

'Think I can resist the temptation to gnaw at it.' Even though she seemed more at ease with him now, she was still watching him carefully and Luke concentrated hard on winding the bandage with absolute precision around her hand. Tried to forget her eyes and the pallor of her skin against her auburn hair. The fragility of her almost-too-slender wrist.

'That should do it.' He fastened the bandage carefully, and she held her hand in front of her face, inspecting his handiwork.

'Very neat.' She was teasing him now, and Luke's stomach tightened. Everything she did and said just seemed to stoke the growing fascination he felt. 'So where do you usually do your bandaging?'

It was an innocent enough question, but Luke was under no illusions. This was a breakthrough of mammoth proportions. Up till now she'd shied away from anything that was even remotely personal, and he'd done so, too. But her mesmerising eyes broke his resolve.

'I have my own practice. I'm also involved with the new nature reserve a couple of miles out of the village on the road towards Knighton. Along with a few other projects.'

'So you're a busy man, then.'

Luke nodded. He'd kept himself busy since Tanya had left. Found the contentment in his work that the sudden end of his marriage had stripped him of, filling his time so that there was no temptation to look elsewhere. 'I stay occupied.'

'Better get you your coffee, then. I don't want to stop the wheels of industry from turning.' She turned away from him, concentrating hard on the coffee machine, and Luke saw the side of her face flush slightly. 'You won't…tell anyone, will you? This is the first time I've opened up on my own.'

Women and their secrets. But this one seemed innocuous enough. 'What's to tell? Why don't you sit down and I'll make the coffee?' He supposed that would have to be their secret, too, and the idea made him smile. 'You…er…might be in shock or something.'

She dismissed the thought with a laugh. 'I don't think so.' She pushed a large cardboard beaker in his direction. 'But thanks for helping. This one's on the house.'

It was almost a week before Luke heard another word from her. On the mornings that she was there in the coffee shop, she somehow contrived to be busy, leaving someone else to serve him. The more she ignored him, the more it intrigued him and finally, in the face of Luke's determined patience, she broke.

'Don't you have a loyalty card?'

It was something. Luke was used to gaining trust by inches, and this sudden leap forward made an indifferent Thursday morning take on a sparkling, gem-like quality. 'About twenty of them, in the glove compartment of my car. Each of them with one stamp.'

She twisted her lips in what might be construed as

a grin. 'That's okay, you only need seven stamps for a coffee. Nothing in the rules that says they all have to be on the same card.'

Luke planted his elbows on the counter, leaning towards her slightly, and she didn't draw back. 'Okay, I'll—'

'No, no, no!' Olenka, the manager of the coffee shop, had been checking stock behind the counter and it was she who leaned towards Luke, her chin jutting belligerently. 'No kitten, no free coffee.'

The spark of excitement that was making Luke's heart beat a little faster fizzled out, and the grimace he shot Olenka wasn't all for show. 'That's blackmail, Olenka.'

'Well spotted. Katya will not give you free coffee until my child has a kitten.'

Katya. She didn't wear a name badge like the others, and Luke had been trying to fit different names to her smile. This one was perfect and it rolled around Luke's brain, leaving happiness in its wake. Katya.

'Do you hear me?' Olenka was waving a finger at him.

'I hear you. And it's still next week, free coffee or not. You can't rush nature.'

Olenka gave a laughing gesture of resignation, slipping into her mother tongue to express her feelings as she turned to Katya.

'Tak.' Katya gave Luke a small shrug. 'Sounds as if you get to pay this week.'

'That's fine.' Luke grinned at Olenka. 'I'll collect next week.'

Katya made his coffee, just the way he liked it, and handed it over, stamping a new loyalty card and stowing it under the counter. 'I'll keep this here, so you can't forget it next time.'

'Thanks.' Time for just one more question before he had to pick up his coffee and go. 'So you speak Polish?'

She nodded. 'My father's…' She stopped herself. Even that small detail was clearly more information than she was comfortable about giving.

'Right. My father's a Scot.' He grinned at her, picked up his coffee and turned before she had a chance to reply. If life had taught him one thing, it had made it very clear to Luke that the best time to leave was when you were winning.

Katya watched him go. He was broad, strong looking, but that didn't necessarily count against him. The man who had ruined her career and put her in her own hospital, as a patient rather than a nurse, hadn't been all that imposing. It was the eyes that mattered and there was kindness in this man's dark eyes.

'Luke.' Katya too was being watched, and Olenka unglued herself from the doorway to the stockroom, letting it drift closed behind her.

'So Peter's getting a kitten, eh?' The best thing to do was to ignore Olenka. The man was easy on the eye but his name was immaterial. All she needed to know about him was that he liked his latte with two shots.

'Yes, he's wanted one for a long time. He's old enough to look after it properly.' Olenka had switched back into Polish. Although Katya was a Londoner, whereas her cousin Olenka had been born and brought up in Poland, they shared a love of the language. It reminded Katya of her father, and Olenka of home.

'It'll do him good to have something to look after. What kind of kitten?'

Olenka shrugged. 'Lucasz says they're a bit of everything. There are seven kittens and they're all different, so I'm going to take Piotr to go and choose one.' She quirked her lips downwards. 'Next week. Lucasz can't rush nature and neither can I.'

'Thought you said his name was Luke.' Katya slipped back into English to make her point.

'I like him. It is a compliment.' Olenka narrowed her eyes. 'You like him?'

'He seems nice enough. I don't really know him.'

Olenka dismissed her with a gesture. 'It only takes one look to find out if you like a man.'

Katya had thought the same once upon a time. 'I don't do first impressions, Ola. My judgement isn't that good.'

Olenka shook her head. 'You made one mistake…'

'One's enough.' Katya hadn't suspected for a moment that everything had been about to blow up in her face so badly when she'd tried to help a patient. You didn't get to make mistakes like that and still keep your faith in your own judgement.

Olenka groaned in frustration. Just the way Katya would have done before it had all happened, but now she knew differently. 'You can look. You don't need to touch.'

That was the trouble really. Katya was beginning to feel that she did need to touch. 'He's not that good-looking.'

'Pftt. Are you blind?' Olenka gave Katya's comment exactly the consideration it deserved.

A clatter at the doorway came to her rescue and

Katya turned, smiling at the man who was hurrying towards the counter. The first of the eight-thirty coffee rush. No time now to think about Luke's dark, slightly dishevelled curls or his kind eyes. Or wonder whether those broad shoulders really were enough to keep someone safe. In all likelihood they were. Just not this someone.

CHAPTER TWO

PETER WAS SITTING obediently at the corner table of the coffee shop, one of his mother's special hot chocolate drinks and a computer game in front of him. Katya took her eyes off him long enough to serve two women who couldn't decide which drink was lowest in calories, and when she flipped her gaze back across the counter, Luke was sitting opposite him.

'Peter…Peter…' Peter was rummaging in his back-pack and ignored her completely, but Luke looked up. Fair enough. This was a coffee shop and she worked here. There was no reason why she shouldn't ask Luke herself. 'Would you like something to drink?'

'The hot chocolate looks nice.' He got to his feet.

'That's okay. Stay there, I'll bring it across.' Katya made his drink carefully, creamy and rich with shaved chocolate sprinkled on top. When she set it in front of him he smiled appreciatively.

'Thanks. What's the damage?'

'It's on the house.' Katya allowed herself a smile in his general direction. 'I hear that the kittens are at home for visitors today.'

'Yeah. Peter tells me he's going to photograph them—' He broke off as Peter passed his new camera across the table, and Luke turned it over in his hands to inspect it carefully. 'Nice one, Peter. You'll be able to take some great pictures with that.'

'Aunt Katya bought it for my birthday,' Peter piped up before Katya could stop him. 'She's not really my aunt, though.'

'No?' Luke gave the boy a conspiratorial smile.

'No. She's not my mother's sister, she's my mother's cousin.' Peter was counting on his fingers, the way he always did when he was trying to get a difficult detail exactly right. 'But I call her Aunt.'

'Fair enough.' Luke nodded, clearly fighting to keep his face straight.

'She's going to help me look after the kitten.' Peter was on a roll now, information leaking out of every new sentence. 'Aunt Katya's come to stay with us for a while.'

Luke already knew her name and now he knew where she lived and who her family were. It wasn't Peter's fault and Katya stopped herself from chiding him for it. She didn't want to teach the boy to be fearful.

She reserved the right to be cautious herself, though. Katya turned, more quickly perhaps than she should, and bolted back behind the counter. Back to her own space, where she was just an anonymous face, who smiled, brewed coffee and took the customers' money. She could feel Luke's eyes on her and she ignored him. Olenka would be finished in the office soon, and Peter would not allow Luke and his mother to stay here a moment longer than necessary. He would be gone soon enough.

Katya followed Luke's SUV as it bumped down the dirt track that led towards a high, brick-built barn standing commandingly on the brow of a hill, a little way back from the road. It was obviously in the midst of renovations and the SUV came to a halt on a levelled area of gravel with a couple of portable cabins at its edge, painted green in an attempt to blend in with the landscape.

Katya had wondered whether it would be forgivable to stay in the car but dismissed the idea. Olenka was embroiled in a crisis with one of her suppliers and Katya had promised her that she would help Peter choose his kitten. That undertaking could not, by any stretch of the imagination, be accomplished from the car so she followed Luke and Peter past the main door at the front to the back of the barn, where the downward slope of the hill revealed an entrance into another storey beneath the one she'd seen from the road. Inside, the large space had been partitioned and washed down, ready to be decorated.

'Which one do you think, Katya?' Luke had made sure that Peter knew how to handle the kittens and then left him to the task of carefully stroking each one of them, taking up a vantage point next to her in the corner of the room.

'The little one with the black patch over his eye looks like a pirate.' The tiny creature was the least outgoing of the brood, keeping to the large box that had been lined with cushions and an old rug.

'Doesn't he just. Unfortunately he really is blind in that eye.'

'He was born that way?'

Luke grimaced, shaking his head. 'Nope. They were abandoned and when someone found them and brought them here, he had an eye infection. We managed to save one eye, but the infection got to the optic nerve in the other and he's completely blind on that side.'

'He'll be difficult to find a home for, then.' The small creature was hurt and disorientated. Frightened by the world. She had more than an inkling of how that felt.

Luke was looking hard at her, and she avoided his gaze. 'He has a home.'

'Good. That's good.' Katya didn't need to ask where. The kitten was already home and he could stay for as long as he wanted. 'So you're renovating this place?' The mellow shades of the old bricks gave it a rustic charm and it seemed a shame to Katya that they'd soon be covered in plaster and paint.

'Yeah. I brought the kittens down here because it stinks of paint upstairs.' He opened a door in the partition wall, which revealed a small hallway with a staircase beyond. 'Peter, you'll be okay here if we go upstairs for a moment, won't you?'

'Yes.' Clearly the only thing Peter wanted right now was to pet as many kittens at once as possible, and Katya and Luke were both bothersome interruptions to the matter in hand. Katya shrugged, grinning, and followed Luke, latching the door closed behind her to stop any of the kittens from escaping.

The staircase led to the ground-level entrance hall at the front of the building. There was a door to the right and a wide arch to the left, which he ushered her through. 'What do you think?'

The evening sunlight shimmered across the exposed brickwork and roof beams, giving a feeling of even more space to the already large room. 'It's huge! And you've left the brickwork.'

'It's too good to hide. They've been repointed and

I had a clear sealant put on there…' Luke regarded the walls thoughtfully. 'Turned out more expensive than just covering them up with plasterboard, but I think it's worth it.'

'Definitely. It looks fantastic.' Katya walked to the middle of the space, turning full circle to see everything. 'What are you going to use this for?'

'This is the public part of the building. It's for small exhibitions, lectures, children's activities.' He jerked his thumb towards the hallway. 'The office space is through there, and my veterinary practice is going to be housed downstairs, where Peter is now.'

His enthusiasm for the project was obvious in every line of his face and those long, strong limbs. If it was at all possible, he seemed to stand taller here, his shoulders even squarer, proud of the vast amount of work that had already been done, and ready for the amount needed to complete the project. There had been a time when Katya had been that immersed in her work, and the sudden feeling of loss almost made her choke.

'Would you like to see the office space?' His voice was suddenly tender, as if he could see the crushing sadness that had just dumped itself on her shoulders. 'It's not finished yet, but…'

'Yes.' Katya gave him a bright, brittle smile. Maybe, one day, she'd find something she could put her heart into, where there was no danger of her messing up. Until then, she'd keep making coffee and smiling.

Luke wasn't quite sure what he'd said or done to set the ghosts swirling in her eyes. Perhaps it would have been better to stay with Peter, but the temptation to show her the project that was so close to his heart had overwhelmed him, and now that he'd brought her up here, he couldn't take her back downstairs again without at least showing her around quickly.

She didn't seem in that much of a hurry, though. If anything, she lingered over the half-finished office space, inspecting the kitchen and tiny shower room and pacing the full length and breadth of the main area.

'It's a huge space.'

'Yeah. I'm going to have demountable partitions made so it can be split up into thirds later on, if necessary. For now, I prefer open-plan.' He was watching her carefully, trying to see the place through her eyes. The value that she put on it had suddenly become unrealistically important.

'Yes. The views are beautiful, too.' She was leaning on one of the windowsills, looking out at the rolling green countryside. 'It'll be better still once you get those prefabs down.'

For the first time Luke saw the two, low, prefabricated units that had been home sweet home for the last two years through someone else's eyes. 'They'll be staying for a while.'

'But surely once you get your new offices and surgery…?'

He shifted uncomfortably. 'That's where I live.'

She reddened slightly. 'Oh! I thought…' Suspicion flickered in her eyes and hardened suddenly. 'I thought that the coffee shop was on your way to work.'

'It is. My surgery's still down in the village. I pick up my coffee on the way there from here.' He shrugged. 'In a few weeks' time I'll be giving up the lease on my practice premises and moving it over here. It's all part of a five-year plan.'

'I see.' She thought for a moment then nodded, obviously finding his answer acceptable. 'So when do you get somewhere permanent to live?'

'That's not at the top of my list of priorities right now. I bought this land two years ago, and I've ploughed every penny I have into getting this place set up. I've got planning permission for a house down by the road there, but it'll have to wait.' He indicated the spot where the house would eventually stand, shaded by trees and currently overrun with brambles. 'In the meantime, I have no shortage of fresh blackberries.'

'Pretty long-term project.' She was craning to see the spot he had indicated, and then her gaze swept back to the temporary buildings. 'Doesn't it get cold in there in the winter?'

Cold, unwelcoming, utilitarian. He didn't spend a lot of time there anyway, and up until this moment he had neither wanted nor needed anything else. The word 'home' had seemed overrated. 'Depends how many pairs of socks I wear.'

She smiled. Really smiled. A smile like that could make anywhere a home. 'This is an amazing place, Luke. It'll be worth it when it's finished.'

He wanted to hug her. No—that was hardly substantial or long-lasting enough. He wanted to hold her. But the last time he'd come too close to her, he'd seen fear in her eyes and she had shrunk back from him. If that happened again, it would shatter everything that Luke had ever believed about himself. A man that a woman feared was no kind of man at all. He turned quickly, cannoning into a workbench, and put his hand out to steady himself.

The blade sliced into his thumb like a hot knife through butter. In the moment before he felt any pain he jerked his hand away from the workman's knife, which had been left out on the bench, and saw blood plume over his fingers.

'Dammit.' Some blood drops had skittered across to a gap in the plastic covering the newly laid flooring and were beginning to soak into the untreated wood. Luke held his injured hand over an empty paint can and bent to repair the damage.

He felt her hands on his, something wrapped around the gash and pressure at the base of his thumb. 'Don't worry about that.'

'It'll stain the wood.' Luke hissed out a curse as the plastic slipped under his feet and more blood spilled onto the floor.

'And you're just making it worse.' Her voice was calm but brooked no argument. 'What's done is done. Come here and we'll sort that out later.' She pulled him away, her green eyes flashing dangerously when he made to resist.

'Hey, that's my fabric sample…' Somehow she'd managed to locate the only clean piece of fabric in the whole place and wrap it around his hand, in the space of time it had taken Luke to half assess the damage to the flooring.

'You're using that colour in here?' She raised one eyebrow. Whatever hesitation she might have displayed in the past was gone now. She was direct, calm and unmistakably in charge. Capital letters, In Charge.

'No. When I got it back here, I thought something a little lighter would be better.'

'Good. You'll not be needing it, then.' She rolled her eyes as Luke tried to move her fingers to inspect his thumb. 'Stop that and come here.'

She hustled him down the stairs and thrust him into a battered armchair that the workmen used during their coffee breaks. 'Peter.' Peter was immersed in trying to disentangle a set of claws from his pullover and Katya's voice increased in intensity if not volume. 'Peter, will you take my keys and go and get the red bag from the back of my car, please?'

Luke took his chance. When she wore her vulnerability like armour, he could do nothing else but treat her gently. But now it was as if her true self had emerged, fearless and capable. He was the one who was at a disadvantage now, and he could afford to flex his muscles a little with her.

'Don't worry about me, I'm fine. I need to see if I can get those bloodspots off the flooring before it stains.'

She dismissed him with a flip of her eyelashes and Luke grinned. 'It's already stained. You might be able to get it off with vinegar. If that doesn't work, try a little bleach.'

'I'd better go and see…' He broke off as she wiggled the thumb of her free hand at him.

'See this?'

'Yep. I cut my hand, not cracked my skull.'

'It's an opposable thumb.' She grinned at him. 'You of all people should know how tricky things get without it.'

'It's a myth that we're the only species with opposable thumbs, lots of animals have them. Gibbons, great apes. Some possums have two digits that oppose the other three. Giant pandas…'

'So many for you to keep up with. Be a shame if you lost your grip.' She lifted the corner of the fabric.

'Seems to have stopped bleeding. Any loss of feeling in your thumb?'

'No.' Luke mimicked the movements of her thumb, circling and bending his own, and she nodded.

'Okay. I'll clean it and tape it up, but you need to get it looked at by a doctor if you experience any loss of sensation or movement or the wound becomes infected.'

'Right.' An idea was beginning to occur to Luke, and when she unzipped the red nylon bag that Peter had brought to her side, it began to gain form and substance. 'Done this before?'

'Once or twice.' She began to clean the wound with alcohol wipes selected from the well-stocked first-aid kit.

'I just want to make sure you know what you're doing. I don't want to trust my valuable opposable thumbs to just anyone.'

'I think you'll be okay.' No explanation. Nothing to reassure him, but then he was getting used to Katya giving the absolute minimum of information and leaving him wondering. Luke didn't need it, though, her attitude and obvious expertise were quite enough.

'It looks horrible.' Peter had been watching carefully.

'It does now. But the miracle of the human body is that it can heal. It'll be just fine in a few days. When we get home, I'll show you exactly what to do if anyone you know cuts themselves like this.' She took a moment to check that Peter was happy with her answer and gave a little satisfied nod. 'Now, have you chosen which kitten you'd like to take home with us?'

'That one.' Peter pointed to an all-black kitten, the boldest of the crew, and the one that Luke had expected him to take to. 'Or that one.' A little white one, with blue eyes and undoubtedly the prettiest. 'Or perhaps…'

Katya laughed. 'Well, I guess you've got a bit more thinking to do.' She paused for a moment to concentrate on taping Luke's wound and then glanced across at Peter's rucksack. 'Perhaps one of them has chosen you.'

Peter caught his breath and ran over to his rucksack, where the tiny kitten with the black patch over its eye had managed to work the zip open and was trying to crawl inside. Carefully he disentangled its claws, and let it attach itself to his chest instead. 'It's licking my hand!'

'Can you let that one go?' She turned to Luke, seeming to know that the weakest of the litter, the one that he had needed to nurse back to health, was the one that he most wanted to find a good home for. 'Olenka will make sure he's looked after properly.'

'I know.' He nodded over towards Peter and his new best friend. 'All he needs now is someone to care for him, and it seems he's found that.'

Luke's gaze found Katya's and she gave him a nod and a shy smile. Now that she was out of the loose-fitting top and apron that she wore at the coffee shop, he could see how slim she was. Almost painfully so. He wouldn't have credited her with the strength to propel him downstairs the way she had just now.

'All done.' She regarded her work for a moment and then began to pack her things back into her bag, pulling her surgical gloves off and stuffing them into the pocket of her jeans. 'You do need to see a doctor if—'

'I know.' Luke thought he saw an echo of his grin in her face. 'I will. Thanks.'

She nodded, and instinct told Luke that now was not the time to press her any further. Or maybe it was, just a little. 'I promised Olenka some things for the kitten if Peter chose one. They're in my cabin. Will you help me carry them back?' Luke made a slightly shamefaced gesture towards his injured hand. There was no point in wasting a good excuse.

'Of course. Peter, you'll be all right here for a minute?'

Peter didn't even bother to answer, he was so absorbed with carefully stroking the small creature that had curled up in his arms.

'He'll be fine. We won't be long.' Luke made his way to the door, sure somehow that Katya would follow.

He could hear her footsteps on the gravel behind him. When he turned, she was hugging the red bag to her chest, and Luke unlocked the door to his temporary home and ducked inside, manners giving way to instinct. She'd make her own decision about whether she wanted to come in or not.

'It looks cosy.' She was craning her head through the doorway, keeping her feet on the rickety steps outside.

Luke shrugged. 'It's enough for me at the moment.' A sofa bed that creaked whenever he turned over. His books, stacked neatly into a couple of packing cases in the corner and his clothes in a chest of drawers. A desk for his laptop, an old easy chair, and that was about it. He didn't spend many of his waking hours here anyway.

'It's very tidy.' She put the red bag down and stepped across the threshold.

'I used to travel a lot, and I found that the best way to keep track of everything was to travel light and keep it orderly.'

She nodded. Most people would have asked where, or why he'd travelled, but he'd learned not to expect that from Katya. It would be too much like striking up a conversation, and you never knew what kind of information sharing that might lead to.

'I was working with a unit of Rescue Dogs. We went wherever we were needed, often at pretty short notice.' There was no reason why he shouldn't volunteer the information.

'Oh.' She was still looking around intently, almost as if there was a prize on offer for shutting her eyes and remembering as many items from the room as she could.

'The aid agency I used to work for is interested in using some of the land here as a training centre for their dogs. I'm hoping to get that up and running next spring.'

'One of the other projects that you're involved with.' She turned to him, the ghost of a smile on her face. She'd remembered, and Luke's heart crowed with triumph. Even if she didn't seem to react much to what he said, she'd clearly been listening all this time.

'Yeah.' He picked up an envelope from the pile on his desk. 'We've got another project that we're trying to get off the ground as well, in partnership with the local hospital. Taking animals into the hospital so that long-stay patients can interact with them.'

A glimmer of interest showed in her eyes. Luke took his chance and handed her the envelope. 'You might be interested in reading about it.'

'Yes...yes, I would, thanks. Aren't there a couple of charities that do that already?'

'Yes, we're working in association with one of them. And directly with the hospital authorities.'

Luke opened the door to the store cupboard and busied himself with sorting out an animal carrier, some kitten food and a few leaflets for Olenka, which he annotated quickly with extra information. When he glanced back in Katya's direction, she was peering inside the envelope, flipping through the papers inside.

'I'm looking to employ someone to help me for the next three months. This place is taking up a lot of time, and I need to concentrate on my veterinary practice in order to finance the building work.'

'Must be quite a juggling act.' She'd now tucked the envelope into her bag.

'It is at the moment. When I've got the visitors' centre and the dog school properly sorted, then the place will begin to pay for itself, but that won't be until next spring. In the meantime, I'm looking for someone with some experience of hospital procedures, who likes animals and who can work well with kids. And the pay's not great either.'

Luke reckoned that he could match whatever Katya was getting at the coffee shop, but that was about all.

'Sounds like a great job, though. I'm sure you'll get some takers.'

'Not so far. I haven't had many applications, and they've all been completely unsuitable. I need someone who actually thinks that this is a good idea, not someone who doesn't care what they're doing as long as the hours suit them.'

She didn't take the bait. For all Luke knew, she might have been thinking about it, but she said nothing, just picked up her bag and tucked the animal carrier under one arm. 'You can manage the rest?'

'Yeah, no problem. Thanks.'

He could wait. Luke had seen something in Katya, something loving and compassionate. Something that would make her fight for whatever cause found a way into that closely guarded heart of hers. In the old days, the charming, happy-go-lucky version of Luke would have wanted that for himself, along with those enchanting eyes and the body that seemed to cry out for the safety of his arms.

Now he wanted it for the only thing that his heart knew how to desire. His work, the land here, and all the possibilities that they held.

CHAPTER THREE

KATYA SAT OPPOSITE Olenka at the dining-room table, a sheet of paper between them. 'So what do you think?'

Olenka picked up the application form, and read it through. 'Sounds great. Really impressive.'

'What would you do?'

'Well, he hasn't offered you the job yet. There's nothing wrong with making an enquiry to find out whether it's what you want…' Olenka twisted her mouth in an expression of resignation. 'That's not the problem, eh.'

'No. I'm going to have to tell him about what happened.'

Olenka sighed. 'Okay, so what did happen? You meet a guy in the course of your work, have a few conversations with him and he decides that he's in love with you. He asks you out, you turn him down nicely and he stabs you. It wasn't your fault. No one said it was your fault.'

'That's not all, though, is it?' Olenka made it all sound so simple but there was so much more to it than that. Enough to fog even the most straightforward decisions.

'Of course not. It's all that matters to any employer, though.' Olenka looked weary. She worked hard, raising a child and running a business, and now it seemed she had Katya to look after as well.

'I'm sorry, Ola. You've enough on your plate, you can do without me turning up and dumping my troubles on your doorstep.'

Olenka grinned. 'Lucky for me that's not what your parents said when I arrived from Poland with a new baby and no husband.' She crooked her little finger and Katya wound hers around it. Shades of the time when Katya had been the one to offer comfort, helping Olenka with her English and babysitting when she went out looking for work. 'Look, the only thing I care about is that you'll be safe and happy. And from what I know of Luke, you will be.'

'You mean from what your spies tell you?' It hadn't escaped Katya's attention that Olenka had drawn a couple of her customers aside, people who, she guessed, knew Luke well, and asked a few hushed but clearly important questions.

'You're not in London now, this is a village. Everyone has spies.' Olenka brushed the accusation off. 'And none of mine have a word to say against him.'

'Right. And what do they have to say about me?'

'Nothing. What happened to you is your business, no one else's. The only thing that Luke has a right to know is whether you can do the job. This other thing is…' Olenka waved her hand dismissively '…nothing to do with it.'

'You think so?' Katya supposed that Olenka was right. On the other hand, this was a position of responsibility. Shouldn't a prospective employer know that she had feet of clay?

'You came here to make a new start. You can leave

it all behind you if you want to. Whatever you want to think, none of what happened was your fault.'

Katya shrugged. She couldn't bear to say that she was innocent when she felt so very guilty, even for Olenka's sake. 'Well, I'll send the application form off and see what happens. Maybe I won't even get the job.'

Clutching the envelope that contained her curriculum vitae, Katya walked through the pub and into the garden behind it, scanning the wooden tables and benches. Luke was there, an untouched pint of beer in front of him and a blond Labrador retriever dozing in the sun at his feet. He frowned when he caught sight of her.

'I thought we decided this wasn't an interview.' His eye travelled from her blouse and skirt to his own work-worn jeans. 'I didn't bother to dress up.'

'Neither did I.' Like hell she hadn't. Katya had spent a good couple of hours deciding what to wear. *Lively and outgoing* the job description had said. She'd reckoned that warranted a bright summer skirt and a pair of strappy sandals, and that her plain blouse would cover the *responsible* part of things.

'Oh. Well, in that case what can I get you to drink?' He grinned up at her, his dark eyes flashing with mischief.

'Water, please. Sparkling.' Katya sat down opposite him, laying her envelope on the wooden trestle table.

'Sure? I can't get you anything stronger? This really isn't an interview, it's just an informal chat…'

'I'd like some water, please.' Katya wanted to keep a clear head for this.

'Of course.' Luke bent and ran his hand down the

sleeping dog's back and it opened its eyes. Dark and soft, like its master's. 'Meet Bruno. Say hello, Bruno.'

The dog rose and lifted its paw, and Katya took it. 'Is he yours?'

'Don't let him hear you say that. Bruno's always earned his own living. He's retired from the rescue business now, though, and I'm the one who gets to feed and look after him.' Luke rose from his seat. 'Ice and lemon?'

'Yes, thanks. Not too much ice.'

Katya watched him go. Pale, washed-out jeans that fitted him far too well and a dark polo shirt, which clung to his broad shoulders. An easy, laid-back gait, which made her want to walk beside him. Any woman would. Luke was by far the best-looking man she'd seen in years, probably for ever, and he had that indeterminate quality about him that turned good-looking into something that made you catch your breath and shiver every time you even thought about his lips.

She'd get used to it, though. After a couple of weeks working alongside him she'd get to see the person and forget all about the gorgeous outer wrapping. And she wanted this job. Katya had come to the conclusion that she wasn't ready to go back to nursing yet, but she'd outgrown the coffee shop. She wanted something more, and this was an ideal stepping stone.

The clink of ice in a glass shattered her reverie. 'I see you've already won the chairman of the board over.' Luke's eyes were flashing with gentle humour as he indicated Bruno's head, resting in her lap.

'He gets a vote?'

'Yeah. I just get to do the talking.' Luke sat down, sliding a bar menu across the table towards her. 'Would you like something to eat?' He saw her hesitate and laughed. 'It's not a trick question. I'm starving. Let's order and we can talk while we're waiting.'

He ordered a home-made burger with steak-cut chips and salad, grinning his approbation when Katya said she'd have the same. He took a draught of beer from his glass and then all his attention was on her. Katya tried not to think about how his gaze always seemed to resemble an embrace.

'I've brought my CV for you.' She laid her two-page résumé on the table between them, along with the fat A4 envelope. She'd brought a handkerchief, too. There was one point in this story that always sent tears coursing down her cheeks, however many times she practised it in front of the bathroom mirror.

'What's in the envelope?'

'Just some supporting documents.' Katya took a sip of water, wondering whether perhaps a little Dutch courage might not have been a good idea. 'There's something I'd like to tell you.'

'No.' Luke was suddenly still. Only his hand moved, to Bruno's head, his fingers absently fondling his ears.

'No?' This was the one reaction she hadn't expected from him. Anything else, but not this flat refusal to even listen to her.

'I don't want to hear it, Katya. The form that you filled out said that you're a nurse. That you had a senior position in one of the top London hospitals but you left more than a year ago.'

'Yes, that's right.' There was still a swell of pride. Muted now, and tinged with bitter experience, but it was still there.

'In my experience, someone with that kind of background, who's working in a coffee shop, is in need of a new start. Is that right?' His manner was kind, but he'd sliced right to the bone.

'Yes. That's right.' Katya felt her spine begin to sag, and pulled herself upright, squaring her shoulders.

'Then let's make one. Look forward instead of back.'

'But you need to know...' Katya knew that she had to put her own feelings aside. Disclosure was one of those things you had to do in this kind of job. 'I'll be working with children, with vulnerable adults...'

'Not yet you won't. It'll be another month before the reserve is open to the public and we get the project going to take animals into the hospital. I need to put an advanced CRB check in motion, and I'll take up the references that you've given, but...'

'The references will be fine. There'll be nothing on the CRB check either.'

'So is there any reason why you shouldn't work with me, setting up procedures and getting things organised?'

'No.' Luke would be in charge, and that was her safety net. She could refer any difficult decisions back to him.

'Then this can wait.' Luke pushed the envelope back across the table towards her. 'Until you're ready.'

He was giving her a chance. Taking her at face value and letting her prove herself. This was not what Katya had expected, but it felt okay. It was a place from which she could move forward.

'Aren't you curious?' She almost wanted him to be.

'Truthfully?' He grinned. 'Yes, of course.'

'But you're not going to do anything about it?'

'No. Bruno and I are unanimous in that.' The old

dog looked up at Luke at the mention of his name and started to lick Katya's hand. 'See?'

There was little else to do but give in gracefully. 'Okay.' Katya sealed the envelope, pushing it back towards Luke. 'Keep that for me, will you? We might be having this conversation again.'

He took the envelope without a word and stashed it, along with her résumé, in the leather document wallet that lay on the bench beside him.

'In the meantime, I'll be giving this job my best. And Olenka can tell you that I've no history of trying to strangle my work colleagues.'

He shrugged. 'That's okay.' The delicious sweep of his gaze, up and down her body, made her shudder. 'I can take care of myself.'

Luke wasn't so sure about that. Something about her, maybe her obvious vulnerability, which she seemed determined not to give in to, stirred feelings that he would rather forget. Feelings that he'd had no trouble forgetting until a few weeks ago.

He couldn't go back on what he'd promised her now, though. It was plain that she needed this job, and someone like Katya, with practical nursing experience and willing to take the paltry amount he could offer to pay her, was a godsend for the project that he was trying so hard to get off the ground. If it took a little bravado to make out that he was indifferent to her charms, then so be it.

They talked all through their meal, until the evening chill drove them inside. Then they talked some more, until the pub landlord called time. By then, her eyes were shining with as much enthusiasm as Luke felt.

'Do I get the job, then?' She'd waited until they were strolling across the car park towards her car before she asked.

'Do you want it?' Being able to tease her, without worrying that she was going to crumple, was something new, which they'd worked their way round to during the course of the evening, and Luke rather liked it.

'I asked first.' She tilted her face up towards him in the darkness. For one sweet moment Luke thought that he might kiss her and the shock of how good that felt bounced him back into reality.

'You got the job about three hours ago. If you get into that car without accepting it, Bruno might have to beg.' That's right. Get Bruno to do the dirty work.

'I'd hate to see that happen. I accept. Thank you.'

'You might not be saying that in a week or so's time. There's a lot on that list we've just made.'

'We'll get through it.' She pressed her lips together in thought, and Luke's head began to swim again. 'We talked about getting some shirts with the name of the nature reserve on them.'

'Yeah. I'll make some calls…'

'I can speak to the guy who does the polo shirts for the coffee shop, if you'd like. When Olenka ordered some for me she said he was very reasonable and I can get his catalogue for you to look at.'

Luke grinned. He'd made the right choice. 'That's okay, I'm sure you'll pick something suitable.' He pulled out his wallet and extracted the last couple of notes from it. 'Will that cover it?'

'It's more than enough. I'll save the receipts for you.'

Accounting had never seemed so delicious. 'Right.

Thanks. If there's room in the budget, perhaps you can get a couple for me, too.'

She folded the notes, putting them into her bag. 'Consider it done. What size…?' In the darkness, Luke couldn't see whether she was blushing or not, but from the way she suddenly looked away from him she probably was. Something inside him crowed with triumph at the thought. 'They only come in small, medium and large, so I'll get large.'

'That'll be fine.' A thought struck him. 'Is Olenka ever going to speak to me again?'

She laughed. Luke could almost feel her breath on his cheek. It was time to step back, but somehow he couldn't. 'Olenka will be fine. She'll probably give you free coffee for a week for taking me off her hands.'

'I doubt it.' How could she think so little of herself? Luke wondered whether the answer to that was in the manila envelope tucked in his notecase. He'd have to lock it away safely somewhere and consider swallowing the key.

She didn't reply. As she turned to unlock her car, the temptation to take her by the shoulders and shake this nonsense out of her gripped Luke and he stumbled backwards. He wasn't her lover, her social worker or even really a friend. He was just a guy who'd offered her a three-month contract, and it didn't matter what either of them thought of each other as long as she did the job.

'I'll see you next week, then.' Maybe he should start as he meant to go on. No popping into the coffee shop just to see her in the meantime.

'Yes. I'm looking forward to it.' She grinned at him. 'Don't forget your coffee run in the morning.'

'Um…no, of course not.' So much for good intentions. When she came to work with him Luke was going to have to do a little better than that.

That wasn't going to be a problem. He only needed to think about his marriage, and how a woman's secrets had almost destroyed him, to know that Katya's personal life would stay locked away in that envelope and that he would stay away from her. Anything else could shatter everything he'd built here, and he wasn't about to do that.

CHAPTER FOUR

KATYA HAD BEEN expecting something approaching an induction session on her first day. Or, if anything as grand as a session didn't seem like Luke's style, maybe a half-hour chat to give her an idea of where to start with the schemes and ideas they'd talked about. When she arrived at the reserve at eight o'clock sharp, the note on the door of the newly finished barn was distinctly underwhelming.

Meet me by the old bridge.

A hastily drawn map showed the location.

Bring waterproofs if you have them.

She had wellingtons in the boot of her car. Katya had fondly supposed that she might be accompanying Luke on a tour of the reserve and had come prepared. The bridge looked to be on the road that ran along the west side and Katya sighed, getting back into her car.

The old bridge turned out to be a single-lane section of road, which spanned a small river. Luke's truck was parked nearby, and Katya pulled off the road and tucked her car into the space next to it. 'Luke. Luke! Are you there?'

'Under here.' His voice echoed out from under the bridge, an edge of annoyance to it that was so unlike Luke that she hardly recognised it. His head and shoulders appeared from the shadow beneath the brick arch and when he caught sight of her his eyes, dark with rage, softened a little. 'Hey, there.' He stood up straight and pulled off one of his heavy work gloves, running one hand through his hair. 'Welcome.'

That might have been a smile, but then again it might not. Katya gave him the benefit of the doubt. 'Thanks. I got coffee from Olenka's. As it's my first day.'

Now, that *was* a smile. 'Thanks. I could do with one.' He began to climb the riverbank towards her.

'What's going on?'

The shake of his head told her that this was one of those situations where words were pathetically inadequate. Taking the cardboard beaker that Katya had fetched from her car, he took a swig. 'Some idiot's been dumping stuff.' He gestured towards the far side of the bridge, where water was building up, haemorrhaging out into the grassland on either side of the stream. On the near side, water was spilling sluggishly through the blocked opening.

'What's down there?'

He rolled his eyes. 'Two old mattresses. Someone must have stopped on the bridge and just tipped them over the side. The water's taken them under the bridge and they've stuck there. I've been trying to shift them, but they're waterlogged and that makes them heavy.'

'Perhaps we can do it between us. You push and I'll pull.' Katya grinned at him. He might have skipped the induction session but there was no doubt that they were working together now.

The lines of tension melted into a smile. 'Yeah. Perhaps we can. Have you got waterproofs?'

'I've got wellies.' Katya reached into her car and brought out the new pair of dark blue wellingtons.

'Very smart. I like the polka dots.' He shrugged. 'I don't think they'll do the job.'

'No. Probably not.' Her own boots looked like a fashion accessory next to Luke's workmanlike waders. Katya shifted uncomfortably. Did it look as if she was just playing at this?

'Never mind.' He grinned at her. 'They'll be great for day-to-day stuff, around the reserve.'

They matched the shirts as well. Katya decided this wasn't the moment to mention that. 'So what are we going to do? Is there someone we can call?'

'We could try towing them out…' He gestured towards the tow bar on the back of his truck. Katya followed his drift. They could position the vehicle on the path by the river and she could ease it forward, while Luke guided the mattresses out, making sure that they didn't catch on anything. But he was waiting for her to approve the plan first.

'Yes. I'll get to keep my feet dry in your truck.' He nodded. 'Let's give it a go.'

It took half an hour, but the extra leverage as Katya inched the truck forward made all the difference. Once the mattresses were out of the water, Katya joined Luke, helping him push them up the sloping riverbank.

'One last push!'

She was trying not to notice the way he encouraged her. How he praised her for jobs well done and egged her on to do more. He was way stronger than her but he made her feel like an equal partner, the extra bit of strength that made all the difference, and when he swung the mattresses onto the back of his truck, it felt like her achievement as well as his.

Katya had been trying not to notice him either. Or the muscles in his arms and shoulders, swelling to meet the challenge of the waterlogged mattresses, which twisted and buckled every time you tried to get a grip on them. Or how there were few things more beautiful than the lines of a male body when it was in good shape. And Luke was in very good shape.

'Nice job.' He inclined his head towards the river. 'See, it's already back to its usual flow.' The gush of water that had surged under the bridge when they had dislodged the second mattress had soaked him.

He wasn't just perfect, he was wet and perfect, and now that she wasn't giving all her energy to shoving as hard as she could, it was difficult not to look at the way his wet shirt stuck to his skin.

He held out his hand as she scrambled up the sloping riverbank, and Katya ignored it. It would be foolish to get any closer to him than necessary at this point.

'Careful!' Almost before she realised that her foot had slipped in the mud and she was falling, he had hold of her. Instinctively she tried to twist away, but he had one arm around her waist, pulling her up and towards him. Her chest hit his with a slight squelch, and all she could feel was his warmth and the safety of his all-too-solid arms around her.

If he'd had the chance to think about it Luke would have hesitated before he'd grabbed her and stopped her from falling, but there had been no time. And she'd been about to careen backwards down the muddy slope of the riverbank and onto the rocks below. Instinctively, her arms had flown outwards, searching wildly for something to hang on to, and instinctively he'd reached out for her and pulled her into his arms.

'I'm…I'm sorry.' *Sorry for touching you. Sorry for intruding into that well-guarded space you keep around yourself.*

She moved against him and it was only by a superhuman effort of will that Luke managed to loosen his arms around her, rather than pull her closer. She was trembling, and Luke wondered if it was from the shock. He'd better let her go before she realised that he was trembling, too. As he did so she stumbled slightly, as if her legs weren't quite ready to hold her yet, and he steadied her. 'Careful. Are you all right?'

'Yes, I'm fine. Just a bit dizzy. Give me a moment.'

Just one? She could have more if she liked.

He let her lean against him, holding on to his shoulder. Wherever she touched, his skin seemed to warm slightly, defying the chill of the morning breeze on his wet shirt. Luke hoped against hope that she wasn't aware of what she was doing to him.

'I'm sorry. I didn't mean to grab at you like that.'

'It's all right, Luke. You can touch me.' She tipped her face up towards him, her emerald eyes clouded in thought.

He didn't know what to say. Wasn't quite sure what she meant by that. If this had been any other woman he would have kissed her right there and then, and he was pretty sure that she would have kissed him back. But if this had been anyone other than Katya, he probably wouldn't have wanted to kiss her.

Luke decided to concentrate on the practical. 'Feeling better now?'

'Yes, I'm fine.' She didn't move. Then, suddenly, she stepped away from him, as if what she was about to say needed a little distance. 'I'm a bit jumpy at the moment.'

'Yeah. I guessed that.' He grinned at her, as if to say that it was okay. He knew that she didn't like him getting too close, and he could handle it. Probably far better than he had handled having her cling to him just now.

'I'm dealing with it. Sometimes better than others.' She shrugged, as if it was really nothing to do with her but something that had been foisted on her. 'It's not you.'

Luke's heart thumped in his chest. Most people wouldn't have bothered to think about what this was doing to him. How hard it was to have someone shy away from him when he knew that he could never do her any harm. But Katya wasn't most people. She wanted to reassure him.

'Thank you for saying that.' He held his hand out to her and she took it, squeezing it slightly before letting it drop. 'I wish I could own my fears as well as you do.'

He respected her for that. When Tanya had left, he'd carried on as if nothing had happened. Let the emotions eat away at him, without ever speaking of them or letting anyone know that he was broken. Maybe that was why it seemed inconceivable now that he would ever mend.

Katya was smiling at him. Her eyes never quite lost their troubled look, but there were times when she hid it well. 'I don't know about that. I hope you're not regretting taking me on already.'

Luke gave that comment the contempt it deserved. 'I'm lucky to have you.' He reached out and removed a piece of green stuff from the river, which had transferred itself from his shirt to hers. 'I don't suppose you have a clean top to wear for this afternoon? We're due at the hospital at half-three for a short meeting with the administrator.'

'I've got the reserve tops I ordered in the car. The guy dropped them off on Saturday.'

'That'll be fine.' He grinned at her. 'Show them that we mean business.'

Luke was already late for his morning surgery by the time they got back to the barn, and he went to his cabin to change his clothes, then left almost immediately. Just pointed her towards her desk in the corner of the vast office space, impressed on her the need for keeping the doors locked while he was gone, and asked if Bruno could keep her company for the rest of the morning.

When he returned, he seemed in no less of a hurry. Katya and Bruno were hustled towards his car, and they were already out onto the main road before she got a chance to ask the obvious question.

'I thought we weren't due at the hospital until three-thirty. We're a little early, aren't we?'

'I thought you might like a chance to have a look around before our meeting.'

'Yes, I would. Thanks.' Katya swallowed hard. So what if she hadn't been back to a hospital since she'd been discharged after the attack? She'd had no particular reason to, other than her follow-up appointment, and a home visit from the district nurse had been a perfectly good substitute.

He didn't utter another word until they drove in through the hospital gates, and neither did Katya. Luke was obviously on a mission, and she already knew better than to try and divert him. The place was quite different from the hospital that Katya still thought of as hers, sprawling outwards instead of upwards, with grass, trees and flower-beds in between an assortment of buildings that looked as if they ranged in age between a hundred years old to only just finished.

'This looks like a nice place.' It did. Apart from the fact that her heart was thumping so loudly that Katya was surprised it didn't drown out the car radio.

'Yeah. There are a lot of good people here. The new paediatric unit is intended to serve the whole county.' He waved his hand towards the large, modern block.

'Looks big enough.'

'Yeah.' He stopped the car at a pedestrian crossing and shot her a glance. 'You okay?'

'Why wouldn't I be?' Katya bit her tongue. A smile and confirmation would have been perfectly adequate.

'You tell me.' He motioned with a grin towards a small group of nurses crossing the road in front of him. 'Do you miss it?'

Yes, she missed it. Being able to go home, feeling that she'd done something that mattered at work that day. Meeting the challenges. 'On my first day of a new job, the tactful answer would be no.'

He nodded. 'And on the second day?'

'Wait and see.' At least she'd have twenty-four hours to think up something that approximated to an answer. 'So the dogs are initially going to be visiting one of the hospital gardens?'

'Oh. Yeah.' Luke seemed to focus back onto the

real purpose of their visit with some difficulty. 'One of them, there are three. The one they're proposing is down there, that's where the hospital administrator says she'll meet us.' He pointed past the main building to a group of newer buildings, arranged in a U-shape around a pretty garden. 'I'll park the car and we can take Bruno for a walk around the place. Give him some exercise so he'll settle when we meet Laura.'

That was an excuse if ever she'd heard one. Bruno was a consummate professional, and he didn't need a walk to settle down, just one gesture from Luke. Katya, on the other hand, did need to calm her nerves. 'Good idea. I'd like to have a look around, too.'

'Good.' His smile broadened. 'Will you get Bruno's lead? It's in the glove compartment.'

Luke and Bruno were clearly working together, and seamlessly fell into maximum protective mode, Luke strolling on one side of her with Bruno so close on the other that Katya's hand brushed against his collar as she walked. Luke took a circular path around the site, pointing out the various departments as they went and stopping some yards from the entrance to the A and E department.

'Do you want to go in? I'll wait here with Bruno.'

'Me? Go in? Why would I want to do that?' As soon as the words had left her mouth Katya realised that, as they'd approached, her gaze had hardly left the paramedics and nurses around the doors of the unit.

'Just for a look around. Get the feel of the place.'

It felt the most natural thing in the world just to go in, be a part of a world that she loved again, even if it was only for a few minutes and she was just a visitor. Luke was giving her every opportunity to do it but Katya couldn't, not yet. 'Maybe another time.'

'Okay.' Katya almost wished that he would push it, but he didn't. 'It's about time we made tracks for our meeting anyway.' He looked around, as if to orientate himself, and then headed off in the direction that Bruno seemed to have already decided was the right one. 'This way.'

CHAPTER FIVE

LUKE WAS QUIETLY pleased with his progress. At one point Katya had looked as if she might leg it out through the hospital gates, with Bruno loping along behind her, but he'd stayed close and she hadn't. And as soon as he'd introduced her to Laura Berry, the hospital administrator, she'd snapped into business mode.

The two women couldn't have been more different. Laura was a small, precise woman in her fifties, with honest eyes, who exuded quiet authority. One of the things that Luke liked about Laura was that you always knew exactly where you were with her. Katya, tall and slender, exuded quiet mystery and Luke never knew quite what she was going to do next. Somehow, though, through a process of women's radar that Luke had never quite got to grips with, there seemed to be an instant understanding between them.

'You're a nurse?' Laura sat down on one of the benches in a quiet corner of the garden.

'I used to be.' Katya sat down next to her, putting her notes on the bench between them. Luke grinned. That was a nice touch. Nothing to hide, complete accountability. He doubted if Katya even knew that she'd done it, it was just her way.

'Is that something you ever stop being? I don't think I have.'

Katya nodded. 'No, I suppose not. I'm taking a break, though.'

'Me, too. Rather a long one. It's been twenty years since I was last on the wards.' Laura smiled in response to Katya's look of enquiry. 'I injured my back. Herniated disc.'

Katya nodded gravely. She didn't waste any words on compassion but it showed, bright and clear, in her eyes. 'Do you miss it?'

'I don't miss shift work. Or being on my feet all day.' Laura pursed her lips. 'The rest of it I miss, even after all these years.'

There was a moment of silence and Luke held his breath. Some kind of understanding, which he wasn't privy to, was flowing between the two women and he dared not break the spell.

'Well.' Laura seemed to know when to speak again. 'Down to business, eh?'

Luke had come well prepared for the meeting, but it seemed that Katya had read all of the notes he'd given her, and she was more than capable of fielding Laura's questions. She reviewed the list of requirements that Laura had supplied him with the last time they'd met, and showed that they could not only meet them, but in some areas that they intended to exceed them.

Leaning back in his seat, watching her work while he soaked up the afternoon sunshine, was a pleasure.

Laura was difficult to persuade. Katya was answering all her questions, thinking on her feet when she needed to and using her knowledge of clinical procedure, but there was still something stopping Laura from giving the project her final approval. Luke had sensed it when they'd met the last time but hadn't been able to put his finger on what it was and had wondered whether it was his imagination.

'I wouldn't want the animals to invade anyone's space…' Laura seemed to falter slightly. 'Some people don't like dogs.'

'And when you're vulnerable and in hospital, the last thing you can do with is something large and threatening bearing down on you.' Katya's eyes lit up with mischief. 'Patients get enough of that with the registrars.'

Laura laughed suddenly. 'Quite.'

Katya thought for a moment. 'We have no intention of forcing the dogs onto anyone. The idea is that we're here, in a corner of the garden, and people can come to us if they want to. You can see that Bruno's very well behaved, he won't be running around all over the place, and neither will any of the other dogs.' She gestured to where Bruno was lying at Luke's feet, and he cocked his head slightly towards her.

Laura was unconvinced. 'But if he has children around him, or he gets overexcited…'

It was time for a demonstration and Luke got to his feet, walking Bruno a few yards away from the benches where they sat and unclipping his lead. 'Watch this.' He tossed Bruno a dog treat and he caught it deftly, wolfing it down. Then he gave Bruno the command to sit and waved a second biscuit above his nose. 'If I tell him to sit, then he sits. Bruno used to be a rescue dog, and lives depended on him being able to follow orders. He's never let any of us down.'

Laura nodded, pressing her lips together as Luke

turned his back on Bruno, walking away from him. Bruno didn't move a muscle, but Katya's head whirled round as Laura jumped.

Maybe it *was* true that vulnerable people saw the vulnerabilities in others more clearly. Whatever, Katya seemed to have an immediate grasp of the situation, while Luke was still grappling with the vague notion that something was wrong. 'Put him back on the lead, Luke.' She turned to Laura. 'I'm sorry.'

'That's all right.' Laura shot a conspiratorial glance towards Katya. 'I'm not the best person to be doing this. I'm not very good with dogs, and that's probably why I'm struggling to see the benefit of having them here.'

'Then that makes you the very best person to be doing it.' Katya grinned. 'If we can persuade you then we can persuade anyone.' She looked up at Luke, her green eyes flashing, and he felt his stomach twist. She seldom took charge of a situation, but when she did she was decisive, unstoppable. She could back him into a corner and take charge of him any time she liked. Luke let go of the delicious thought and led Bruno over to a shady spot at the edge of the garden, looping his lead around the railings and telling him to stay put.

'If anyone isn't comfortable around any one of our dogs, we take them away.' Katya was flipping through the proposal and found the paragraph that made that clear. 'No questions, no shoving the animal in their face, trying to persuade them that they're not that bad really.'

Laura read the paragraph that Katya indicated. 'You don't know how refreshing that is. Mostly dog owners tell me that their dog's different from any other dog and that if I only got to know it, I'd realise that it wasn't the biting machine I think it is.'

'And there isn't much point in trying to rationalise someone out of an irrational fear.' Katya reddened. She'd clearly said more than she'd meant to.

'No.' Laura laughed. 'There isn't. You have to do that all for yourself.' She looked up at Luke, her lips pursed in thought. 'When can you start?'

The sudden breakthrough caught Luke off balance. 'We'll have to think about that and get back to you with a definite date. But it shouldn't be more than three weeks from today.'

Laura nodded. 'Okay. I'll need to get back to my committee, but that's just to rubber-stamp my decision. If you can get back to me with the date, I'll include it in my formal letter to you.' She held her hand out towards Luke and he shook it.

'Thank you. I hope that you'll drop in on one of the sessions.'

'You can be sure of that. I'll be wanting to see that you live up to your promises.' Laura smiled. 'I think you will. Maybe I'll even end up getting to know Bruno a little.'

'So what happened there?' Luke had been thinking hard as Laura had strolled with them back to the car, and now they were on the road they could talk.

'What do you mean? You got what you wanted, didn't you? Even if it is going to concentrate our minds a bit to get everything sorted in the next three weeks.'

'Concentrate *your* mind—I'll be busy.' He grinned across at her. 'I meant how did you pick up that Laura was afraid of dogs? She never mentioned it to me.'

'Ah. And you're miffed about being beaten to the punch, are you?' That slight teasing tone again.

'No. I'm annoyed with myself for not having noticed it sooner. Laura seemed okay with Bruno. You know he wouldn't do anyone any harm.'

'Fear isn't necessarily rational. If I jump when I see a spider, it's not because I actually think it's going to do me any harm. I know it won't, it's a lot smaller than me and spiders in this country aren't poisonous.'

'*Do* you jump when you see a spider, then?' He'd come to think of Katya as fearless when it came to material things. It was everything else that seemed to bother her.

'No. Not really. It was an illustration.' She shrugged. 'To Laura, Bruno's probably quite a different proposition when he's off his lead or shut up in her office with her. A lot of these types of fears come from childhood, and she's probably lived most of her life with this and learned to handle it to some extent. It just comes out when she's put in certain situations that happen to press her buttons.'

Luke took the opportunity of negotiating a roundabout to think about that one. 'Aggression. Being unable to escape. Pretty universal fears, right?' It seemed that whatever was behind them featured on Katya's list as well. She'd tried not to stretch too often to see in the rear-view mirror, but Luke had noticed.

'Yes. Those and other things.'

'What things?' This was about as close as Luke dared go to asking.

She shrugged. 'Falling from heights, I suppose. Drowning.' She'd deftly switched the conversation to a different aspect. Those things really could hurt her, but they weren't the things that made her start suddenly.

'Yeah, I guess.' Luke left it at that. The road behind

them was clear, but it still seemed to occupy her more than the way ahead. If he was going to find out what she saw there, what she'd run from but not truly been able to escape, he was going to have to formulate his questions carefully.

Luke's car was there when Katya parked outside the barn the following morning. He had to be around somewhere. As she opened the unlocked door of the barn and poked her head tentatively inside, the smell of coffee and the sound of a radio told her where.

'Morning.' He was in the kitchen, arguing back with the early-morning talk programme, and jumped when she spoke. Somehow the incongruity of it made her smile. Jumping was generally her move.

'Oh! Hey, there. Have you eaten yet?'

'No. Not yet.' Although she had stopped off at the coffee shop this morning for two coffees and croissants. They could stay in the car. The pastries that Luke had set out on the table looked, and smelled, mouthwatering. 'You went out and got these this morning?'

'Yep. Thought we could have a breakfast rota. Since you've taken it upon yourself to turn up early for work two days in a row now.'

A breakfast rota with Luke. Katya dismissed the thought. Far too delicious. 'I might decide to have a lie-in tomorrow.'

'I can wait. Will you pour the coffee? I've got some things I want to show you.' He winked at her, and Katya felt herself redden. 'I like to get the most I can out of my employees, so this is a working breakfast.'

He reappeared with a bundle of papers and a carrier bag, and sat down opposite her at the table. 'Recognise the blend?'

'Of course I do. It's Olenka's, isn't it?'

He nodded. 'She slipped me a couple of bags of it the other day. Along with a few thinly veiled threats about what might happen to me if I don't turn out to be a model employer.'

At least he hadn't repeated what Katya reckoned Olenka's words would have been. She wouldn't have worried about the model employer bit, she'd have told Luke to look after her. 'Olenka can be a bit protective at times.'

He nodded. 'Nothing wrong with that. It's good to have people around you who want to protect you.'

Katya supposed so. In the last few months that had been all everyone seemed to have wanted, her friends, her family and particularly her parents. She'd come here for a measure of freedom, away from the suffocating concern that seemed to surround her, and that had only been allowed because everyone knew that Olenka would call immediately if there were any signs of her wavering from a perfect recovery.

'So what's that you've got there?'

'This is for you.' He pulled a box out of the bag and handed it to her. Luke hadn't made any comment when he'd asked for her mobile number and she'd told him she didn't have a mobile, but he'd obviously remembered. 'So I can get hold of you, just as any model employer should.'

Right. So he could keep an eye on her more likely. And so she could phone him when the inevitable happened and she found herself unable to cope. 'I don't need this…'

He waved her into silence, chewing on his pastry.

'I don't need it, Luke. I can manage perfectly well without a phone.'

'I'm sure you can. But this place is isolated and I'm not always going to be around. It's basic health and safety at work. You need to carry a phone when you're working on your own.'

There was a flash of something in his eyes, and his voice was firm. Luke might be a little laissez-faire about other things, but he'd clearly made his mind up about this. In which case, he could just unmake it.

'I'm perfectly capable of working on my own. We talked about it the other day, and I knew exactly what the job entailed when I took it.'

'I don't doubt that. But anyone who works alone at times, including me, needs to have some way of calling for help if the unexpected happens. It's just common sense.' He flipped through the stack of notes in the pile next to him and handed her a leaflet. 'Here. Ten safety points for lone workers. This is number three.'

'But—'

'No buts. I have a duty of care to people who work for me. If you don't like it…' he shrugged '…that's tough.'

'What, you'll sack me?' Katya had no idea why she was arguing with him over this. It was, as he'd said, simple common sense. But she liked this new Luke. The one who didn't back off and let her have her way with everything.

'Yeah, actually. Which would be a pity because this is only your second day, and I thought that day one went pretty well. And as you went to all the trouble of getting a pair of wellingtons to match your T-shirt.'

Was there anything that Luke didn't notice? 'I just

happened to see them. But since I've got them now…' The box had already been opened, and when she looked inside the phone was charged and ready to go. 'I dare say you've programmed your number into it already.'

'Very perceptive. If you press the shortcut key on the right…' He broke off as Katya pressed the key and a tone sounded from his pocket. 'Okay. You've got the phone under control, then.'

Katya ignored him, and turned her attention to the printed leaflet. 'What about this?' She pointed to item six. 'How are we going to manage that?'

His lip gave a brief, unmistakable curl of triumph. 'There's a whiteboard through there, next to your desk. I'll fix it to the wall and we can both write our movements for the day on it, where we'll be and when we expect to be back.'

'Okay. That'll work.' Katya nodded, scanning the rest of the leaflet. He hadn't given her The Concerned Look once. Neither had he told her that anything was *for her own good.* She had that, at least, to be grateful to him for. 'What arrangements have you made for security when you bring your practice up here? There'll be drugs on the premises then.'

'The layout of the barn helps. You'd have to tunnel to get to the back of the ground floor, and I've had a secure room built there. It's beyond the specification needed to store drugs.' Luke shifted almost awkwardly. 'I'm not worried so much about theft, we have good security here, it's everyone's personal safety that is my main concern.'

She'd given him a hard enough time about being over-protective already. In truth, he wasn't, he was just being responsible. Maybe if she had thought about some of these things, she wouldn't have got herself into such a mess. She'd still be loving her job back in London, instead of sitting here, eating breakfast with Luke. Suddenly the change in tempo didn't seem quite as bad as it usually did.

'Right. I'll tell you what, why don't we find some time to do a safety at work risk assessment together? Maybe just codify everything, so that when you have more people on site, it's all written down.'

His look of surprise turned into a grin, as if she'd just offered something beyond his wildest dreams. In truth, she'd offered something that was beyond *her* wildest dreams. She hadn't thought that she was ready to approach those issues yet, but apparently she was. Fair enough. Katya decided to go with the flow.

'Good. Yeah, we'll do that. How's tomorrow morning suit you?'

'Won't you be at your practice?'

His grin turned sheepish. 'Well, actually, that was the other thing I was going to say. I've got a locum starting this morning, just until the end of next week. I was thinking through the amount of work we'll have to get through in the next couple of weeks and it just wasn't going to happen. So I gave a friend of mine a call, and he's going to step into the breach for a little while.'

'Really? You think that's necessary?'

He gave her a long, thoughtful look. 'Yeah. I think that's necessary.'

CHAPTER SIX

KATYA HAD GONE to fetch a large cardboard box from her car, which apparently contained everything she needed to be comfortable in her office environment, and by nine o'clock she looked as if she had been there for months, sitting by the window, surrounded by plants, a brightly decorated coffee mug and a pot with yellow pencils.

'Do you really need that many pencils?' Luke looked up from fixing the legs to the frame of his own desk.

'No. They're pretty, though, aren't they?' She moved some of the pencils in the pot, as if she was putting the finishing touch to a flower arrangement, and then picked up the backup computer drive that Luke had left in its box on her desk. 'What am I supposed to do with this?'

'Just plug it into your computer… No, look, at the back there…' She was usually so capable, so self-sufficient with practical things. Her sudden bewilderment made Luke smile.

'In here?' She was staring helplessly at the machine in an unmistakable signal that he should come and look.

'That's it.' Luke wondered whether she'd break and actually ask for his help. He wanted her to, rather more than he was willing to admit. 'Then you have to install the software.'

'Right.' She frowned, rummaged in the box and extracted a DVD, putting it into the computer and staring at the screen. 'It says that it can't find the drive.'

'Did you plug it in properly?'

'I thought I did.' She pulled the connector cable out of the back of her computer and replaced it. 'Ah, that's better.' She wrinkled her nose, deliciously. 'No, it's not, it wants me to reformat something now….'

Her head sank into her hands, light from the window shining across her hair. It almost physically hurt not to drop what he was doing, go over there and run his fingers through it, smoothing the little strands that dropped across her face. 'Would you like me to have a go?' It appeared that he was the one who had broken first.

She looked up, grinning. 'Would you?' In a flash she'd jumped to her feet so that he could sit down in front of the screen. 'I thought you'd never ask.'

Suckered. Luke sat down and began to type. 'Here, aren't you going to finish this?' The plate, which contained the remaining half of her morning pastry, had followed her from the kitchen to her desk, and he pushed it towards her.

'Thanks.' She looked at it as if she might finish it and then changed her mind. 'Think I'll wrap it up and put it into the fridge for later.'

Along with the rest of her lunch from yesterday, no doubt. She had all the right intentions. She brought food, she started to eat, but she never seemed quite able to finish. Luke imagined that the pastry would still be in the fridge in three days' time, and she'd dispose of it then.

'What do you say we take a stroll around the reserve

when I've finished this?' She needed to see the layout of the place, and a brisk walk might help her work up a bit more of an appetite.

'Yes, I'd like that.' She was craning over his shoulder to see what he was doing, hovering maddeningly close. Luke's fingers began to tremble, and he clicked *Cancel* instead of *Install* by mistake.

'Right, then, let's go.'

Bruno trotted at Luke's heels, alert to the smells of the woodland. The trees and the quiet sunshine were doing just as he had hoped, and Katya seemed to relax from her state of perpetual watchfulness. She even seemed to be able to breathe more deeply here.

'Exactly what did Bruno do?' She was strolling next to him, the early-morning sun caressing her hair, making it shine like burnished gold.

'He was a search and rescue dog. Travelled all over the place with his handler, to disaster areas. He was ready to retire, and I was coming back to the UK so I took him.'

She looked down at Bruno, nodding slightly. 'So you weren't his handler?'

'No. I was a part of the team, though. I used to look after the dogs. Other animals that had been affected.'

'Not the human survivors?'

Luke laughed. Everyone said that. 'There were doctors on the team, too. And I did my share of digging, everyone did.' A little girl's face flashed into his mind. There was always one that you couldn't quite shake. Luke had dug for her in the wreckage of her family's house, given her water and then carried her to the medical tent. She was out there somewhere right now, and he often wondered if she remembered him the way he did her.

'I suppose…in poor rural communities people's animals can be the only thing that stands between them and starvation.'

'Exactly. And compassion doesn't make distinctions.'

She nodded. 'I expect you've seen a bit.' She was smiling at him, biting her lip. Wondering, perhaps, whether he'd seen enough to understand whatever it was that she hid so carefully.

'A bit. Some good and some bad.' He grinned at her. 'Actually, good and bad don't really cover it.'

'I imagine not.' The little grimace she gave him told Luke that she understood exactly what he was talking about. 'What made you decide to come home? If you don't mind my asking.'

He minded. Luke was about to give her the same carefully constructed sham of a story that he gave everyone else, but something stopped him. Maybe it was the sunshine. Or maybe this was a down payment on the honesty he planned on getting from her sometime soon.

'I came home because my wife asked me to.' He saw the shock in her eyes. 'My ex-wife. We'd been married for more than four years, and only just about clocked up two of them together. I was always only just back or just about to leave.'

'Oh.' She was lost for words, but seemed to be trying hard to find something to say. 'Yes. That's a good reason.'

'Seemed like it at the time. It turned out that my marriage worked a lot better when I wasn't around.' That was it. Luke was starting to feel sick, and that was generally a sign that he needed to leave this subject alone.

Katya appeared to have called time on the conversation as well. She murmured an apology, and let the subject slide. Just as well. If she'd shown any understanding of even these bare details of what Tanya had done, that would have just been another thing he needed to add to the list of things he had to come to terms with but couldn't. Luke took a sharp right turn and forged a way from the trees towards the steep incline, which had been a part of his morning run for the last two years, in an effort to escape those thoughts.

Katya fixed her eyes on Luke's back, concentrating on keeping up. Her legs were beginning to get shaky, but they were almost at the top of the hill and she concentrated on counting her footsteps.

'You okay?' His pace slackened and he turned for a moment.

Her lungs were bursting and her cheeks were probably redder than a tomato. 'Yes, fine.'

'We're nearly there. It's worth it for the view.'

Yeah, right. It was going to be worth it for the chance to stand still for a while and pretend to admire said view. Katya didn't have any breath to spare to answer him.

'What do you think?' He sat down beside her on a flat rock, right at the top. 'I thought I could put a couple of benches up here and a board with pointers to the various landmarks. You can see a long way from here on a good day.'

'Good idea.' Even if she couldn't manage more than a couple of words yet, sitting down had freed up enough energy for Katya to consider the landscape around her. It was beautiful. Rolling hills, farmland and in the distance the village. With a pair of binoculars she reckoned that she could pick out Olenka's coffee shop.

'There used to be a beacon up here. You can just about see the sea if you look hard.' Katya followed the line of his arm, and saw a faint, bluish haze in the distance. 'They lit a fire up here to warn of the approach of the Spanish Armada in 1588. Since then this place has been used for all kinds of things. There are stories of smugglers, witches and even a pair of lovers who flew off from the highest point here while being pursued by the young lady's father.' He paused, looking speculatively up at the clouds. 'I don't think that one's true. They probably just hid somewhere.'

'You prefer that explanation?'

'Yep. Give me stone-cold reasoning every time.' He grinned. 'It's what's got me this far.'

'How so?'

'The woodland we've just walked through was part of a big estate in the eighteenth century, owned by one of the wealthy families in the area. One of the men who owned it was a keen naturalist and he parcelled it off, stating that it must be kept as it was in perpetuity. I have a one-hundred-and-twenty-five-year lease on the land, granted by the trustees, and I had to jump through all sorts of hoops to get it. Show that I could maintain it properly, how I was going to use it for the community and for educational purposes.'

'But you've built on it…'

Luke shook his head. 'No, I bought the old barn and the land surrounding it, everything from here down to the road, as a separate parcel of land. In the last couple of years I've ploughed everything I have into making it work, so that I can develop the reserve properly.' He shrugged. 'There's nothing romantic about that, it's all a matter of calculating just how far the money that I can earn will stretch.'

Maybe that was just a matter of hard facts. But the idea behind it, the passion that had made Luke want to do it in the first place was a great deal more than just pounds and pence. Katya opened her mouth to answer but the shrill sound of his mobile phone cut her short.

'Yeah, Amanda. What's up? Has Charlie managed to frighten all my clients away yet?' Luke grinned at Katya and mouthed an apology.

'Mrs Charlton? She asked for a home visit? Did she say what the matter was?'

A voice sounded at the other end of the line, talking quickly, and Luke listened carefully. 'Yeah…okay, that's probably best.' His brow furrowed. 'No, on second thoughts, leave it with me. I'll go and see her… Yes, that's fine. Thanks for letting me know.'

'What's the matter?' Luke had finished the call, but he was still staring at the phone, obviously thinking about something.

'Oh, that was my practice nurse. It's probably nothing.' He got to his feet, and Katya followed him as he made his way towards the path that led back down to the foot of the beacon. 'I've got to go and see a patient of mine. I'd like you to come along with me.'

He kept up a punishing pace all the way back to the barn, and it wasn't until they were in the car that Katya had enough breath to ask the obvious question. 'Why do you want me to come, Luke?' She didn't want to voice the suspicion that he was reluctant to leave her on her own. Not until she had a bit more to go on.

He shrugged. 'I've just got a feeling about this one…

In any case, it'll give you a chance to see another side of the work.'

'What's your feeling?' The part about seeing another side of what Luke did sounded like an excuse.

'Like I said, it's probably nothing.'

'Come on, Luke, spill it. "Probably nothing" generally means "almost certainly something" in human medicine. I imagine it's much the same in veterinary medicine, too.'

He gave her a wry grin. 'Rosie was Maisie Charlton's husband's dog. He died last year and now Rosie's her only companion. She looks after her scrupulously.'

'And…?'

'So why is she calling the surgery, asking if someone could pop by sometime in the next few days because Rosie's looking a bit off colour? I know Maisie. If she thought there was something wrong with Rosie, she'd bring her straight round to the surgery, and if she couldn't get there herself, she'd have her daughter do it. She's only two streets away.'

'So you think there's something wrong with Maisie?'

'I don't know. Maybe. If there is, you're the one who's better qualified to deal with that than I am. If not, I'm sure you'll be very pleased to have the opportunity to see what I do for a living.'

'Shouldn't you call her doctor? He'd be the person to deal with this.'

'On what basis? Amanda said she asked Maisie if she was all right and she said she was fine. It's just a hunch.'

'All the same…' Katya wasn't exactly comfortable with the idea of just stopping by to give an opinion on anything, let alone medical issues. 'You can't rely on me to—'

'I'm not relying on you to do anything other than just accompany me, and possibly hold a few things if required.' He slowed the car, negotiating an almost blind corner, and then shot her a dark, melting look. 'We're human beings, Katya. It's okay to just call in on an old lady to see if she's all right, isn't it?'

Of course it was. 'You need me to answer that?'

He chuckled. 'No point in wasting your breath.'

CHAPTER SEVEN

MAISIE'S COTTAGE WAS in the newer part of the village. Not quite as picturesque as the ones on the main street, it was still a pretty place, with flowers in the front garden and a brightly painted door. And, as the ever practical Olenka had pointed out on more than one occasion, a newer property had fewer draughts.

Luke grabbed his bag from the back seat and strode up the front path. When there was no answer to the doorbell, he tried rapping with his knuckles and then calling through the letterbox.

'Perhaps she's gone out, Luke. Or decided to take Rosie to the surgery after all.'

He shook his head. 'I don't think so. Her handbag's on the hall table, along with her walking stick. She doesn't need it inside the house, but she always takes it with her when she goes out.'

'So what shall we do?' Katya stepped over the flower-beds, cupping her hand against the glass of the front window so she could see inside, but there was no one in the little sitting room.

'The back door's probably open.' Luke strode to the high gate that blocked the way through to the back of the house, pulling at it and finding it locked. 'If I gave you a leg up…'

Katya rolled her eyes, put her foot into his clasped hands and allowed him to hoist her upwards. 'If I get arrested for breaking and entering, I'm going to sing like a canary, Luke. I'll tell them this was all your idea.'

'Can you climb over?'

'Don't need to.' Katya reached down on the other side of the gate and undid the bolts. 'There, that's it. Let me down.'

He lowered her back onto the ground and pushed the gate open, following the path that ran around the house, Katya hard on his heels. When he twisted the handle, the back door gave inwards and he disappeared inside.

'Maisie. It's me, Luke.' He was kneeling down in front of a small, white-haired woman, sitting at the kitchen table.

'Luke.' Maisie smiled at him. 'I'm so glad you came. I'd like you to have a little look at Rosie if that's all right. She doesn't seem at all herself. I can't get her to wake up.'

Katya had already bent down to touch the dog, curled up in its basket by the door. There wasn't any point in Luke looking at her. She didn't need to be a vet to be able to tell that it was already dead. It had probably happened during the night sometime, rigor mortis having already set in. Luke shot a glance at her, and she shook her head.

'Okay, Maisie. I'll look at Rosie and my friend Katya will sit here with you. Is that all right?'

'Yes, dear. Thank you.'

Luke rose, moving one of the chairs so that it was facing Maisie, and Katya slipped past him and sat down.

'Hello, Maisie.' She took the old lady's hand. 'How are you feeling?'

'Oh, I'm all right.' Katya recognised that tone of voice. A bit more wishful thinking than veracity there. 'Katya. What a pretty name.'

Katya smiled at her, reaching out to lay her fingers on Maisie's flushed cheek. 'You feel very hot, Maisie. Are you having trouble breathing?'

'A little, dear.' Maisie tried to stifle a cough and failed. 'I've had a nasty cough for the last couple of days, but I think I'm on the mend now.'

Katya could hear Luke's voice behind her. Talking quietly to the animal as if it were still alive, soothing it. She'd seen some of the better doctors do that when they examined a patient to pronounce them dead. She'd done it herself. It was a last gesture of respect towards someone who had lived and been loved.

'Maisie, will you come through into the sitting room? I'll make you a cup of tea if you'd like.'

'No!' Maisie's grip was surprisingly strong, her nails digging into Katya's wrist. 'I want to stay here and hear what Luke says about Rosie.'

She knew. It just wasn't real to her, until someone said it. Katya didn't envy Luke the task. 'Okay, that's fine. Luke's just looking at her now…' She could hear Luke moving behind her, and the sound of him washing his hands at the kitchen sink.

He was there in the space of two laboured, wheezing breaths from Maisie. Kneeling down on the floor next to her. 'Maisie, I'm sorry. Rosie's dead.'

The old lady didn't cry. Hardly even flinched at his words. 'Thank you, Luke. I think I needed someone to tell me.'

'I know.' He took Maisie's hand. 'Does she have a rug or something I can cover her with?'

'Her favourite rug's in the cupboard under the stairs.' Maisie was almost choking, and it was hard to gauge whether it was illness or grief that was causing it.

'I'll go and get it.' Luke rose and disappeared for a moment, returning with a red-and-green plaid blanket, and tucking it carefully over Rosie. 'Now it's time to leave her to sleep, Maisie. Come with us.'

This time Maisie allowed herself to be supported to her feet and into the small sitting room. By the time they'd lowered her into an easy chair, her breathing was shallow and laboured.

'Maisie.' The old lady seemed unaware of her presence, and Katya took hold of her hand. 'Maisie, listen to me, this is important. You seem very breathless, particularly when you try to walk. Can you tell me how long you've been like this?'

'Just this morning. When I came downstairs, I had to stop halfway and sit down.' Maisie paused to gulp in a couple of breaths. 'I thought I might have to bump down on my bottom, like a frog.'

'And you were all right yesterday? Last night?'

'Just the cough, dear.' Maisie licked her lips. 'I'm very thirsty.'

'I'll go and make a cup of tea. Just close your eyes and rest for a minute.' Maisie's eyes fluttered closed, and Katya beckoned to Luke to follow her into the hall.

'What do you think?' Concern was written all over his face.

'I don't know. She's obviously upset about losing Rosie, and it's probably doubly difficult for her because Rosie was her husband's dog. She really doesn't seem well, though. I think we should try and get in touch with her family and call the doctor.'

He nodded. 'She has a daughter in the next village. I'll get her number and give her a call. Will you call the doctor? Maisie's probably with the high street medical practice, everyone around here is.'

'Okay, thanks.' Katya heaved out a sigh. Someone would be here soon, and the responsibility for Maisie's welfare would no longer be hers. The sooner the better, for Maisie's sake. 'Go back and sit with her and I'll call the doctor while the kettle's boiling.'

Katya was away in the kitchen for a while and when she returned she didn't have the promised cup of tea with her. She was clutching her phone, her face ashen.

'Did you get through to the doctor?' Luke had left a message on Maisie's daughter's answering machine, asking her to call him back.

'Yeah.' She was biting her lip. Almost crying. 'The receptionist finally put me through to him.'

'And?' Luke looked at Maisie. Her eyes were closed and she seemed to be asleep, her breathing a little less laboured now. He took Katya's arm and guided her to the doorway, just in case Maisie could hear them. 'What did he say?'

'I went through it all with him. He says that he'll come and see Maisie as soon as he can. Tonight, between six and eight.'

'Tonight? Can't he come any sooner?'

'He says not. I told him all my concerns, Luke, and he reckons she has a feverish cold. He said she should take some paracetamol.'

From what he'd seen of Maisie's condition and the look on Katya's face, that wasn't right. 'What do you think?'

There was clearly a battle going on in Katya's head. 'He's her doctor. He knows her best…'

And a doctor's word was law. Maybe Luke could tip the balance a little. 'What's your gut feeling?'

Her eyes inexplicably misted. 'My only gut feeling is that it's probably not a good idea to trust my intuition.' She leant one shoulder against the wall, seeming to need its support, and fixed her gaze on her feet.

'Katya, if you think there's something wrong, you have to act on it.'

'I could do more harm than good by interfering. If Maisie does just have a chest cold, then dragging her up to the hospital is only going to tire her out and upset her even more. Perhaps we should wait until her daughter gets here.'

'That could be hours. Katya, you did the right thing when I cut myself. You didn't even stop to think about it.' He held out his hand, daring her to look at the fading scar.

'You were hardly going to die from that. And I hadn't been on the phone with a doctor who practically told me to back off.'

The woman who knew what was right and had the guts to do it, whatever anyone said, was in there somewhere. It was just a matter of dragging her out of retirement. Luke strode through to the kitchen, opening drawers and cupboards until he found a little home first-aid box. Bending, he drew his own stethoscope from his bag.

'Here. Take these, there's a thermometer in the box. Go and make a decision. If you don't, I will.'

She took the stethoscope, seeming to lose some of her hesitancy as soon as it was in her hands. 'The lead's a bit longer than I'm used to.'

'Yeah, my patients are all shapes and sizes. Apart from that, it's pretty standard. You go and see to Maisie and I'll get that cup of tea you were threatening her with.'

When Luke tapped on the door a few minutes later, a cup of tea in his hand, he heard Katya's voice calling him inside. She was squinting at a thermometer, smiling in the face of Maisie's remonstrations that she was all right really.

'Well, you've got a temperature. And your chest sounds very bubbly. I'd like to call an ambulance and have the paramedics take a look at you, if that's okay.'

Maisie capitulated surprisingly quickly. Perhaps she'd just been waiting to be told that, too. 'All right, dear. If you think it's best.'

'Yes. Let's just be on the safe side, eh?' She picked up the phone and started to dial, leaving Luke to administer the tea.

She'd spoken quickly and authoritatively to the controller, but as soon as the ambulance arrived she seemed to melt away, leaving Luke to answer the door and speak to the crew. She was watching carefully, though, making sure that nothing was missed. Maisie seemed brighter now, but no one was disposed to take any chances.

'You were right to call us.' One of the crew drew Luke to one side, speaking softly. 'We're going to give her oxygen and we need to take her to hospital, get her checked out. Are you family?'

'No. I'm a vet, I called round to see Maisie's dog.'

'Ah, yes, you said that the dog had died and that it's given Maisie a bit of a shock.' The paramedic frowned. 'What do you think was the matter with it?'

'I can't say at the moment, but Rosie was pretty old. My first thought is a heart attack or stroke—it doesn't appear to be anything that could be connected with Maisie's illness.'

'Right. Well, I'll put that in my notes. I don't suppose you have a contact number for the family?'

'Yeah, right here. I've left a message for her daughter already, and I'll keep trying her until I reach her.'

The paramedic was nodding, scribbling all the information down on the form on his clipboard. 'Looks as if you've done a bit of human diagnosis this morning as well.'

'Not me. My colleague here is a nurse. She was the one who called you.'

Katya flushed bright red, and the paramedic looked up, acknowledging her with a nod. 'Are you going to ride with us?'

'Er...yes, I'd like to if that's all right.'

'Glad to have you along.' The paramedic finished writing and turned back to his colleague. 'Tony, what do you reckon? Will the trolley bed fit around that bend in the hallway?'

Luke turned back to Katya. 'I'll take Rosie down to the surgery. We'll look after her until Maisie's well enough to let us know what she wants to do. I'll ask Amanda to keep trying Maisie's daughter, and come down to the hospital to meet you.'

She hesitated. 'I may be a while...'

'That's okay. I can wait.'

If Katya had hesitated in going into the A and E department yesterday, she seemed to have no such reservations today. Luke had caught up with the ambulance, following it to the hospital, and watched as Katya climbed down from the back of the vehicle and accompanied

Maisie inside, without so much as a glance behind her. He parked the car and made his way back in time to see Katya and Maisie being shepherded towards a cubicle.

'I'll wait here,' he called after her, and she turned quickly and shot him a smile. 'Do you want me to get you anything?' The offer fell on deaf ears as the door closed behind them, and Luke supposed not. Searching in his pocket for change, he approached the two elderly women, obviously volunteers, who sat knitting behind the counter of the snack bar.

'That lettuce looks as if it's seen better days.' Luke had been concentrating on extracting the token piece of wilted greenery from his cheese salad roll and hadn't seen Katya approach.

'Yeah. Do you want some?'

She shook her head. 'Think I can resist the temptation.'

'Chocolate?' Luke offered her the bar he'd bought.

'Oh, now you're talking.' She flashed him a smile, taking the chocolate and tearing at the wrapper, breaking a square off. 'They're pretty well set up here.' She looked around her with obvious approval.

'Yeah, they're very good. How is she?' Luke couldn't imagine that Katya would be out here talking to him unless Maisie had already been seen.

'They're going to do some X-rays, but the doctor reckons it's probably pneumonia. He's going to keep her in for observation tonight.'

'So it's as you thought.' Luke wasn't about to let her forget that.

'Hmm.' She still couldn't give herself even that much credit. 'Any luck with Maisie's daughter?'

'Yes, Amanda managed to reach her, and she's on her way. She'll be here in about half an hour.'

'Good.' She wrapped the foil around the rest of the chocolate and put it back in his hand. She seemed distracted, worried about something, and Luke wondered whether it was Maisie or just her surroundings.

'What's on your mind, Katya?'

'Nothing.' She twisted her mouth apologetically. She wasn't a very good liar.

'What's on your mind?' He tried to imbue the request with as much authority as he could, but it still sounded something like a plea. It was becoming increasingly difficult to insulate himself against her thoughts and feelings.

'Nothing. Nothing, I…' Her eyes seemed to shine suddenly in the overhead strip lighting and she turned her head away from him.

'You what?' The words were rougher than he meant them to be. Weeks of wondering what on earth was going on with her lent an edge to them.

'You were right, Luke. And I might not have done anything if you hadn't pushed me.'

'You really think that?'

She plonked herself down on the seat next to him. 'I was about to just take her doctor's word for it. I didn't like it, and I knew it was wrong…' She shook her head slowly, staring at the floor.

Luke sighed. She was a very tough nut to crack. 'So you're going to beat yourself up about not being capable of making a decision then, when you do, you'll beat yourself up all over again for having thought about whether you should.' He shrugged. 'I'm sure there's logic to that somewhere, but I'm failing to see it at the moment.'

She rose to the challenge and faced him, eyes flashing. 'You're making me sound irrational.'

'Just saying.' He grinned at her provocatively.

'Oh! And I was going to thank you for believing in me.'

'Don't thank me. You did that one all by yourself.'

'Liar.' She leaned in to whisper the word in his ear then stood up and flounced away, leaving Luke chuckling to himself. That was better.

CHAPTER EIGHT

THEY WORKED UNTIL late that evening, Katya insisting that they should make up the time that they'd spent at the hospital. At eight o'clock Luke called a halt to their endeavours.

'Stop that now, or I'll pull the plug on you.' His hand hovered over the power switch of her computer in an effort to show that he meant business.

'Don't you dare! If I lose this document…'

'Save it, and shut your computer down. You're coming with me.' It was getting late and there was still something that Luke had to do that night.

'Okay, okay. Where are you going?'

He switched the lights out in the office and she followed him out of the barn, waiting while he locked the doors. As he led her across the uneven ground to his makeshift home, he was gratified to find that she followed him willingly, stroking Bruno's head as she went.

'Do you like tomato soup?' Luke moved to the area that he liked to call a kitchen and opened the refrigerator.

'Doesn't everyone?'

He shrugged. 'Suppose there must be someone who doesn't.' He held up the carton and she nodded her approval. 'Sit down. I won't be a minute.'

When he returned with the tray she was curled up in his easy chair, Bruno's head in her lap. She made to stand but Luke waved her back down again. 'Stay there.' He nudged Bruno out of the way and put the tray onto her knees. 'It's a bit makeshift, I'm afraid.'

'It's fine. Thanks, I was getting hungry.' She picked up one of the rolls and broke it in two, and Luke went to fetch his own tray and sat down on the sofa.

It was nice to have someone to eat with. Someone to pass the pepper and the Parmesan cheese. A reason to switch the lamp on so that he could see her face in the growing dusk. She had the sort of face that a man could fall in love with, without even having to try. If falling in love happened to be anywhere on that man's radar.

They were just two people, that was all. Luke couldn't think of a definition for it. 'Friends' seemed a bit presumptuous, and 'work colleagues' didn't quite cover it. He guessed he'd find out soon enough.

He cleared away the plates, noticing with approval that she'd finished her soup and one of the rolls, and sat back down. He couldn't go back now. 'Katya, I want to ask you something.'

She didn't even see it coming. Raised her gaze to his face, her lids heavy in the soft light, a little smile on her face. 'Yeah? What's that?'

'I said that I didn't need to know what happened to you.'

'Yes?' Her face stiffened into a mask.

'Well, I think that I do.'

She'd thought that he would ask that afternoon, but he hadn't. Then he'd put her off her guard with tomato soup and crusty rolls. Luke's interest in getting her to eat was second only to Olenka's and she'd thought that this was what he'd invited her over to his cabin for. He'd waited until she was relaxed, ready to stretch and think about making her way home, and then he'd hit her with it.

'Yeah. I suppose you do.' She'd known that this moment would come, but she hadn't reckoned on the panic that would twist her stomach when it did. Hadn't realised that she would care so much what Luke thought of her afterwards.

'You can tell me to mind my own damn business if you want. But as a friend…' He paused and considered the word. 'As a friend, I'm asking you.'

'So you can help me?' Defiance broke through the panic and saved her from crying, right there in front of him.

'No. So I can know you.'

At least he didn't make her sound like his good deed for the day. And strangely it was almost a relief. Katya wanted him to know her. What good was his approval when he didn't really know who she was?

'Okay. It's probably good to get this out of the way.' Right. Rationalise it. That was the way to go.

'I think so.' His face was soft in the light from the lamp. Tender almost. No, that wasn't true, it was definitely tender but Katya wasn't going to think about that. She was going to get this over with.

'Fourteen months ago I was working as a nurse in the renal health department. Our patients often came in for treatments regularly, and we got to know them well.'

'I imagine it's a difficult job.'

'Difficult. But very rewarding.' It didn't matter any more, that was over. 'There was a patient, Carl Davies, who was doing well physically, but mentally he was a mess. Didn't seem to have any family or friends and was obsessed with his own death, even though he wasn't critically ill. He refused to see the mental health team, but he would talk to me, and his doctor asked me if I could try and persuade him to take some help. It seemed to me that I was getting through, that I was making a difference.'

'What happened to him?'

'One night I was walking to the Underground from the hospital, and he was just there, in front of me. Talking so quickly, telling me that he…he loved me and that everything was going to be all right, we'd get married and have children.' Katya almost choked on the words. It must sound to Luke as if she'd led Carl on.

'That must have been terrifying.' His gaze was on her but, try as she may, Katya couldn't make out what Luke was thinking. 'Was anyone else there to help you?'

'We were in a little alleyway that ran behind the hospital buildings, it was a short cut through to the main street. I tried to reason with him but he was very insistent. He grabbed hold of me and told me that if he couldn't have me then no one would.' Katya brushed the tears from her face. They didn't matter, they were just her body's reaction to saying the words. 'Corny, eh?'

Luke smiled. At that one expression of solidarity from him, Katya felt her shoulders begin to shake, and she pulled herself upright. She couldn't let go, not now. 'It was only twenty yards to the street, and I tried to run, but he slammed me up against some railings. Afterwards I had a bruise, all the way down the side of my face.' In the scheme of things that had been nothing. But that little thing always seemed to hurt the most.

It was as if she'd slapped him. Luke whispered something that she didn't catch, shaking his head slowly.

'At first I thought that he was hitting my back. Then I felt blood, running down inside my clothes. He'd stabbed me six times.'

'Katya.' His hands were clenched tightly together now, in front of him, the knuckles showing white from the pressure. 'Katya, I'm so sorry.'

'It's okay. Really, it's okay.' He moved towards her and she waved him away. He'd thought that was all, but she hadn't got to the worst of it yet. 'I was lucky. The hospital staff used that alleyway all the time, and the people who found me were doctors. If they'd tried to move me the wounds would probably have ruptured and I would have bled out, but they knew what to do and saved my life.'

'And the man who attacked you? Did they catch him?' He seemed to know that there was more now.

'I was taken straight up to the operating theatre and couldn't give a statement, but the police made enquiries and the next day they went to his flat and found him dead. He'd gone back there and taken an overdose.' She knotted her fingers together in her lap, twisting them tightly until they hurt.

'He hadn't done it until the following morning. If they'd found me a little sooner, if I'd just been able to tell someone, perhaps they could have saved him.'

'And perhaps they wouldn't have been able to. You're not responsible for his actions.'

That didn't stop her from wondering, though, trying to piece together the fleeting moments of consciousness, before darkness had finally taken over. 'I guess that's just one of the things I'll never know. The police said he'd been following me for a couple of months, photographing me, and he had things from my flat.'

'And you never suspected?'

'No. Sometimes I had an odd feeling when I got back home, as if something wasn't quite right, but I never dreamed that anyone had been there. The police psychologist said that he might have spent whole days there while I was at work, he had lists of everything that I kept in the drawers and cupboards.' Katya wiped her face with her hand and Luke jumped to his feet, almost running into the kitchen and reappearing with a roll of kitchen towel.

'Here.' He knelt in front of her, tearing off a piece, but he didn't give it to her. Gently, tenderly he dried her tears himself. 'Katya, you can't think for one moment that any of this was your fault.'

'I thought that I was making progress with him. I was wrong. I was just tearing his life apart.'

'But he must have had some mental problems. No sane person does those things.'

Katya shrugged. He was trying his best to make excuses for her, but even Luke couldn't lift the blame from her shoulders. 'That all came out at the inquest. It wasn't on his medical notes, he'd moved cities and that part of his medical history hadn't followed him. But I should have seen. I spent time with him, I should have realised.'

So many people had been there for her, and now it was Luke. Holding her as if she'd break, and in truth Katya wasn't sure that she wouldn't. Murmuring soft words, telling her that she was safe now and that it hadn't been her fault. She couldn't believe him. Maybe in another thirty years she would. Perhaps she should keep in touch with Luke so she could write and tell him that he'd been right all along.

She was as crazy as Carl had been. Trying to build a future that didn't exist. Looking for absolution where there was none. This was her life now, and there were plenty of other people who had to put up with a great deal more. Regretfully, she pulled away from him, tearing another piece of kitchen towel from the roll and blowing her nose.

'Six times.' The number seemed to give him more pain than it did her. Six was just a number, and all it showed was that she'd been too bloody pig-headed to die.

'Yep. Got the scars to prove it. For a while it was touch and go, but I didn't know anything about that at the time. The surgeons repaired me and stitched me back up and here I am.'

Her flippancy was too much for him. He sat back on his heels, dipping his head, and she saw him wipe his eyes quickly. When he looked at her again his eyes were naked. All the pain that she felt, with a bit more on top, was written across his face.

'It's okay, really, Luke.'

He grinned at her. 'That's my line, isn't it?'

It occurred to Katya that this was the one thing he hadn't said. He hadn't told her that everything was okay, the way that most people did. The look on his face told her that he knew damn well that it wasn't okay and that it wouldn't be for the foreseeable future.

'Thanks. For not judging me.'

'Why would I?'

Bruno was pawing at his arm and Luke turned, trying to quiet him. 'Get off, Bruno.' He shrugged. 'He wants me to let him rescue you.'

Katya giggled through the last of her tears and stretched her arms around the dog's neck. 'Go on, then, boy.' Bruno planted his front paws on her lap, nuzzling her neck, his tail wagging, and Luke got to his feet.

'I'll make a cup of tea.'

That was the end of it, then. No questions, no wanting to know what the police had said, what the coroner's verdict had been. Luke didn't seem to need to know those things.

'Thanks. I could do with one.' She needed to know something first. 'Do I still have a job, then?'

Shock registered on his face. 'If you don't turn up for work tomorrow, I'll be coming to get you.' He tapped Bruno on the shoulder, motioning him away from her, and took her hand, pulling her to her feet. 'Do you hear me, Katya?'

'Yes. I hear you. I'll be here.'

The world seemed to stop. Luke's hands moved, and she could almost feel them on her waist, pulling her towards him. He'd be gentle but insistent. His fingers would skim her back, soothing the throb of her scars, and then he would give her the passion that was bursting in his eyes. Luke's kiss would be everything that her mind could not frame but that her instinct knew all about.

She felt his fingers on her shoulder and something inside began to beg for more. His lips skimmed her cheek and she shivered at the sharp brush of his chin. Then he stepped back.

'Don't be late. And don't forget that it's your turn to fetch breakfast.'

* * *

He'd insisted on running her home last night and Katya had given in, not altogether unhappy in the knowledge that his eyes had been on her as she'd hurried through the darkness to Olenka's front door. It hadn't been until she was inside, the door closed firmly behind her, that she had heard the engine of his SUV choke into life and drive away. And now, at seven-thirty sharp the next morning, he was back.

She'd wondered whether he would follow her into the coffee shop, the way her parents had followed her everywhere once she'd been well enough to go out again. But he stayed put, one arm draped across the steering wheel, looking just drowsy enough to remind Katya that she'd felt something had been missing when she'd woken up that morning. That before she'd opened her eyes to make absolutely sure where she was, she'd almost reached out for him.

'Luke...last night.' This probably wasn't the best time to bring it up. Luke was negotiating the narrow country lanes and she was concentrating on balancing the coffee on her knees. On second thoughts, that made it the perfect time. Both of them had their hands full with other things.

'Yes?'

'I wanted to know if it changed anything. Anything about the work, I mean, going into the hospital.'

The car skidded to a halt, and he directed it off the road into a lay-by. Luke turned and gave her the full force of his stare. 'Why would it?'

'You might be having second thoughts. On my role.' Yesterday might have changed a lot of things. Her indecision over Maisie. Telling him about what had happened with Carl. Luke had to see now that he couldn't rely on her judgement.

'Well, since you ask, I have.' He reached forward and took one of the cardboard beakers from the holder on her lap, and Katya snatched her hand away for fear that his fingers might touch hers.

'I thought a lot about things last night. I realise that maybe I've been pushing you too hard. Making you take the phone. Making you make a decision about Maisie yesterday. It can't have been easy for you, taking on a new job, doing all that, having to look over your shoulder all the time.'

He'd noticed. Of course he had, Luke noticed everything, the way she couldn't help checking if anyone was following her, how she couldn't trust herself any more. And here came his verdict on it all. He was going to say that she couldn't cope.

Katya hung her head, closing her eyes so he couldn't see her tears. Heard the seat creak as he moved. Caught his clean, intoxicating scent. Something new seemed to wake in the pit of her stomach. Something that railed against what was about to happen. 'You were right to push me, Luke. I needed to do those things, and I'm glad I did.'

'Good. In that case, I was thinking you might like to consider becoming more involved with the hospital side of the operation. Take sole responsibility for liaising with Laura and supervising the visits. You can make this project more successful than I ever could.'

'But…I said…' Katya's eyes flew open in surprise, sending a tear down her cheek. She'd just wanted to be able to continue with what she was already doing. This sounded like a promotion.

'I know what you said, and if you don't want to do it, that's fine.' He stretched in his seat and took a sip of coffee. 'Eugh! That's yours, I think.' He handed the beaker back and took the other from her shaking fingers.

'I don't know...' Katya didn't want to mess things up for him. She knew how much this project meant to Luke.

He nodded, making no move to start the engine again. Drank coffee. Waited. Katya took the lid off her own coffee and took a swig. She could wait, too.

'I've been with you at the hospital twice now, and each time you showed me something. You're in your element there. Why punish yourself by not allowing yourself to do what you do best?'

'I'm not...' Okay. Maybe she *was* punishing herself. But she'd messed up and there were consequences to that, even if Luke didn't see them.

'Will you think about it? It's not a yes or no thing, you can try it out and see how it goes.' He opened the car door and got out, and the SUV rocked to one side slightly as he leant against it. 'It's a beautiful morning.'

It was. The sun-dappled fields, almost ready for harvest, the hedgerows buzzing with life. Katya gave in and joined him.

'Bring the bag with you, we'll walk down to the stream.' Luke didn't wait for her assent, just strolled down to a small gulley and perched himself on a patch of grass on its bank.

'We have to make this project work, you know. This is not my personal rehabilitation scheme.'

He laughed, retrieving a muffin from the bag she carried and taking a hungry bite. 'Never thought for one minute that it was. I was reckoning that it would take some of the weight off my shoulders.'

It would at that. 'Okay. I'll think about it.'

'Good.' Now that he'd got his way, his attention seemed to wander. 'This is a nice spot for breakfast, don't you think?'

Katya laughed. He was almost boyish sometimes, so ready to drink in the simple pleasures of life. 'Yes, it is.' There was no harm in taking this just as long as she remembered not to get greedy and start wanting everything.

CHAPTER NINE

THE WEEKS PASSED in a blur of activity. Katya could barely remember when she'd slept or eaten so well, and even though they worked hard, there was usually a break at some time during the day for a walk through the wooded reserve. She was getting to know the places where the foxes had raised their young that spring, where the badger sets were and which birds made which calls.

Luke seemed happy, too. That was a problem in itself, because when he was happy he was even more difficult to resist. Impulsive, sometimes angry when red tape got in his way, but never for very long, and creative with his solutions. And, dammit, every time he smiled it made Katya's head spin slightly, as if only Luke could give her the oxygen she needed to keep on breathing.

The place was beginning to come alive. The dog school was going to open ahead of schedule in two months' time and another desk, dedicated to volunteers helping with the reserve, joined theirs in the large, bright office space. When Luke's practice was moved up to the new surgery, the car park began to fill and empty at regular intervals.

'Are we ready for the nature tour this afternoon?'

The one thing that Luke always made time for in his day was breakfast with Katya. This morning, though, he seemed a little out of sorts.

'Pretty much. I still have to get crayons and paper for the drawing session afterwards and set up the tables.' At the moment the large exhibition space had nothing to exhibit, so Katya had turned it into an activities area for the time being.

'Frank's coming in later, he'll help with that.' A retired carpenter and avid amateur naturalist, Frank had taken to drifting into the reserve a couple of times a week, and when he wasn't off somewhere with Luke, he'd sit by Katya's desk, drinking tea.

'Do you think I can get him to come on the walk with us? I think he'd love it and he can fill in on the bits I'm not sure of.'

'I dare say he would. Just ask him.' Luke was fiddling with some printed sheets that he'd pulled out of his notecase, cursing under his breath when he almost dropped them, spilling his coffee in the process.

'You okay?'

'I'm fine.' He pursed his lips, as if that was only a provisional assessment. 'I've had an email.'

'Yes? What about?'

He put two sheets of paper on the table in front of her. The top one, dated the previous day, was a simple covering note from her old boss at the hospital. 'What does Evan want with you?' She pushed the bowl in front of her aside and focussed on the second sheet.

'A reference.'

'What does he want that for?' She scanned the paper in front of her and the university logo answered her own question. 'Oh. I see.'

'Not sure that I do.'

'This is from last year. I had a place at university for a community health practitioner course. I couldn't take it up because I was still in hospital when term started.' The look in Luke's eyes was making her nervous.

'But you're thinking of taking it up now.'

So that was it. He thought she'd gone behind his back and applied for a place at university. 'If I was, I would have said something. Evan contacted the university last year and requested that they keep my place open for this year. There must be some kind of mix-up.'

'It's a great opportunity for you…' One that Luke didn't seem too pleased about.

'It's what I wanted to do last year. Not now. I don't understand why this was sent to you.' Katya wondered if she was protesting too much. Luke wasn't looking particularly convinced.

He picked up the sheets of paper, studying them carefully. 'I wouldn't stand in your way, Katya. If you want to leave, you should just say so, I'd give you a great reference.'

He seemed determined on making something out of nothing. 'I don't need a reference, Luke. The university must have assumed I was taking up my place this year and sent this to Evan because he was shown as my line manager on my application form. And he forwarded it on to you. He must have got your email address from when you took up my references.'

Luke nodded. 'Yeah.' The look of dull betrayal was ebbing out of his eyes. 'So this is all a mistake?'

'It's just paperwork, Luke. I expect they send these things out to everyone.' Katya didn't know why she was trembling. How 'just a job' had suddenly become so personal. And how she of all people should feel such inexplicable joy because Luke didn't want her to leave.

Luke felt as if his blood had finally started to circulate again in his veins. Ever since he'd looked at his email inbox last night and found this, he'd felt cold, as if autumn had skipped a beat and winter had set in. He had been thinking about how Tanya had lied to him, stringing him along until she had been ready to leave. It had taken an almost superhuman effort to believe Katya, but acting suspicious over every little thing she did wasn't going to help anyone.

All the same, even if it was all a mistake, she'd wanted to do this once. Would have done it if she hadn't been attacked. 'You know, if you haven't already been thinking about whether you can take your place up this year, perhaps you should now.' He wouldn't beg her to stay. Not the way he'd begged Tanya.

She twisted her mouth in a grimace. 'Don't you believe me, Luke?' Tears welled up in her eyes and the enormity of what Luke had done hit him suddenly, rushing up at him as if he'd thrown himself off the roof above his head with no clear plan about where he might land.

'Katya, don't, please. I believe you.' He'd made a fool of himself. Actually, it was worse than that, he'd done the very thing that had made her fearful in the first place. The way he'd jumped to conclusions and shown so little trust in her. He might just as well have sneaked into her room and rummaged through her underwear drawer, the way that other guy had.

He had to show her that this was different. 'Will you do something for me?'

'What's that?' Her beautiful eyes were dull with resentment. She seemed to want to leave this alone as much as he did, but Luke couldn't let her move on just yet.

'Will you give this university place some serious thought? Don't just dismiss it out of hand.'

She frowned at him. 'I told you, Luke…'

'You wanted to go last year. What's changed?'

'I'm not ready for it. It's community based medicine, it involves working on my own with people in their homes…' She tailed off into silence. Everything had changed for her since last year, he should have been more sensitive to that. But still he pushed her, not sure quite what he wanted to hear from her now.

'You can only put your dreams on hold for so long, Katya. Sometime you're going to have to either follow them or give them up.'

She didn't answer. This *was* her dream, then. It was so right for her it was almost laughable that she should be hesitating.

'I'll write the reference anyway.' He picked up his newspaper from the table as a sign that this was an end to it.

She narrowed her eyes at him, and he ignored her. One of the things he loved about Katya was that she never could hold on to her anger. That gross, destructive thing that curled around his heart every time he thought about what Tanya had taken away from him was alien to her. She wouldn't be cross with him for long. 'You're not writing anything unless I say you can.'

'Is that just about you, or in general?'

She shook her head slowly, the hint of a smile on her lips. 'You drive me crazy sometimes.'

Luke spread the newspaper and reached for his coffee. Crazy he could deal with. 'Yeah. I know.'

It had rained steadily all morning, summer beginning to give way to an autumn chill. Just as Katya was beginning to despair of what she was going to do with a group of rowdy seven-year-olds, the skies cleared and she and Frank were able to lead them through the woodland paths without getting soaked to the skin.

Luke was nowhere in evidence. Perhaps he was trying to work out what had happened between them that morning. If he got anywhere with that, he might give her a couple of clues. Whatever he was doing, he was taking his time, because it wasn't until the school bus had come and gone and she and Frank were clearing away the mess of crayons and paper that he made a brief appearance.

'Nice to have something in here to brighten the place up at last.' He was smiling, surveying the pictures that Katya had pinned to the long cork board that ran the length of one wall. Clearly he'd made the same decision as Katya, and reckoned that this morning was better forgotten. 'I like that one.'

He pointed out one that showed a figure with an unruly mop of orange hair, standing underneath a tree. 'That butterfly looks as if it's about to take your head off.'

'How did you know it was supposed to be me?' It was her. Joanne had presented the picture to Katya, telling her so, and Katya had thanked her profusely.

'Well, it's not going to be me, is it?' Frank nudged her, running his hand over his bald head.

'The colours on the chalk blue are just right.' Luke

ignored the fact that in comparison to the tree and the figure standing beneath it, the butterfly had a wingspan of about fifteen feet.

'Yes, we saw some.' Katya grinned at him. 'Not that big, of course.'

'No.' He stuck his hands into the pockets of his jeans. 'Probably just as well. It'd make a great B movie, though. *Rampage of the Killer Butterflies.*' There was something different about him. He was trying just that bit too hard to be nice, as if there was something he wanted to say but wouldn't. Katya wondered whether he'd be around when she brought breakfast tomorrow morning or whether he'd find some excuse not to be there.

'Well, I'd better be off.' Frank picked up his coat and pulled it on. 'Looks as if it's about to rain again.'

Frank didn't need his countryman's instinct to tell him that. The sky was almost black and it was so dark that you could have been forgiven for thinking that an early dusk had fallen.

'Yeah. Thanks, Frank. See you next week?' Luke turned and shook Frank's hand. He never failed to acknowledge the efforts of the volunteers and friends who popped in to help out.

'You will. The wife's sister is coming to stay, so I might be camping out here.'

Luke laughed. 'You're always welcome. Why don't you get Helen to bring her sister up here one day? We'll arrange for tea and cakes and someone will show them around.'

'As long as it's not me.' Frank grimaced. 'I'll be here for a bit of peace.'

'That's okay, I'll show them round and you can

mosey off with Luke and build your tree house.' Frank and Luke had plans for a tree house, which were looking more and more elaborate by the day.

'Don't think we're quite ready to start yet, do you?' Luke shot Frank a glance and Frank shook his head.

'No. Spring's the time.' Frank spoke authoritatively. The tree house was clearly one of those projects where the thinking was more important than the doing and Katya guessed that a few long winter evenings in the pub with Luke, ruminating over materials and structure, were critical to the plan. 'I'll tell Helen. She'll be pleased.'

With that he was gone. Katya was alone with Luke. Not for long enough to even wonder what to say next, though. 'I'd better be getting down to my surgery. See you tomorrow, for breakfast.'

It was almost a question, but not quite. 'Yeah. See you then.'

Katya hadn't meant to stay behind this long, but the incessant nag at the back of her mind of something unresolved had kept her at her desk, answering emails that she could just as well have left until the morning. The rain came, rattling against the huge picture windows, and headlights curved in and out of the car park as Luke's patients were ferried by their owners to and from the surgery. She pulled a thick cardigan around her shoulders and concentrated on the report that Laura had sent, giving feedback from patients and staff on the first phase of hospital visits.

'What are you still doing here?' She hadn't heard Luke come upstairs, and she could hardly see him, right over there by the door, away from the pool of light around her desk.

'I was just finishing off an email to Laura. I guess I should be making tracks.'

Luke advanced towards her, just enough so she could see him nod. 'Yes, you should. It's a filthy night.'

And he was going to be out here, on his own, in a prefabricated cabin. Here, in the main building, it was warm, dry and comfortable, and for the first time Katya realised that Luke had given that up in order to get this place started. 'Are you going to be all right?'

He shrugged, as if the idea had never occurred to him. 'Of course. My cabin's just fine, it was home for the whole of last winter and I seem to have survived. A few leaks, but nothing major.'

Now wasn't the time to persuade him that he really ought to do something about his living arrangements. Maybe she'd mention it tomorrow. Not that it was any of her business. Katya pulled on her jacket and shut down her computer.

'I'll walk you to your car.'

'No, don't bother…'

He caught her arm as she walked past him. 'Then I'll have to say it here. I'm sorry, Katya.'

There was no point in pretending that she didn't know what he was talking about. 'Again?'

'The first time wasn't enough.' He knew as well as she did that there was more to say, before they could leave this behind. It was too hard, though. Too much of a risk.

'It doesn't matter, Luke. It was just a misunderstanding.'

He didn't believe that any more than she did. This

morning he'd been jealous and possessive and she'd been upset and defensive. Those weren't the kinds of things that friends or work colleagues did: it looked a lot more like the way that lovers behaved. And now they were stuck in some kind of no man's land, between the two.

Somehow, he'd got too close. Or maybe she had moved towards him. Their bodies were almost touching. And his fingertips had found their way to hers.

'Luke...?'

He answered the question that she didn't dare ask. 'You don't need to be afraid. It's okay.'

The simple movement involved in stretching her body upwards, moving her face towards his, seemed to throw off all her doubts. His hands around her waist steadied her and she kissed him, feeling the sensation juddering through her own body and into his. 'Is that...?'

'Anything's okay. Let's just find our own way, shall we?'

He held her hand. Brought it slowly to his lips and kissed the knuckles, one by one. Waited, before moving his mouth to the sensitive spot on the inside of her wrist. Kissed her on the lips, a sweet summer breeze that turned into a hurricane, tearing a shaking response from her.

She backed him against the wall. He unhooked her handbag from her shoulder and slid her coat off, dropping them both on the floor. Then he pulled her in, holding her tight, kissing her slowly.

She moved against him and heard his sharp intake of breath. Felt his body harden. Good. That was good. That was just exactly what she wanted. It was killing her as well, though. Katya was hardly aware of having expressed the sentiment, but she must have done because Luke answered.

'You'll survive. You're a lot tougher than I am.'

'Do you really think so?' Suddenly it mattered that these weren't just words. She wanted Luke to mean them.

'Yes, I do.' There was no doubt about the sincerity in his voice. No doubt about the passion either. They'd driven each other to the very edge of distraction, and along with all the finer feelings there was pure wanting now, which echoed deep in the pit of her stomach.

Where next? She knew exactly where she wanted to be with Luke. Naked somewhere, in the darkness. Wrapped in his tenderness while he coaxed the fury of her passion out of the prison she'd held it in for so long. Where would they go? There was nowhere in the office, and his cabin seemed like an interminable trek from here.

Luke would find somewhere. She trusted him to do this right. Katya reached forward and undid one of his shirt buttons.

'Do that again.' There was an edge of command in his voice.

'You mean…' She undid another, this time daring to let her fingers trace lightly across the magnificent, uncharted territory of his chest. 'Like that?'

He groaned. 'Just like that, honey.'

She explored some more, just to feel the way his body moved under her touch. To hear his sharp intake of breath when her thumb found the sweet, sensitive spot at the base of his ear.

'Katya, I…'

Excitement shimmered through her body. She hung on to him and he held her tight, seeming to brace himself against its force. 'I know, Luke.' This was so sweet. Such heady pleasure.

'We belong together, Katya.'

She was suddenly blind to everything else. Instinct took over, and before she knew quite what she was doing her foot had connected with his shin, and she was staggering backwards.

CHAPTER TEN

SHE'D BEEN BLOOMING in his arms, like some exotic flower. Heavy lids over her bright, liquid eyes. Clinging to him as her body started to shudder, trusting him to take her softly into the arms of sweet oblivion. He couldn't help it. It had just slipped out.

'Ow! Katya?' The overhead lights flipped on and for a moment Luke was blind as well as lame.

She took a rasping lungful of air. Then another. She was backing away from him, a look of horror on her face.

'Katya, what's the matter?' The sudden plunge from all-consuming pleasure to sheer panic hit him like a fall from thirty feet, and Luke's head spun. What had he done?

He knew exactly what he'd done. That morning he'd acted like a jealous lover, and he'd tried to justify that by transforming aching want into deed. He'd said the same things that he'd said to Tanya, in the unconscious hope that Katya's response might be something different. He'd damned himself with his own words.

'Sorry. Sorry. I'm so sorry.' Luke wondered whether he should fetch a paper bag as she looked as if she was about to have a panic attack. 'Your ankle.'

'It's okay, Katya. It's all right.' Once again the instinct to hold her grappled with the knowledge that if he tried she'd probably make a bolt for the bathroom and lock herself in. 'You don't need to be sorry for anything.'

She was twisting her fingers together, as if trying to snap them off. The kick she'd given him was clearly now hurting her more than it did him. 'Are you sure your ankle's okay?'

The thought occurred to Luke that if he'd been rolling on the floor in agony she'd probably be at his side. Perhaps the pain of a knee to the groin would have been worth it. Maybe not. Even if it was a little more in keeping with what he deserved.

'It's fine.' He tentatively put his weight on the ankle. 'See, I think I'll walk again. Might even be able to play the piano.'

The joke fell on deaf ears. 'Luke, I'm so sorry.'

'Hey. It's okay. I said that anything was okay.' Granted, he hadn't exactly had this in mind. Perhaps he should be a little more precise next time. Although there obviously wasn't going to be a next time. He wouldn't say those words again, not to anyone.

She was looking at him, her face twisted with some emotion that Luke couldn't divine, her chest rising and falling quickly. There was no right thing to do next. 'I don't suppose you'd like a cup of tea?'

'What?' She looked at him as if he was stark, staring mad. If anyone ever needed proof that her judgement was sound, there it was, written all over her face.

'Peace offering. If I go to the kitchen and make a cup of tea, it gives us both a chance to take a breath. I give you the tea, which is nurturing, and you take it, which shows that you're considering not killing me. Then we talk a bit…' He shrugged. He didn't much want to talk about it, but maybe she did.

Relief showed in her face. 'I'm not considering killing you. Can we pass on the tea?'

'Yeah, sure.' From the look of it, she wanted to pass on the talking, too. That was fine with Luke. He just wanted to pretend that today had never happened.

Katya couldn't stop the words from repeating, over and over, like a phrase from some sick song. As Luke had spoken them, the memory had shot into her head, how she'd been pinned to the railings, feeling the warm trickle down her back. How the last time that Carl Davies had pushed the knife in, he'd whispered them into her ear, intending that they should be the last words she ever heard.

Maybe if Luke hadn't seemed so possessive that morning, she wouldn't have panicked. The only slim thread of positivity in all of this was that she hadn't remembered the moves she'd learnt at that self-defence class she'd gone to and tried to do some more permanent damage.

'We haven't broken the law, Katya.' He was still keeping his distance. Probably staying out of kicking range.

'No, we haven't. Maybe we broke the rules.' Luke was a good friend, and as sexy as hell, and that lethal combination had drawn her into something that she clearly couldn't handle. Territory where cold logic no longer applied, and feeling… She couldn't rely on feeling, and that was that.

'I won't tell if you don't.' He was offering her a way back. 'We made a mistake. We can pretend it never happened.'

It had, though. But maybe Luke was right. Maybe they could just ignore what they'd done and it would obligingly go away. She ventured a smile and the one she got in return emboldened her. 'Are you up for breakfast tomorrow? It's my turn…'

'Yeah, of course.' He was smiling still, but beyond that she saw nothing. It was as if an impenetrable barrier had rolled down over his thoughts and feelings and they were now shut up tight, away from prying eyes.

'Good. I'll get off home now, then. If you're sure you're okay.'

'I'll manage. Just to prove it to you, I'll walk you to your car.'

'No need. Really.'

He grinned at her, shaking his head. 'It's dark and wet out there. Stay here, while I fetch a torch.'

He jogged across the newly laid car park, which glistened with a fine sheen of water now that tarmac had replaced gravel, leaving her to stand in the shelter of the entrance to the barn. One long stride to avoid the mud around his cabin and he was inside.

The rain got heavier again, and water seemed to slough off the hard surface of the car park, draining off down the hill. The lights in the cabin went on as Luke shut the door behind him, and the whole place seemed to shiver as the wind drove around it, rain hitting its sides in waves.

It wasn't seeming to shiver, it actually was shivering. A cracking noise sliced through the sound of the storm, and almost in slow motion the cabin tipped and slid, nearly breaking in half as the brick supports beneath it disintegrated. It teetered for a moment and then gracefully tipped onto its side.

CHAPTER ELEVEN

'LUKE! LUKE!' KATYA screamed his name in the darkness, starting forward towards the cabin. One of the windows had flopped open and hung against the wall, almost touching the ground, and she saw Bruno appear, jumping down and careening towards her.

'I'm coming!' Bruno was darting back and forth, as if urging Katya to help his master.

She didn't need any encouragement. Stumbling through the mud towards the open window, she braced herself against the frame, ready to lever herself inside.

'Stay there!' Luke's voice rang out in the darkness, so urgent that for a moment she froze.

'Luke! Are you all right?'

'Yes. Stay where you are, don't come inside. And don't let Bruno back in here.' A torch came on, its beam flipping around the remains of the cabin and then swinging towards her, almost blinding her. She could hear Luke moving around and then his unsteady footsteps came towards her.

Katya caught Bruno's collar and held tight, pulling him away from the open window. Some scrapes and a soft curse, and then Luke appeared at the window, climbing out painfully and lowering himself to the ground. Even in the darkness she could see that he was hurt. 'Are you okay, Luke? Take my arm.'

Now that his master was here, Bruno wasn't about to go back inside, and she let go of his collar, letting him follow them as she took Luke's arm, wrapping it around her neck to steady him as she led the way slowly back to the barn.

He sank onto the wooden settle in the hallway. 'Katya, could you go downstairs to the surgery? There are some clean towels in the cupboard in my consulting room.' Bruno was sitting at his feet, anxiously nosing at his master's hand.

'Are you all right, Luke?'

He waved away her concern. 'Please, Katya. Go.'

He was obviously not going to allow her to tend to his needs until he'd satisfied himself that Bruno was unhurt. There wasn't much point in arguing with Luke, and the only thing she could do was to hurry things along a bit. 'Okay. Don't move until I get back.'

He couldn't even follow that simple instruction. When she returned he was checking Bruno's legs and body, nodding in satisfaction with what he found. 'All right, then, old boy. Open up.' He gently tugged at Bruno's jaw, and the animal yawned widely at him. 'Good. Well done, mate.'

He looked up at Katya, his face full of relief. 'Thanks. Could you hand me one of those towels, please?' He winced as he reached for it.

'Stay there, Luke. I'll do it.' She opened up a towel, called Bruno over and started to dry him. Bruno's eyes never left his master and he twisted fretfully in Katya's arms.

'What happened? Did you hit your head?' She was still rubbing Bruno vigorously.

'No. I think that's about the only part of me I didn't hit.'

'Are you sure? I couldn't hear you moving around when I first got to the cabin. I thought you must be unconscious.'

'Nah. I felt the cabin begin to go, grabbed Bruno and tried to get him out. When it tipped over, he landed right on top of me.'

'So he winded you?'

'Yeah. Seems that I broke his fall.' He pulled a face. 'The sofa didn't help much either. That thing's got a few sharp edges I didn't know about.' He flexed one arm experimentally but seemed to decide that wasn't a good idea.

'Any trouble breathing?'

'No. As long as I don't get too enthusiastic about it.' He grinned at her. 'I'm okay.'

'You let me be the judge of that.' Katya gave him the sternest look that she could muster and let Bruno go. 'No…Bruno!' He took three steps and shook himself vigorously, spraying the remains of the water in his coat all over the walls.

'Okay, boy.' Bruno had returned to nuzzle at Luke's hand, and he was grinning at the dog. 'Leave it out, mate.'

'Stop it, both of you.' Katya could feel tears pricking at her eyes. This wasn't a boy's adventure with his dog; Luke could have sustained some major damage. 'Luke, you've got blood on you, and as it's clearly not Bruno's or mine, it must be yours. Bruno, over there.' She pointed to the corner.

'Go on.' Luke motioned Bruno quietly away from him, and the animal sat, watching intently as Katya carefully began to ease Luke's jacket off. 'Sorry.'

'That's okay. People in shock do a lot of odd things. I'm used to it.' Katya dropped his jacket on the floor and set about rolling up his sleeve, to trace the source of the blood, which, diluted with rainwater, seemed to be all over the place.

'I'm not…' He heaved a sigh. 'I'll leave you to be the best judge of that, shall I?'

'You do that. You've got a nasty graze on your elbow but you'll live. I'll clean that up in a minute.' She took a deep breath. This next bit was going to be tricky. 'I'm going to take your shirt off.'

Luke didn't reply. The two top buttons of his shirt were still undone from when taking his shirt off had been an entirely different proposition. His hands moved to the next three, and he undid them himself, letting her slip the garment from his shoulders.

Faint red marks were already beginning to show across his ribcage. That had to hurt and it was going to hurt a good deal more in the morning. Brisk professionalism was about the only option available to Katya at the moment, and she started to carefully feel her way down his ribs, applying gentle pressure.

'Ow! Your hands are cold.'

'Be quiet.' He wasn't making this very easy.

'Thought you nurses were supposed to be angels.'

'Even angels don't have X-ray vision.' A sharp intake of breath from Luke indicated that she'd found a spot that really did hurt. 'Is that painful?'

'Yeah, a little.'

'Okay, deep breath.' She placed her hands around

his ribcage. 'And again… Can you twist to one side. And the other?'

Luke obeyed her without a word. Clearly, good sense, or pain, was beginning to set in and he was letting her get this over and done with.

'Right, lean forward a bit so I can see your back. Any pain there, or in your legs?'

'No.'

'Good.' She caught up the other towel and wrapped it around his shoulders. 'I think you're good to go. But you might like to go down to A and E and get it looked at.'

'It's okay. They'll only do what you've just done.'

'Probably. But it can't hurt to get a second opinion.'

'Yours is enough.' He turned his dark eyes on to her and something melted deep in the pit of her stomach. 'Anyway, I know what a busted rib feels like, and this isn't it.'

'Okay, we'll see how you are in the morning. In the meantime…' Katya scrubbed her hand across her brow. 'In the meantime, have you got a spare shirt downstairs?' She knew that he used the washing machine in the utility room for his own clothes as well as the washing from the surgery.

'Yeah.' He rose painfully. 'I'll go and get it.'

'I'll go. I'll call Olenka as well. She'll have a hot bath and something to eat ready by the time we get there.'

'There's no need to trouble Olenka…'

'You can't stay here, Luke, you've nowhere to sleep. You need some hot food inside you and to rest tonight. I'll get anything you can't leave until the morning out of your cabin.'

'There's nothing there.' The assertive spark was back in his eyes. 'My laptop and papers are all downstairs in the surgery, and anything of any value is in storage. You're not going anywhere near that cabin.'

'Fair enough.' Katya didn't want to admit how good his protectiveness felt. 'I'll pop downstairs, and then we'll go straight to Olenka's.'

Luke opened his eyes the following morning to the thing he'd been trying not to dream about for what seemed like the whole of his life. A pair of green eyes. Katya's subtle scent, mingling with the stronger smell of coffee. Half-asleep still, he tried to reach for her and reality kicked him in the ribs like a mule with attitude.

'Steady on. How are you feeling this morning?' She set the tray down on the small table by the bed and gave him an inquisitorial frown.

'Uh. Better.' Luke tried to move again, and pain shot through his back and legs. 'I think.'

'You must be pretty stiff—you took quite a fall last night. Take it slowly.'

There wasn't much choice about that. Luke sat up in bed, pulling the covers along with him. 'Where's Bruno?'

She tipped her head to the corner of the room, to where Bruno lay on a pile of old cushions. 'He wouldn't settle last night unless he was here with you, and, anyway, Peter was afraid he'd pester his kitten. So the kitten's downstairs, locked in the kitchen, and Bruno's up here.' She completed the roll call. 'Olenka's gone to work and Peter's at school.'

'What's the time?' Luke looked for his watch, and found that it wasn't on his wrist. He didn't remember taking it off last night, and the disturbing thought that someone else might have occurred to him.

'Nine-thirty. I left you to sleep. Sleep's good for you.'

He'd take her word for it. At the moment it felt as if he'd been dragged from his bed and beaten up during the night. 'Thanks.' Luke turned his attention to the tray, where an empty cup stood next to a full cafetière. 'You've brought coffee.'

'Yes. I thought you might like to take it easy this morning. Charlie's going in to do your surgery.'

'Yeah, I remember that.' He pulled at the old T-shirt he was wearing. 'Did you…?'

'Olenka.'

He remembered now. He'd been so tired that he'd fallen asleep on the sofa downstairs, and Olenka had good-naturedly shooed him up the stairs. She'd made to take his shirt off for him, and when he'd protested drowsily that she wasn't Katya, she'd snorted and left him to it. Good. That was good. As long as Olenka hadn't reported back on what he'd said.

'Would you like me to take a look at those bruises?'

Last night had been one thing. This morning, with soft pillows at his back and light streaming through the blinds, the only person who got anywhere near him would have surgical gloves and a mean look, and currently Katya had neither. The loss of his home seemed to have effectively wiped away the events that had preceded it, and Luke wasn't about to repeat them.

'No. Thanks, that's okay. If I'm worried about anything…'

'You'll go and see the doctor.'

'Yeah.'

She looked pleased. She had clearly been steeling herself for an argument on that very point. 'Okay. Good.

Well, I'll leave you to it, then. Your clothes are there, and some towels. The bathroom's just along the hall.'

His clothes had been washed overnight and were neatly folded in a pile, along with a garish pink striped towel. Luke supposed that he was going to have to wind that around himself for his trip to the bathroom and decided that any complaint might be construed as lack of gratitude. 'Thanks.' She seemed to brush his appreciation aside, turning to leave, and he caught her hand, noting that this time the pain in his shoulders wasn't so intense when he moved. 'I mean it, Katya. Thank you.'

She tried to get him to take it easy, cooked him a full breakfast, and lingered over coffee afterwards. It was nice to sit in Olenka's bright kitchen with her, eating and talking, but it made Luke feel uneasy. He could get used to this without any difficulty at all.

Finally, he managed to persuade her that he was both fit enough to go back home and eager to do so. She hurried the washing up, and then bundled him and Bruno into her car.

'Why don't you go and see how Charlie's doing with the morning surgery?' It was an innocent enough question, but Luke got the feeling that she was packing him off somewhere warm and dry, so she could go and inspect the cabin on her own.

'He's okay. He doesn't need me looking over his shoulder.' Luke was aware that she was watching him, and tried to get out of the car without wincing.

'Where are you going, then?'

'I'm going to have a look at the cabin.' He wanted to walk away from her. For a few hours, last night and this morning, he'd succumbed to the temptation of letting her take care of him. That had to stop.

She pursed her lips but followed him across the car park and into the mud. 'Careful…'

'Yeah, I see it.' He slithered around the perimeter of the cabin, avoiding a large puddle, and found that she had followed him.

'Perhaps there hasn't been too much rain in there overnight.' She was surveying what had been the underside of the cabin, which was now rising upright out of the mud.

'Katya.' He frowned at her. 'Watch out, will you? This thing's unstable.'

'I'm not touching it.' Her cheeks coloured in protest.

'No, well, keep clear of it. If it slides down the hill, I don't want it taking you along with it.'

'Or you.' She muttered the words under her breath, and Luke pretended he hadn't heard her.

He reached the open window of the cabin and bent to peer inside. It was okay. The roof had split, but the side that was uppermost was relatively undamaged and had protected the inside from last night's downpour. There was evidence of smashed crockery in the kitchen area, but the sofa bed looked to be in one piece, even if it was upside down.

'Not too bad.' Her voice was close to his ear, and Luke smiled despite himself. She was unstoppable. 'There's a bit of mess to be cleared up, but at least the furniture looks salvageable. Apart from that table…' She squinted sideways at the smashed legs of the table, which doubled up as a dining area and a desk.

'Good excuse to get another one. I never much liked it.' Luke straightened and felt in his pocket for his mobile. It would take days to clear this, and they were days he didn't have. He was going to have to bite the bullet and call for reinforcements.

Luke's builder had been able to send a couple of men right away, as last night's rain had stopped work at another site. Their heavy-duty tools had made short shrift of what remained of the cabin, and by mid-afternoon all of Luke's salvageable possessions had been stacked carefully in the large office space in the barn.

Katya was rather more worried about Luke than his furniture. Consigning a broken table to a skip was easy enough, but you couldn't just go out and buy a new ribcage. He seemed all right, though. Stopped for a rest more often than usual, and let the builders take on the heavy lifting work, but he was obviously pacing himself, working within his capabilities.

'This'll be workable.' He lowered himself down onto the sofa bed. There was little danger of either getting the other dirty as both Luke's clothes and his sofa were covered in dust and grime at the moment.

'I'll run the vacuum cleaner over the sofa. That might clean it up a bit for tonight.' Luke had made it plain that he intended to stay here tonight, and rather than argue with him Katya had turned her attention to making sure that he'd be comfortable. 'I'll take the bedding downstairs and put it in the washing machine.'

'Thanks.' He nodded, surveying the room from his seat. 'This'll do me fine for a couple of weeks, until I can get a new home delivered.'

Katya sighed, turning away from him. She probably shouldn't say it. On the other hand, it was the obvious solution, even if Luke had been studiously ignoring it all day. 'Have you thought there might be a better option?'

'Not really.'

Yeah. Pull the other one. It was staring him straight in the face. 'Why not move in here? The office has all you need—bathroom and kitchen facilities, it's warm and dry, and it's much more comfortable than your cabin was. We can relocate the desks somewhere else.'

He didn't even take the time to think it over. 'There's nowhere else. I'm fine where I am.'

'Right. Which is why you're currently homeless, and if the look of you last night was anything to go by you're black and blue. I don't think having your home collapse around your ears is anyone's definition of "fine".' That sounded rather sharper than she'd meant it to. Too late now. It was true, anyway.

'That's not fair, Katya. When the tarmac was laid for the new car park, they didn't put all the drainage gullies in properly. When it rained, the water just ran off the surface of the car park and collected under the cabin. The ground under there was like a sponge.' Something seemed to goad him to his feet. 'I've had a word with my builder and he's going to rectify the mistake and supply a new cabin. Which I can site in a more sheltered spot now that the work on the barn's finished.'

'But, Luke, this is crazy. Why bother with a cabin at all? Why not just stay here? It's the obvious solution.' She should leave it alone. Finish this conversation in a couple of days' time, when he wasn't hurting like hell and smarting from the loss of his home. But there was something about the insistence in his voice that told Katya that his answer would probably be just the same then, and she knew that what she had to say wouldn't be any different either.

'No, Katya!' He turned on her, the sudden vehemence in his voice making her jump, and his anger turned to something that looked a lot like panic. 'I'm sorry. I didn't mean to shout at you.'

Right. That was it. She'd just about had enough…

'Do me the courtesy of a straight answer, Luke. Stop tiptoeing around me.'

Something dangerous ignited in his eyes. Flared for one delicious second and then died. 'I don't know what you mean.'

'Yes, you do. I'm not made of glass. I won't break if you speak your mind, I've survived far worse than that.' Not fair. There had been a time when she would have broken and run if he'd raised his voice to her. She'd made a pretty spectacular fool of herself just last night. Not tonight, though. This was different.

'I know. Don't ever think that I don't know how strong you are.'

She could have taken the compliment, smiled at him and let the matter slide. Gone home and left him to get on with it. Or she could have grown wings and flown home, or anything else from a whole range of impossible things. Katya marched up to him, stopping just before their bodies touched. Dangerous. Reckless even. She didn't care. 'So what's wrong with a straight answer, then?'

Anger exploded in his eyes. 'I gave you one. My answer's no.'

'Logical, Luke. That's very logical. Why not freeze your butt off in a cabin all winter when there's space here for you to live comfortably? What must I be thinking?'

'Yeah, what are you thinking?' His words dripped

sarcasm. 'I was under the impression that I was the one who got to choose where I live. That I might have some kind of say around here.'

'And if I'd known that I was supposed to be impressed by all this self-sacrifice, I wouldn't have mentioned it. Helping yourself once in a while isn't going to tarnish that precious halo of yours.'

His face hardened and he turned away from her, his hands clenched by his sides in frustration, pain at the sudden movement, or perhaps both. 'Of course. You're the one who's supposed to be able to see everything, control the world, aren't you? Must be tough, carrying all that responsibility around with you.'

That stung. It really stung. 'Not as tough as not trying, Luke. Just keeping on punishing yourself for whatever sins you've committed and never ask whether you might be making a mistake.'

'Your job description does *not* include organising my life for me, Katya.'

'Oh, don't give me that, Luke. I'm allowed to show a bit of concern, aren't I?'

Suddenly he was cold, still, as if they'd finally reached the eye of the storm. 'No, Katya, actually, you aren't. You can't just breeze in, put me to rights and then breeze back out again. It doesn't work like that.'

Rage and hurt rose in her chest, battering its way out. 'In that case, you don't get to pick my life apart either. I quit.'

Katya marched over to her desk and grabbed her coat and handbag. He could do whatever he wanted to do. She didn't have to sit by and watch.

The door slammed behind her, as if by sheer kinetic

energy. He didn't follow. Didn't catch up with her as she marched to her car, tears of rage prickling in her eyes. Fine. Good riddance.

CHAPTER TWELVE

THE FOLLOWING DAY he sent her flowers. Katya dumped them into the bin and Olenka pulled them back out again.

'Not a smart move.' Olenka inspected the note on the Cellophane. 'Keep the flowers.'

They'd already been over this. Olenka's practical nature didn't see wasting a perfectly good bunch of flowers on a gesture that Luke would never know about as anything other than misguided. Katya didn't want to think about the fact that Luke could probably ill afford such beautiful blooms, and didn't care to even consider that he might be going out of his way to effect a reconciliation.

'What does it say?'

'Thought you weren't interested.'

'I'm not. Just tell me what it says.'

Olenka shrugged. 'You can't quit.'

'Oh, can't I? I just did.'

'All right.' Olenka dropped the florist's card and held her hands up in surrender. 'Don't shoot me, I'm just reading what it says.'

'Yeah. Sorry.' Katya swiped her hand across her face.

'Why don't you take the flowers? Put them in your bedroom, somewhere that I can't see them.'

Olenka nodded and started to unwrap the tape that bound the stems together. For a moment Katya wanted to snatch them back. They were *her* flowers. Even if she didn't want them. 'When you go to work on Monday, I'll put them back downstairs.'

'I'm not going back, Olenka. He practically called me a control freak.'

'And he was wrong?'

'That's not the point. It was the *way* he practically called me a control freak.'

'I like a man who speaks his mind.' Olenka was arranging the flowers deftly.

'I don't think he does speak his mind, Ola. Nothing about what he's doing makes any sense to me. There must be more to it than just male stubbornness.'

Olenka shrugged. 'I don't know. He's a stubborn guy. Must be to have done as much as he has with that place in the last couple of years.'

'I think it's called determination. Anyway, that's not really it.' Katya shifted uncomfortably, feeling her cheeks warm with embarrassment. 'He kissed me.'

'Yeah? What did you do?'

'Kissed him back. Then I kicked him.' A thrill of shame made Katya shudder.

'That bad, eh?'

'No. That good, actually.'

'Right. When did this happen?'

'On Thursday evening, before the cabin collapsed. It was all wrong, Ola, for both of us. We were going to just forget it happened, but ever since…'

'Once you go there, it's hard to take it back.'

'I know.' There was one part of her that didn't want to take it back. 'It's made things uncomfortable. He doesn't talk to me any more, not the way he used to. I wish I knew what he was thinking.'

'You could ask.'

'No, I couldn't. Not now.'

Olenka gave one, pinky-white bud a final tug and nodded slightly. 'Shame.'

'Yeah. And as of Monday morning I'm officially unemployed. Want a hand down at the coffee shop?'

'No. Too many cooks spoil the broth.' Olenka gave a quiet, self-mocking smile at the quintessentially English saying. Her spoken English was perfect, but she still considered that the most universal truths were framed in Polish.

'So they do. Well, maybe I'll just go and find something on my own this time.' She was ready now. Moving on wasn't the impossible, terrifying thing that it had appeared to be three months ago. If leaving Luke behind was the price she had to pay, then so be it.

Olenka seemed surprised when Katya was up and out of the house by eight o'clock on Monday morning. But presumably she hadn't spent most of Sunday night staring at the ceiling, wondering how Luke was going to deal with the projects that she had left half-finished. And she hadn't seen the envelope that had been dropped through the letterbox on Sunday afternoon.

It contained Katya's final pay cheque, including an extra week's money, clipped to a copy of her

P45 form, which irrevocably severed the working relationship between her and Luke. And a note, which couldn't go unanswered.

Never thought you'd be a quitter.

Katya wasn't sure what she was going to say when she saw Luke, but she was stone-cold certain of two things. If she went back to work for him, she'd do so on her own terms. And she didn't let anyone call her a quitter, without being held to account for their words.

'You came.' Luke answered the door to the barn with a slight smile. Katya still had her keys, but using them wasn't an option when she didn't work here any more.

'You didn't give me much choice.' Katya stepped inside.

'There's always a choice.' He pursed his lips. 'I'll admit to doing everything I could to persuade you to make the right one.'

'This is the right one?'

'It's…' He took a moment to weigh the question. 'It's the one I wanted you to make.'

It was a start. It warmed the chill that had settled on her as she'd walked away from him the last time. She'd been achy and shivering all weekend, and one smile from Luke had the power to dispel all that. How could something that felt so right be so terrifying?

Katya ducked the question and gestured towards the closed door to the office. 'Can we go inside?'

He smiled. Really smiled. The sensation of wanting to hug him, like an old friend she hadn't seen for years, tingled through her veins and before there was time to think about whether it was wise, she'd smiled back.

'I want to show you something.' He opened the door to the office space and motioned her through.

The office wasn't an office any more. It wasn't even a space where Luke was camping out for the duration. A new easy chair, which still bore its warehouse tag, sat at right angles to a long cream-coloured sofa, which Katya hadn't seen before. There was an oak-and-glass coffee table, which she recognised as one of those from the waiting room downstairs in the surgery. A couple of bookshelves, which stood ready to receive the piles of books on the floor next to them.

'Come in. Sit down.' The words held all the warmth of someone inviting her into his home. And although it wasn't quite a home yet, that was clearly his intention. Framed pictures were stacked in the corner, waiting to be hung, and in the window was a long table with matching chairs, the wood uneven and knotted but polished up to make a virtue out of its flaws.

'You've been busy.' Katya walked over to the window, running her fingers across the surface of the table. 'This is nice.'

He nodded. 'I salvaged the wood and had it made when I cleared the woodlands here after I first took them over.'

'Where have you been hiding all this away?' Luke had never given any indication that he actually did have a home somewhere, stored away under lock and key.

'Downstairs. There's a large back room next to the secure area and I've been using it for storage. The sofa's my sister's old one—she was redecorating and it didn't match her new colour scheme so she gave it to me.'

'And you put it into storage.'

He shrugged, rubbing the back of his neck uneasily. 'Yeah. You were right, Katya. These things should be used.' His gaze focussed on one leg of the table, and he bent to remove a scrap of sticky tape that still clung to it.

The chairs were neatly tucked under the table and Katya pulled one out and sat down. Ran her hand over the smooth wooden surface in front of her.

'Would you like some coffee?' He seemed to realise that she needed time to take all this in, and then some more to think.

'Yes, that would be nice.' An idea struck her. 'Is this the first time you've used this table?'

'Yeah.' He shifted uncomfortably. 'When I brought it back here, I didn't even take the wrappings off, just put it straight into storage.'

'Then what do you say we christen it? Have breakfast here?'

For a moment he was uncertain and then he grinned. 'Good idea. I've not got much in the way of groceries here yet, but it'll only take ten minutes to pop down to the village and get something. Will you stay here?'

'Get some bacon and eggs, eh? I could do with a proper cooked breakfast.' Something to face the day on. Something to make this place really feel like home.

'Bacon and eggs it is.' He caught his car keys and wallet up from the coffee table, and pulled on his jacket. 'Don't go anywhere.'

'I won't.'

Now that she was alone, she could think more clearly, weigh things up a little better. Everything, something, nothing. They were the choices. They'd both managed to prove beyond any shadow of a doubt that everything, tantalising as that was, wasn't an option. And nothing was like returning to the dead void she'd struggled so hard to move on from.

Something was… Something was his friendship. Working here, feeling that she was making some headway. It seemed that was what Luke wanted, too, and if she had to let her questions go unanswered for the sake of peace, maybe that was the best thing to do.

The relief in finding that Katya was still there when he returned, after an almost frantic dash to the shops and back, almost made Luke cry out in triumph. Maybe this was enough. He would have begged her if she'd wanted, apologised for his blind bull-headedness and literally thrown himself at her feet, but she hadn't asked that of him.

She hadn't asked the questions that he'd most feared either. It seemed enough that he had moved in here now, and why he hadn't done it sooner was no longer important. And that was just as well, because he wasn't sure that he knew how to explain why he suddenly cared about having a home, when up till now it had been an irrelevance without the family that he had so longed for.

She'd been outside, picked a couple of late-summer blooms from the meadow behind the barn, and arranged them in an old metal jug that Amanda used for watering the plants downstairs in the surgery. Suddenly the place looked welcoming, like home, instead of an almost random arrangement of items that happened to belong to him.

'That looks nice.' He grinned at her.

'That smells wonderful.' She nodded towards the bag

that held the bread, still warm, from the bakery. 'I'll set the table and you get the coffee on.'

The smells of bread and coffee, and then crispy bacon, which mingled with the soft scent of the flowers when they sat down to eat, almost overwhelmed him. He'd denied himself the simple, everyday pleasures for so long now. But if Katya knew how delicious this novelty was, she said nothing.

'So what's behind there?' She laid her knife and fork down on her empty plate and gestured towards the partition, which he'd drawn across the room to make a separate bedroom for himself.

'Somewhere to sleep.' That wasn't what she'd meant. She was checking up on him, but that was okay. 'I had a proper bed in storage, too. My old sofa bed's in the skip. I moved the shelves in the built-in cupboard around a bit, bought a couple of clothes hangers and it makes a perfectly good wardrobe.'

She nodded, as if that was what she'd been wanting to hear, but gave no indication that she might like to inspect his handiwork. Some things would remain private. His bed was number one on that list. And his past came a close second.

'I was hoping you weren't going to say you'd put the desks in there.'

'No, they're downstairs, in the office next to the waiting room. I originally intended that to be Amanda's but she prefers to sit at the reception desk so she can see what's going on and greet people.'

'Hmm. That sounds practical.' Nothing about whether she approved of his lifestyle reorganisation, even though she clearly did. 'Perhaps we can go and take a look when we've done the washing up.'

He could breathe again. Take in a deep draught of air, which made his head spin with possibilities. 'I'm afraid there isn't as much space down there.'

She shrugged. 'There was always too much up here. I like to have at least one wall close at hand to beat my head against if I feel like it.' Laughter danced in her eyes. She was happy with this. So was Luke. Bruno didn't care, and was curled up in his basket, snoring quietly in the morning sunshine. It was best to let sleeping dogs lie.

Katya squeezed around the edge of her desk and plumped herself down in her office chair. Swivelled two full circles, as if to test out her new working area, and smiled. 'This is great.' She reached over and tipped her pencil sharpener out of her coffee mug.

'I hope there's enough room here.' Luke sat down at his own desk and surveyed the room. It had seemed okay last night, when he'd brought the desks down here, but this morning it seemed smaller, as if somehow his horizons had widened overnight.

'Plenty.' She opened the desk drawer and surveyed it carefully, as if to check that he hadn't raided her stock of stationery. 'And everything's in the right place… mostly.' She retrieved a stray rubber band and, stretching it across her fingers, pinged it in his direction. 'Your desk's well within shooting range.'

'Right. So you can keep me in line.' The thought was delicious. On a professional level, of course.

'You think you need it?'

Oh, yes. Luke let that one go and asked the other question that seemed to be burnt across his retinas, obscuring his view of everything else. 'Will you stay, Katya? Please.'

She pretended to think about it. 'Since you asked.' She opened her bag and withdrew the envelope that he'd posted through Olenka's letterbox yesterday. 'If you want to take this back…'

Luke leaned over the desks, grabbing it out of her hand. Shrugged and smiled, in an attempt to disguise the eagerness of the motion. 'Guess I could.'

Her lips twitched in a smirk, which looked suspiciously as if she'd got what she wanted. 'I suppose that's settled, then.' She looked at her watch. 'You'd better be getting ready for your morning surgery.'

He wanted to sit here and watch her. Listen to the steady tap of her fingers on the keyboard, let the sound of her voice as she made phone calls swirl over his senses. But it was too late to phone Charlie to ask if he'd fill in for him, and she was here to work, not provide a sideshow for his pleasure.

'I'll be getting on, then. Are you going to the hospital this afternoon?'

'No, tomorrow. The session's being held in the morning and Laura says she wants a word with me afterwards, so I won't be back until after lunch.' She seemed to have slipped effortlessly back into the routine of the office. 'Are you free this afternoon? I've got some ideas for some events we could hold here during the winter.'

'Yeah? Be good to start getting people interested in this place as soon as we can.' Luke wondered for the hundredth time what he would have done if she hadn't come back. 'But there are some things still packed up in the storeroom that I need to go through…' Things that he hadn't been able to bring himself to open yesterday. Maybe, now he knew that Katya was back, he could today.

'Oh, well, I'll give you a hand with that, if you like. We can talk afterwards.'

Luke shook his head and then changed his mind. Why not? Sorting through everything this weekend had been a hard job, both physically and emotionally. And Katya had seemed to understand, had been so supportive, without trying to turn his head inside out, looking for answers that he couldn't give. 'Yeah. Thanks. If you don't mind, that would be great.'

After lunch, he led the way through to the storeroom and turned the key in the lock. Almost faltered at the doorway, but she'd slid around him and breezed in, looking around. 'These boxes here?'

'Yeah. Those two are all china.'

'Plates and cups?' Luke nodded in reply. 'Shall we start there? You could do with some, everything in the cabin was shattered.'

He used the key in his hand to split the packing tape sealing the boxes and opened them up. Katya waited, watching as he drew out one of the plates from the set his sister had bought him when he'd moved here and unwrapped it for her to see, nodding in approval when he set the box to one side to take upstairs. 'What's in the other box?'

'Ah. That's something special.' Luke opened the box and unwrapped a cup, handing it to her.

'That's beautiful, Luke!' She held it up to the light. 'Porcelain. It's old, isn't it? From the thirties?'

'That's right. My grandmother left it to me. She knew I always liked it, even when I was a kid. She used to give me milk and soda in a cup and saucer.'

'She was never afraid you'd break it?'

'She used to say that things that aren't used are

wasted…' Luke laughed at the thought of his tiny, irrepressible grandmother. She would have really liked Katya. 'I suppose that's my answer, then.'

'Suppose it is. Sounds as if she'd like it if you got the china out and used it.'

'Yeah.' Luke moved the box over towards the door with the other one. 'There are some woven rugs I brought back from South America in that bag…'

She nosed inside the bag and drew out the bright, multicoloured fabric. 'Oh, that's nice. It would look great across the back of your sofa. What else is in here?'

'Have a look.' It felt better when she did this. Sorted through his memories and pulled out the things that he could use now. It made everything feel as if it was a part of a new start, not relics from a past he'd rather forget.

She gave him a smile and started to dig around in the bag, pulling out a large padded envelope. 'What's in here?'

'That? Nothing.' Luke tried not to move too fast as he reached over and took it out of her hand. The trouble with trying to bury your memories was that they just wouldn't stay down. They squeezed through the cracks at all the wrong moments. This one last piece of evidence of past mistakes was going to have to go. Even if it was the quilt that his mother had lovingly fashioned for the child that Tanya had told him was his. Tanya had lied. His mother had never mentioned the quilt again, and probably thought that it was already lost or had been thrown away.

Katya was looking at him thoughtfully. The envelope clearly wasn't empty, and Luke obviously didn't want her to see what was inside. She nodded and then gave him a bright smile, turning her attention back to the bag. 'Okay, so what else is in here?'

CHAPTER THIRTEEN

KATYA'S SHAKING FINGERS pushed the 'call' button on her phone, and she regretted it almost immediately. Held the phone to her ear, hoping that Luke wouldn't answer. He'd said that he would be out working in the woods this afternoon while she was at the hospital with Bruno, so maybe he wouldn't hear his phone.

He did, of course.

'Hey, there. What's up?'

'Oh! You're not in the middle of something, are you? This can wait.' Pathetic and needy weren't exactly model employee characteristics.

'What is it, Katya?'

'It's not important.'

'Right. So what is it?'

'I've just seen Laura. She's asked me to go and see a particular patient…'

'With Bruno?' Bruno was nosing at her hand, and Katya stroked his head automatically.

'No, on my own.' Katya sighed. 'Laura knows why I gave up nursing, we went for a coffee after one of the sessions and I told her.' Laura had listened and understood, the way that Luke had. 'She's got a patient who's a victim…' She couldn't go on. She'd told everyone that she didn't want to get involved with individual patients. She wasn't ready for this yet.

'I'll be there in fifteen minutes. Wait for me there.'

'No! No, it's okay, Luke. It's outside the scope of the animal visiting scheme, it's just something that Laura asked me to do. I can think about it…' Katya broke off. The silence at the other end of the line wasn't because Luke was listening to what she had to say. He'd hung up on her.

He obviously had been doing something, and he had clearly dropped it in a hurry when she'd called. When he arrived, sauntering into the garden as if he hadn't just made the twenty-minute journey in fourteen minutes flat, mud was still clinging damply to the knees of his jeans.

She met him at the edge of the little group of patients and volunteers. 'You didn't need to come, Luke.' She was angry with herself. She had taken on full responsibility for these groups, and she shouldn't be calling him every time a problem came up. She was also very glad to see him.

He shrugged. 'I was just thinking that I could do with a break. What's up? Laura wants you to go and meet someone?'

'Yeah. A woman in the hospital who's been very badly beaten. She won't talk about it, and Laura seems to think that I can do something. I've told Laura that I'll think about it. There was no need for me to phone you and drag you all the way over here.'

'I gave you that phone so you could call when you needed me.' He grinned. 'So far I'm disappointed at how little you seem to use it. It would be churlish of me not to take notice when you do decide to take my advice on something.'

'Right. So I'm taking your advice now, am I?' She folded her arms, trying to pretend that this wasn't just what she had wanted. Someone to lean on. Someone to test her decisions against, to see if they were sound.

He perched himself on the arm of a bench. 'You could. Advice is generally optional.'

She'd give it a go. 'So what do you think?'

'Not sure yet. I need a bit more information.' He grinned at her. 'Are you happy to talk about what happened to you with her? Without getting too upset?'

'Yes, I don't see why not. I think I'm getting better at talking about it.' Luke deserved a lot of the credit for that.

'Good. And do you think that if someone who'd been through the same as you had approached you in hospital, it might have helped?'

'Yes, I do. It's the little things, you know? The things that you think are stupid and no one will understand.'

He nodded. 'So you can do it. She could benefit. What's the problem?'

When he said it like that, it seemed so easy. 'I just don't want to set myself up as some kind of expert on the subject. All I know is what happened to me. If I'd known the right things to do, I wouldn't have ended up in the hospital.'

'Which is where this lady is now.' His voice was tender. 'You think she's not feeling the same?'

Katya tried to turn away from him, but his gaze wouldn't let her go. Even if she did walk away from him now, the simple logic of his reasoning would follow her. The warmth that was spreading in her chest at the thought of Luke's faith in her wouldn't suddenly cool and disappear.

'I…suppose.'

'So what's bugging you?'

'Suppose I do the wrong thing, Luke? Some of the people I worked with said that they'd known there was something wrong with Carl Davies. I didn't see it.'

His expression hardened. 'Right. And did anyone put it on his notes? Anyone raise the matter with you? Did anyone say anything about that at all?'

'No. Perhaps it was just obvious.'

'Perhaps it's just a case of being wise after the event. Or loading their own feelings of guilt on to you.' Disgust sounded in his voice.

'I don't know, Luke. I just don't know.'

'Okay, perhaps that's one to think about later.'

She raised her eyebrows. He was giving her homework now?

'Or not. Whatever you like. In the meantime, why don't you go and see this woman, introduce yourself and say that you're a volunteer here, and ask if she wants you to do anything for her? You don't need to pitch straight in with the other thing. That would probably frighten her anyway.'

'Yes… Yes, I was thinking that might be the best approach.' Before panic had driven reasoning straight out of the window. 'That's what you think?'

'Yeah, it's what I think.' He grinned at her.

That hadn't been too bad. Quite easy, really. 'Well, I guess I'll go and see Laura, then. I could pop in now, and say I'll go back after work tomorrow.'

'Or during the day might be better.' Luke grinned at her. 'It's about time you had some time off, you've done far more overtime than you ever put down on your timesheet.'

'Maybe...'

That was enough for Luke. He was done with talking, and his restless urge to take action as soon as a decision had been made had got the better of him. He got to his feet briskly and set off in the direction of the entrance of the building that led to Laura's office, seeming to know that Katya would follow him. 'Let's go and find Laura.'

Despite a couple of very heavy hints, which would have penetrated even the thickest of skulls, and an explicit invitation to go home, Luke was still there. Sitting outside the door of the room, just off the main ward, that Laura had shown her to. Probably listening.

Laura had stayed a moment to introduce Katya to Jackie and then disappeared, leaving Katya to sit down, uninvited, next to the bed.

'Hello, there.' She was aware of speaking slightly louder than she might have otherwise done. Nerves perhaps. Or perhaps it was because she knew beyond all doubt that Luke was listening.

'Hello.' Jackie gave the smallest of smiles, which didn't even touch the hollow look of suspicion in her eyes.

'My name's Katya. I'm a volunteer, here at the hospital. I work at the nature reserve, just outside Knighton.' Jackie nodded, giving away nothing. 'We're piloting a scheme to bring animals into the hospital. Some patients find them comforting.'

Another small nod. Katya wondered whether she had been such hard work for the people who had breezed into her ward and sat down next to the bed, trying to talk to her, and decided that very probably she had.

'I'm coming in tomorrow as well, and I wondered whether you'd like me to get you anything.' Katya hadn't wanted to talk about her injuries, or how well they were healing, or how she'd got them either. She imagined that Jackie was sick to death of people trying to interrogate her, however kindly they went about it.

'Thanks. That's kind of you.' Another smile, this one edged with relief.

'You might like some hand and face wipes so you can clean yourself up instead of having to wait for the nurses.' Jackie was obviously confined to her bed, and from the equipment to help her breathe, Katya guessed she had broken ribs, which had penetrated her lung.

A small laugh, cut short by breathlessness. 'No one thinks of that. They bring fruit.'

'Yeah, and you end up with sticky fingers.' Katya grinned at her. 'I'll get something from the chemist that doesn't smell of hospital antiseptic.'

'I've got some money in my handbag.' Jackie gestured towards the cabinet beside the bed.

'That's okay. We can settle up tomorrow. Anything else?'

Jackie's hand went to her mussy dark hair. 'Don't suppose you could get me my comb, could you? It's in my bag.'

'Of course.' The almost painfully tight muscles in Katya's stomach were beginning to relax. Reaching to open the cabinet, she pulled out the dark leather bag inside. 'Here.'

Katya watched as Jackie slowly unzipped the bag

and drew out a comb. Painfully tried to fix her hair and then dropped her arms with a sigh.

'Will you let me do it for you?' That was another thing that Katya had hated about being in hospital. However much the doctors and nurses asked first whenever they touched her, told her what they were about to do, she knew that if she refused they'd find another way. They had to as they were charged with her care. Jackie could make her own decision about whether she wanted Katya to help her.

'Okay. Thanks.' Jackie gave her the comb and Katya carefully combed her hair. It would have been easier to have lifted her a little to get her head off the pillow, and the temptation to do so was strong, but she mustn't. She didn't know exactly what Jackie's injuries were. She wasn't her nurse.

'How's that?'

'Can you do the back?' Jackie lifted her head from the pillow, and Katya carefully complied with the request, trying not to tug too hard on the knots. When Jackie relaxed against the pillows again, she was smiling. 'Thanks. That feels so much better.'

'Good.' A thought struck Katya and she opened her own handbag. 'Would you like to try a little of this?' She held the small atomiser spray out to Jackie.

'Oh, that's nice…' Jackie sprayed a little on her wrist, tried to rub it against the other and found that her hospital tags and the cannula in her arm were in the way. Holding her arm up she blew on her wrist, to dry it. 'Lovely smell.'

'Why don't you take it?' Jackie shook her head and made to give the atomiser back, but Katya pressed it into her hand. 'Helps with the hospital smell.' And perhaps the smell of a man. The one that Katya had scrubbed at her skin for weeks to get rid of.

'Thanks.' When Jackie smiled she was really pretty. 'You're very kind.' Suspicion crept back into her dark blue eyes.

'No, I…' Katya stopped herself. It was too soon. Much too soon. 'I was in hospital myself last year. A friend of mine brought me hand wipes and perfume and I really appreciated it.' She shrugged. 'Just passing on the favour.'

It was time to go. Hopefully she could leave the scent of kindness behind her. 'I'll be back tomorrow, right after lunch. Is there anything else I can get for you?'

Jackie shook her head, and Katya stowed her handbag away for her, leaving the comb and the atomiser within reach beside the bed. Chatted a little, said her farewells, and then walked away, even though her instinct was to stay. She had to take this gently.

'Okay?' Luke rose as she walked out of the room.

'Not really. But she's getting good care.'

'I meant you.'

'Me? I'm…' Katya caught the slight arch of his eyebrow and realised that the last half-hour had taken more out of her than she'd thought. 'It wasn't easy, but I'm glad I did it. It felt like fighting back, you know? Not just for Jackie but for me.'

He nodded, apparently satisfied. 'So you didn't push her too hard.'

'I didn't think that would be a good idea.' Somehow she knew that Luke would have done just the same. It occurred to Katya that he had. Hadn't pushed her but had just been there, like a persistent note of pleasure in her day.

'I think that was a good call.' He started to walk before she could either dismiss his statement or disagree with it. 'By the way, keep Friday evening free.'

'Why?' Hopefully they wouldn't be staging a re-enactment of last Friday evening.

'Laura's invited us to the hospital's Friends' Evening. Lots of people go, staff from the hospital, administrators, various people who are helping out in one way or another. They do it once every three months or so, it helps to get people talking. The official line is that it helps create a sense of community, but actually it just gives everyone an excuse to dress up a bit and have an evening out.'

'Where's it held?'

'They've got a room at the back of The Crown. Just along from the hospital gates. Starts at eight-thirty, so I can pick you up at about eight—'

'I didn't say I could come yet.'

'Why, are you doing anything else?'

'No, but—'

'Good. Just as well, because I told Laura that we'd both be there.' Katya huffed out a breath and he grinned. 'You'll need a long lunch-hour every day this week if you're going to see Jackie, so consider this as making the time up.'

'Hey! I thought you said that I'd already covered the time for that!'

'Think I liked it better when you didn't give me quite such a run for my money…' He was grinning. He did nothing of the sort.

'Yeah, in your dreams. You love it.' She quickened

her pace, grabbing the swing door up ahead, and opened it, motioning him through with an ostentatious gesture.

Luke walked through, rolling his eyes. 'A monster. I've created a monster.'

CHAPTER FOURTEEN

LUKE HAD INSISTED that there was something he had to do in town, and dropped Katya at the hospital the next day, leaving her to visit Jackie and saying he would pick her up on his way back. From what she said, Jackie was beginning to trust her, and Luke guessed that he should do the same, contenting himself with being there when she left for the hospital the day after that, watching her car disappear along the road and looking for its return.

Every day she seemed to get stronger. She no longer hesitated, looking at him for approval and perhaps protection whenever anyone new came to the barn. She was like a wounded bird who had somehow found its way to him and who was now ready to fly. Trouble was, he'd rather got used to having her around.

All the same, he had Friday evening to look forward to. He probably shouldn't, but no one was going to know. He'd rejected the option of buying a new tie on the basis that his best navy blue shirt—actually, his only decent shirt—looked better with just a matching pair of trousers and a jacket and he was overdue for a haircut anyway. He'd done nothing that anyone could point to that even remotely suggested this might be a date.

'You've scrubbed up well.' Olenka's voice floated

from the hallway behind Peter, and he frowned at her over the boy's shoulder. The idea that maybe he was a little overdressed occurred to him, and then crashed and burned on the carpet. Katya had appeared on the stairs.

She looked lovely. Hair like the russet woodland colours in autumn, fixed up at the back of her head in a gravity-defying bundle. A black dress, which made her eyes seem even more luminous, paired with silver jewellery, dark stockings and pumps. Seeing her for the first time in ages in something other than jeans and a sweater, Luke realised she'd put on a little weight. Just a couple of pounds, but it was definitely in exactly the right places.

'Doesn't she look…?' Peter yelped as Olenka dragged him off into the kitchen and slammed the door behind them.

Didn't she just. Luke waited for her to descend the stairs, almost breathless. When she got close, he noticed that she smelled as gorgeous as she looked.

'You look…different.'

She seemed pleased by the compliment, however inadequate. The thing to do now was to brush her cheek with a kiss, and Luke ached to do it. He stepped back so he wasn't tempted beyond his strength. They'd been there, not quite done that, and decided it wasn't for them. There was no going back now.

'I thought that jeans and wellingtons probably weren't appropriate.' She'd pulled on a red coat, which covered up her slim curves, and Luke found himself able to think better. Then his senses exploded again into a million shards of tingling pleasure as she unashamedly looked him up and down, gave a little nod as if she liked what she saw, took his arm and made for the front door.

'Shouldn't we say goodbye to Olenka?' Luke twisted his neck round towards the kitchen door, still firmly closed.

'No. She knows where I'm going.' And when she'd be back, no doubt. 'She's been trying to impress on Peter that he's not supposed to be surprised that I am capable of smartening myself up a bit when I go out. Let's not tempt fate.'

A comment about kids getting the wrong end of the stick was on the tip of his tongue, but Luke swallowed it. It wouldn't be fair. If pressed for the truth, and he was glad that Katya showed no indication of being about to do so, Peter had a point. It wasn't her clothes or her make-up or her jewellery. It was the subtle shine about her, the way she smiled and the answering thud of his heart that said this evening was special.

'So I've got Olenka to thank for escaping without the third degree, then.'

She laughed. 'As far as Peter's concerned. I suspect we're under surveillance.'

'You think so?' He guided her through the front gate and stopped a yard short of the car. 'So would it be a bad idea if I opened the car door for you?'

She thought for a moment. 'Not particularly. You've done it before.'

Whenever he could get to it before she did. It was just good manners. 'Okay, then, perhaps we'll do it right.' He really shouldn't. But Luke couldn't help himself. She was so beautiful tonight and it could do no harm. They were just messing around, having a laugh. Right?

He reached the car in one stride, and with a flourish

of his hand gave a small bow as he grabbed the door handle. It didn't budge. Katya squealed with laughter. 'You forgot something.'

'Yeah.' Luke felt in his jacket pocket for the car keys and flipped the central locking. 'Let's try that again.'

This time the car door opened and she glided into the front seat like a princess entering a carriage. He tucked her coat inside and closed the door, looking back at the house as he did so, just in time to see the curtains twitch and Peter's head appear, then a disembodied arm curling around his shoulders and pulling him back.

He was chuckling to himself as he got into the car. Katya had obviously seen the same thing as he had, and gave him a look of grinning reproach. 'Stop. We've done it now. I'll never hear the last of this.'

Luke shrugged. 'That's okay. When you get back, you can say that I ignored you all evening.'

'And is that what you're going to do?'

'I might. Or you could ignore me.'

She grinned, turning her head away from him to look straight ahead of her. 'Just drive, Luke.'

Perhaps she'd told Olenka about the kiss. If she had, she couldn't have gone into much detail or Olenka would have had no scruples about making her displeasure known to him. Perhaps Katya had said that she'd liked it. He dismissed the thought, and twisted the key in the ignition. They'd had their fun for the night, and things hadn't got out of hand. He'd have to make sure that when he brought her back home he stopped at the front gate, and didn't walk her to her doorstep.

The room was large and full of people. Laura had greeted them and made some introductions, and Katya had floated away from his side, but Luke never quite lost track of her. She seemed to shine in the dimly lit room, bobbing like a lantern on a river, talking first to a group of nurses, who Luke recognised from the ward, and then being commandeered by one of the hospital board of directors, who obviously wanted to gauge her opinion on something at quite some length.

He reckoned that he couldn't be accused of crowding her if he drifted back in her direction now, and Luke worked his way across the room, smiling at new acquaintances as he did so. She was alone for a moment, and Luke approached her from behind and laid his hands on her shoulders, feeling her start slightly. Time had been when he would have jumped back as quickly as she, but now the sudden tension was accompanied by a shiver of pleasure and a laughing exclamation.

'What have you been doing?' He bent towards her ear, almost whispering.

'You're supposed to circulate at these things, aren't you?' She'd turned round now, her face bright.

'And you've been circulating very well. Was that one of the board of directors I saw you in deep conversation with?'

'If you saw me then I expect it was.' She grinned mischievously, as if somehow she'd known that his eyes had never left her all evening. 'No harm in buttering up the people who hold the purse strings.'

'No, I suppose not.' No harm at all. Other than while she had been doing that she hadn't been by his side.

He didn't hear her phone ring over the hubbub in the room, but it must have done because she pulled it out of her bag, and pressed it to her ear. 'Hello…' She pressed her fingers against the other ear. 'I can't hear you very well…'

Suddenly her face darkened. 'Have you told someone?' She shook her head slowly, as if she somehow knew she wasn't going to get the answer that she wanted. 'Do that, then. I'll be there in five minutes.'

She cut the line and stuffed her phone back into her bag. 'Sorry. Got to go.' Without another word of explanation she turned on her heel, pushing past the knots of people in her way towards the door.

Had she thought for one moment that Luke wasn't going to follow? She seemed surprised to find him there as she caught her coat up from the row of hooks outside the reception room, throwing it on as she hurried to the main doors.

'What's the matter?' He stayed doggedly on her heels.

'It's Jackie. Probably nothing, but I'll just go and check on her. It's okay, you stay here.'

Luke ignored her. She was going out into the darkness alone. Okay, so it was nine o'clock and the road outside was still full of people. That didn't matter. She'd come with him and if she was going to leave now, she'd do it with him. That was an unwritten rule of the universe.

'You really don't need to…' They were at the hospital gates before she seemed to realise that he was still there.

'I know.'

'I won't be long.'

'Good. I'll wait for you, then.'

She huffed at him, never slackening her pace. Luke supposed that was an acceptance of sorts and decided that leading rather than following was now in order.

Lengthening his stride, he hurried to the closed doors of Jackie's ward, Katya almost running to keep up with him.

A ward orderly finally answered the bell. 'I'm sorry but visiting time's over.'

'I've had a call from one of the patients here. She says that she's in some kind of trouble, and I'd just like to see her.' Katya gave the orderly her most persuasive smile but somehow he failed to be melted by it. 'We'll only be a couple of minutes.'

He wasn't going to open the door. It was probably more than his job was worth. Katya was listening to him politely and Luke caught sight of the ward sister behind them, and beckoned to her. Sometimes it was good to know people.

Sarah hurried over, listened to Luke's quick explanation and made her decision. 'Let them in.' Katya hurried to Jackie's room, not stopping to knock before she went in, leaving Luke and Sarah to follow.

Jackie was gasping for breath, red-faced and crying. Luke felt Sarah's hand on his arm, gently holding him back. She knew as well as Luke did that Katya was the person to deal with this.

'Hey. Hey, Jackie, what's going on?' She was at the side of the bed, her hand automatically finding Jackie's. 'It's okay, sweetheart, just tell me what the matter is.'

Katya was checking the monitors by the side of the bed, without seeming to divert her attention from Jackie. When Sarah quietly put the oxygen mask into her hand, Katya acknowledged it with the slightest of nods.

What Jackie really seemed to need was Katya's arm tight around her shoulders, and she began to breathe more easily. 'He… My ex. He called me. He's coming…' Jackie was gripping her phone tightly.

'Okay. What did he say? It's okay, Jackie, this ward is locked up for the night. He can't come in.'

'He'll get in. He will. He goes out for a drink with his mates on a Friday night and…' Jackie trailed off, dissolving into tears again.

Katya turned to Sarah, a quick look of understanding passing between them. 'I'll go and call hospital Security.' Sarah hurried out of the room.

'There. See, he can't get in.' Katya paused, obviously weighing up her next move. 'Jackie, I need you to help me.'

'What?' Katya had done her work well this week. Jackie was looking at her with trust in her eyes, waiting for Katya to come up with a solution to her problem.

'We can stop your ex from coming onto the ward but unless he does something to someone here, there's only so much we can do. You understand that?'

Jackie nodded, biting her lip. She knew as well as Luke did what was coming, and all Luke could do was to hope that she trusted Katya well enough to do what she was about to ask.

'Did he do this to you, Jackie?'

Jackie dissolved into tears, clinging to Katya as if she was the only one who could save her. Katya gently prised Jackie's fingers from her arm, grasping her hands between hers. 'Jackie, I have to know. Help me here. Did he do this to you?'

Jackie seemed to calm down slightly. 'Yeah. Mark pushed me down the stairs.'

'Deliberately?'

Jackie nodded.

'And he kicked you?' Jackie's eyes flared in questioning panic. 'You can cover up for him but your injuries tell a different story.'

'Everyone knows, then…' Jackie dissolved into tears.

'Not everyone. And everyone who does know understands. I understand, because it happened to me.'

The words seemed to jolt Jackie out of her misery. 'You…?'

'Yeah.' The overhead lights caught the glint of tears in Katya's eyes. All Luke wanted to do was to go to her and comfort her, but he knew she wouldn't thank him for it. This wasn't about her, however much his own instincts were screaming to him that everything was always about Katya.

'Stabbed six times. Got the scars to prove it.' Katya grinned at Jackie, as if somehow that would make it okay. 'But that's in the past now. What I need from you is for you to say that you'll give a statement to the police.'

Jackie gulped on her tears. 'Did you?'

'No, I didn't. I couldn't because I was in Intensive Care. I didn't have to do what I'm asking of you now.'

'W-would you have?'

'I don't know. By the time I'd woken up, it was all over.' Katya pressed her lips together and Luke wondered how many times she'd wished that could have been different. How many times she'd thought that she might have saved her attacker's life if she could have spoken and the police had got to him in time. 'You've got a chance to make things right, in a way that I couldn't.'

'Will you stay?'

'Try telling me to go. I'll be here for you, whether you want me or not.'

Jackie nodded. 'Okay. I'll do it.'

'That's the spirit.' Katya was still holding on to Jackie, but twisted round towards Luke. 'Can you find Sarah?'

All Luke's instincts told him that he should stay put, that he could fight off anyone who came anywhere near either Jackie or Katya. That wasn't going to help anyone, though. He couldn't protect them both, twenty-four hours a day, and any long-term solution to Jackie's problem was going to be a team effort. Swiftly he scanned the ward, and found Sarah on the phone at the nurses' station.

'Jackie says that this ex of hers was the one who—' Luke broke off as a bell started to clang raucously.

'Shit. Fire alarm.' Sarah looked around quickly. 'Alan, Carole, check the ward. Marie, get everyone else to prepare for evacuation.'

Everyone seemed to have a job to do. Everyone but him. Luke saw Katya appear at the entrance to Jackie's room, look around and then disappear again, closing the door behind her. The fire doors had swung shut and now they had to wait until it was clear where the fire was.

'Could this be malicious?' Sarah was looking up at him.

'Maybe. I don't smell smoke.'

'Me neither. We can't take the risk, though.'

The best thing he could do was to try and determine whether there really was a fire or not. 'When Security turns up, will you send someone into Jackie's room? I'll go outside, see if I can locate anything.' He wished

Bruno was here, instead of dozing in his basket back at the barn. His sensitive nose would be able to sniff out if there was a fire.

'Thanks, that would be good. The combination for the door is three seven four six. The bell's continuous, so the alarm's originated from somewhere in this sector.'

'Right. I'll be back.' Luke made for the entrance to the ward. Somewhere out there someone was either trying to burn the place down or make everyone think that. He had to find that someone.

Luke worked carefully, methodically. He checked the entrances to the six wards on the wing. Corridors. Cupboards. Then outside, jogging around the perimeter of the building. Nothing. By the time he punched the combination on the keypad and let himself back onto the ward, the fire alarm had stopped and the initial hurried activity had given way to alert watchfulness.

'Nothing?' Sarah was still at the nurses' station, manning the phone and directing operations.

'I can't find anything.'

Sarah pushed out a sigh of relief. 'Probably a false alarm, then. The fire brigade's on its way and they'll check everything out to make sure.'

'Suppose it's malicious. Perhaps someone's trying to get the ward to evacuate so that they can get to Jackie.'

'It's possible. But if that's the case they don't know hospital policy. We don't evacuate without knowing where the fire is.'

'And you have one of your security people with Jackie?'

'Yes. By the way, Katya was looking for you. She went to see if you were in the corridor outside.'

'What?' He must have just missed her. She hadn't been there when he'd got back to the ward. 'Did she come back in again?'

'No, I haven't seen her. She would have had to come past here.'

Cold fear thudded in his chest. 'Don't leave Jackie on her own.' He flung the instruction over his shoulder, knowing that Sarah would comply, and ran out of the ward.

Katya's name was sounding in his head, each one of his instincts calling for her. Luke made his way silently back around the perimeter of the building, this time taking note of everyone he saw, instead of looking for sparks and smoke.

Katya.

Anger ignited in his gut. Why couldn't she have just stayed put, where she was safe? He knew the answer, without having to even ask. Katya was facing her demons. It was what he had led her to, what he'd wanted her to do. Not like this, though.

Katya.

Luke plunged into a knot of brambles that grew at the back of the ward, tearing his hands on them as he made his way through to the enclosed garden area. Then he saw them. Two dark figures, standing next to one of the benches. One was undoubtedly a man. The other smaller, slighter, was Katya.

Something about the way she was standing made him slow his frantic pace. She was gesturing as she talked, as if she was speaking to an old friend. This wasn't a friend, though. There was only one person who could have kept Katya from Jackie's side at the moment. The thought of what she must be feeling right now made

Luke sick to his gut. How she was keeping her fear and her loathing under control, just to talk to the man.

He gestured aggressively and Luke started forward. Slowed again when Katya laid her hand on his arm and he seemed to calm. If Luke could just get to them, without spooking the guy, then he could grab him, pull him away from the one person who should never have to face anything like this again.

Suddenly the man grabbed her arm and Katya began to struggle. Luke thought he heard her call out for him. The instincts that he had been ignoring for so long now broke their bonds and he ran as fast as he could towards her.

CHAPTER FIFTEEN

AS SOON AS the alarm bells had gone off, Katya had known what had happened. Jackie's eyes had flashed a warning signal to her, and she'd nodded when Katya had asked whether Mark had done this before.

She'd been so angry. Angry for Jackie, angry for herself. When Jackie's phone had rung and she had looked at the caller ID and burst into tears, it had been Katya who had answered it.

'I dealt with the guy who was prowling around out here. I'll deal with all of you if you get in my way.'

The voice sounded drunken and the threat was probably an empty one, but Katya hadn't taken that chance. She'd gone to the corridor outside and opened the door that led into the garden, meaning to call out to Luke. Someone had grabbed her, pulling her out into the darkness.

Something had snapped inside her, and all she'd been able to think about had been that she wasn't going to take this. She'd managed to talk Mark down and he'd let go of her. But then he'd changed again, cursing her and grabbing her arm.

This time she wouldn't go down without a fight. And she wouldn't go down quietly either. She yelled Luke's name in the hope that he might hear her, lashing out at Mark, but he dodged her fists, catching hold of her wrist and swinging his other arm back.

Katya braced herself for the blow but it didn't come. The deep roar of anger that reached her ears hadn't come from Mark either. Suddenly she was free, stumbling back from what seemed like a whirlwind force, passing so close by her that she could feel the air brushing against her cheek in its wake.

'Katya. Are you okay?' The words brought her to her senses, and when she looked down she saw that it wasn't some freak of nature that had saved her. Luke had come.

'I'm okay. I'm okay!' She gulped the words out. Luke wasn't being too gentle about pinning Mark face down on the ground and looked as if he was thinking about delivering a punch to his kidney.

'Are you sure? He got hold of you.'

Yes, and she was going to have the bruises to show for it tomorrow. Katya decided to keep that information to herself for the time being. 'And you've got hold of him now. Careful, you'll suffocate him.'

A grin broke through the granite determination on his face. 'He's all right.' Mark tried to twist free and Luke pulled his arm an inch further up his back, getting an oath in return. 'See, he's breathing.'

'Stop it, Luke. We're better than that.'

'She may be.' Luke's hissed reply was directed at Mark. 'I'm not.'

'Luke!' If he kept on like this, she was going to have to wade in on Mark's behalf. Then Katya saw that it was all for show. Mark's arm was still pinioned behind his back but at a more comfortable angle. Luke was holding him down, but all the fight had gone out of his opponent, and he wasn't about to do him any more damage.

All the same, the menace in Luke's voice when he addressed Mark was real. 'Did you start a fire?' Mark cursed again, this time a whine in his voice. 'Come on. Tell me now.'

'Luke, he didn't. He said that he just set the fire alarms off.' Mark's overweening self-pity had disgusted her. 'He'd said that Jackie had pushed him into it, given him no choice after she'd refused to see him.'

Luke snorted in disgust. 'Clever guy.' He pulled Mark to his feet, and started to march him towards the fire engine that had just turned in through the main gates of the hospital.

Katya wasn't sorry to see Luke hand his captive over to the firemen who jumped out of the cabin. They didn't seem disposed to give Mark much sympathy when Luke explained what had happened, but at least they'd hand him over to the police in one piece. For a moment there, the cold, hard fury that had burned in Luke's eyes had made her doubt that he would.

There was nothing there now except tenderness. Catching her hand, he led her back over to a bench underneath one of the large windows of the ward, light spilling out onto it. 'Sit down for a moment, Katya. Talk to me.'

He sat down, throwing his arm across the back of the bench, and Katya joined him. Just one minute, before she had to get back to Jackie. She moved closer than was probably necessary, feeling the reassurance of his bulk. Safe. She was safe.

'I mustn't be long.' She had to keep going, do something positive, before her mask slipped. Before someone saw that she had been more than frightened back there.

'I won't keep you.'

Katya could feel her hands begin to tremble and she twined her fingers together in her lap. 'You weren't going to hurt him, were you, Luke?'

He shook his head slowly. 'I doubt that hitting the ground with me on top of him was an entirely painless experience.'

'I don't mean that. Afterwards…'

'I wanted to.' His words were full of anguish.

'But you didn't.'

'No.' He shifted closer to her, and she felt his arm around her shoulders. 'You said that we're better than that. I'm not sure that I am, but I reckoned the least I could do was try.'

'You did fine.' She snuggled up close to him, and felt his arm tighten around her. 'If I were you, I would have hit him.'

'Now you tell me.' Katya felt him chuckle.

She could have sat there for hours. Watching the sky. Feeling the breeze on her cheek. With Luke to guide and protect her. 'I've got to get back to Jackie. I promised her.'

'Yeah. I know.' He didn't move for a while, seemingly aware of the fact that while he stayed here, Katya couldn't tear herself away. 'You okay?'

'Yes. I'm fine.' She'd cry later. She could fall to bits when she knew that Jackie was all right.

'Right, then.' He got to his feet, waiting for Katya to stand. 'Saving your tears for your pillow, eh?' For a moment she thought that he was mocking her, but his face was deadly serious. And he was right. She'd do just that.

* * *

Luke had stuck with her the whole time. Through the interviews with the police, waiting for the duty doctor to come and see Jackie to make sure she had suffered no ill-effects from the evening, talking to Laura and the hospital social worker, who had both been summoned from the party over the road. He had been there for all that, and what had seemed like the interminable waiting in between.

Finally, Jackie settled down to sleep. As soon as she did, Sarah ushered Katya and Luke away from the bed and back out of the ward. 'She'll be okay. We'll take good care of her.'

Katya grimaced. 'I must have said that about a million times myself.' It felt different to be on the other end of the reassurances.

'You know that we will, then.' Sarah caught Katya's eye with a knowing look and closed the door of the ward firmly behind them, before hurrying away.

Luke looked at his watch. 'I guess the party's probably broken up by now.'

'Guess so. What time is it?'

'Ten past three.' He turned and Katya automatically followed him along the quiet corridors. 'Will you come home with me?'

Katya stopped short, and he turned, aware that the sound of her footsteps had died away. 'I have cocoa. Those pecan biscuits you like.' Ten feet of empty air separated them, and he made no effort to close the gap. 'We could talk.'

'I should get some sleep. I promised Jackie I'd come by in the morning.'

'I've got a sofa…'

'No. I couldn't make you sleep on the sofa.'

He grinned. 'Fair enough. You can take the sofa, then.'

It would be good to talk. If she went back home, she'd probably just wake Olenka up on her way in, and then lie staring at the ceiling herself. Katya wondered if a no-kissing clause might be added to the promise of cocoa and pecan biscuits, and decided that it should go without saying between friends.

'No, Luke. Thanks, but I'd like you to take me home.' She wanted his solid reassurance so badly, which was the best reason she could think of to put as much space as possible in between them.

'Okay.' He leaned back against the wall, folding his arms. 'Guess I'll say it here, then.'

'Or in the car?' Whatever it was that was so important it couldn't wait until later might be better discussed under cover of darkness. If Luke couldn't see her face he might not know what she was thinking.

'Here will do.' He didn't move. 'Katya, about tonight…'

'Yes?'

'I wish you hadn't gone out of the ward to find me.'

She'd heard his sharp intake of breath when she'd got to the part in her statement to the police about the phone call. 'I…' She shrugged. 'I just went to the door.'

'I know. It wasn't your fault. But I still wish you hadn't.'

Katya almost felt the weight lift from her shoulders. 'You know, I'm almost glad I did. When I was stabbed everything happened so quickly and I couldn't fight back. I've always wondered if I would have.'

'This wasn't the way to find out. There's no shame

in not being able to fight. You never needed to redeem yourself.'

He was right. 'It's taken what's happened tonight for me to be able to see that. I wouldn't have gone outside the ward if I'd known, but the way things turned out…' She shrugged. 'I faced him, Luke. I fought him.'

He leaned forward, brushing a strand of hair back from her forehead. 'You've been fighting back ever since I met you. And tonight you were a force to be reckoned with. You looked out for Jackie and for me in a situation that you had every right to back off from. You were very brave.'

'I was very scared.'

'Good. That shows excellent judgement on your part.'

Warmth washed over her, like a great, tranquil wave. 'I think I've had enough of all this for tonight, you know. Probably enough for an entire lifetime.'

'Yeah. I think so, too.'

'I still don't understand, though, Luke.' She walked over to the seats on one side of the corridor and sat down. Luke followed, coiling his long limbs into the seat next to her.

'Maybe that's all you need to know. That there's no understanding the things that some people do.'

His hand, resting on his knee, was just inches away from hers. Less than that. Almost as if she had suddenly become magnetic and he was fighting to resist the inevitable attraction.

'He was just so totally on another planet. He said that they were keeping his girlfriend here and that she'd told lies about him and they wouldn't let him see her. He made it sound as if it was all her fault.'

'And was it?'

'No! Of course not.'

'Right.' He swivelled towards her, reaching out to brush her cheek with his fingertips. The sensation was delicious and calming, all at the same time. 'And when it happened to you. Was that your fault?' She went to answer and he laid his finger across her lips. 'Think about it now. Tell me what you really believe.'

Katya thought about it. The automatic 'no' that everyone seemed to want to hear. The incessant 'yes' that thundered in the back of her head.

'No. It wasn't… It wasn't my fault.'

It was far more difficult to say when the words came from her heart, and weren't just a way of keeping everyone quiet on the matter. Tears slid down her face before she had a chance to blink them away, and Luke coiled his arm around her shoulders. 'Hey. It's all right.'

'It's three o'clock in the morning and I'm crying in a hospital corridor. That's not all right.'

'I'm the only one here to see you. And I'll keep quiet about it.' He felt in his pocket and pulled out one of the red paper napkins from the party. 'Here. It's more or less clean.'

She tried to grin. 'It smells of those awful salmon vol-au-vents.' Katya took it and blew her nose. He smelled of…something. Reassurance. Solidity. Wild, head-spinning sex.

This was more than reckless. She moved away from him, and Luke drew back.

'You want to go now?'

'Yes. Thanks, Luke.'

He got to his feet. 'Let's get you home, then, while it's still worth getting into bed before you have to get up again.'

CHAPTER SIXTEEN

LUKE LAY AWAKE, staring at the ceiling. He'd taken a walk before going to bed, but somehow his racing thoughts just wouldn't switch off. Dawn was breaking now, and his body ached with weariness.

He pulled his duvet over his head, turning over in a pathetic attempt to sleep. He wasn't kidding anyone, not even himself. The blur of unsatisfied longing that he'd been fighting for weeks now was stronger, and much more immediate, than exhaustion. He had to make a decision.

He'd justified his campaign to keep Katya here on the grounds that this was a safe place, where she could begin to spread her wings. But tonight she'd relived her worst nightmare and proved to Luke, and to herself, that she could face her fears. He had become irrelevant. Worse than irrelevant. He wanted—needed—her to love him, completely and unequivocally, the way that Tanya had refused to do. But that was too much to ask of any woman. No one just fell in love like that in a matter of months.

He was going to have to let her go. Like a wild animal, given shelter to heal its wounds, she was ready to go free. It would only take a nudge from him and she'd see that. Luke rolled onto his back, staring upwards again. The decision was made.

He was unused to not putting his decisions into action straight away, but the weekend only strengthened his resolve. Her voice on the phone, when he called to see how she was doing, was clear and steady, and when he saw her on Monday, there was a new assurance about her. It suited her.

'Did you think any more about your university place?' He tried to keep the question casual.

The tips of her ears went pink. He'd hit a nerve. 'I… Yes, I was thinking about it over the weekend. Next year maybe.' She turned her attention back to measuring out the coffee for the machine.

'Not this year?'

The back of her neck was burning now, and Luke began to feel sick. 'No. Not this year. I've got things to do here.'

'Actually, that's what I wanted to talk to you about. I'm not sure how much longer I can afford to keep you on here. Your three-month contract's up soon and…'

She swung round to face him, her expression unreadable. 'But last week you were asking me to come back. You said you needed me.'

'Yeah, I know. I'm sorry. I was going over the books at the weekend and it seems that I've miscalculated. I have another couple of months' grace, but after that I'm going to have to make some drastic cuts in order to get through the winter.' Luke almost choked on the lie. It was down to Katya's efforts with the dog school and the business plan that the budget was looking far healthier than he'd hoped.

'So…what, you're making me redundant?'

'Not yet. But I may have to soon. I don't want you to pass up any opportunities in favour of your job here, because it might not last too much longer.'

She seemed to be fighting some internal battle. It was a lot for her to take in all at once. He should give her time to think. 'There's no need to say anything right away. I just wanted to raise it…as something to think about.'

'I…I have to admit I've been thinking about it over the weekend. My university place.'

'Do you think you're ready to go now?'

'I'm not sure. I'm beginning to think so.'

Luke suddenly realised what people meant when they talked about the bottom dropping out of their world. It felt as if he was in free-fall, spinning downwards, with nothing beneath him.

'If you're ready, then you should go.'

Tears spilled out of her eyes, and the part of him that wanted to make her stay crowed in miserable triumph. 'Are you sure?'

'It makes sense, Katya. If you have a definite offer for something you really want to do…' He shrugged. 'I can't match that. You have to look at it in terms of what's best for you.'

'If you say so.' She pressed her lips together. Whatever else she had to say on the subject wasn't for his ears. 'Give me twenty-four hours to think about it.'

'Sure. Take your time, Katya, you need to make the right decision.' He no longer had any right to persuade her. Actually, he'd never had that right, but for a while it had seemed that it was okay to pretend he did. That was over now. 'I've got to go somewhere after my surgery this morning and I doubt I'll be back before evening surgery. Will you be okay here?'

'Yes, sure. Frank's coming in later and I've got to go out myself. Have you written it down on the board?'

'No. It's…personal time.' Luke couldn't think of a better excuse at this short notice. 'Just mark me down as out of the office.' He rose, picking up the untouched mug of coffee that she'd put in front of him. 'See you tomorrow.'

Tomorrow had seemed like a different country, some place a million miles away from everything that they'd built together. But it came, with horrible speed, bearing down on Luke like a train with a full head of steam. Katya was in the office early, as usual, and Luke could hear her, moving around downstairs.

She used the kettle in the surgery to make a cup of instant coffee, seemingly unwilling to venture into the kitchen that was now part of his living quarters. When Luke finally decided that if she wasn't going to come to him, he'd better go to her, she was sitting at her desk, looking as weary as he felt.

'I've made up my mind, Luke.' Before he had a chance to wish her good morning she'd skipped the pleasantries in favour of the one thing that was on his mind.

'Okay.' He sat down. 'What's the verdict?'

She gave him a pained look. 'I want to ask you something.'

'Fire away.'

'Is there anything you want to say to me?'

Only about a hundred things. None of them for her ears, though. 'Just what I said yesterday. That you have to think about your own career now. What's best for you.'

She nodded. 'In that case…' She seemed to have as much difficulty in getting the words out as Luke reckoned he'd have hearing them. 'In that case, it might be best if I took my university place up this year. Get back on track.'

'Good. I think it's the right decision.'

'Yeah. In the circumstances…' She shot him a questioning look and Luke ignored it.

'When does the course start?'

'Second week in September.' She was looking at her hands now.

'Nearly three weeks.' It sounded like a death sentence. Luke administered a hard mental slap to his head. He mustn't do this. He mustn't hold her back. 'There's not much time.'

'I've thought about it. I can stay here for the rest of this week and next week, try to get some of the loose ends sorted, and then go down to London after that. I'll have to open up my flat again, give it a bit of a spring clean and get settled.'

'You'll have some support there?' He could ask that, at least. His protective instinct wouldn't allow him not to.

'Yes. Thanks. My parents live close by and I have friends…' She tailed off. Perhaps she divined that he didn't much want to hear about the people who would be giving her love and support when he wasn't around.

'You'll have your work cut out to do all you need to do in London in a week.' Luke knew how important it would be to Katya to get her flat cleaned, perhaps a coat of fresh paint on the walls to make it hers again.

'You've got plenty of time until your course starts. Why don't you take it?'

The offer wasn't strictly unselfish. Having Katya here for almost two weeks, when he knew that she was leaving him, would be torture. He couldn't imagine the hurt that tonight would bring if she left today, but he'd always preferred to rip a plaster off in one go. It would hurt for a while, but at least it would be over quickly.

She gulped, and a tear ran down her cheek. 'Are you sure?'

'I'm sure. Katya, this is a new opportunity for you. If you're going to do it, do it properly. Take some time to get yourself settled back into your flat and ready for your course.' He wished she'd stop crying. If she didn't then the urge to hold her, dry her tears, would become irresistible. And if he did that, Luke knew he could never let her go.

She wiped her face with one hand. Gave him a watery smile. That was better. 'I'll make a few enquiries. About getting a replacement for me here…'

'Don't worry about that. I can sort that out.'

She wouldn't be put off. 'I spoke with the head of the land management department at the horticultural college last week…about some of the students coming to lend a hand. He was really enthusiastic about it. I can call him again, see if we can firm a few things up.' Luke nodded. 'And now that the procedures are all in place for the project at the hospital…'

'That'll run itself for a while.' Luke leaned back in his chair. What the hell was he going to do without her? 'Katya you've done a fantastic job here. Got things started, helped me establish projects for the future. It's time for you to move on.'

She nodded. Looked as if she was about to cry again, and then pulled herself together with an obvious effort of will. 'Thanks, Luke. For everything.'

He'd thought he could leave it at that but now the moment was here, he couldn't. 'I'll only ask one more thing of you.'

She smiled. 'Whatever it is, the answer's yes.'

He really, really wished she hadn't said that. All the things he might have asked suddenly popped into his head, exploding with the force of a grenade. He ignored them and stuck with the original request. 'That idea of yours, for a Guy Fawkes Night display. Will you come?'

A smile transformed her face from sorrowfully beautiful to achingly bright. 'Yes, of course. When is it? The weekend of the fifth of November?'

'I'll phone you and let you know the arrangements.' He knew that this was just a trick, to allow himself to think that maybe this wasn't the end. That he'd see her again sometime. That wasn't going to happen. When the time came he'd invite her and she'd politely decline. There was nothing that could change what this was. It was the end.

'I'll give you my number…'

'I've got it.' He pointed to the mobile phone on her desk.

'But this is yours. I was going to give it back.'

She fell silent as Luke shook his head. 'Take it. If I've got to get to grips with your filing system, I might need to call.' He wouldn't. He'd work it out somehow. But he needed the fantasy to get him through the day, today. Tomorrow, when he gave it up, he could punch the walls in private.

She picked the phone up, running her finger across

the small screen, and he almost choked with grief. It was the little things he was going to miss. Strike that. He was going to miss everything about her, and most of those things were already beginning to play in his head, like a home movie that needed to be watched over and over again, far into the night.

'Okay. Thanks.' She stared at the phone and put it into her bag. 'Make sure you do call.'

Katya hadn't thought that it would be over so quickly. Just one afternoon spent handing over everything she'd done in the last three months and packing up her things from her desk. It wasn't enough. She'd planned on having more time, but when she thought about it, that wouldn't have been enough either.

She'd done it, though. Kept herself together, and managed not to show him any more of her tears, even when she'd kissed him lightly on the cheek to say good-bye.

'You're late…you told him, then?' She found Olenka in the kitchen when she returned to the house.

It was probably obvious from her red, tear-worn eyes. She might have kept her composure in front of Luke, but stopping the car on the way home to have a good cry was allowed. 'Yes. I told him.'

'How did he take it?' Olenka didn't look up from the pie crust that she was carefully rolling over the top of a dish.

'He was really good about it. Said that I should go straight away, so that I can get everything sorted up in London before I start my course.'

The pastry flopped, unnoticed, in a heap on the floured board. 'That's it?'

'Yeah. That's it.' Katya dropped her bags onto the floor, falling into Olenka's waiting arms, and started to cry again. Not that she'd really stopped properly yet from the last time.

'Didn't you ask him? If he wanted you to stay?'

'Sort of. He doesn't, Olenka. Why would he have suggested it otherwise?'

'Men are…' Olenka gave a gesture that took in the full, incomprehensible, pig-headed contrariness of the beast. 'Men are men.'

'Luke isn't like that.' Katya bit her tongue. She could stop defending him now. 'We're just no good together. I thought that if we ignored all the things that Luke won't talk about, they'd go away. But they don't, do they?'

'Not generally. They just get bigger…'

'And bigger.' Katya coiled her little finger around Olenka's. 'Some things just aren't meant to be.'

'You believe that?'

Katya didn't know what to believe. All she could do was rely on what Luke had said and on the generally accepted wisdom on the subject. If a guy said he didn't want you around, then he didn't want you around.

'It's too much of a leap into the darkness not to.'

Olenka nodded. 'I get that. For what it's worth, I think you've done the right thing. This course is what you want. You know I like Luke, but you only have one life.'

'I know.' For once, Olenka's solid logic failed to comfort her. One life without Luke didn't seem much of a prospect.

'So.' Olenka wasn't giving up yet. 'Tomorrow you can get up late, wear your pyjamas all day and watch TV. I have ice cream in the freezer. Friday evening we pack your bags, and Peter and I will come to London with you.'

'You don't need to…' However much Katya didn't want to make it on her own, she knew that she could. Luke had given her that, at least.

Olenka waved away her objections. 'I haven't seen Papa Jozef for months. You want to keep my child from his family?'

Katya smiled. 'You know that Mum and Dad are always happy to see you and Peter.'

'Then I will call them. I may bring a bottle.'

'No! You know what happened the last time when you brought my dad a bottle.' Katya's father and Olenka had sat up far into the night together, drinking and talking, and the next morning they'd found the two of them still in his study and fast asleep.

Olenka shrugged. 'Maybe we'll drink it now, then.' She reached for the freezer. Olenka always kept a bottle of Polish honey vodka in the freezer, although she only broke it out for emergencies.

'Later. One glass. I can't hold my liquor like you can.' Honey vodka wasn't going to heal the pain of parting from Luke any more than the love of her family or knowing that she'd done the right thing could. It might dull it a little, though.

CHAPTER SEVENTEEN

REMEMBER, REMEMBER THE *fifth of November. 18:00*

Katya dropped her phone back into her bag. No word from Luke for the last two months, and even now he'd just sent a text. It was Luke all over. Too little, too late.

Maybe she'd go, just to show him. She wanted him to see that she'd made a success of things. Wanted to find out whether Olenka's faithful reports about him seeming fine whenever he dropped into the coffee shop were really true.

It was tempting, but it was just asking for trouble. She'd learned to handle the searing pain of their parting, just like she'd learned to handle everything else. No point in reopening old wounds. If she didn't reply, she knew that Luke wouldn't press the invitation.

She eased her heavy satchel further onto her shoulder. If she didn't hurry, she'd be late for her tutorial. The autumn colours of the trees on the campus seemed to be calling her back to the wild, beautiful woodland that she had come to know so well. Turning her back on them, Katya pushed the swing doors of the medical sciences block and headed for the stairs. She'd made her decision. No going back now.

* * *

A good crowd had turned up for the fireworks display, and Luke noticed with approval that the student fire marshals were all doing their jobs. Frank and his wife had control of the camp kitchen, and the fireworks were safe in the hands of the approved team. Everything was running smoothly, and he should be getting on with his job of meeting and greeting.

There was only one person he really wanted to meet and greet. She hadn't replied to his text, and Luke supposed that meant she wasn't coming. Actually, he was sure that meant she wasn't coming, but these days he seemed to be giving dreams rather more house room than strictly necessary. And he hadn't failed to notice that Olenka had taken three tickets for herself from the supply he'd left at the coffee shop for her to sell.

If she wasn't here now, she wasn't coming. Half past six, the tickets said, and Katya was never late. He turned, signalling to Frank that he was going to light the beacon now, surveying the crowd in one last grim confirmation of what he knew to be true.

Luke froze. Olenka was walking across from the car park with Peter. Just the two of them. And then, running to catch them up, he saw her. She had a short coat on that he'd never seen before, a scarf and gloves and a knitted beret. Even the way she moved was different. More confident and relaxed. Olenka had been right. She was doing well. Olenka pointed in his direction and Katya's face swung towards him then turned away again.

Oh, no. There were some things in this life that you just allowed to pass you by. This wasn't one of them.

Luke strode towards her, his heart beating out the ever-increasing pace of his steps.

'Hey.' She gave a guilty smile, as if she'd been caught doing something she shouldn't. 'Great turnout. This is wonderful.'

It was suddenly easy to smile. He didn't have to think about it, the way he'd been doing for the last two months—it just happened. 'Guy Fawkes Night is a bit of a tradition in Sussex. We know how to do it properly.'

'Yes, I heard. Olenka told me about the bonfire parties down here.' In the lights from the barn he could see that her cheeks were red from the cold. That her coat was dark green, and about the closest that man's manufacture could get to the colour of her eyes.

'I'm glad you could make it, Katya.'

'I didn't think… Sorry I didn't get back to you. I wasn't sure whether I could come or not.'

'It doesn't matter.' She was here, and that was all that mattered. 'Come with me.'

She protested and Olenka ignored her. Luke caught her gloved hand in his and practically dragged her away from the crowd of people around the tent where Frank and his wife were dispensing hot food and drinks.

'Where are we going?' She was matching his pace now.

'Wait and see.' He gave her the heavy-duty torch he was holding and let go of her hand, confident that she'd follow, if only out of curiosity.

She was breathless by the time they reached the hilltop. 'I think I'm getting out of shape. All that sitting at my desk, studying.'

'Yeah? How's it going?'

'Good. The course is great and I'm learning a lot.'

'Getting good marks?' Of course she was. Katya worked hard at whatever she did, and failure wasn't generally an option for her.

He could feel her grinning in the darkness. 'Since you ask, yes, not so bad.'

'Good for you.' He guided her to the wooden post some twenty yards from the sturdy tower, built of local stone, that housed the beacon. 'The fuse runs from this switch. Wait for the countdown and then hit the button.'

'What happens then?'

'I told you to wait and see. I just hope it works.' Luke jogged over to where the signal rocket was primed and ready to go, lit the fuse and backed away. There was a short silence and then a *whoosh* as it flew upwards and a loud bang, accompanied by a shower of stars and Katya's yelp of delight. 'Not yet… Don't hit the button yet…' He wanted this to be perfect.

The sound of voices floated across the still night air. The crowd was responding to the marshals' instructions and they were counting. 'Ten, nine, eight…'

She was laughing with delight, almost dancing on the spot. 'When can I press it?'

'When they get to one.' The sight of her like this almost made his heart burst. When the crowd finished counting, she reached forward, grabbed his hand and slammed it with hers down onto the switch. There was a flicker of light inside the beacon and then flames shot up into the night sky.

The crowd below them cheered. Fireworks started to shoot up from the roped-off enclosure in the car park, and Katya turned her face to the night sky. Perfect. It was all perfect.

'Luke!' He revised his definition of 'perfect' when

he heard her shout out his name excitedly. Now it was perfect. It was only one short step before he reached her, and he took that step. When he caught her by the arm, she spun round, her face tilted up towards his. The meaning of 'perfect' was revised again. When his lips touched hers, the moment was finally, irrefutably perfect.

'Katya.' He could hardly breathe. The fireworks flying up into the sky around them were forgotten. This was better in every way. No hesitation, not like before. Her mouth met his and Luke pulled her into his arms, all the frustration and longing of the last months fuelling the heat and the tempo.

She met him halfway. Wound her arms around his neck, pulling his head down, so that he couldn't have backed off if he'd wanted to. Her kiss was sweet, but there was more than just that. Passion. Assurance. When she turned her mind to it, Katya was one hell of a kisser.

She swept all of his reticence, all of the holding back, aside. Met his demands on her and then some. Only took her lips from his to whisper his name.

'Say it again, Katya.' He couldn't believe that this was happening to him. That she could be so nerve-meltingly, deliciously bold.

She laughed, twisting away from him. 'Lu-u-ke!' She shouted his name into the night sky, still ablaze with fireworks and echoing with the sound of exploding stars, and Luke roared with delighted laughter.

He pulled her back, confident now. Crushed her in his arms and kissed her again. This time it was even better. How the hell did perfect get to be any better? Luke didn't care any more.

They couldn't keep this up for much longer. She broke away from him, her lungs searching for air, and Luke held her, feeling the swift rise and fall of her chest against his. Held her for precious moments, which seemed to obliterate all the pain of the last two months.

'No more fireworks?' The first part of the display had finished now. Had they really been up here for so long?

'There are some more later. This is the first time the beacon's been lit for nearly a hundred years and I wanted to make a bit of a thing of it.'

She nodded, breaking away from him. 'Luke, I'm sorry…'

He laid his finger over her lips. 'Don't lie to me, Katya. You've never lied to me before and now isn't the time to start.' No one kissed like that when they didn't mean it. No one.

She heaved a sigh. 'Okay. But you know this isn't going to work.'

'What, you're thinking of kicking me again?'

He was pretty sure that she was flushing red in the darkness. 'I wasn't. Now you mention it, though…'

He chuckled. 'Yeah. I suppose that wasn't very fair.' Luke took a breath and said the words that he'd been wanting to say. The ones that had formed and re-formed in his head, each time a little differently, for weeks. 'Katya, I didn't give you a chance. I'm sorry.'

'What do you mean?'

She knew damn well what he meant but he didn't blame her for wanting to hear it. She'd left because he wouldn't talk to her and she'd been right to.

'I wouldn't let you close. There were things that I

felt that I didn't own up to and that drove a wedge between us.'

She nodded. 'It's done now, Luke.'

'I know.' He couldn't ask for any more from her. Just this. 'But will you listen to me now? It's too late but if you'll let me explain…'

'Then you'll feel better about it?' She shot the accusation at him.

'No. I'll feel as if I was honest with you. I can't change the past, but I can own my mistakes.' He shoved his freezing hands into his jacket pockets. 'It's a harder route to absolution than just saying sorry.'

A sharp intake of breath that might have been accompanied by a wry smile, but it was difficult to tell in the shadows. 'Yeah. It is, that. A surer route, though.'

'Maybe. I hope so. And you deserve an explanation of why I drove you away.'

'Because you didn't care enough.' Her voice was suddenly hard, controlled. Was this what she'd been telling herself for the past two months?

'It was because I wasn't strong enough to own my fears, Katya. When my marriage broke up, it left me with a lot of issues. I couldn't let go of my anger. I couldn't even make a proper home here for myself. But you changed all that.' He was jumping the gun. He had to start at the beginning, tell her everything. 'I gave up rescue work and came home because my ex-wife asked me to. And because she was pregnant.'

He heard Katya catch her breath. She was listening now.

'Things didn't seem right between us, but Tanya insisted that everything was okay. Then three months later I found out that they weren't. She'd been having an affair and the baby wasn't mine.'

'What? Luke, why did she do that?'

'I don't know. I guess she was having a hard time making a decision and didn't want to burn any of her bridges. Whatever. It doesn't matter.' None of that mattered any more. 'I begged her to stay, told her that I'd raise the child. That I could love it as my own and that was all that mattered, we'd work something out.'

'But she wanted to be with the father?' There was a precious note of outrage in her voice.

'Yeah. But that's okay, she made her choice, and I can honestly say that I hope she's happy.'

'It's pretty hard to trust anyone after something like that.' As usual she'd hit the nail right on the head.

'Yes. I made you pay for her lies. I wanted everything from you before I'd give anything. I didn't have it in me to make the leap of faith that every new relationship demands.' He shrugged. 'Things don't work that way.'

'No. They don't.' She moved a step nearer to him. 'It wasn't all your fault, Luke. If I'd been—'

'It's okay, Katya. You don't have to say anything. I only wanted you to listen, and you've done that. Thank you.'

She nodded, turning to scan the horizon as if there was some answer there. Then gave a sharp, explosive gesture of frustration. 'What on earth…?'

Luke followed her gaze and saw the group climbing the beacon. Clearly someone had thought it was a good idea to lead a party up here to take in the view. Fair enough, it was pretty spectacular. But the only thing he'd wanted to see was Katya, and neither of them had noticed the torchlights bobbing towards them until they were nearly on them.

There was no more time. He could see Olenka and Peter near the front of the group, and Peter broke away, running towards Katya. Whatever he did now, it had better be quick.

He caught her arm, leaning towards her. 'Remember this. I'll always be here for you if you need me. Don't be afraid any more. Of anything.' If these were going to be the last words he ever spoke to her, he would make them count.

She nodded, and then turned. Peter reached her, flinging his arms around her waist, and she bent to talk to him. One of the volunteers appeared with an urgent message from Frank about the soup. In the tide of the growing crowd on the hilltop they were carried apart and Luke stumbled away, able only to catch a glimpse of Katya and make sure that she was with Olenka and Peter, before he was urged back down the hill.

Katya put her coat on. Then padded downstairs to the hallway, slipped her feet into her wellington boots and craned around the door of the living room, where Olenka was watching TV. 'I'm just going out, Olenka.'

'At this time of night? It's eleven o'clock!'

'If I'm not going to be back in an hour, I'll call you.'

Olenka gave her a quizzical look and when Katya ignored the unspoken question, she shrugged. 'Okay. Stay safe, Kat, there are still a lot of firework parties going on out there.'

'I will.'

She kept her eye on the pinpoint of light ahead of her as she drove. She knew where Luke was right now.

Stopping the car at the foot of the beacon, and grabbing a torch from the glove compartment, she began to climb.

He must have been watching her, and as she approached he rose from the old deckchair, placed at the foot of the beacon. 'You came, then.'

'Yes. You knew I would.'

'Hoped you would. With a degree of optimism.'

'It's a leap in the dark, Luke. Do you think we can do it? I'm scared, too.'

He let out a deep sigh. Almost as if he'd been holding his breath ever since they'd stood here alone together, nearly three hours ago. 'I think we've both just done it, haven't we? I waited here for you. You came. There were no guarantees for either of us, but we're both here.'

'I love you, Luke.'

He took one step forward. Wrapped his arms around her shoulders and pulled her close. 'I love you, too, Katya.'

This was bliss. Here in Luke's arms, the crackle of the flames above their heads and beyond that the night sky. Luke loved her. She loved him. And even though the practical obstacles hadn't disappeared, they didn't matter any more.

His fingers brushed her cheek and she shivered. 'Luke, you're freezing. How long have you been up here?'

'A little while. I didn't want to miss you.'

'What, you thought I'd give up and go home if you weren't here? I would have waited.'

He shrugged. 'Didn't want to take the chance. I just hoped that you'd know that I'd be here if you did decide to come back.'

'I knew. I'd have come sooner if I'd known you were

going to take "being here" so literally. Or I'd have brought a Thermos flask with me.'

'Can't you think of another way to warm me up?'

'One or two.'

'Feel free, then.'

She kissed him. The passion that had flared in her veins earlier that evening burst across her senses, blinding her to everything but Luke. The scent of his body. His lips. The way he took everything, and then came back for more.

'Katya.' The words were whispered, softly, against the sensitive skin behind her ear. 'I want you so badly.'

'I do, too…want you…'

'There are some things… I have to take care of something first.'

'This is more important.' She clung to him, kissing him again, and he seemed to forget about whatever it was he had to do.

'No…no, Katya, please. I need to…' He changed his mind, backing her against the stone wall at the foot of the beacon and unzipping her coat so that he could wind his hands around her waist.

'What's so important?'

'You and me. In my bed. As soon as possible.'

'Right answer. I knew you'd get there in the end.'

He chuckled quietly. 'I need to shut the beacon down, too. Fire safety.'

'Yeah.' She felt in her pocket, found what she wanted and pressed it into his hand. 'Just in case you were thinking that we might need to make a detour. On the way to your bed.'

'Do you always walk around with a packet of

condoms in your pocket? Or are you just pleased to see me?'

'I stopped off at the all-night chemist on the way here.' She nipped at his lower lip. 'Just to show that I'm serious in my intentions.'

'Hmm. You didn't need to, but I guess an extra packet might come in handy.'

'Think so?' This was something she had to hear.

'I know so. Only fair you should know what *my* intentions are.' He whispered low into her ear and Katya squirmed with anticipation against him.

'Sure about that, are you?'

'Yeah.' His hand found her breast and pleasure shot through her like a bolt of lightning. 'Try me.'

He could do whatever he wanted. And the thought that he probably would made her tremble with anticipation. 'Shut the beacon down, Luke. Now.'

Somehow they made it back to the barn. At one point, Katya thought that they wouldn't as he pressed her against the oldest oak tree in the woods, kissing her as if it was the last thing he'd ever do. Her legs were about to give way from their last careening rush across the open ground that separated the woods from the barn, and Luke caught her up in his arms, taking the steps up to the porch in long strides.

'Keys. In my pocket.' She slid her hand into his jeans pocket and purposely took her time in finding the keys. 'Katya!'

She knew that he was reaching the limits of his control and quickly slid the key into the lock. They burst inside, and Luke kicked the door closed behind them and made straight for the bedroom.

She hadn't seen his bedroom before. Apart from the

built-in cupboards, painted the same cream colour as the walls, the bed was the only furniture in the room. A large, spectacular bed, smooth, dark mahogany curling up and back at the head and foot of it. No mirrors, or pictures, or knick-knacks. Somehow the fact that this was all there was was enormously erotic. The only thing there was to do here was to sprawl on the crisp, cream-coloured sheets and make love with Luke.

That was clearly exactly what he had in mind, too. He practically threw himself down onto the soft mattress, taking her along with him. There was no question about her getting home any time tonight.

'Luke. Wait. I've got to call Olenka and let her know what I'm doing.'

'Really?' A broad grin spread across his face. 'In detail?'

'No, you idiot. She'll be expecting me home.'

He nodded, and his hand slipped into the pocket of her coat, withdrawing her phone. 'Well, you won't be going home for a while.'

'Yeah. I might have to call my course supervisor as well, then.'

He chuckled, finding Olenka's number in the phone's contacts list, and dialling. A short pause, and he started to speak. 'Hi, Olenka, it's Luke. Katya's staying here with me tonight, so don't expect her back.' His grin broadened as Katya eased herself out of her coat and dropped it next to her wellingtons on the floor.

'Yeah… Tomorrow… Not first thing, she'll give you a call about lunchtime.' His eyes were following her every movement as she pulled her sweater over her head. 'Yeah. Good thought… Bye, Olenka.' He cut the line and slipped her mobile into one of her wellington boots.

'What did Olenka say?'

'No idea. Probably something insightful, it was in Polish.' He slung himself down on the bed next to her, supporting himself on one elbow. 'Don't stop what you're doing.'

'Turn the light out.'

He shook his head. 'Why would I do that?'

'I…I just thought…' Her hand wandered to her right side. She was suddenly conscious of the scars. Six of them, along with a couple of neat surgical incisions.

'What, that I'd want to grope around in the dark? Katya, that's not what this is about.'

'They're not exactly pretty…' She'd got used to them, didn't give them a second thought any more. But that was because she saw them every day in the mirror.

'I don't care. I want you to see me just as I am, and take me anyway. Give me the chance to do the same with you.'

The honesty in his eyes gave her courage. Slowly, she slid out of her jeans, and then her shirt, and his lips curved into a smile. 'You always wear lace underwear?' She could see from his face that he liked it.

'Only on special occasions.'

He grinned, laying his hand on her arm to stop her as she reached for the catch at the back of her bra. 'Think I can handle things from here. You can lose the socks, though.' He pulled at the toe of one of her thick, woollen socks and threw it backwards over his shoulder, then leaned in to kiss her.

'Not yet, Luke.' She pushed him away. These were the last delicious moments before the rising tide of their passion carried them away. She wanted to make the most of them. 'Now you.'

Katya stretched herself out on the bed as he rolled upright, taking his shirt off. In here, silhouetted against the pale walls, his body seemed more powerful. Sharp, angular lines, broad curves of muscle. She wanted him so much.

He came to her naked, and beautiful in every regard. Kissed her tenderly. Let her gasp in a few precious breaths of air and then kissed her again, until she moaned, bucking against him. His hands slid across her back, his fingertips skimming the scars. Luke didn't falter but kissed her again, and this time it was hotter, sweeter.

He rolled her over, nuzzling at her neck. Running his thumb down her spine, so she shivered. Planting a kiss in the small of her back. 'You're beautiful, Katya. More so than I could ever have imagined.'

He was neither afraid to touch the scars nor fascinated by them. He just accepted them, the way that she had learned to do. There were no words to say. She just wanted to kiss him again, look straight into his eyes, and she turned to face him again.

His gaze told her everything. Nothing hidden, no excuses or little white lies. Just the two of them. Moving against the tides that had drawn them apart. Knowing they were strong enough.

Luke made sure that she was ready for him. Not content with her whispering it in his ear, he kept going until she screamed it. Took her right to the edge of begging and then unleashed his own passion. With deft, delicious movements he practically tore the lacy scraps of underwear away, finally taking her in one rapid movement. Katya squeezed her eyes shut and he kissed the lids, demanding that she open them. When she did his gaze awaited her, dark and delicious. If sex had been invented solely for that look then it would have been well worth the trouble.

'Luke.' He seemed to love nothing better than for her to say his name. She goaded him on, her hands and mouth finding the places that made his body jerk and his muscles pump to straining point.

'Katya…Katya, I can't…'

Too late, she was already there. The shimmering pleasure that had been coursing through her body suddenly broke loose, whipping through her and making her cry out. He caught its rhythm, dragging it out into long moments of sheer bliss, before she felt him lose all control, his voice deep and guttural as he called out her name.

Sunlight filtered through the wooden slats of the window shutters. She was warm, and everything was right with the world. Luke was still sleeping.

Well, he may, he'd been tireless last night. He did hot and hard just as well as he did tender, and in equal degrees. Katya snuggled into his body and took a moment to consider which she liked best. It was a question without an answer. She liked both. She needed both.

Sliding out of his arms, she padded over to the high cupboards, opening the doors. She found a towelling bathrobe and pulled it out, wrapping it securely around herself and rolling up the sleeves.

Before she headed for the kitchen, she checked again to make sure he was sleeping soundly. She didn't want

Luke waking up to find her gone. She made the coffee and then slid back into the bed next to him.

He stirred, opening his eyes. Saw her face and smiled, stretching like a big cat in the sun. 'Mmm. You smell gorgeous.'

'I smell of you.' That musky scent, which she'd taken through with her into the kitchen, reminded her that last night he'd made every part of her body his.

'You smell of roses…and lavender.' He grinned, rolling her over onto her back and pressing his body onto hers, nuzzling her neck. 'And sex and coffee. Fabulous combination.'

'Which do you want first?'

He snorted with laughter. 'Trick question, Katya. I want you before anything…everything. Didn't I say that?'

'I think you mentioned it. But the coffee's getting cold. I'll still be here when we've drunk it.'

'Mmm. You've got a point.' He twisted round, reaching for one of the mugs on the floor by the bed and handing it to her. 'Guess I really should get a table for beside the bed.'

'I like it like this. Just you, me and the bed.'

He laughed. 'And all our clothes on the floor.'

'Maybe an easy chair. By the window, there.'

He considered the option. 'In case we don't make it to the bed, you mean.'

'Oh, so you're planning for us to work our way around every piece of furniture in the place, are you?'

The twist of his lips told her that the idea had probably already occurred to him. 'It's a thought.'

'Dream on, Luke. I'm not making love on the kitchen table. It'll collapse.'

'Yeah, probably. That wasn't my first option. Did I mention that your practicality really turns me on?'

Katya aimed a play punch at his shoulder. 'Drink your coffee.'

They drank coffee together, showered together and then made love again. It was almost noon, and Katya was beginning to be aware of the fact that Luke hadn't actually asked her to stay yet.

'We should get up. It's almost midday.' The words seemed like a breaking point. Time to find out what it was that Luke really wanted from her.

'You'll stay here.' His arm curled around her waist possessively. 'I'm not letting you go.'

The thrill that quivered through her wasn't so much excitement as joy. 'We have to get up sometime.'

'Yeah, I know. You have to go back to London on Monday. I have responsibilities here.' He pulled her close. 'Things are no different from how they were last night. But then we talked about trust.'

'And now?'

'We work it out. I can travel down to see you on Friday evening…'

'Or I can come here on Thursday, after lectures. Friday's my study day, so I could spend the day here with my books, if you can find a corner for me.'

'I've got plenty of corners, you know that. I've got a place for you on Thursday night, too.'

It sounded wonderful. But if post-coital, rose-coloured spectacles had anything to do with his offer…

'Is this going to work, Luke? Long-distance relationships can be hard. You know that better than I do.'

'We can make it work. Don't chicken out on me now.'

'But—'

'But nothing, Katya. We're taking this on trust.' The charming, playful Luke who had shared his bed with her for the whole of the morning was gone. He was earnest, sure of himself. 'I trust you, and I trust myself enough to know a good thing when I see it. I'm not letting you go without a fight.'

She sank into his arms. The man she loved was going to fight to keep her and that was all she really needed to know for now. 'Me neither, Luke.'

EPILOGUE

THEY HADN'T NEEDED to fight at all. Luke and Katya had fallen into a blissful routine and in the three days and four nights each week that she was with him he gave her enough loving to carry her through her days away.

He was waiting at the station for her, as he always did on Thursday evenings. This time she flew into his arms, full of excitement. 'Four whole weeks, Luke.' She had the whole of the winter break to spend with him.

He lifted her off her feet, hugging her as if he'd never let her go. He never really did let her go, even when they were miles apart. 'We've plenty to do. You have to study, and I've got a new project to work on, too.'

'What? What is it?'

'Come and see.'

As they got closer to home, she could see the light. Not quite in the sky but just touching it, on the highest piece of land in the area. Luke parked the car at the foot of the beacon, reached behind him for a large envelope which lay on the back seat and got out. 'You'll have to walk a bit.'

He took her hand, leading her over the steep ground to where the beacon flamed. 'What are you up to, Luke?' There was a little frisson of excitement emanating from him that told her that, whatever this was, it was something important.

'Here.' He sat down on the new bench that he'd constructed, at the foot of the beacon, and took a wad of folded paper from the envelope. A lantern light that he must have fixed to the side of the beacon while she was away shone over her shoulder, illuminating the building plans.

'This is your house?'

'Nope. Our house. What do you think of putting it down there?' He pointed towards a space in the trees, several hundred yards away from the original site that he'd earmarked for the house. 'More secluded there. I think it'll be nicer.'

'Yes, I think it will.'

'You can change anything you don't like.' He shrugged. 'You can change the whole thing if you want. I've been working on some ideas with the architect for the last month, and this is what he came up with. It's just a concept for us to agree.'

'It's lovely. It's going to be beautiful, Luke.'

'And if all goes well, we can start to build in the spring.'

'So soon?'

'It'll be a while before we can move in. But the practice is doing well and there's enough cash to make a start. There is one more thing I need, though.'

'What's that?'

He pointed to the lettering in the corner of the sheet in front of her. *'Client: Mr and Mrs Kennedy.'* Katya held her breath. 'This house is for both of us, it's not going to work without you. Marry me.'

Everything fell into place. Luke was the thread

that bound all the pieces of her life together. Made her whole. She loved him so much. She felt him strip her glove off her hand and something cool nudged against the tip of her finger. 'Hey! Wait until I say yes!'

'Say it quickly. Say it now.' He kissed her. That slightly heady feeling was familiar now, but always brand-new.

'I want you to kiss me a bit more before I do.'

'What, I won't be able to kiss you when we're engaged?'

'Of course you will. When we're engaged it'll be your duty to kiss me regularly.'

'Sounds good. Looking forward to that bit of it. Along with the house-building, the child-raising…' he ran his hand inside her coat '…keeping my wife happy.'

'Mmm. I like the sound of that.'

'Say yes, then. Or do I have to pull out all the stops to persuade you?'

'There's more?'

His quiet laugh was one of pure happiness. 'There's always more. Marry me and find out.'

There was only one thing for it. Katya got to her feet, climbed up on the bench and filled her lungs with the evening air. 'I love him!' she yelled at the top of her voice. 'I'm going to marry him!'

* * * * *

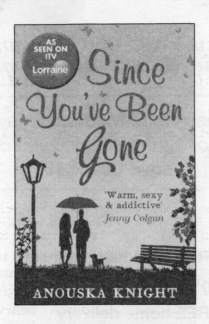